THE AFTERLIFE OF FRANKENSTEIN

A Century of Mad Science, Automata, and Monsters Inspired by Mary Shelley, 1818-1918

Edited by David Sandner

LANTERNFISH PRESS
Philadelphia, PA

THE AFTERLIFE OF FRANKENSTEIN

Lanternfish Press
21 S. 11th Street
Philadelphia, PA 19107

lanternfishpress.com

Cover
Design by Kimberly Glyder
Images courtesy of the Wellcome Library: 1. The fall of Babylon; Cyrus the Great defeating the Chaldean army. Mezzotint by J. Martin, 1831, after himself, 1819; 2. Mikroskopische Untersuchungen über die Uebereinstimmung in der Struktur und dem Wachsthum der Thiere und Pflanzen / Von Th. Schwann. Mit vier Kupfertafeln.

Printed in the United States of America.
27 26 25 24 23 1 2 3 4 5
Library of Congress Control Number: 2023932912
ISBN: 978-1-941360-79-8
Digital ISBN: 978-1-941360-80-4

Dedication

To everyone who sees an image of themselves in Mary Shelley's Creature. To those she influenced to make their own monsters, misunderstood or not. To all that these monsters have taught us. And to all they have left to teach us still.

SOURCES

Anonymous (attributed to William Maginn), "The New Frankenstein," *Fraser's Magazine for Town and Country*, No. XCVII (January 1838), 21-30.

Anonymous, "The Monster Made by Man; or, the Punishment of Presumption," *Endless Entertainment: A Series of Original Comic, Terrific, and Legendary Tales*, No. 7 (Friday, June 17, 1825), 99-112.

Emily Brontë, *Wuthering Heights*, Thomas Cautley Newby, 1847.

Lord Byron, "A Fragment," *Mazeppa: A Poem*, John Murray, 1819, 57-69.

Mrs. W.K. Clifford (Lucy Lane Clifford), "The New Mother," *Anyhow Stories, Moral and Otherwise*, Macmillan, 1882, 8-47.

Charles Dickens, "Chapter XL," *Great Expectations*, in *All the Year Round*, Vol. V, No. 108 (Saturday, May 18, 1861), 169-174.

Paul Laurence Dunbar, "Chapter XIV. Frankenstein," *The Sport of the Gods*, Dodd, Mead, and Company, 1902, 197-209.

Edward S. Ellis, *The Steam Man of the Prairies*, 1868. Reprinted as *The Huge Hunter; or The Steam Man of the Prairie*, Beadle's Half Dime Library, Vol. XI, No. 271 (October 3, 1882), Fourth Edition, 1-14.

Alice W. Fuller, "A Wife Manufactured to Order," *The Arena*, Vol. XIII, ed. B.O. Flower, Arena Publishing, 1895, 305-312.

Elizabeth Gaskell, *Mary Barton: A Tale of Manchester Life*, Chapman and Hall, 1848.

Jerome K. Jerome, "The Dancing Partner," originally an untitled interpolated story in "Novel Notes," Part XI, *The Idler Magazine*, February to July, 1893, eds. Jerome K. Jerome and Robert Barr, Chatto & Windus, 1893, 185-192.

E.E. Kellett, "The Lady Automaton" (original version title: "The New Frankenstein," 1900), *Pearson's Magazine*, Vol. XI (January–June, 1901), 663-675.

Jack London, "A Thousand Deaths," *The Black Cat*, 1899. Reprinted in The Black Cat, 1917.

W. C. Morrow, "The Monster-Maker" (originally titled "The Surgeon's Experiment," *The Argonaut*, 1887), in *The Ape, The Idiot and Other People*, Lippincott, 1897.

E. Bland (Edith Nesbit), "The Third Drug," *The Strand* (February, 1908), 179-188.

Richard Brinsley Peake, "Presumption; or, The Fate of Frankenstein," 1823. *Dick's Standard Plays* #431, c. 1865.

Edgar Allen Poe, "The Facts in the Case of M. Valdemar," *Broadway Journal* (December 20, 1845), reprinted in *The Works of Edgar Allen Poe*, Vol. 2: Tales (1850), ed. E.C. Stedman and G.E. Woodbury, Stone and Kimball, 1894, 322-334.

John William Polidori, "The Vampyre; A Tale" (originally attributed to Lord Byron), *New Monthly Magazine*, Vol. 11, No. 63 (April, 1819), 195-206.

Christina Rossetti, "Goblin Market," *Goblin Market and Other Poems*, MacMillan, 1862, 1-30.

Mary Shelley, "The Mortal Immortal," in *The Keepsake for MDCCCXXXIV* (1833). Reprinted in *Tales and Stories*, collected by Richard Garnett, William Patterson, 1891, 148-164.

_____, "Roger Dodsworth: The Reanimated Englishman," 1826. First published in *Yesterday and To-day*, by Cyrus Redding, T.C. Newby, 1863, 150-165.

Robert Louis Stevenson, *The Strange Case of the Dr. Jekyll and Mr. Hyde*, Longmans, Green, and Co., 1886.

Jane Webb, *The Mummy! A Tale of the Twenty-Second Century*, Henry Colburn, 1827.

H. G. Wells, *The Island of Dr. Moreau*, Heinemann, 1896.

CONTENTS

PART TWO
Byronic Heroes and Sympathetic Monsters

PART THREE
Mad Science!!!

PART FOUR
From Automatons to Robots

THE AFTERLIFE OF *FRANKENSTEIN*

INTRODUCTION

DAVID SANDNER

Mary Shelley's *Frankenstein* is among the most widely read novels in the world today, and its influence on current literature and film is immense. However, though the novel is two hundred years old, its current standing as an undisputed "classic" is a more recent development of perhaps the last fifty years. Feminist scholars like Sandra Gilbert and Susan Gubar did much to rehabilitate the novel's reputation in works like 1979's *The Madwoman in the Attic*. In response, the critic Fred Botting went so far as to say in the 1990s that *Frankenstein* as we know it "is a product of criticism, not a work of literature." Botting's claim is a gross overstatement, but for much of its existence many did read the novel as merely an entertaining "monster story." Academics might have allowed it some insight into the canonical male poets Shelley knew so well, her husband Percy Shelley and the infamous Lord Byron. But more complex readings that recognize, say, the far-reaching gender implications of a novel centered on men by the daughter of the extraordinary proto-feminist Mary Wollstonecraft, or claims for the powerful ways the work addresses itself to matters of race, identity, and culture, appear to be contemporary critical concerns.

Is Mary Shelley's influence really of so recent a date? Isn't a novel already itself even before critics discover it to be so? The collection you are about to read traces Mary Shelley's influence through its first hundred years, considering work produced from 1818 to 1918. "Influence" is a tricky matter, so let me state up front that I am not concerned with "proving" connections. Instead, my goal is to bring to light rich and suggestive associations. These short stories and excerpts from novels and plays demonstrate *Frankenstein* to be a pioneering work from the beginning, quickly spreading into adaptations and influencing the course of literature. *Frankenstein* is a startling novel of firsts: it is not only the first science fiction novel (as Brian Aldiss influentially claimed in the 1970s) but the first appearance of the iconic mad scientist figure. And perhaps its most important "first" is Shelley's now-ubiquitous modern twist on the monster: the "sympathetic monster" we can identify with instead of simply trying to kill.

Mary Shelley's abject Creature has become a powerful cultural force. Most readers, as my own classroom teaching attests, identify with the Creature instead of Victor Frankenstein (even though his name is on the cover); yet Shelley's Creature remains murderous in its outrageous violence, creating an existential problem for the reader. What is it we see when we see ourselves in the Creature? Shelley wrote what many of us take to be our own autobiography as monsters *inside*: we recognize the Creature's loneliness and thwarted desires as a portrait of our own wounded psyches. Shelley's text is an origin point for monsters who move us not only to sympathy but to empathy as we come to consider the nameless Creature more human than Victor. Her true "hideous progeny" (as she called the novel in her introduction to the 1831 edition) is the modern reinvention of the monster as ourselves—a peculiar but now widely embraced and recycled subset of the "monster" category proper.

Along with the "sympathetic monster," Shelley's tale is also influential for what we can identify as the "Frankenstein monster" motif, a shorthand widely used (in *The Encyclopedia of Science Fiction*, for example) to describe the story of the created being who turns on its creator, destroying both. The term "Frankenstein monster" also neatly encompasses the common confusion of Creator and Created that has led many readers to call both entities by the name "Frankenstein," a far-reaching and influential "misreading" that still *gets at* the intimate connection between the two central figures of Shelley's novel. We, as readers, sense that the creator and created are so closely connected as to be nearly one. Though the Creature is not named Frankenstein, we recognize in the monster the destructive mirror image or double or shadow side of its mad scientist maker. "I ought to be thy Adam," the Creature tells Victor. It should have been considered the creator's son; "Adam Frankenstein" might have been its name; instead, the Creature is, pathetically, nameless and so without a separate identity of its own.

***

I. Of Creatures and Monsters

This study of Shelley's literary influence is divided into four sections in order to highlight the development of key themes. These sections are not mutually exclusive but rather, again, suggestive: groupings to think about. The first section, "Of Creatures and Monsters," looks to the vision of monstrosity that emerges from the shadow of Shelley's extraordinary, wretched, hand-fashioned being. The first two works are a pair: Lord Byron's "Fragment" and John William Polidori's "The Vampyre," those remarkable *other* productions related to the famous "ghost story compact" that inspired *Frankenstein* itself. While there had been hints of vampiric elements in earlier works, such as Samuel Taylor Coleridge's poem "Christabel" from 1800, Polidori's story is considered the first appearance of the vampire in English literature, leading directly to *Dracula* at the end of the century and to our own continued production of vampire stories today. Published in *New Monthly Magazine* in 1819, and in book form later that year, Polidori's tale is a reaction to Byron's unpublished vampiric "fragment" written as his entry in the 1816 "compact." Byron had proposed the writing of "ghost stories" to his guests—both the Shelleys and Polidori—at his palatial Villa Diodati on the shores of Lake Geneva during a rainy summer, but he left his work undone to wander with Percy Shelley in the Alps. Both the magazine version and the initial book version of "The Vampyre" were published as written "by Lord Byron," infuriating both authors and convincing Byron to append his unfinished tale to *Mazeppa: A Poem*, also published in 1819.

Lord Ruthven, the vampire of Polidori's tale, borrowed its name from Lady Caroline Lamb's thinly veiled caricature of Byron in her 1816 novel *Glenarvon*. Her Ruthven was not a vampire but might as well have been. Lord Byron, a darkly brooding, infamous poet whom Lamb dubbed "mad, bad, and dangerous to know," can be figured all too easily as a monster, preying on the weak. He is, in fact, also one of the models for Victor Frankenstein. In proposing a writing contest of ghost stories, Lord Byron himself, and not ghosts, became the central monstrous theme (although, if you think about it, the protagonists in the "compact" stories, including Victor, are all "haunted" by the monsters that plague them). The Creature and vampires would remain intimately connected.

Take, for instance, the first stage adaptations of Shelley's work. Polidori's tale was adapted first: by Frenchman Charles Nodier in 1820 as a melodrama, *Le Vampire*, performed in Paris. Dramatist James Robinson Planché adapted Nodier's play into a successful English version, *The Vampyre*, performed at the Lyceum English Opera House, also in 1820. The first stage production of *Frankenstein*—titled *Presumption; or, the Fate of Frankenstein*, adapted by Richard Brinsely Peake in 1823—cast the same actor who'd played Lord Ruthven in *The Vampyre*, T. P. Cooke, as the Creature. The present collection includes an excerpt of the famous moment when the Creature comes to life in Peake's play.

Watching the production herself, Mary Shelley noted that "the story was not well managed," but also exclaimed: "Lo & behold, I found myself famous." In short, the success of *The Vampyre* directly promoted Peake's adaptation of Shelley's novel. Peake's success with *Frankenstein* became, in turn, a likely reason for the revival of *The Vampyre* at the end of the 1823 season, with Cooke again in the starring role. When Universal Pictures made both *Dracula* and James Whale's *Frankenstein* in 1931, they were only repeating the original pairing of these "monster tales."

An early surviving "penny dreadful" version of Shelley's story, "The Monster Made by Man; or, The Punishment of Presumption" (1825), shows the story stripped down, as in Peake's drama (which clearly influenced it), to its "Frankenstein monster" core. Appearing in the publication *Endless Entertainment: A Series of Comic, Terrific, and Legendary Tales*, the "terrific" or terror-filled story is perhaps most of interest for the way the Victor-figure, Ernest Wallberg, first models his man in clay before somehow grafting in "fibres, muscles, veins and skin" and infusing the whole with an "elixir of life." An excerpt from Jane Webb's *The Mummy!* (1827) connects another 1930s-era Universal movie monster to *Frankenstein*. Both "The Monster Made by Man" and *The Mummy!* take pains to clarify that their creatures only come to life by virtue of a "supreme power" and as an explicit punishment for the supposed usurping creator's "presumption." Webb's work also points toward Shelley's value for other women writers with "hideous" monster stories to tell. According to early reviews of her debut novel, Shelley, as both female and a teenager, should not have written her horror book at all—she was a monster to have done it. Like her Creature, she desired more, and achieved more, than allowed. For other women writers, her work became, from the beginning, an inspiration.

Christina Rossetti's "Goblin Market" (1862) follows Shelley's original in using monsters to covertly explore the consequences of male desire in woman's lives. *Frankenstein* is notably a story all about men, but it is a story written by a woman, the daughter of outspoken early feminist Mary Wollstonecraft, and so a double reading of Shelley's text suggests itself: *Frankenstein* is a story *of* men in conflict, but also *about* men's actions and lives from the perspective of a woman who knew the consequences of male lives on the women around them. Shelley's novel develops penetrating comments *on* men and power, and on the meaning of intimacy between men, exploring a "toxic masculinity" in which selfishness and a death drive are paramount. Shelley's critique of male power and intimacy rewards attention to its perception of how men are negatively shaped by patriarchy. Rossetti's narrative poem is told from the point of view of two sisters in a world where the only men to be found are "goblin men," men as monsters who prey on the unwary by selling their deadly, seductive fruit. Her validation of love between women covertly suggests an alienation between the sexes where inequality estranges the possibility of "true" love itself and means that men can only be realized as monsters. One wonders, if the young women in Shelley's novel—Elizabeth, Justine, and the unnamed female creature—had held to each other like Rossetti's two sisters, could they have weathered their monsters as well?

II. Byronic Heroes and Sympathetic Monsters

The second section, "Byronic Heroes and Sympathetic Monsters," gathers representatives of the modern monster that makes us care as much as recoil—the one in which we see ourselves uncannily reflected. It is worth remembering that even Victor Frankenstein, who is generally excoriated by modern readers sympathetic to the Creature's plight, is based on men Mary Shelley knew and loved: Lord Byron and Percy Shelley, her husband, whose childhood nickname was "Victor."

"Byronic hero" is a name for a gloomy, brilliant antihero. Mary Shelley's friend Lord Byron was obviously the most famous model for the figure in his day (unless it was Napoleon); Victor Frankenstein is perhaps the most famous iteration in our own time (unless it's Batman). The figure is embodied in Gothic villains from Manfred in *The Castle of Otranto* (1764) forward to Byron's own play *Manfred* (1817) and beyond. Sublime in his swift-darting intellect and willed achievement, the figure appears in many of Byron's extremely popular narrative poems, such as *Don Juan* (1818-24) or "The Corsair" (1814). Drawing directly on contradictions in the original source—Lord Byron himself—Victor and the Creature are *both* Byronic heroes, making Shelley's novel a complex interrogation of the figure.

Like the Creature, the Byronic hero is an outcast, alienated from society. However, like Victor, the emphasis is on his rarified position and unique, gloomy vantage on the rest of us that seemingly penetrates into the "secret of life" itself. The fascination of Byron's and Polidori's vampires is a manifestation of this aspect of the Byronic. Mary Shelley pens stories of men outcast from time in both "Roger Dodsworth, The Reanimated Englishman" (1826) and "The Mortal Immortal" (1833). Dodsworth is unfrozen after being in the ice for nearly 200 years. The "mortal immortal" draws on the legend of the restless Wandering Jew (a character who emerged in the thirteenth century as a man who supposedly taunted Jesus at the crucifixion and so was cursed to wander, undying, until the end of time). The story depicts a mortal made immortal by an experiment (another one!) gone awry. Like the Creature at the end of *Frankenstein*, both are lost, irrevocably, "in darkness and distance." Both figures find themselves alienated from the lives of ordinary people and society, questioning, by their very presence, the limits of our circumscribed lives.

While Lord Byron is upper class (as are, uncoincidentally, Victor Frankenstein, Dracula, and, for that matter, Bruce Wayne), the Creature is notably "unclassed," with no place in society. *Frankenstein* is a novel born of the Age of Revolutions, a time still absorbing in particular the reverberations of the French Revolution of 1789, which centered on class conflict. One of the first cultural uses of Mary Shelley's Creature was in the allusions of contemporary news, journal illustrations, and political speech to the fear of working-class "mobs," especially Irish ones—a connection that speaks to the invention of "race" as well as to the stratification of class. *Wuthering Heights* (1847) by Emily Brontë provides a towering presentation of the Byronic Heathcliff, whose love lies beyond the bounds of the quotidian world, rooted in "the eternal rocks beneath," and in a radical identification between him and Catherine Earnshaw: "I am Heathcliff!" Heathcliff must transform his class and does so through an act of stubborn will, and yet remains estranged by his nature. *Mary Barton* (1848) by Elizabeth Gaskell as well as *Great Expectations* (1861) by Charles Dickens use allusions to Shelley's novel to raise sympathy for the monstrous underclass, locating part of the Creature's power in its representation of the laboring lower classes, immigrants, and racial others emerging in the wake of the Industrial Revolution. Such readings of Shelley's original are borne out by her own radical political leanings; she supported revolutionary organizations like the Carbonari, a group fighting for Italian independence, even late in her life, long after some critics claimed a more conservative turn in her thinking.

Influential modern critical readings have developed the argument that *Frankenstein* advances a critique of "othering" that includes not only the marginalization of the underclass but of the foreign or exotic based on racialized fear. Key texts in that tradition include Gaytri Spivak's "Three Women's Texts and a Critique of Imperialism" (1985) and Anne Mellor's "Frankenstein, Racial Science, and the Yellow Peril" (2001). In response to our own era's greater attention to matters of race, "Black Frankenstein" is a new term offered by Elizabeth Young in *Black Frankenstein: The Making of an American Metaphor* (2007), a spectacular reading of *Frankenstein*'s influence that crystallizes and describes the use of the Creature in complex ways to represent slavery, black bodies, violence against people of color, and more in American society and culture. Young's powerful readings offer *Frankenstein* as an important precursor text not only for science fiction but for the emergence of Afrofuturism and other futurities imagined by people of color. Just as women writing genre fiction find a key ancestor in Mary Shelley, so her text and its notably non-white Creature offer a point of contact for the embodiment and voicing of othered, racialized bodies. The Creature's longing to be accepted as "human" resonates. *The Sport of the Gods* (1902) by Paul Laurence Dunbar excerpted here marks one of the first stories to present an intense reconsideration of what Mary Shelley's invention of the modern monster can mean in matters of race.

III. Mad Science!!!

Next, "Mad Science!!!" puts the focus on Creator instead of Creature. The mad scientist is a ubiquitous figure in the pulp science fiction magazines of the 1930s onward but has also had many, many iterations outside of the pulps, both before and after. Consciously indebted to *Frankenstein*, "mad science" stories explore the responsibility of the Creator as the ill-conceived experiment careens out of control. There is always a sense in the mad scientist's character of "presumption," the word used in the title of Peake's initial adaptation of Shelley's novel into a play. Readers, and so many adaptations of Shelley's work, often associate the figure with blasphemy, though that seems more tied to over-readings of Shelley's changes to the 1831 edition than to the original themes of the 1818 first edition. The mad scientist is a kind of debased Byronic hero, often flattened of complexities. Still, this stock SF character has provided a key trope in the rich shared storytelling tools that make up the genre. One irony is that while Victor is the first mad scientist (a few decades before the term "scientist" actually existed), with numerous "mad" doctors in his wake, he is not, as many call him, "Dr. Frankenstein." Victor fails to get his degree, leaving university early to complete his experiment. (So, perhaps the lesson is to stay in college, listen to your professors, and take your degree—or else calamity follows?) Victor Frankenstein might be described as a natural philosopher, especially with his reliance on alchemy. However, it has been strongly established that Shelley's work is steeped in the cutting-edge science of her day, from galvanism to air pumps. As a working writer, Shelley wrote many of the entries for *Lives of the Most Eminent Literary and Scientific Men* (1829-46), so we can rightly see Victor as another "Scientific Man." Iconic tales of mad science with mad doctors at work include two novels excerpted here: Robert Louis Stevenson's *The Strange Case of Dr. Jekyll and Mr. Hyde* (1886) and H. G. Wells's *The Island of Dr. Moreau* (1896).

The "sublime" is the Romantic-era term for a confrontation at the limits of human understanding, in which the mind and imagination are challenged by conceptions "too large" for comprehension; often, in what has been called the "natural sublime," the sublime is figured as an attempt to apprehend what we cannot comprehend: nature in totality. The "sublime moment" breaks understanding, and then it either promises a possible reintegration of the self with nature in some sort of transcendence, or threatens a dissolution of the self, an end. *Frankenstein* remains an important example of the sublime in SF, and an influence on stories about breaking limits, both evolutionary and ecological, and of the effect of humanity on nature as recorded in a term like "Anthropocene." In Shelley's novel, we can note numerous sublime elements: a Byronic hero (or two), a final, nearly impossible confessional narrative of fantastic events from the dying Creator, and a sense of a confrontation with nature and evolutionary change itself in the reconstituted Creature. The Creature is sublime in size but also in its startling intellect and in its "othering" animal nature (for it is an impossible synthesis of human and animal body parts, with Victor finding what he needs in the charnel- *and* the slaughter-house). The Creature is directly and continually conflated with sublime natural scenery in the Alps and elsewhere, throughout the novel. Stories of scientific breakthroughs that bring wonder and terror (like Frankenstein's breaking of the bounds between life and death) include Edgar Allen Poe's "The Facts in the Case of M. Valdemar" (1845) with its impossible claim—"I am dead"—and Edith Nesbit's "The Third Drug" (1908) with its mad scientist's desire to make a "superman."

A mad science story that is now lesser known but was more prominent in the nineteenth century is the vivisection story, a curious subset of the scientific breakthrough story. They still proliferated through the early twentieth century (H. P. Lovecraft's "Herbert West—Reanimator" from 1922, for example) before fading from view. The bloody physicality of the vivisection story points not only toward the horror genre side of Shelley's original tale but to the usurpation of the physically trying birth process itself by men. In these stories, men, violently but with a disturbing intellectual coolness, "give birth" to monstrosities. From grave-robbing to stitching patchwork bodies, sometimes mixed with animals, the mad scientist creates an artificial but humanlike being. Mythic originals include Athena memorably breaking out of Zeus's head. Adam's rib also comes to mind. The iconic modern take on the theme is, quite simply, Mary Shelley's novel. Examples here include W. C. Morrow's "The Monster-Maker" (1887) and Jack London's "A Thousand Deaths" (1899).

IV. From Automatons to Robots

The final section brings together nineteenth- and early twentieth-century stories along the cutting edge of "humanlike" or android technological creations, taking us up to the moment just before we arrive at the word "robot," a designation which first appeared in Karel Ĉapek's play *R.U.R.* (1920; translated into English in 1923). The word implies, it is worth noting, "forced labor," slavery, or serfdom, connecting it consciously with a class critique. The famous bolts in the neck of Boris Karloff as Frankenstein's Creature from Whale's preeminent 1931 movie version point toward the slippage between human and machine in Shelley's creation. If that is not clear enough, one story in this section about automatons is simply titled "The New Frankenstein" (from 1844, anonymous but attributed to William Maginn) and another's original version was also titled "The New Frankenstein" ("The Lady Automaton," 1901, by E. E. Kellett).

The question "What is Human?" is key in *Frankenstein* and has a long afterlife in the SF tradition of robots. The issue moves through the extraordinary "supermen" and alien encounters in early pulp SF, but robots hold a special place in the history of the field and its existential questioning, from Isaac Asimov's robot stories to Philip K. Dick's "Andys" to James Tiptree Jr.'s "The Girl Who Was Plugged In." The 1980s subgenre of cyberpunk, for example, blurred the line between our humanity and the tech we inhabit, wear, and implant. Norman Spinrad, in his essay "The Neuromantics" (1986), argues that one meaning of *Neuromancer*, the title of William Gibson's central cyberpunk text, is "new Romancer." Cyberpunk writers, he suggested, should be called "Neuromantics," as their work was "a fusion of the romantic impulse with science and technology." Cyberpunk frequently tests the limits of the human in the remaking of humanity through machine augmentations and biological engineering. Bruce Sterling defines the subgenre by the presence of such modifications (see the introduction to his foundational 1986 collection *Mirrorshades: The Cyberpunk Anthology*). Suffice it to say, the limit of the human is a constant SF concern and Mary Shelley's novel is the origin point for this ongoing, vital discussion. So perhaps it is no surprise that Shelley's organic, biological creation of life has so easily served to inspire stories of technological, artificial "life."

A work like *The Steam Man of the Prairies* (1868) by Edward S. Ellis offers a seemingly unproblematic use of the automaton, one more in line with Asimov's later positive spin on the robot, which labeled anyone who irrationally feared the coming of such "lifelike" helpers as suffering from what Asimov called "the Frankenstein Complex." But *Steam Man* enacts a disturbing colonial discourse for modern readers that supports the coming of white supremacy over the American frontier, as the "steam man" marches forth to subdue Native Americans as much as to catch criminals and perform physical feats.

Other stories are more wary of their created automata. Most of the works here engage with a fear of the consequences in the creation of an emergent, self-aware intelligence. Many of the stories raise questions about our roles in society and even the nature of existence itself. A new being, even one who serves us, tasks its maker with existential questions from an alien mind. The central connection to *Frankenstein*, of course, is the Creature's questioning of its own humanity and the limits of the human, and the way the Creature threatens at once to be all too human and yet to be more than human.

Interesting here is how strongly the gender issues of Shelley's original reappear, though they are not always as well handled, in a set of stories on the creation of female automatons, including "A Wife Manufactured to Order" (1895) by Alice W. Fuller and "The Lady Automaton" (1901) by E. E. Kellett. Are women actually—gasp!—intelligent autonomous beings? Should they be allowed to be? All these stories pick up most closely on the fate of the "mate" that Frankenstein made and destroyed before the Creature's eyes, before he could bring it to life, exploring how the feminine gender is a manufactured thing figured, all too often, only in relation to the desires of men.

An especially frightening version of a female creation is Lucy Lane Clifford's "The New Mother" (1882), in which the kindly human mother has to leave when her children misbehave and is replaced with the new mother, whose wooden tail and glass eye point to her mechanical coldness and severity. In "The Dancing Partner" (1893) by Jerome K. Jerome, the tables are turned and a fatherly male scientist's creation of the "ideal" male dancing partner, as abstracted from the gossiping of a group of young women, has a disastrous result.

Stories of Byronic antiheroes and monsters are still with us, as are tales of mad science and its mad scientists (especially as we face the calamity of the world we have made in the Anthropocene), and we still tell stories of lifelike robots and of machines coming to life, and we wonder what the Singularity—the moment when "thinking machines" outthink us—might bring. Versions of the Creature rise again and again, like undead vampires, coming back to life once more in the high style of any respectable horror icon. Mary Shelley's story is, after all, a "ghost story," as Byron tasked it to be. *Frankenstein* haunts us with the limits of the human—both "what is human?" and "what does it mean to be human—in our society, in the world, or inside ourselves?" While our age did not invent Shelley's story, we need it still. But that has been true from the beginning, since even as the text was dismissed as a mere monster story, it was still read and adapted frequently. Shelley's text loved us all too well long before we, as a culture, learned to call it a "classic."

Read what follows here and find what other writers from the first hundred years after Shelley's creation have wrought out of it, stitched from what they found in Shelley's "workshop of filthy creation." And after that? Her original patiently waits for you to jolt it to life—to read her story, not a version of it—both *once again* and *still*—for we have never stopped.

May these stories offer you fresh perspectives and insights on her original genius. Enjoy!

PART ONE

Of Creatures and Monsters

THE VAMPYRE

(1819)

John William Polidori

It happened that in the midst of the dissipations attendant upon a London winter, there appeared at the various parties of the leaders of the town a nobleman, more remarkable for his singularities, than his rank. He gazed upon the mirth around him, as if he could not participate therein. Apparently, the light laughter of the fair only attracted his attention, that he might by a look quell it, and throw fear into those breasts where thoughtlessness reigned. Those who felt this sensation of awe, could not explain whence it arose: some attributed it to the dead grey eye, which, fixing upon the object's face, did not seem to penetrate, and at one glance to pierce through to the inward workings of the heart; but fell upon the cheek with a leaden ray that weighed upon the skin it could not pass. His peculiarities caused him to be invited to every house; all wished to see him, and those who had been accustomed to violent excitement, and now felt the weight of ennui, were pleased at having something in their presence capable of engaging their attention. In spite of the deadly hue of his face, which never gained a warmer tint, either from the blush of modesty, or from the strong emotion of passion, though its form and outline were beautiful, many of the female hunters after notoriety attempted to win his attentions, and gain, at least, some marks of what they might term affection: Lady Mercer, who had been the mockery of every monster shewn in drawing-rooms since her marriage, threw herself in his way, and did all but put on the dress of a mountebank, to attract his notice:—though in vain:—when she stood before him, though his eyes were apparently fixed upon her's, still it seemed as if they were unperceived;—even her unappalled impudence was baffled, and she left the field. But though the common adultress could not influence even the guidance of his eyes, it was not that the female sex was indifferent to him: yet such was the apparent caution with which he spoke to the virtuous wife and innocent daughter, that few knew he ever addressed himself to females. He had, however, the reputation of a winning tongue; and whether it was that it even overcame the dread of his singular character, or that they were moved by his apparent hatred of vice, he was as often among those females who form the boast of their sex from their domestic virtues, as among those who sully it by their vices.

About the same time, there came to London a young gentleman of the name of Aubrey: he was an orphan left with an only sister in the possession of great wealth, by parents who died while he was yet in childhood. Left also to himself by guardians, who thought it their duty merely to take care of his fortune, while they relinquished the more important charge of his mind to the care of mercenary subalterns, he cultivated more his imagination than his judgment. He had, hence, that high romantic feeling of honour and candour, which daily ruins so many milliners' apprentices. He believed all to sympathise with virtue, and thought that vice was thrown in by Providence merely for the picturesque effect of the scene, as we see in romances: he thought that the misery of a cottage merely consisted in the vesting of clothes, which were as warm, but which were better adapted to the painter's eye by their irregular folds and various coloured patches. He thought, in fine, that the dreams of poets were the realities of life. He was handsome, frank, and rich: for these reasons, upon his entering into the gay circles, many mothers surrounded him, striving which should describe with least truth their languishing or romping favourites: the daughters at the same time, by their brightening countenances when he approached, and by their sparkling eyes, when he opened his lips, soon led him into false notions of his talents and his merit. Attached as he was to the romance of his solitary hours, he was startled at finding, that, except in the tallow and wax candles that flickered, not from the presence of a ghost, but from want of snuffing, there was no foundation in real life for any of that congeries of pleasing pictures and descriptions contained in those volumes, from which he had formed his study. Finding, however, some compensation in his gratified vanity, he was about to relinquish his dreams, when the extraordinary being we have above described, crossed him in his career.

He watched him; and the very impossibility of forming an idea of the character of a man entirely absorbed in himself, who gave few other signs of his observation of external objects, than the tacit assent to their existence, implied by the avoidance of their contact: allowing his imagination to picture every thing that flattered its propensity to extravagant ideas, he soon formed this object into the hero of a romance, and determined to observe the offspring of his fancy, rather than the person before him. He became acquainted with him, paid him attentions, and so far advanced upon his notice, that his presence was always recognised. He gradually learnt that Lord Ruthven's affairs were embarrassed, and soon found, from the notes of preparation in —— Street, that he was about to travel. Desirous of gaining some information respecting this singular character, who, till now, had only whetted his curiosity, he hinted to his guardians, that it was time for him to perform the tour, which for many generations has been thought necessary to enable the young to take some rapid steps in the career of vice towards putting themselves upon an equality with the aged, and not allowing them to appear as if fallen from the skies, whenever scandalous intrigues are mentioned as the subjects of pleasantry or of praise, according to the degree of skill shewn in carrying them on. They consented: and Aubrey immediately mentioning his intentions to Lord Ruthven, was surprised to receive from him a proposal to join him. Flattered by such a mark of esteem from him, who, apparently, had nothing in common with other men, he gladly accepted it, and in a few days they had passed the circling waters.

Hitherto, Aubrey had had no opportunity of studying Lord Ruthven's character, and now he found, that, though many more of his actions were exposed to his view, the results offered different conclusions from the apparent motives to his conduct. His companion was profuse in his liberality;—the idle, the vagabond, and the beggar, received from his hand more than enough to relieve their immediate wants. But Aubrey could not avoid remarking, that it was not upon the virtuous, reduced to indigence by the misfortunes attendant even upon virtue, that he bestowed his alms;—these were sent from the door with hardly suppressed sneers; but when the profligate came to ask something, not to relieve his wants, but to allow him to wallow in his lust, or to sink him still deeper in his iniquity, he was sent away with rich charity. This was, however, attributed by him to the greater importunity of the vicious, which generally prevails over the retiring bashfulness of the virtuous indigent. There was one circumstance about the charity of his Lordship, which was still more impressed upon his mind: all those upon whom it was bestowed, inevitably found that there was a curse upon it, for they were all either led to the scaffold, or sunk to the lowest and the most abject misery. At Brussels and other towns through which they passed, Aubrey was surprized at the apparent eagerness with which his companion sought for the centres of all fashionable vice; there he entered into all the spirit of the faro table: he betted, and always gambled with success, except where the known sharper was his antagonist, and then he lost even more than he gained; but it was always with the same unchanging face, with which he generally watched the society around: it was not, however, so when he encountered the rash youthful novice, or the luckless father of a numerous family; then his very wish seemed fortune's law—this apparent abstractedness of mind was laid aside, and his eyes sparkled with more fire than that of the cat whilst dallying with the half-dead mouse. In every town, he left the formerly affluent youth, torn from the circle he adorned, cursing, in the solitude of a dungeon, the fate that had drawn him within the reach of this fiend; whilst many a father sat frantic, amidst the speaking looks of mute hungry children, without a single farthing of his late immense wealth, wherewith to buy even sufficient to satisfy their present craving. Yet he took no money from the gambling table; but immediately lost, to the ruiner of many, the last gilder he had just snatched from the convulsive grasp of the innocent: this might but be the result of a certain degree of knowledge, which was not, however, capable of combating the cunning of the more experienced. Aubrey often wished to represent this to his friend, and beg him to resign that charity and pleasure which proved the ruin of all, and did not tend to his own profit;—but he delayed it—for each day he hoped his friend would give him some opportunity of speaking frankly and openly to him; however, this never occurred. Lord Ruthven in his carriage, and amidst the various wild and rich scenes of nature, was always the same: his eye spoke less than his lip; and though Aubrey was near the object of his curiosity, he obtained no greater gratification from it than the constant excitement of vainly wishing to break that mystery, which to his exalted imagination began to assume the appearance of something supernatural.

They soon arrived at Rome, and Aubrey for a time lost sight of his companion; he left him in daily attendance upon the morning circle of an Italian countess, whilst he went in search of the memorials of another almost deserted city. Whilst he was thus engaged, letters arrived from England, which he opened with eager impatience; the first was from his sister, breathing nothing but affection; the others were from his guardians, the latter astonished him; if it had before entered into his imagination that there was an evil power resident in his companion, these seemed to give him sufficient reason for the belief. His guardians insisted upon his immediately leaving his friend, and urged, that his character was dreadfully vicious, for that the possession of irresistible powers of seduction, rendered his licentious habits more dangerous to society. It had been discovered, that his contempt for the adultress had not originated in hatred of her character; but that he had required, to enhance his gratification, that his victim, the partner of his guilt, should be hurled from the pinnacle of unsullied virtue, down to the lowest abyss of infamy and degradation: in fine, that all those females whom he had sought, apparently on account of their virtue, had, since his departure, thrown even the mask aside, and had not scrupled to expose the whole deformity of their vices to the public gaze.

Aubrey determined upon leaving one, whose character had not yet shown a single bright point on which to rest the eye. He resolved to invent some plausible pretext for abandoning him altogether, purposing, in the mean while, to watch him more closely, and to let no slight circumstances pass by unnoticed. He entered into the same circle, and soon perceived, that his Lordship was endeavouring to work upon the inexperience of the daughter of the lady whose house he chiefly frequented. In Italy, it is seldom that an unmarried female is met with in society; he was therefore obliged to carry on his plans in secret; but Aubrey's eye followed him in all his windings, and soon discovered that an assignation had been appointed, which would most likely end in the ruin of an innocent, though thoughtless girl. Losing no time, he entered the apartment of Lord Ruthven, and abruptly asked him his intentions with respect to the lady, informing him at the same time that he was aware of his being about to meet her that very night. Lord Ruthven answered, that his intentions were such as he supposed all would have upon such an occasion; and upon being pressed whether he intended to marry her, merely laughed.

Aubrey retired; and, immediately writing a note, to say, that from that moment he must decline accompanying his Lordship in the remainder of their proposed tour, he ordered his servant to seek other apartments, and calling upon the mother of the lady, informed her of all he knew, not only with regard to her daughter, but also concerning the character of his Lordship. The assignation was prevented. Lord Ruthven next day merely sent his servant to notify his complete assent to a separation; but did not hint any suspicion of his plans having been foiled by Aubrey's interposition.

Having left Rome, Aubrey directed his steps towards Greece, and crossing the Peninsula, soon found himself at Athens. He then fixed his residence in the house of a Greek; and soon occupied himself in tracing the faded records of ancient glory upon monuments that apparently, ashamed of chronicling the deeds of freemen only before slaves, had hidden themselves beneath the sheltering soil or many coloured lichen. Under the same roof as himself, existed a being, so beautiful and delicate, that she might have formed the model for a painter wishing to pourtray on canvass the promised hope of the faithful in Mahomet's paradise, save that her eyes spoke too much mind for any one to think she could belong to those who had no souls. As she danced upon the plain, or tripped along the mountain's side, one would have thought the gazelle a poor type of her beauties; for who would have exchanged her eye, apparently the eye of animated nature, for that sleepy luxurious look of the animal suited but to the taste of an epicure. The light step of Ianthe often accompanied Aubrey in his search after antiquities, and often would the unconscious girl, engaged in the pursuit of a Kashmere butterfly, show the whole beauty of her form, floating as it were upon the wind, to the eager gaze of him, who forgot the letters he had just decyphered upon an almost effaced tablet, in the contemplation of her sylph-like figure. Often would her tresses falling, as she flitted around, exhibit in the sun's ray such delicately brilliant and swiftly fading hues, it might well excuse the forgetfulness of the antiquary, who let escape from his mind the very object he had before thought of vital importance to the proper interpretation of a passage in Pausanias. But why attempt to describe charms which all feel, but none can appreciate?—It was innocence, youth, and beauty, unaffected by crowded drawing-rooms and stifling balls. Whilst he drew those remains of which he wished to preserve a memorial for his future hours, she would stand by, and watch the magic effects of his pencil, in tracing the scenes of her native place; she would then describe to him the circling dance upon the open plain, would paint, to him in all the glowing colours of youthful memory, the marriage pomp she remembered viewing in her infancy; and then, turning to subjects that had evidently made a greater impression upon her mind, would tell him all the supernatural tales of her nurse. Her earnestness and apparent belief of what she narrated, excited the interest even of Aubrey; and often as she told him the tale of the living vampyre, who had passed years amidst his friends, and dearest ties, forced every year, by feeding upon the life of a lovely female to prolong his existence for the ensuing months, his blood would run cold, whilst he attempted to laugh her out of such idle and horrible fantasies; but Ianthe cited to him the names of old men, who had at last detected one living among themselves, after several of their near relatives and children had been found marked with the stamp of the fiend's appetite; and when she found him so incredulous, she begged of him to believe her, for it had been, remarked, that those who had dared to question their existence, always had some proof given, which obliged them, with grief and heartbreaking, to confess it was true. She detailed to him the traditional appearance of these monsters, and his horror was increased, by hearing a pretty accurate description of Lord Ruthven; he, however, still persisted in persuading her, that there could be no truth in her fears, though at the same time he wondered at the many coincidences which had all tended to excite a belief in the supernatural power of Lord Ruthven.

Aubrey began to attach himself more and more to Ianthe; her innocence, so contrasted with all the affected virtues of the women among whom he had sought for his vision of romance, won his heart; and while he ridiculed the idea of a young man of English habits, marrying an uneducated Greek girl, still he found himself more and more attached to the almost fairy form before him. He would tear himself at times from her, and, forming a plan for some antiquarian research, he would depart, determined not to return until his object was attained; but he always found it impossible to fix his attention upon the ruins around him, whilst in his mind he retained an image that seemed alone the rightful possessor of his thoughts. Ianthe was unconscious of his love, and was ever the same frank infantile being he had first known. She always seemed to part from him with reluctance; but it was because she had no longer any one with whom she could visit her favourite haunts, whilst her guardian was occupied in sketching or uncovering some fragment which had yet escaped the destructive hand of time. She had appealed to her parents on the subject of vampyres, and they both, with several present, affirmed their existence, pale with horror at the very name. Soon after, Aubrey determined to proceed upon one of his excursions, which was to detain him for a few hours; when they heard the name of the place, they all at once begged of him not to return at night, as he must necessarily pass through a wood, where no Greek would ever remain, after the day had closed, upon any consideration. They described it as the resort of the vampyres in their nocturnal orgies, and denounced the most heavy evils as impending upon him who dared to cross their path. Aubrey made light of their representations, and tried to laugh them out of the idea; but when he saw them shudder at his daring thus to mock a superior, infernal power, the very name of which apparently made their blood freeze, he was silent.

Next morning Aubrey set off upon his excursion unattended; he was surprised to observe the melancholy face of his host, and was concerned to find that his words, mocking the belief of those horrible fiends, had inspired them with such terror. When he was about to depart, Ianthe came to the side of his horse, and earnestly begged of him to return, ere night allowed the power of these beings to be put in action;—he promised. He was, however, so occupied in his research, that he did not perceive that day-light would soon end, and that in the horizon there was one of those specks which, in the warmer climates, so rapidly gather into a tremendous mass, and pour all their rage upon the devoted country.—He at last, however, mounted his horse, determined to make up by speed for his delay: but it was too late. Twilight, in these southern climates, is almost unknown; immediately the sun sets, night begins: and ere he had advanced far, the power of the storm was above—its echoing thunders had scarcely an interval of rest—its thick heavy rain forced its way through the canopying foliage, whilst the blue forked lightning seemed to fall and radiate at his very feet. Suddenly his horse took fright, and he was carried with dreadful rapidity through the entangled forest. The animal at last, through fatigue, stopped, and he found, by the glare of lightning, that he was in the neighbourhood of a hovel that hardly lifted itself up from the masses of dead leaves and brushwood which surrounded it. Dismounting, he approached, hoping to find some one to guide him to the town, or at least trusting to obtain shelter from the pelting of the storm. As he approached, the thunders, for a moment silent, allowed him to hear the dreadful shrieks of a woman mingling with the stifled, exultant mockery of a laugh, continued in one almost unbroken sound;—he was startled: but, roused by the thunder which again rolled over his head, he, with a sudden effort, forced open the door of the hut. He found himself in utter darkness: the sound, however, guided him. He was apparently unperceived; for, though he called, still the sounds continued, and no notice was taken of him. He found himself in contact with some one, whom he immediately seized; when a voice cried, "Again baffled!" to which a loud laugh succeeded; and he felt himself grappled by one whose strength seemed superhuman: determined to sell his life as dearly as he could, he struggled; but it was in vain: he was lifted from his feet and hurled with enormous force against the ground:—his enemy threw himself upon him, and kneeling upon his breast, had placed his hands upon his throat—when the glare of many torches penetrating through the hole that gave light in the day, disturbed him;—he instantly rose, and, leaving his prey, rushed through the door, and in a moment the crashing of the branches, as he broke through the wood, was no longer heard. The storm was now still; and Aubrey, incapable of moving, was soon heard by those without. They entered; the light of their torches fell upon the mud walls, and the thatch loaded on every individual straw with heavy flakes of soot. At the desire of Aubrey they searched for her who had attracted him by her cries; he was again left in darkness; but what was his horror, when the light of the torches once more burst upon him, to perceive the airy form of his fair conductress brought in a lifeless corse. He shut his eyes, hoping that it was but a vision arising from his disturbed imagination; but he again saw the same form, when he unclosed them, stretched by his side. There was no colour upon her cheek, not even upon her lip; yet there was a stillness about her face that seemed almost as attaching as the life that once dwelt there:—upon her neck and breast was blood, and upon her throat were the marks of teeth having opened the vein:—to this the men pointed, crying, simultaneously struck with horror, "A vampyre! a vampyre!" A litter was quickly formed, and Aubrey was laid by the side of her who had lately been to him the object of so many bright and fairy visions, now fallen with the flower of life that had died within her. He knew not what his thoughts were—his mind was benumbed and seemed to shun reflection, and take refuge in vacancy—he held almost unconsciously in his hand a naked dagger of a particular construction, which had been found in the hut. They were soon met by different parties who had been engaged in the search of her whom a mother had missed. Their lamentable cries, as they approached the city, forewarned the parents of some dreadful catastrophe. —To describe their grief would be impossible; but when they ascertained the cause of their child's death, they looked at Aubrey, and pointed to the corse. They were inconsolable; both died broken-hearted.

Aubrey being put to bed was seized with a most violent fever, and was often delirious; in these intervals he would call upon Lord Ruthven and upon Ianthe—by some unaccountable combination he seemed to beg of his former companion to spare the being he loved. At other times he would imprecate maledictions upon his head, and curse him as her destroyer. Lord Ruthven, chanced at this time to arrive at Athens, and, from whatever motive, upon hearing of the state of Aubrey, immediately placed himself in the same house, and became his constant attendant. When the latter recovered from his delirium, he was horrified and startled at the sight of him whose image he had now combined with that of a vampyre; but Lord Ruthven, by his kind words, implying almost repentance for the fault that had caused their separation, and still more by the attention, anxiety, and care which he showed, soon reconciled him to his presence. His lordship seemed quite changed; he no longer appeared that apathetic being who had so astonished Aubrey; but as soon as his convalescence began to be rapid, he again gradually retired into the same state of mind, and Aubrey perceived no difference from the former man, except that at times he was surprised to meet his gaze fixed intently upon him, with a smile of malicious exultation playing upon his lips: he knew not why, but this smile haunted him. During the last stage of the invalid's recovery, Lord Ruthven was apparently engaged in watching the tideless waves raised by the cooling breeze, or in marking the progress of those orbs, circling, like our world, the moveless sun;—indeed, he appeared to wish to avoid the eyes of all.

Aubrey's mind, by this shock, was much weakened, and that elasticity of spirit which had once so distinguished him now seemed to have fled for ever. He was now as much a lover of solitude and silence as Lord Ruthven; but much as he wished for solitude, his mind could not find it in the neighbourhood of Athens; if he sought it amidst the ruins he had formerly frequented, Ianthe's form stood by his side—if he sought it in the woods, her light step would appear wandering amidst the underwood, in quest of the modest violet; then suddenly turning round, would show, to his wild imagination, her pale face and wounded throat, with a meek smile upon her lips. He determined to fly scenes, every feature of which created such bitter associations in his mind. He proposed to Lord Ruthven, to whom he held himself bound by the tender care he had taken of him during his illness, that they should visit those parts of Greece neither had yet seen. They travelled in every direction, and sought every spot to which a recollection could be attached: but though they thus hastened from place to place, yet they seemed not to heed what they gazed upon. They heard much of robbers, but they gradually began to slight these reports, which they imagined were only the invention of individuals, whose interest it was to excite the generosity of those whom they defended from pretended dangers. In consequence of thus neglecting the advice of the inhabitants, on one occasion they travelled with only a few guards, more to serve as guides than as a defence. Upon entering, however, a narrow defile, at the bottom of which was the bed of a torrent, with large masses of rock brought down from the neighbouring precipices, they had reason to repent their negligence; for scarcely were the whole of the party engaged in the narrow pass, when they were startled by the whistling of bullets close to their heads, and by the echoed report of several guns. In an instant their guards had left them, and, placing themselves behind rocks, had begun to fire in the direction whence the report came. Lord Ruthven and Aubrey, imitating their example, retired for a moment behind the sheltering turn of the defile: but ashamed of being thus detained by a foe, who with insulting shouts bade them advance, and being exposed to unresisting slaughter, if any of the robbers should climb above and take them in the rear, they determined at once to rush forward in search of the enemy. Hardly had they lost the shelter of the rock, when Lord Ruthven received a shot in the shoulder, which brought him to the ground. Aubrey hastened to his assistance; and, no longer heeding the contest or his own peril, was soon surprised by seeing the robbers' faces around him—his guards having, upon Lord Ruthven's being wounded, immediately thrown up their arms and surrendered.

By promises of great reward, Aubrey soon induced them to convey his wounded friend to a neighbouring cabin; and having agreed upon a ransom, he was no more disturbed by their presence—they being content merely to guard the entrance till their comrade should return with the promised sum, for which he had an order. Lord Ruthven's strength rapidly decreased; in two days mortification ensued, and death seemed advancing with hasty steps. His conduct and appearance had not changed; he seemed as unconscious of pain as he had been of the objects about him: but towards the close of the last evening, his mind became apparently uneasy, and his eye often fixed upon Aubrey, who was induced to offer his assistance with more than usual earnestness—"Assist me! you may save me—you may do more than that—I mean not my life, I heed the death of my existence as little as that of the passing day; but you may save my honour, your friend's honour."—"How? tell me how? I would do any thing," replied Aubrey.—"I need but little—my life ebbs apace—I cannot explain the whole—but if you would conceal all you know of me, my honour were free from stain in the world's mouth—and if my death were unknown for some time in England—I—I—but life."—"It shall not be known."—"Swear!" cried the dying man, raising himself with exultant violence, "Swear by all your soul reveres, by all your nature fears, swear that, for a year and a day you will not impart your knowledge of my crimes or death to any living being in any way, whatever may happen, or whatever you may see."—His eyes seemed bursting from their sockets: "I swear!" said Aubrey; he sunk laughing upon his pillow, and breathed no more.

Aubrey retired to rest, but did not sleep; the many circumstances attending his acquaintance with this man rose upon his mind, and he knew not why; when he remembered his oath a cold shivering came over him, as if from the presentiment of something horrible awaiting him. Rising early in the morning, he was about to enter the hovel in which he had left the corpse, when a robber met him, and informed him that it was no longer there, having been conveyed by himself and comrades, upon his retiring, to the pinnacle of a neighbouring mount, according to a promise they had given his lordship, that it should be exposed to the first cold ray of the moon that rose after his death. Aubrey astonished, and taking several of the men, determined to go and bury it upon the spot where it lay. But, when he had mounted to the summit he found no trace of either the corpse or the clothes, though the robbers swore they pointed out the identical rock on which they had laid the body. For a time his mind was bewildered in conjectures, but he at last returned, convinced that they had buried the corpse for the sake of the clothes.

Weary of a country in which he had met with such terrible misfortunes, and in which all apparently conspired to heighten that superstitious melancholy that had seized upon his mind, he resolved to leave it, and soon arrived at Smyrna. While waiting for a vessel to convey him to Otranto, or to Naples, he occupied himself in arranging those effects he had with him belonging to Lord Ruthven. Amongst other things there was a case containing several weapons of offence, more or less adapted to ensure the death of the victim. There were several daggers and ataghans. Whilst turning them over, and examining their curious forms, what was his surprise at finding a sheath apparently ornamented in the same style as the dagger discovered in the fatal hut—he shuddered—hastening to gain further proof, he found the weapon, and his horror may be imagined when he discovered that it fitted, though peculiarly shaped, the sheath he held in his hand. His eyes seemed to need no further certainty—they seemed gazing to be bound to the dagger; yet still he wished to disbelieve; but the particular form, the same varying tints upon the haft and sheath were alike in splendour on both, and left no room for doubt; there were also drops of blood on each.

He left Smyrna, and on his way home, at Rome, his first inquiries were concerning the lady he had attempted to snatch from Lord Ruthven's seductive arts. Her parents were in distress, their fortune ruined, and she had not been heard of since the departure of his lordship. Aubrey's mind became almost broken under so many repeated horrors; he was afraid that this lady had fallen a victim to the destroyer of Ianthe. He became morose and silent; and his only occupation consisted in urging the speed of the postilions, as if he were going to save the life of some one he held dear. He arrived at Calais; a breeze, which seemed obedient to his will, soon wafted him to the English shores; and he hastened to the mansion of his fathers, and there, for a moment, appeared to lose, in the embraces and caresses of his sister, all memory of the past. If she before, by her infantine caresses, had gained his affection, now that the woman began to appear, she was still more attaching as a companion.

Miss Aubrey had not that winning grace which gains the gaze and applause of the drawing-room assemblies. There was none of that light brilliancy which only exists in the heated atmosphere of a crowded apartment. Her blue eye was never lit up by the levity of the mind beneath. There was a melancholy charm about it which did not seem to arise from misfortune, but from some feeling within, that appeared to indicate a soul conscious of a brighter realm. Her step was not that light footing, which strays where'er a butterfly or a colour may attract—it was sedate and pensive. When alone, her face was never brightened by the smile of joy; but when her brother breathed to her his affection, and would in her presence forget those griefs she knew destroyed his rest, who would have exchanged her smile for that of the voluptuary? It seemed as if those eyes,—that face were then playing in the light of their own native sphere. She was yet only eighteen, and had not been presented to the world, it having been thought by her guardians more fit that her presentation should be delayed until her brother's return from the continent, when he might be her protector. It was now, therefore, resolved that the next drawing-room, which was fast approaching, should be the epoch of her entry into the "busy scene." Aubrey would rather have remained in the mansion of his fathers, and fed upon the melancholy which overpowered him. He could not feel interest about the frivolities of fashionable strangers, when his mind had been so torn by the events he had witnessed; but he determined to sacrifice his own comfort to the protection of his sister. They soon arrived in town, and prepared for the next day, which had been announced as a drawing-room.

The crowd was excessive—a drawing-room had not been held for a long time, and all who were anxious to bask in the smile of royalty, hastened thither. Aubrey was there with his sister. While he was standing in a corner by himself, heedless of all around him, engaged in the remembrance that the first time he had seen Lord Ruthven was in that very place—he felt himself suddenly seized by the arm, and a voice he recognized too well, sounded in his ear—"Remember your oath." He had hardly courage to turn, fearful of seeing a spectre that would blast him, when he perceived, at a little distance, the same figure which had attracted his notice on this spot upon his first entry into society. He gazed till his limbs almost refusing to bear their weight, he was obliged to take the arm of a friend, and forcing a passage through the crowd, he threw himself into his carriage, and was driven home. He paced the room with hurried steps, and fixed his hands upon his head, as if he were afraid his thoughts were bursting from his brain. Lord Ruthven again before him—circumstances started up in dreadful array—the dagger—his oath.—He roused himself, he could not believe it possible—the dead rise again!—He thought his imagination had conjured up the image his mind was resting upon. It was impossible that it could be real—he determined, therefore, to go again into society; for though he attempted to ask concerning Lord Ruthven, the name hung upon his lips, and he could not succeed in gaining information. He went a few nights after with his sister to the assembly of a near relation. Leaving her under the protection of a matron, he retired into a recess, and there gave himself up to his own devouring thoughts. Perceiving, at last, that many were leaving, he roused himself, and entering another room, found his sister surrounded by several, apparently in earnest conversation; he attempted to pass and get near her, when one, whom he requested to move, turned round, and revealed to him those features he most abhorred. He sprang forward, seized his sister's arm, and, with hurried step, forced her towards the street: at the door he found himself impeded by the crowd of servants who were waiting for their lords; and while he was engaged in passing them, he again heard that voice whisper close to him—"Remember your oath!"—He did not dare to turn, but, hurrying his sister, soon reached home.

Aubrey became almost distracted. If before his mind had been absorbed by one subject, how much more completely was it engrossed, now that the certainty of the monster's living again pressed upon his thoughts. His sister's attentions were now unheeded, and it was in vain that she intreated him to explain to her what had caused his abrupt conduct. He only uttered a few words, and those terrified her. The more he thought, the more he was bewildered. His oath startled him;—was he then to allow this monster to roam, bearing ruin upon his breath, amidst all he held dear, and not avert its progress? His very sister might have been touched by him. But even if he were to break his oath, and disclose his suspicions, who would believe him? He thought of employing his own hand to free the world from such a wretch; but death, he remembered, had been already mocked. For days he remained in this state; shut up in his room, he saw no one, and ate only when his sister came, who, with eyes streaming with tears, besought him, for her sake, to support nature. At last, no longer capable of bearing stillness and solitude, he left his house, roamed from street to street, anxious to fly that image which haunted him. His dress became neglected, and he wandered, as often exposed to the noon-day sun as to the midnight damps. He was no longer to be recognized; at first he returned with the evening to the house; but at last he laid him down to rest wherever fatigue overtook him. His sister, anxious for his safety, employed people to follow him; but they were soon distanced by him who fled from a pursuer swifter than any—from thought. His conduct, however, suddenly changed. Struck with the idea that he left by his absence the whole of his friends, with a fiend amongst them, of whose presence they were unconscious, he determined to enter again into society, and watch him closely, anxious to forewarn, in spite of his oath, all whom Lord Ruthven approached with intimacy. But when he entered into a room, his haggard and suspicious looks were so striking, his inward shudderings so visible, that his sister was at last obliged to beg of him to abstain from seeking, for her sake, a society which affected him so strongly. When, however, remonstrance proved unavailing, the guardians thought proper to interpose, and, fearing that his mind was becoming alienated, they thought it high time to resume again that trust which had been before imposed upon them by Aubrey's parents.

Desirous of saving him from the injuries and sufferings he had daily encountered in his wanderings, and of preventing him from exposing to the general eye those marks of what they considered folly, they engaged a physician to reside in the house, and take constant care of him. He hardly appeared to notice it, so completely was his mind absorbed by one terrible subject. His incoherence became at last so great, that he was confined to his chamber. There he would often lie for days, incapable of being roused. He had become emaciated, his eyes had attained a glassy lustre;—the only sign of affection and recollection remaining displayed itself upon the entry of his sister; then he would sometimes start, and, seizing her hands, with looks that severely afflicted her, he would desire her not to touch him. "Oh, do not touch him—if your love for me is aught, do not go near him!" When, however, she inquired to whom he referred, his only answer was, "True! true!" and again he sank into a state, whence not even she could rouse him. This lasted many months: gradually, however, as the year was passing, his incoherences became less frequent, and his mind threw off a portion of its gloom, whilst his guardians observed, that several times in the day he would count upon his fingers a definite number, and then smile.

The time had nearly elapsed, when, upon the last day of the year, one of his guardians entering his room, began to converse with his physician upon the melancholy circumstance of Aubrey's being in so awful a situation, when his sister was going next day to be married. Instantly Aubrey's attention was attracted; he asked anxiously to whom. Glad of this mark of returning intellect, of which they feared he had been deprived, they mentioned the name of the Earl of Marsden. Thinking this was a young Earl whom he had met with in society, Aubrey seemed pleased, and astonished them still more by his expressing his intention to be present at the nuptials, and desiring to see his sister. They answered not, but in a few minutes his sister was with him. He was apparently again capable of being affected by the influence of her lovely smile; for he pressed her to his breast, and kissed her cheek, wet with tears, flowing at the thought of her brother's being once more alive to the feelings of affection. He began to speak with all his wonted warmth, and to congratulate her upon her marriage with a person so distinguished for rank and every accomplishment; when he suddenly perceived a locket upon her breast; opening it, what was his surprise at beholding the features of the monster who had so long influenced his life. He seized the portrait in a paroxysm of rage, and trampled it under foot. Upon her asking him why he thus destroyed the resemblance of her future husband, he looked as if he did not understand her—then seizing her hands, and gazing on her with a frantic expression of countenance, he bade her swear that she would never wed this monster, for he— But he could not advance—it seemed as if that voice again bade him remember his oath—he turned suddenly round, thinking Lord Ruthven was near him but saw no one. In the meantime the guardians and physician, who had heard the whole, and thought this was but a return of his disorder, entered, and forcing him from Miss Aubrey, desired her to leave him. He fell upon his knees to them, he implored, he begged of them to delay but for one day. They, attributing this to the insanity they imagined had taken possession of his mind, endeavoured to pacify him, and retired.

Lord Ruthven had called the morning after the drawing-room, and had been refused with every one else. When he heard of Aubrey's ill health, he readily understood himself to be the cause of it; but when he learned that he was deemed insane, his exultation and pleasure could hardly be concealed from those among whom he had gained this information. He hastened to the house of his former companion, and, by constant attendance, and the pretence of great affection for the brother and interest in his fate, he gradually won the ear of Miss Aubrey. Who could resist his power? His tongue had dangers and toils to recount—could speak of himself as of an individual having no sympathy with any being on the crowded earth, save with her to whom he addressed himself;—could tell how, since he knew her, his existence, had begun to seem worthy of preservation, if it were merely that he might listen to her soothing accents;—in fine, he knew so well how to use the serpent's art, or such was the will of fate, that he gained her affections. The title of the elder branch falling at length to him, he obtained an important embassy, which served as an excuse for hastening the marriage, (in spite of her brother's deranged state,) which was to take place the very day before his departure for the continent.

Aubrey, when he was left by the physician and his guardians, attempted to bribe the servants, but in vain. He asked for pen and paper; it was given him; he wrote a letter to his sister, conjuring her, as she valued her own happiness, her own honour, and the honour of those now in the grave, who once held her in their arms as their hope and the hope of their house, to delay but for a few hours that marriage, on which he denounced the most heavy curses. The servants promised they would deliver it; but giving it to the physician, he thought it better not to harass any more the mind of Miss Aubrey by, what he considered, the ravings of a maniac. Night passed on without rest to the busy inmates of the house; and Aubrey heard, with a horror that may more easily be conceived than described, the notes of busy preparation. Morning came, and the sound of carriages broke upon his ear. Aubrey grew almost frantic. The curiosity of the servants at last overcame their vigilance, they gradually stole away, leaving him in the custody of an helpless old woman. He seized the opportunity, with one bound was out of the room, and in a moment found himself in the apartment where all were nearly assembled. Lord Ruthven was the first to perceive him: he immediately approached, and, taking his arm by force, hurried him from the room, speechless with rage. When on the staircase, Lord Ruthven whispered in his ear—"Remember your oath, and know, if not my bride to day, your sister is dishonoured. Women are frail!" So saying, he pushed him towards his attendants, who, roused by the old woman, had come in search of him. Aubrey could no longer support himself; his rage not finding vent, had broken a blood-vessel, and he was conveyed to bed. This was not mentioned to his sister, who was not present when he entered, as the physician was afraid of agitating her. The marriage was solemnized, and the bride and bridegroom left London.

Aubrey's weakness increased; the effusion of blood produced symptoms of the near approach of death. He desired his sister's guardians might be called, and when the midnight hour had struck, he related composedly what the reader has perused—he died immediately after.

The guardians hastened to protect Miss Aubrey; but when they arrived, it was too late. Lord Ruthven had disappeared, and Aubrey's sister had glutted the thirst of a VAMPYRE!

A FRAGMENT

(1819)

Lord Byron

In the year 17—, having for some time determined on a journey through countries not hitherto much frequented by travellers I set out, accompanied by a friend, whom I shall designate by the name of Augustus Darvell. He was a few years my elder, and a man of considerable fortune and ancient family—advantages which an extensive capacity prevented him alike from undervaluing or overrating. Some peculiar circumstances in his private history had rendered him to me an object of attention, of interest, and even of regard, which neither the reserve of his manners, nor occasional indications of an inquietude at times nearly approaching to alienation of mind, could extinguish.

I was yet young in life, which I had begun early; but my intimacy with him was of a recent date: we had been educated at the same schools and university; but his progress through these had preceded mine, and he had been deeply initiated into what is called the world, while I was yet in my noviciate. While thus engaged, I had heard much both of his past and present life; and although in these accounts there were many and irreconcileable contradictions, I could still gather from the whole that he was a being of no common order, and one who, whatever pains he might take to avoid remark, would still be remarkable. I had cultivated his acquaintance subsequently, and endeavoured to obtain his friendship, but this last appeared to be unattainable; whatever affections he might have possessed seemed now, some to have been extinguished, and others to be concentred: that his feelings were acute, I had sufficient opportunities of observing; for, although he could control, he could not altogether disguise them: still he had a power of giving to one passion the appearance of another in such a manner that it was difficult to define the nature of what was working within him; and the expressions of his features would vary so rapidly, though slightly, that it was useless to trace them to their sources. It was evident that he was a prey to some cureless disquiet; but whether it arose from ambition, love, remorse, grief, from one or all of these, or merely from a morbid temperament akin to disease, I could not discover: there were circumstances alleged, which might have justified the application to each of these causes; but, as I have before said, these were so contradictory and contradicted, that none could be fixed upon with accuracy. Where there is mystery, it is generally supposed that there must also be evil: I know not how this may be, but in him there certainly was the one, though I could not ascertain the extent of the other—and felt loth, as far as regarded himself, to believe in its existence. My advances were received with sufficient coldness; but I was young, and not easily discouraged, and at length succeeded in obtaining, to a certain degree, that common-place intercourse and moderate confidence of common and every day concerns, created and cemented by similarity of pursuit and frequency of meeting, which is called intimacy, or friendship, according to the ideas of him who uses those words to express them.

Darvell had already travelled extensively; and to him I had applied for information with regard to the conduct of my intended journey. It was my secret wish that he might be prevailed on to accompany me: it was also a probable hope, founded upon the shadowy restlessness which I had observed in him, and to which the animation which he appeared to feel on such subjects, and his apparent indifference to all by which he was more immediately surrounded, gave fresh strength. This wish I first hinted, and then expressed: his answer, though I had partly expected it, gave me all the pleasure of surprise—he consented; and, after the requisite arrangements, we commenced our voyages. After journeying through various countries of the south of Europe, our attention was turned towards the East, according to our original destination; and it was in my progress through those regions that the incident occurred upon which will turn what I may have to relate.

The constitution of Darvell, which must from his appearance have been in early life more than usually robust, had been for some time gradually giving way, without the intervention of any apparent disease: he had neither cough nor hectic, yet he became daily more enfeebled: his habits were temperate, and he neither declined nor complained of fatigue, yet he was evidently wasting away: he became more and more silent and sleepless, and at length so seriously altered, that my alarm grew proportionate to what I conceived to be his danger.

We had determined, on our arrival at Smyrna, on an excursion to the ruins of Ephesus and Sardis, from which I endeavoured to dissuade him in his present state of indisposition—but in vain: there appeared to be an oppression on his mind, and a solemnity in his manner, which ill corresponded with his eagerness to proceed on what I regarded as a mere party of pleasure, little suited to a valetudinarian; but I opposed him no longer—and in a few days we set off together, accompanied only by a serrugee and a single janizary.

We had passed halfway towards the remains of Ephesus, leaving behind us the more fertile environs of Smyrna, and were entering upon that wild and tenantless track through the marshes and defiles which lead to the few huts yet lingering over the broken columns of Diana—the roofless walls of expelled Christianity, and the still more recent but complete desolation of abandoned mosques—when the sudden and rapid illness of my companion obliged us to halt at a Turkish cemetery, the turbaned tombstones of which were the sole indication that human life had ever been a sojourner in this wilderness. The only caravanserai we had seen was left some hours behind us, not a vestige of a town or even cottage was within sight or hope, and this "city of the dead" appeared to be the sole refuge for my unfortunate friend, who seemed on the verge of becoming the last of its inhabitants.

In this situation, I looked round for a place where he might most conveniently repose:—contrary to the usual aspect of Mahometan burial-grounds, the cypresses were in this few in number, and these thinly scattered over its extent: the tombstones were mostly fallen, and worn with age:—upon one of the most considerable of these, and beneath one of the most spreading trees, Darvell supported himself, in a half-reclining posture, with great difficulty. He asked for water. I had some doubts of our being able to find any, and prepared to go in search of it with hesitating despondency—but he desired me to remain; and turning to Suleiman, our janizary, who stood by us smoking with great tranquillity, he said, "Suleiman, *verbana su*," (i.e. bring some water,) and went on describing the spot where it was to be found with great minuteness, at a small well for camels, a few hundred yards to the right: the janizary obeyed. I said to Darvell, "How did you know this?"—He replied, "From our situation; you must perceive that this place was once inhabited, and could not have been so without springs: I have also been here before."

"You have been here before!—How came you never to mention this to me? and what could you be doing in a place where no one would remain a moment longer than they could help it?"

To this question I received no answer. In the mean time Suleiman returned with the water, leaving the serrugee and the horses at the fountain. The quenching of his thirst had the appearance of reviving him for a moment; and I conceived hopes of his being able to proceed, or at least to return, and I urged the attempt. He was silent—and appeared to be collecting his spirits for an effort to speak. He began.

"This is the end of my journey, and of my life—I came here to die: but I have a request to make, a command—for such my last words must be—You will observe it?"

"Most certainly; but have better hopes."

"I have no hopes, nor wishes, but this—conceal my death from every human being."

"I hope there will be no occasion; that you will recover, and—"

"Peace!—it must be so: promise this."

"I do."

"Swear it, by all that"—He here dictated an oath of great solemnity.

"There is no occasion for this—I will observe your request; and to doubt me is—"

"It cannot be helped,—you must swear."

I took the oath: it appeared to relieve him. He removed a seal ring from his finger, on which were some Arabic characters, and presented it to me. He proceeded—

"On the ninth day of the month, at noon precisely (what month you please, but this must be the day), you must fling this ring into the salt springs which run into the Bay of Eleusis: the day after, at the same hour, you must repair to the ruins of the Temple of Ceres, and wait one hour."

"Why?"

"You will see."

"The ninth day of the month, you say?"

"The ninth."

As I observed that the present was the ninth day of the month, his countenance changed, and he paused. As he sat, evidently becoming more feeble, a stork, with a snake in her beak, perched upon a tombstone near us; and, without devouring her prey, appeared to be steadfastly regarding us. I know not what impelled me to drive it away, but the attempt was useless; she made a few circles in the air, and returned exactly to the same spot. Darvell pointed to it, and smiled: he spoke—I know not whether to himself or to me—but the words were only, "'Tis well!"

"What is well? what do you mean?"

"No matter: you must bury me here this evening, and exactly where that bird is now perched. You know the rest of my injunctions."

He then proceeded to give me several directions as to the manner in which his death might be best concealed. After these were finished, he exclaimed, "You perceive that bird?"

"Certainly."

"And the serpent writhing in her beak?"

"Doubtless: there is nothing uncommon in it; it is her natural prey. But it is odd that she does not devour it."

He smiled in a ghastly manner, and said, faintly, "It is not yet time!" As he spoke, the stork flew away. My eyes followed it for a moment, it could hardly be longer than ten might be counted. I felt Darvell's weight, as it were, increase upon my shoulder, and, turning to look upon his face, perceived that he was dead!

I was shocked with the sudden certainty which could not be mistaken—his countenance in a few minutes became nearly black. I should have attributed so rapid a change to poison, had I not been aware that he had no opportunity of receiving it unperceived. The day was declining, the body was rapidly altering, and nothing remained but to fulfil his request. With the aid of Suleiman's ataghan and my own sabre, we scooped a shallow grave upon the spot which Darvell had indicated: the earth easily gave way, having already received some Mahometan tenant. We dug as deeply as the time permitted us, and throwing the dry earth upon all that remained of the singular being so lately departed, we cut a few sods of greener turf from the less withered soil around us, and laid them upon his sepulchre.

Between astonishment and grief, I was tearless.

EXCERPTS FROM

PRESUMPTION; OR, THE FATE OF FRANKENSTEIN

(1823)

Richard Brinsley Peake

ACT I, SCENE III

The Sleeping Apartment of Frankenstein. Dark. The Bed is within a recess between the wings, enclosed by dark green curtains. A Sword (to break) hanging. A Large French Window; between the wings a staircase leading to a Gallery across the stage, on which is the Door of the Laboratory above. A small high Lattice in centre of scene, next the Laboratory Door. A Gothic Table on stage, screwed. A Gothic Chair in centre, and Footstool. Music expressive of the rising of a storm. Enter Frankenstein, with a Lighted Lamp, which he places on the table. Distant thunder heard.

FRANKENSTEIN. This evening—this lowering evening, will, in all probability, complete my task. Years have I laboured, and at length discovered that to which so many men of genius have in vain directed their inquiries. After days and nights of incredible labour and fatigue, I have become master of the secret of bestowing animation upon lifeless matter. With so astonishing a power in my hands, long, long did I hesitate how to employ it. The object of my experiment lies there (*pointing up to the laboratory*)—a huge automaton in human form. Should I succeed in animating it, Life and Death would appear to me as ideal bounds, which I shall break through and pour a torrent of light into our dark world. I have lost all soul or sensation but for this one pursuit. I have clothed the inanimate mass, lest the chilly air should quench the spark of life newly infused. (*Thunder and heavy rain heard.*) 'Tis a dreary night, the rain patters dismally against the panes; 'tis a night for such a task. I'll in and complete the wondrous effort.

Music.—Frankenstein takes up lamp, cautiously looks around him, ascends the stairs, crosses the gallery above, and exits into door of laboratory. Enter Fritz, with a candle.

FRITZ. Master isn't here—dare I peep. Only think of the reward Mr. Clerval promised me, a cow and a cottage, milk and a mansion. Master is certainly not come up yet. My candle burns all manner of colours, and spits like a roasted apple. (*Runs against the chair and drops his light, which goes out.*) There, now, I'm in the dark. Oh my nerves. (*A blue flame appears at the small lattice Window above, as from the laboratory.*) What's that? Oh, lauk; there he is, kicking up the devil's own flame! Oh my cow! I'll venture up—oh my cottage! I'll climb to the window—it will be only one peep to make my fortune.

Music.—Fritz takes up footstool, he ascends the stairs, when on the gallery landing place, he stands on the footstool tiptoe to look through the small high lattice window of the laboratory, a sudden combustion is heard within. The blue flame changes to one of a reddish hue.

FRANKENSTEIN. (*Within.*) It lives! it lives!

FRITZ. (*Speaks through music.*) Oh, dear! oh, dear! oh, dear!

Fritz, greatly alarmed, jumps down hastily, totters tremblingly down the stairs in vast hurry; when in front on stage, having fallen flat in fright, with difficulty speaks.

FRITZ. There's a hob-hob-goblin, seven-and-twenty feet high! Oh, my nerves; I feel as if I had just come out of strong fits, and nobody to throw cold water in my face—if my legs won't lap under me, I'll just make my escape. (*Crosses.*) Oh, my poor nerves!

Exit Fritz, crawling. Music.—Frankenstein rushes from the laboratory, without lamp, fastens the door in apparent dread, and hastens down the stairs, watching the entrance of the laboratory.

FRANKENSTEIN. It lives! I saw the dull yellow eye of the creature open, it breathed hard, and a convulsive motion agitated its limbs. What a wretch have I formed, I had selected his features as beautiful—beautiful! Ah, horror! his cadaverous skin scarcely covers the work of muscles and arteries beneath, his hair lustrous, black, and flowing—his teeth of pearly whiteness—but these luxuriances only form more horrible contrasts with the deformities of the monster. (*He listens at the foot of the staircase.*) What have I accomplished? the beauty of my dream has vanished! and breathless horror and disgust now fill my heart. For this I have deprived myself of rest and health, have worked my brain to madness; and when I looked to reap my great reward, a flash breaks in upon my darkened soul, and tells me my attempt was impious, and that the fruition will be fatal to my peace for ever. (*He again listens.*) All is still! The dreadful spectre of a human form—no mortal could withstand the horror of that countenance—a mummy embued with animation could not be so hideous as the wretch I have endowed with life!—miserable and impious being that I am! Elizabeth! brother! Agatha!—fairest Agatha! never more dare I look upon your virtuous faces. Lost! lost! lost!

Music.—Frankenstein sinks on a chair; sudden combustion heard, and smoke issues, the door of laboratory breaks to pieces with a loud crash—red fire within.—The Monster discovered at door entrance in smoke, which evaporates—the red flame continues visible. The Monster advances forward, breaks through the balustrade or railing of gallery immediately facing the door of laboratory, jumps on the table beneath, and from thence leaps on the stage, stands in attitude before Frankenstein, who had started up in terror; they gaze for a moment at each other.

FRANKENSTEIN. The horrid corpse to which I have given life!

Music.—The Monster looks at Frankenstein most intently, approaches him with gestures of conciliation. Frankenstein retreats, the Monster pursuing him.)

FRANKENSTEIN. Ficnd! darc not to approach mc—avaunt, or dread the fierce vengeance of my arm.

Music.—Frankenstein takes the sword off the nail and points with it at the Monster, who snatches the sword, snaps it in two and throws it on stage. The Monster then seizes Frankenstein—loud thunder heard—throws him violently on the floor, ascends the staircase, opens the large window, and disappears through the casement. Frankenstein remains motionless on the ground.—Thunder and lightning until the drop falls.

ACT III, SCENE V

Wild Border of the Lake. At the extremity of the stage, a lofty overhanging mountain of snow. Music.—All the Gipsies discovered in various groups. A pistol shot is heard. The Gipsies start up alarmed. A second pistol is fired nearer. The Monster rushes on with the locket worn by Agatha during the piece. The Gipsies scream out and fly in all directions. Hammerpan is on the point of escaping, when the Monster seizes him, and Hammerpan falls down on being dragged back. The Monster points off, to intimate that Frankenstein is approaching, throws down the locket, commands the gipsy, Hammerpan, to show it to Frankenstein—the Monster threatens him, and rushing up the mountain, climbs, and disappears. Enter Frankenstein, with two loaded pistols and a musket unloaded. At the same time Hammerpan rises.

FRANKENSTEIN. In vain do I pursue the wretch, in vain have I fired on him. (*Throws his gun from him.*) He eludes the bullet. Say, fellow, have you seen aught pass here?

HAMMERPAN. The giant creature, who aroused us in the forest, rushed upon me but this instant, and pointing to the path by which you came, intimated that I should give you this.

(Presents locket to Frankenstein.)

FRANKENSTEIN. 'Tis Agatha's—the murdered Agatha! Malicious fiend! it will joy you to know that my lacerated heart bleeds afresh. Revenge shall henceforth be the devouring and only passion of my soul. I have but one resource—I devote myself either in my life or death to the destruction of the Demon! Agatha! William! you shall be avenged.

HAMMERPAN. See yonder (*points*), the monster climbs the snow.

FRANKENSTEIN. Then this rencontre shall terminate his detested life or mine!

Music.—Frankenstein draws his pistol—rushes off at back of stage—The Gipsies return at various entrances—At the same time, enter Felix and Clerval with pistols, and Safie, Elizabeth, and Ninon following.—The Monster appears at the base of the mountain, Frankenstein pursuing.

CLERVAL. Behold our friend and his mysterious enemy.

FELIX. See—Frankenstein overtakes him—let us follow and assist him.

Is going up stage with Clerval.

HAMMERPAN. Hold, master! if the gun is fired, it will bring down a mountain of snow. Many an avalanche has fallen there.

Music.—Frankenstein discharges his pistol.—The Monster and Frankenstein meet at the very extremity of the stage.—Frankenstein fires his second pistol—the avalanche falls and annihilates the Monster and Frankenstein.—A heavy fall of snow succeeds.—Loud thunder heard, and all the characters form a picture as the curtain falls.

THE MONSTER MADE BY MAN; OR, THE PUNISHMENT OF PRESUMPTION

(1825, abridged)

Anonymous

In every age of the world woman's curiosity has been equaled by man's presumption, and one of the most astonishing events produced by the latter is related in Germany, that native country of every thing non-natural.

In one of the most romantic parts of it resided Wallberg, a magistrate, whose eldest son Ernest had from his youth evinced a studious disposition and gloomy cast of thought, seldom enlivened by the usual vivacity belonging to his years, though of an amiable disposition. Some of his ancestors had held a high rank amongst the learned men of their times, a library collected by them had descended from father to son for several generations, the reading of which formed the chief delight of Ernest. A large portion of it consisted of a certain kind of philosophical works, which the superior light of modern science has proved to be absurd and rendered obsolete. To that species of study, for want of a judicious director, Ernest unfortunately devoted his chief attention, and the consequence was that instead of storing his powerful mind with useful knowledge, he became an admirer of the explored mysteries of astrology, and filled with a desire to attain possession of those two unattainables, the philosopher's stone, and the elixir of life.

Wallberg had a younger son; but the chief ornament of the family was an orphan niece of Madame Wallberg's. Agnes was as lovely in person as she was excellent in disposition. It had long been the wishes of their friends that at a proper age she should be united to Ernest. Their attachment appeared to be reciprocal, though had her's been defined it would have been found to have partaken more of a sister's love than the affection of a destined wife. His most intimate friend was Lewis Hartmann, in whose society and that of Agnes, was spent the few hours that Ernest could be tempted to allow from the pursuit of those studies he became daily more attached to. Hartmann much regretted the deep influence such a pernicious course of reading was getting over the mind of Ernest, more especially as he saw in it the probable seeds of unhappiness to Agnes, for who he entertained feelings which, looking upon her as the intended wife of one who he regarded, he would never allow himself to consider of a deeper kind than those of friendship. With a view to their happiness he endeavoured to detach Ernest from such useless studies, and to cheer his mind with innocent amusement. But all in vain, for he daily became attached to the acquirement of ignorant knowledge, until it appeared to absorb his whole faculties.

When the mind of Ernest had been thus occupied a few years, it became worked up to that pitch of enthusiasm so nearly allied to lunacy, as to be fully impressed with the belief that he had found out the mysterious spark of life to a being perfectly endowed with all the faculties and attributes of human nature. Wrapt in the contemplation of such supernatural power, all other knowledge seemed valueless, and his mind was bent on giving effect to the strange idea he had formed. His attention was now given to studying the structure of the human body, nor could the necessary disgusting researches turn him from his purpose; scenes loathsome to the mind were sources of delight to him, and he might be said to banquet on the revolting objects of decaying nature. For the place of his operations he chose a retired cave, and for his assistant a simple rustic lad, who only thought his employer was going to make a similar statue to those he had often seen in gardens. Of the purest and best tempered clay he there began to form a figure, modelled after the finest sculptures he could procure; the fibres, muscles, veins and skin, he supplied according to the preconceived ideas of his distempered imagination, while his mind reveled in the idea of being the creator and master of a set of beings, that should be the living proofs of his superior knowledge and power. When his prolonged absences from home were mentioned by his friends, his replies consisted of such incomprehensible hints as alarmed them for his sanity. At length, after many hours of toil he proudly surveyed an outwardly perfect representative of human beauty. He now began to collect the instruments that were to give life and animation to the mass he had compounded; and Frantz, his assistant, when he saw the proceedings, sometimes thought his master a madman, and sometimes a wonderful genius, that might in the end learn even him to be a clever fellow. Scarcely, however, had Ernest commenced those operations, which were to produce what he thought would be the elixir of life, the infusing of which into his figure would give it vitality, then chancing to look at it, it seemed to his amazed senses to have a slight convulsive motion. While gazing on it with all the intentness his almost bewildered mind would allow, a peal of thunder broke directly over the cave, that seemed as if it would level it with the ground, and bury him and his presumptuous work in its ruins. Ere it had subsided the form again began to move, and as it gradually arose from the platform on which he had modelled, it, its perfect proportions were enlarged to an unnatural size, its regular features were distorted into hideousness, the eyelids opened, and displayed two green balls, bedded in a yellow fluid, and the alabaster whiteness of its exterior turned to a leaded blue colour; at length it stood erect, every nerve and muscle writing with convulsive agitation. Ernest was transfixed with astonishment and horror at the result of his toils, and Frantz threw himself on the ground, a picture of fear; at length recovering he rushed from the cave, exclaiming "A man devil! A man devil!" When motion was restored to Ernest, he shrunk with abhorrence from the object he beheld, rolling its detestable eyes at him, its jaws alternately opening and shutting, and its bosom heaving as if endeavouring to give vent to sounds that at length seemed to proceed from it. Ernest, unable to bear the torturing sight, left the horrid scene and hastened home, where he threw himself on his bed in all the agony of despair. After some hours of wretchedness, during which he called down imprecations on his daring folly, he began to reflect on how he should act towards a being so unexpectedly called into existence. At length he resolved if it was alive to provide for its wants in a place of safety if tractable, and to destroy it if it showed tokens of being possessed of a mischievous spirit; providing himself with the means of either to sustain or deprive it of life, he returned to the cave.

In the meantime the monstrous being observing that the two principal objects on which its eyes had rested moved and then were not seen, using the instinct which along with animation had been given to it, essayed to do the same, stepped from the platform, and issued from the entrance of the cavern; but the brilliant light of the day striking suddenly upon its weak and glassy eyes gave them such a painful shock that, uttering a hideous cry, he returned into it, and seated himself on the ground. In that position Ernest found it, and for some time stood looking on the singular being mute with astonishment at the past, and apprehension for the future. The monster in return sat gazing at him, his distorted face rapidly changing in expression, at each variety of which Ernest felt that it was also becoming endowed with the accompanying passion, but its growl of rage gave him a feeling of horror that was only exceeded by his disgust at its attempts at laughter. Seeing it shake with cold, he threw a cloak on it; from the warmth thus produced evident pleasure was derived. Ernest next produced some bread, and putting a little in his own mouth gave part to the being who did the same; that a want of nature was thus supplied became evident, for no sooner was the portion given him eaten, than he seized on all the rest with the eagerness of a hungry wolf, and ravenously devoured it, while the expression of his face made Ernest fearful of interfering. Revolving in his mind how best to act towards the detested creature after what he had witnessed, he determined to place it under such confinement as would prevent its inflicting injury on others. To effect this he bound its arms with a cord, and then attempted to lead the monster out by it; not liking the twitch the rope gave he struggled and resisted, at which Ernest struck him with a large stick; furious with the pain the blow evidently gave the monster, it with an effort broke the cords asunder as though they were only pack-thread, and seized Ernest with so powerful a grasp as proved that in point of strength the one was not more than as a child in the hands of the other. Ernest's feeling of abhorrence was for a time changed into terror as the monster fixed his eyes on him, while his whole frame appeared convulsed as if some new sensation within him was struggling to find vent, at length in a hollow voice, in which was discernable none of the usual tones of human nature, he uttered, "I am the punishment of thy presumption." He then released Ernest from his hold, who immediately fled, fully impressed with the truth of the few words he had heard, and though he had impiously dared to mould the figure of a fellow creature, it was a supreme power that had imparted to it the principal of vitality, and would make it an instrument of retribution. These thoughts operating upon his previous irritation of mind caused a fever and delirium which reduced him to the brink of the grave.

Frantz, when he rushed from the cavern at the animation of the monster, stopped not until he reached his own home, continuing his outcry of "A man devil!" the whole way.

[Frantz tells his story, but is disbelieved.]

Nor was it long before there were full proofs of Frantz's story having some truth in it; for the monster being endued with a singular combination of animal instinct and human sense, was forced by the cravings of hunger to leave the cave in search of food, he found what at first satisfied him in wild berries and roots, and when his appetite was appeased returned to his abode. Gradually he extended his walks, till at length he was seen by labourers in the fields. Struck with terror at the approach of a being of such gigantic stature, and frightful visage, whose appearance was that of savage wildness and ferocity, they all fled at his approach; the provisions and clothes they left he immediately converted to his own use. Having thus tasted food more pleasing to his palate than the wild produce of the hedges, he repeated his visits, fear constantly driving the men away, till at length the annoyance became so great they determined to end it by his destruction. For that purpose all the villagers assembled, watched, and surrounded him; the shout they raised to keep up their own courage deprived him of his, and filled him with an instinctive desire to fly, rushing on them he seized the two that were nearest, hurled them from him with a power that fully proved his strength was equal to his stature, and ran with such speed as set all their endeavours to secure him at defiance. Finding however that he never attempted to injure them beyond devouring their food, a kind of silent bargain was made between the parties. The villagers regularly placed provisions for him in one place, and he after having eaten them, suffered the men to pursue their labours unmolested, and would even mount some elevated spot and quietly look at them until the close of day ended their toils. One day he wandered beyond his usual bounds, approached a cottage, and was tempted to enter it. It was the residence of Frantz's father, but none of its inhabitants were at home except his three sisters. They had heard of, but never seen their strange visitor, the uncouthness of whose figure naturally filled them with terror. His continuing to stand in the door-way prevented their being able to run away, while he stood motionless with wonder at the new objects that he saw. One of the girls summoning courage and remembering his partiality for eating, placed some victuals as near to him as she durst venture, while the other two barricadoed themselves with furniture in the furthest corner of the room. Having satisfied his eyes, he was just approaching the food when Frantz entered, who seeing the unwelcome guest, and the fears of his sisters, instantly felt bold in their defence. Seizing the cudgel that had preserved his head from the barber's razor, he applied it with good will to the shoulders of the monster, who in a moment wrested it from his attacker, dashed him to the ground, and raising the stick was about to strike a blow that would have deprived Frantz of power if not of life, when the sisters seeing his danger threw themselves before him in a supplicating attitude. The beauty of their innocent faces, and mute imploring eloquence arrested his arm, he gazed on them with as much pleasure as could be pictured in so unnatural a face, gradually dropped the weapon, and after an expressive action in which surprise, feeling, and delight were singularly blended, left the cottage, thus proving that in a lovely innocent woman's countenance there is silent language that speaks to and subdues the most untutored heart, when its possessor is undepraved by vice.

Ernest's illness was of long continuance; the mysterious exclamations he made during it were naturally attributed to delirium; the attentions of his mother and the lovely Agnes were unremitting. Hartmann witnessed them, and it far more firmly rivetted the attachment which he was unwilling to allow, but could not subdue, for the excellent girl; while his mind was filled with the deepest anxiety for her happiness when united to Ernest, as the latter's mind, when he began to recover, appeared more than ever burthened with gloom and approaching misanthropy. Madame Wallberg's health had also suffered by her attendance on her son, and they were both advised to retire a few miles into the country for change of air, thither they repaired. Youth and exercise soon renewed the son, but could not remove his excessive agitation of mind whenever the portentous words of the monster rose to his mind. The mother's health received not so much benefit from the change of air as her spirits did from her son's improved looks. They were one day walking in a plantation near their residence, when the frightful being suddenly appeared before them, to the horror (though from different causes) of them both. Madame Wallberg, appalled by the terrific appearance of a creature, in size and looks so unlike aught human, fell senseless in the arms of her son, who, convulsed with agony, had scarcely power to support her. The monster, after eyeing Ernest for some time with the malice of a demon, gave vent to a howl, in which all the bad passions of human nature might be fancied as combined together in a sound of a most unearthly description. Ernest remembered the superior strength of the other, and shuddered at what would be his mother's fate should hate prompt its possessor to use it; at length his feelings found utterance, and he cried out, "Monster! pernicious fiend! avaunt! if thou art destined, as the penalty of my folly to torment me with thy accursed presence, the innocent must be beyond thy appointed power, away then! and disturb not those who have not sinned like myself." The being seemed to understand the import of his words, but not to regard them; for after a loud contemptuous laugh he appeared on the point of rushing on Ernest, like a hyena on its prey, when casting his eye on the placid, but death-like countenance, of Madame Wallberg, as she lay supported on her son's bosom, its almost more than mortal look seemed to arrest him; gazing on it for some time, his eyes rolled alternately on the face of the mother and son, as if tracing a similarity between them; after some time, starting from his fixed attitude, the terrific being again uttered the dreadful words, "I am the punishment of thy presumption," and then disappeared. Madame Wallberg soon after began to recover, and looked fearfully round to see if the cause of her horror was still present, and then asked her son if some threatening words had not been spoken by it, he endeavoured to assure her not. Supported by Ernest, she was able to reach the house, but her delicate frame had received a shock it was not able to sustain, and before many days it became evident to all her family that her time on earth was drawing rapidly to a close. To lose so excellent a being wrung the hearts of all her relatives with grief; but their feelings were comparative happiness to the wretched misery of Ernest, at the knowledge that his daring folly had led to the death of one of the most excellent women, and that she who gave him existence was deprived of her's, as the first victim sacrificed by his presumption. Madness would have almost been welcome to him, but there was a sentiment always prevalent in his mind that his senses were to be preserved, that he might bear the inflictions of further sufferings. Feeling her last hour approaching, after an heart-breaking farewell of her beloved family, his mother intreated him to endeavour at a more composed state of mind, for the sake of those who would need his consolations; then, placing his hand in the hand of Agnes, prayed for a blessing on her son and daughter, and soon resigned her pious spirit into the hands of her Creator.

Wretched at having been the cause of such an irreparable loss to his family, Ernest subdued as much as possible his own feelings, that he might be the more capable of assuaging their grief; resolved afterwards to seek and destroy the monster whose appearance had produced the lamentable event. When time therefore had softened the violence of their sorrow, he armed himself and repaired to the cavern, as the most likely place to meet with the object of his hatred. When he arrived at the entrance, the monster was just issuing from it, who, on seeing Ernest, gave one of those howls which equally with his looks were nearly indescribable, being neither angelic, demonic, or human, but a combination of the extreme of all. Ernest, after recovering [from] the sensation of horror which his presence raised, said, "Detestable wretch! whose appearance in the face of day carries destruction with it, for in thy hideous aspect is death, forbear to contaminate the earth by showing thy abominable presence; submit thyself to my commands and keep within the cavern, or I will this moment end thy life, and rid the world of such a monster." The being's looks shewed that he understood what was addressed to him, while his countenance marked both contempt and defiance of the threat; after a malignant laugh, in his usual unearthly tone, he answered as before, "I am the punishment of thy presumption." "Thy mission has already been fulfilled," Ernest replied, "by the death of one most dear unto me; but the innocent shall not again suffer for my presumptuous misdeeds, even if I forfeit my own life in the attempt I will extinguish they existence."—"Canst thou?" was the answer, accompanied by the same contemptuous defying look. Ernest felt that the supreme power that had endued the being with life might also have placed him above his vengeance, but he also felt that he had with his own life rather make an atonement for his sin, than let further injury attend the innocent. "And why cannot I?" exclaimed Ernest; "the strongest beasts of the field are subservient to the power of man, thy strength may be superior to mine, but then it is only brutal strength, unaided by the influence of reason; the beasts that are not useful are deemed pernicious, and driven from the abodes of men, as thou shalt be, for thou art—" "The punishment of thy presumption," interrupted the being; then after a pause, changing from the tone he had hitherto spoken in to one of deep solemnity, continued, "thyself, a created being, presumed in thy pride of knowledge to become a creator: like the heathen who raises the funeral pile on which he perishes, thou hast only built up an edifice too frail to last, but which, falling, will destroy thee." In the voice he now heard there was that which was more appalling to the mind of Ernest than the one that had before made him tremble at the sound. It first filled him with awe, then with desperation. "Be this the moment then of its fall and my destruction:" so saying, Ernest pointing his gun fired; his intended victim was unhurt, and said, "it is not the hour appointed for thee, but may be that fixed for one of thine." He then rushed on Ernest, and with ease wrenched the weapon from him, who immediately drew his sword, and furiously attacked the hated being, who returned not the blows but caught them on the gun.

Ernest's younger brother, Henry, was rambling in the fields, and being near heard the report of Ernest's gun when he fired, thinking he was out shooting, he hastened to the spot, and beheld what appeared such an unequal combat. His terror at the super-human appearance of the monster was lost in fear for his brother's safety, to aid whom, he, with the broken branch of a tree that he found on the ground, struck at the hideous being, who instantly returned the blow by one with the butt end of the gun, which levelled him to the earth, and a moment sufficed to extinguish life in the affectionate, but unfortunate, Henry. Ernest flew to his brother, the monster pointed to the victim with terrible expression, and then left them. The miserable Ernest finding life extinct in Henry, threw himself frantic on the ground beside him, in which state they were found in the course of the day, and conveyed to that home again rendered the scene of mourning. Conjecture attributed the fatal event to accident; for when Ernest recovered his faculties, every inquiry or allusion to the dreadful occurrence drove him to the verge of madness.

[The friends all console one another.]

Time at length began to produce again its usual soothing effects on the mourners; short excursions to amuse their minds by change of scene were proposed and executed. One day Ernest, Hartmann, and Agnes were sailing in a small boat near their residence, the two latter endeavouring by the conversation to interest the former, who, though he appeared to listen, was only occupied by his own thoughts. Looking towards the land, he suddenly uttered an exclamation of horror, and starting up with great force, the violence of the action overset the boat, and in a moment they were all plunged in the water. Ernest had mechanically seized the boat, and was supported by it; Hartmann, when he rose to the surface, looked around for Agnes, and to his horror saw that the current was hurrying her towards an eddy that would inevitably be fatal long before he (though an excellent swimmer) could reach and rescue her from the danger. He was exerting himself to the utmost to save her, when he heard a violent plunge into the lake near her, and she totally disappeared. Almost frantic he made a hopeless effort to save her by diving; obliged to return above the water for air, what was his astonishment at beholding a being, monstrous in size and appearance, just emerging from the water with the lovely insensible girl in its arms, and which it deposited with every mark of care on the grass. He hastened towards the shore and was just landing when the being who had stood intently looking at the sufferer, saw him approach, and instantly fled into an adjoining grove.

> [Sensing the growing affection of Hartmann and his intended, Agnes, but too sorrowful to love anyone himself, Ernest secludes himself in the Alps and urges his friends to be a couple.]

One day wandering further than usual from his habitation, the being unexpectedly stood before him, and appeared to welcome the sight of Ernest with one of his unnatural howls, which rivetted him to the spot, and for some time made his tongue refuse to do its office. "Monster," at length Ernest exclaimed, "hast thou again come to torment me? thou heretofore proclaimed thyself the punishment of my presumption; if that punishment is to cease but with my life, let both now end together: use thy super-human strength and at once annihilate me; it will be an act of kindness, for I am weary of the world."—"I owe thee no kindness," answered the being, "thou, in the vanity of knowledge, aimed at that which one alone has power to perform; thy presumption began that which has called me into existence, wretched to myself, and hateful to others: from where I first saw light and found a shelter, I have been hunted as though I were a beast of the forest, than which once I was little better; but now (for what purposes I know not), my nature seems changed, and I feel within me workings that make me nearer allied to human nature!"—Ernest said, "Thou! hideous to look on; unlike every object that moves upon the earth, art of no species, and can claim kindred with none, and yet dares to call thyself human."—"Mock me not," replied the being: "deride not the mass of misery thou hast been the cause of; rather seek to lessen it, and be my benefactor by repairing the evil thou hast done to me; find me a place of shelter, where, though I have no companion, I may be safe from injury. If my mind continues tractable as now, teach me the difference between good and evil, so that while I am cursed with life, though I may not be able to practice the former, I may avoid inflicting the latter upon others."—Ernest stood gazing with astonishment at the calm voice and manner of this singular being; a change wonderful as that which first gave him existence seemed to have taken place in the inward not the outward man, for that remained unsightly as it had ever been; but the contemplation of this unlooked-for rationality in the one, seemed to deprive the other of his reason; suddenly his eyes began to roll with fury, and in a frenzied tone he exclaimed, "Why thou art a sensible monster now, and fit company for those who think they are most learned, as I once thought myself! I hate the world, and thou art hated by the world; we, therefore, are the right associates for each other, and henceforth will live together; nay, if thou continues to acquire knowledge as thou hast lately done, I will be thy pupil; what I learned from musty books, that puffed me up with vanity, and taught me to deceive myself. What thou knowest is from nature, and therefore drawn from a source of truth and purity; thou, therefore, must be the real philosopher, and so shall be my friend and master: come, then, let us away, and leave the hateful world to the ignorant who think they are wise."

As soon as Ernest had ceased speaking, he seized the Being by the hand, and proceeded with a hurried agitated pace towards the Alps, sometimes stopping to look earnestly, but wildly, in his companion's face; at other times bursting into laughter, in which madness had evidently usurped the place of mirth.—They soon began to ascend some of the steepest acclivities of that tremendous chain of mountains, and before night closed in, had nearly reached to that height which remains constantly covered with the undissolving snows of winter.

That same evening Agnes, Hartmann, and Mr. Wallberg, arrived at the place of Ernest's residence, and began to feel alarm in addition to disappointment when he returned not home at night. His servant told them it was the first time he had been so long absent, they therefore concluded he had walked further than usual, and that the next day should see him. In the morning they amused themselves with viewing the magnificent Alpine scenery. After walking some time, they stood to admire the objects that presented themselves. Before them rose a mountain, the upper part of which was capped with snow; just below it a narrow path winded round its side overhanging a tremendous precipice, at the foot of which lay a beautiful valley. Suddenly two figures appeared on the ridgy path. One was using the most violent gestures, as if endeavouring to force himself away from his companion, a man of gigantic proportions. Ernest and the being had wandered throughout the night amongst the mountains, the more than human strength of the one, and the burning frenzy of the other, enabled them to bear the excessive cold of that elevated region uninjured. He who at his first starting into supernatural existence had possessed reason scarcely exceeding brutal instinct, was now the most rational of the two, and had several times preserved Ernest from rushing on destruction.

Indescribable was the consternation when the friends discovered the lesser man to be Ernest, and the other the unknown monster that had saved Agnes. Ernest's reason had entirely left him, and he was only restrained by the other from plunging down the precipice. While all were thus situated one of those thunder storms so usual in the Alpine regions burst upon them; the concussion of the air occasioned one of those tremendous avalanches so magnificent to the spectator, but so destructive to all within its range. The snow in its descent swept Ernest and the monster from the narrow ridge into the abyss below, and inextricably buried them in the fallen mass. Mr. Wallberg did not survive the shock of thus witnessing the destruction of the last of his family, and the punishment of Ernest's presumption as in the effects of crime is too often to be deplored, involved the innocent equally with the guilty in ruin. The examination of his papers explained the mystery of Ernest's conduct to the survivors. At the expiration of the time demanded by their own grief, and the respect due to the memory of their friends, the hands of Agnes and Hartmann were united as their hearts had long secretly been.

Sincere was their affection for each other, the successive loss of so many friends prevented those rejoicings usual at the celebration of a marriage; but what was wanting in the outward expressions of joy, was amply supplied by the inward feelings of their excellent hearts. In a short time after their nuptials, Hartmann, guided by the direction in Ernest's papers, sought out the cavern that had been the scene of his labors, and destroyed every vestige of his presumption. A tablet was erected in the church as a memorial of the unfortunate family of Wallberg. When the sun had dissolved the snow in the valley the two bodies were found, the size and strange appearance of one of them filled all who saw it with wonder; the simple and superstitious inhabitants never approached the place where they were discovered without shuddering, and long continued to call it the Valley of the Monster.

EXCERPTS FROM

THE MUMMY! A TALE OF THE TWENTY-SECOND CENTURY

(1827)

Jane Webb

From Vol. I, Chapter I

[Like Mary Shelley's *The Last Man* (1826), Webb's story is set in the future—but her embrace of conservative politics makes a pointed contrast to Shelley's democractic idealism.]

In the year 2126, England enjoyed peace and tranquillity under the absolute dominion of a female sovereign. Numerous changes had taken place for some centuries in the political state of the country, and several forms of government had been successively adopted and destroyed, till, as is generally the case after violent revolutions, they all settled down into an absolute monarchy. [...]

From Vol. I, Chapter II

[...] Edric [the son of an English squire, Sir Ambrose] was, as usual, engaged in those abstract speculations with Dr. Entwerfen, which now formed the only pleasure of his existence, and which he pursued with an eagerness that made all the ordinary affairs of life appear tasteless and insipid. His imagination had become heated by long dwelling upon the same theme; and a strange, wild, indefinable craving to hold converse with a disembodied spirit haunted him incessantly. He had long buried this feverish anxiety in his own breast, and tried in vain to subdue it; but it seemed to hang upon his steps, to present itself before him wherever he went, and, in short, to pursue him with the malignancy of a demon.

"What is the matter with you, Edric?" said Dr. Entwerfen to his pupil, the day we have already mentioned. "You are so changed, I scarcely know you, and your eyes have a wild expression, absolutely terrific."

"I am, indeed, half mad," returned Edric, with a melancholy smile; "and yet, perhaps, you will laugh when I tell you the reason of my uneasiness. I am tormented by an earnest desire to communicate with one who has been an inhabitant of the tomb. I would fain know the secrets of the grave, and ascertain whether the spirit be chained after death to its earthly covering of clay, condemned till the day of final resurrection to hover over the rotting mass of corruption that once contained it; or whether the last agonies of death free it from its mortal ties, and leave it floating, free as air, in the bright regions of ethereal space?"

"You know my opinion," said the doctor.

"I do," replied the pupil; "but forgive me if I add—I do not feel satisfied with it: in fact mine is not a character to be satisfied with building my faith upon that of any other man. I would see, and judge for myself."

"I do not blame you," resumed the doctor; "a reasonable being should believe nothing he cannot prove;—however, to remove your doubts, I am convinced we have only occasion to step into the adjoining church-yard, and try my galvanic battery of fifty surgeon power, (which you must allow is surely enough to re-animate the dead,) upon a body, and then—"

"Hold! hold!" cried Edric, shuddering. "My blood freezes in my veins, at the thought of a church-yard:—your words recall a horrible dream that I had last night, which, even now, dwells upon my mind, and resists all the efforts I can make to shake it off."

"Tell it to me, then," resumed the doctor; "for when the imagination is possessed by horrible fantasies, it is often relieved by speaking of them to another person."

"I thought," said Edric, "that I was wandering in a thick gloomy wood, through which I had the utmost difficulty to make my way. The black trees, frowning in awful majesty above my head, twined together in masses, so as almost to obstruct my path. Suddenly, a fearful light flashed upon me, and I saw at my feet a horrid charnel house, where the dying mingled terrifically with the dead. The miserable living wretches turned and writhed with pain, striving in vain to escape from the mass of putrescence heaped upon them. I saw their eye-balls roll in agony—I watched the distortion of their features, and, making a violent effort to relieve one who had almost crawled to my feet, I shrank back with horror as I found the arm I grasped give way to my touch, and a disgusting mass of corruption crumble beneath my fingers!—Shuddering I awoke—a cold sweat hanging upon my brows, and every nerve thrilling with convulsive agony."

"Mere visionary terrors," said the doctor. "You have suffered your imagination to dwell upon one subject, till it is become morbid.—However, though I do not see any reason why your dream should make you decline my offer, I will not urge it if it give you pain."

"Is it not strange," continued Edric, apparently pursuing the current of his own thoughts, "that the mind should crave so earnestly what the body shudders at; and yet, how can a mass of mere matter, which we see sink into corruption the moment the spirit is withdrawn from it, shudder? How can it even feel? I can scarcely analyse my own sensations; but it appears to me that two separate and distinct spirits animate the mass of clay that composes the human frame. The one, the merely vital spark which gives it life and motion, and which we share in common with brutes, and even vegetables; and the other, the divine ethereal spirit, which we may properly term the soul, and which is a direct emanation from God himself, only bestowed upon man."

"You know my sentiments upon the subject," replied the doctor, "therefore I need not repeat them."

"I know," resumed Edric, "you think the organs of thought, reflection, imagination, reason, and, in short, all that mysterious faculty which we call the mind, material; and that as long as the body remains uncorrupted they may be restored, provided circulation can be renewed: for that you think the only principle necessary to set the animal machine in motion."

"Can any thing be more clear?" said the doctor. "We all know that circulation and the action of the lungs are inseparably connected, and that if the latter be arrested, death must ensue. How frequently are apparently dead bodies recovered by friction, which produces circulation; and inflation of the lungs with air, which restores their action. If your idea be correct, that the soul leaves the body the instant what we call death takes place, how do you account for these instances of resuscitation? Think you that the soul can be recalled to the body after it has once quitted it? Or that it hovers over it in air, attached to it by invisible ligatures, ready to be drawn back to its former situation, when the body shall resume its vital functions? You cannot surely suppose it remains in a dormant state, and is reawakened with the body; for this would be inconsistent with the very idea of an incorporeal spirit."

"Certainly," resumed Edric, "the spirit must be capable of existing perfectly distinct from the body; though how, I own candidly my imperfect reason cannot enable me to comprehend."

"I wish you would overcome your childish reluctance to trying an experiment upon a corpse, as that must set your doubts at rest. For if we could succeed in re-animating a dead body that has been long entombed, so that it might enjoy its reasoning faculties, or, as you call it, its soul in full perfection, my opinion would be completely established."

"But where shall we find a perfect body, which has been dead a sufficient time to prevent the possibility of its being only in a trance?—For even if I could conquer the repugnance I feel at the thought of touching such a mass of cold mortality, as that presented in my dream last night, according to your own theory, the organs must be perfect, or the experiment will not be complete."

"What think you of trying to operate upon a mummy? You know a chamber has been lately discovered in the great pyramid, which is supposed to be the real tomb of Cheops; and where, it is said, the mummies of that great king and the principal personages of his household have been found in a state of wonderful preservation."

"But mummies are so swathed up."

"Not those of kings and princes. You know all travellers, both ancient and modern, who have seen them, agree, that they are wrapped merely in folds of red and white linen, every finger and even every toe distinct; thus, if we could succeed in resuscitating Cheops, we need not even touch the body; as the clothing it is wrapped in will not at all encumber its movements."

"The idea is feasible, and, as you rightly say, if it can be put into execution, it will set the matter at rest for ever. I should also like to visit the pyramids, those celebrated monuments of antiquity, whose origin is lost in the obscurity of the darker ages, and which seem to have been spared by the devastating hand of time, purposely to perplex the learned."

"You say right," cried the doctor with enthusiasm. "And who can tell but that we may be the favoured happy mortals, destined to raise the mystic veil that has so long covered them? we may be destined to explore these wonderful monuments—to revive their mummies, and force them to reveal the secrets of their prison-house. Cheops is said to have built the great pyramid, and it is Cheops whom we shall endeavour to re-animate!

what then can be more palpable, than that it should be he who is destined at length to reveal the mystery."

> [Edric travels to Egypt via balloon, a common method of travel in Webb's future, as it was in Shelley's earlier *The Last Man*.]

From Vol. I, Chapter IX

They had now entered the Pyramid, and were proceeding with infinite difficulty along a low, dark, narrow passage. [...]

"We must descend that shaft," said the guide, "and that will lead us to the tomb of King Cheops; but as the road is dark, and rather dangerous, we had better, each of us, take a torch."

As he spoke, he drew some torches from a niche where they were deposited, and began to illuminate them from his own. The red glare of the torches flashed fearfully on the massive wails of the Pyramid, throwing part of their enormous masses into deep shadow, as they rose in solemn and sublime dignity around, and seemed frowning upon the presumptuous mortals that had dared to invade their recesses, whilst the deep pit beneath their feet seemed to yawn wide to engulf them in its abyss. [...]

No one spoke; and after proceeding for some time along the narrow path, or rather ledge, formed on the sides of the cavity, which gradually shelved downwards, the guide suddenly stopped, and touching a secret spring, a solid block of granite slowly detached itself from the wall, and, rising majestically like the portcullis of an ancient fortress, showed the entrance to a dark and dreary cave. The guide advanced, followed by our travellers, into a gloomy vaulted apartment, where long vistas of ponderous arches stretched on every side, till their termination was lost in darkness, and gave a feeling of immensity and obscurity to the scene.

"I will wait here," said the guide; "and here, if you please, you had better leave your torches. That avenue will lead you to the tomb."

The travellers obeyed; and the guide, placing himself in a recess in the wall, extinguished all the torches except one, which he shrouded so as to leave the travellers in total darkness. Nothing could be now more terrific than their situation: immured in the recesses of the tomb, involved in darkness, and their bosoms throbbing with hopes that they scarcely dared avow even to themselves, with faltering steps they proceeded slowly along the path the guide had pointed out, shuddering even at the hollow echo of their own footsteps, which alone broke the solemn silence that reigned throughout these fearful regions of terror and the tomb.

Suddenly, a vivid light flashed upon them, and, as they advanced, they found it proceeded from torches placed in the hands of two colossal figures, who, placed in a sitting posture, seemed guarding an enormous portal, surmounted by the image of a fox, the constant guardian of an Egyptian tomb. The immense dimensions and air of grandeur and repose about these colossi had something in it very imposing; and our travellers felt a sensation of awe creep over them as they gazed upon their calm unmoved features, so strikingly emblematic of that immutable nature which they were doubtless placed there to typify.

It was with feelings of indescribable solemnity, that the doctor and Edric passed through this majestic portal, and found themselves in an apartment gloomily illumined by the light shed faintly from an inner chamber, through ponderous brazen gates beautifully wrought. The light thus feebly emitted, showed that the room in which they stood, was dedicated to Typhon, the evil spirit, as his fierce and savage types covered the walls; and images of his symbols, the crocodile and the dragon, placed beneath the shadow of the brazen gates, and dimly seen by the imperfect light, seemed starting into life, and grimly to forbid the farther advance of the intruders. Our travellers shuddered, and opening with trembling hand the ponderous gates, they entered the *tomb of Cheops*. [...]

Innumerable folds of red and white linen, disposed alternately, swathed the gigantic but well-proportioned limbs of the royal mummy; and upon his breast lay a piece of metal, shining like silver, and stamped with the figure of a winged globe. Edric attempted to remove this, but recoiled with horror, when he found it bend beneath his fingers with an unnatural softness; whilst, as the flickering light of the lamp fell upon the face of the mummy, he fancied its stern features relaxed into a ghastly laugh of scornful mockery. Worked up to desperation, he applied the wires of the battery and put the apparatus in motion, whilst a demoniac laugh of derision appeared to ring in his ears, and the surrounding mummies seemed starting from their places and dancing in unearthly merriment. Thunder now roared in tremendous peals through the Pyramids, shaking their enormous masses to the foundation, and vivid flashes of light darted round in quick succession. Edric stood aghast amidst this fearful convulsion of nature. A horrid creeping seemed to run through every vein, every nerve feeling as though drawn from its extremity, and wrapped in icy chillness round his heart. Still, he stood immoveable, and gazing intently on the mummy, whose eyes had opened with the shock, and were now fixed on those of Edric, shining with supernatural lustre. In vain Edric attempted to rouse himself;—in vain to turn away from that withering glance. The mummy's eyes still pursued him with their ghastly brightness; they seemed to possess the fabled fascination of those of the rattle-snake, and though he shrunk from their gaze, they still glared horribly upon him. Edric's senses swam, yet he could not move from the spot; he remained fixed, chained, and immoveable, his eyes still riveted upon the mummy, and every thought absorbed in horror. Another fearful peal of thunder now rolled in lengthened vibrations above his head, and the mummy rose slowly, his eyes still fixed upon those of Edric, from his marble tomb. The thunder pealed louder and louder. Yells and groans seemed mingled with its roar;—the sepulchral lamp flared with redoubled fierceness, flashing its rays around in quick succession, and with vivid brightness; whilst by its horrid and uncertain glare, Edric saw the mummy stretch out its withered hand as though to seize him. He saw it rise gradually—he heard the dry, bony fingers rattle as it drew them forth—he felt its tremendous gripe—human nature could bear no more—his senses were rapidly deserting him; he felt, however, the fixed stedfast eyes of Cheops still glowing upon his failing orbs, as the lamp gave a sudden flash, and then all was darkness! The brazen gates now shut with a fearful clang, and Edric, uttering a shriek of horror, fell senseless upon the ground; whilst his shrill cry of anguish rang wildly through the marble vaults, till its re-echoes seemed like the yell of demons joining in fearful mockery.

[The mummy, by accident, travels by balloon back to England, where, reappearing suddenly at numerous points throughout the rest of the narrative, it terrifies various characters who are "conspiring mischief" in the settled conservative politics of the future Empire. The mummy alternately goads and condemns these usurpers, as in the following.]

From Vol II, Chapter XIII

[Father Morris, one of Edric's teachers, now conniving for political power,] was going on when a fiendish laugh rang in his ears; and, looking up, he beheld the gigantic form of Cheops standing over him. The bright moonbeams showed, with horrible distinctness, the strange attire, savage features, and unearthly gaze of the Mummy, as his horrid laugh echoed from the wall behind them and pealed across the water. Rosabella had not before seen him, except when she knelt before the dying Queen; and, shrieking with horror, she fled for refuge to her uncle's garden, whilst Cheops thus tauntingly addressed the priest.

"You were conspiring mischief. Though the language your lips employed was unknown to me, that of your looks was clear. Men do not cast their eyes upon the earth, and murmur forth their accents as though they trembled at the sound of their own voices, when their purposes are such as will bear avowal. Make me your confidant, and by the aid of my serpent deity, my guardian Cneph, I may assist you: but force me to become your enemy, and Typhon himself never pursued Isis and the infant Horus with more unrelenting vengeance than I will follow you and destroy your plans."

Dreading alike to trust, or enrage this mysterious being, and cursing the evil chance that had led him to that spot, Father Morris, who, like all the English in those days, was an universal linguist, found himself obliged partially to obey this injunction, and inform the Mummy of his design. Cheops burst into one of his terrific laughs of derision. "And so," he said, "you would make yonder feeble girl who fled screaming at my approach, a Queen. A fit monarch for a warlike people. Can a woman's arm resist an invasion of the Palli, or a woman's hands direct the reins of Mizraim's government? Alas! alas! where am I wandering? I forgot the change wrought in my destiny, and that your people seem powerless as the sovereign you would give them. Be satisfied, I will not betray thee. Indeed, so do I hate thy countrymen, that I shall rejoice to see thee triumph in deceiving them. Beware, however, how thou attemptest to deceive me, lest my vengeance, quick, sure, and unforeseen as the secret agency of the Epoptæ, should fall upon and crush thee at the very moment of the fruition of thy wishes."

Fearing, whilst he hated the mysterious being thus strangely thrust into his most inmost secrets, Father Morris promised obedience, and the Mummy retreated within the walls of Mrs. Montagu's garden; ere he left the priest, however, he held out his hand to him. "Give me your hand," said he, "and let us seal our compact." Father Morris shuddered as he obeyed; for the words of the Mummy recalled those he had just employed, when this fearful apparition broke in upon him, and brought with them a train of thoughts he would now willingly have shaken off. He did not dare, however, to refuse, and reluctantly held out his hand: the Mummy seized it with an iron grasp, and an icy chill seemed to creep from his hand to Father Morris's heart, as he burst into one of his demon-like laughs and left him.

> [Through many turns of plot, the Mummy reappears again and again at key moments to seemingly aid but actually enact vengeance on all who wrongfully conspire for power. In the final pages, the Mummy confronts Edric and reveals that no human power raised him, as only his maker could have restored him. Edric's dream had all been folly.]

From Vol. III, Chapter XXXII

Edric entered the grove, and threw himself upon that very bank where he had reclined only a few months before, under such different feelings. The river, the grove, the bank, were all the same; he only was changed. "And yet," said he, "is not my mind still as unsettled as before? Am I not still wandering in a labyrinth of doubts? Unknowing where to turn; and yet tormented with a restless desire to discover my way. What can have become of the Mummy, I so strangely resuscitated? It is strange, that since the restoration of Elvira it seems to have vanished, and yet all here speak of it as of a living animated being. Would that I could see it. O Cheops! Cheops—"

Suddenly a strange unearthly voice seemed to murmur harshly in his ear—"Go to the Pyramid! There and there only can thy hopes be gratified." Edric started upon his feet—no one was near him, and not a sound broke the awful stillness that reigned around, save the gentle rippling of the river that flowed at his feet. He gazed wildly on every side, hoping, yet fearing to behold the ghastly being, he fancied his words had conjured up. It was in vain; no dark figure interposed between him and the clear bright sunshine; no gloomy shadow stretched along the plain; all looked gay as youth and happiness; yet still that awful voice rang in his ears, and thrilled through every nerve.

"I *will* go the Pyramid," cried he energetically; "I will again enter that horrid tomb—but I will go alone."

In pursuance of this sudden, but irresistible desire, Edric hastily prepared to return to Egypt; and feigning that he was called to London by business of importance, to satisfy the anxious curiosity of Pauline, he departed. Indescribable emotions throbbed in his bosom as he took his seat in the stage balloon which was to convey him to Egypt; but when he saw the towers and temples, and, above all, the pyramids of this mysterious country, lying beneath his feet, his agitation increased almost to agony. It was with infinite difficulty that he obtained permission again to visit the objects of his journey; as, since the mysterious disappearance of the Mummy, the tomb of Cheops had been closed from mortal eyes. The interference of the British consul, however, at length obviated all objections, and Edric (whose impatience had become absolute torture from the delay) once more entered that awful receptacle of fallen greatness.

Scarcely a twelvemonth had elapsed since he had last trodden those solemn vaults, yet what a change had taken place in his destiny! When he considered the number and variety of the events that had befallen him, he could scarcely fancy it possible that they had been crowded into so short a space of time; and, instead of a year, centuries seemed to have rolled over his head. His feeling of personal identity seemed confused—his senses became bewildered, and he mechanically followed his conductor almost without knowing whither he was going.

At last the guide stopped—"This is the tomb of Cheops," said he; "I suppose, Sir, you will enter it alone."

Edric started—the words of the guide seemed to ring in his ears as the knell of death, and he shuddered as the thought crossed his mind that some horrid and appalling punishment might even now await him for his presumption. Desperately he snatched the torch from the hands of his guide and advanced ALONE. [...]

The brilliant light of the lamp now glowed with noon-day radiance, and showed distinctly every corner of the fatal chamber. Edric looked timidly around, and shuddered as each well-remembered object met his eyes; but what was his horror and surprise when, glancing at the marble sarcophagus of Cheops, he beheld the gigantic figure of the Mummy standing erect beside it! It was again simply wrapped in the garments of the tomb, and its glassy eyes, rigid features, and statue-like form, chilled Edric to the heart. He looked at it a few moments in silence, till it raised its arm and seemed about to address him; when, shrinking back with indescribable horror, he uttered a faint shriek, and hid his face in his hands.

"Why dost thou tremble?" asked the Mummy in a deep hollow voice that thrilled through Edric's very soul. "Didst thou not come here to seek me, and dost thou shudder to behold my form? I am now before thee. Ask what thou wilt,

I am permitted to reply. Why art thou silent? Why does thy heart seem to wither in my presence? Alas! alas! is no mortal to be found free from the debasing influence of fear? Thou art called bold, courageous, and noble. Thou hast dared to soar above thy fellow-men, and thou hast ardently wished to see me. Behold I am here, and now, weak, fearful, and inconsistent as thou art, thou shunnest my approach."

"I do not shun thee," said Edric, removing his hands, and endeavouring to look calmly on the fearful being before him, though the flesh seemed to quiver on his bones with the effort—"I do not shun thee; but the nerves will shrink though the mind be firm. I did wish to see thee; for ardently do I still desire to know the secrets of the tomb."

Cheops burst into one of his fearful laughs. "Weak, silly worm! are you not satisfied then? How would this knowledge avail you? Has any thing but misery attended your former researches? And can any thing but misery attend the knowledge you now covet? Learn wisdom by experience! Seek not to pry into secrets denied to man! If you wish still, however, to be resolved of your doubts, behold me ready to satisfy them; but, I warn you, wretchedness will wait upon my words."

"Then I no longer seek to hear them; for, even weak as you esteem me, I can learn wisdom from experience. Thus, then, I tear the tormenting doubts, that have so long haunted me, from my mind, and bid them farewell for ever!"

"It is well," said Cheops, his eyes beaming with joy. "Then my task is accomplished. I have at last found a reasonable man. I honour you, for you can command yourself, and now you may command me."

"I wish it not," said Edric.

"Have you no curiosity?" asked the Mummy, with a ghastly smile.

"None," returned Edric; "unless it be that I would fain know your history, and the meaning of the sculptures upon your tomb."

"What are they?" demanded Cheops.

"A youthful warrior is bearing off a beautiful woman in his arms, whilst an old man laments bitterly in the distance."

"I was the warrior," said Cheops; "and the beautiful female was Arsinoë. I loved her, and to gratify my impetuous passion I tore her from the arms of her father by force."

"The warrior is afterwards contending with the old man who falls beneath his blows—"

"He did, he did," cried Cheops; "he died by my hand; and eternal misery haunts me for the deed."

"And this old man was—"

"My father!" cried the Mummy, writhing in agony.

"And Arsinoë—"

"My sister—my own, my beloved sister!"

A solemn pause followed this speech, for Edric was too much shocked to speak again to the awful being who had avowed such crimes, and upon whose face were traced passions too horrible to be imagined. After a short silence Cheops again exclaimed—

"Yes, yes; I see your horror, and it is just; but think you that I do not suffer? know that a fiend—a wild, never-dying fiend rages here," continued he, pressing his hand upon his breast. "It gnaws my vitals—it burns with unquenchable fire and never ceasing torment. Permitted for a time to revisit earth, I have made use of the powers entrusted to me to assist the good and punish the malevolent. Under pretence of aiding them, I gave them counsels which only plunged them yet deeper in destruction, whilst the evil that my advice appeared to bring upon the good was only like a passing cloud before the sun: it gave lustre to the success that followed. My task is now finished;—be happy, Edric, for happiness is in your power; be wise, for wisdom may be obtained by reflection; and be merciful, for unless we give, how can we expect mercy? Rely not on your own strength—seek not to pry into mysteries designed to be concealed from man; and enjoy the comforts within your reach—for know, that knowledge, above the sphere of man's capacity, produces only wretchedness; and that to be contented with our station, and to make ourselves useful to our fellow-creatures, is the only true path to happiness."

The Mummy ceased to speak, and his features, which had appeared wild and animated during his conversation with Edric, became fixed—the unearthly lustre that had flashed from his eyes, faded away, and gave place to a glassy deadness—his limbs became rigid, and as the light of the lamp gradually sunk to less distinctness, the ghastly form of the Mummy seemed rapidly changing into stone. Edric felt that the moment when it was possible for him to hold communion with this strange being was rapidly passing away, and almost shrieked as he exclaimed, "One question! only one ere it be too late." The Mummy feebly raised his languid eyelids, but Edric felt his blood freeze at the unnatural glare. With a violent effort, however, he roused himself to speak. "Was it a human power that dragged you from the tomb?"

"The power that gave me life could alone restore it," replied the Mummy in slow measured accents, as it sank gradually back into its former tomb. Edric shuddered, and involuntarily rushed forward, but the Mummy no longer lived or breathed. Cold, pale, and inanimate it lay, as though its sleep of two thousand years had never been broken.

'Oblivion laid him down upon his hearse!'

and no mortal ever more could boast of holding converse with The Mummy.

GOBLIN MARKET

(1862)

Christina Rossetti

Morning and evening
Maids heard the goblins cry:
'Come buy our orchard fruits,
Come buy, come buy:
Apples and quinces,
Lemons and oranges,
Plump unpecked cherries,
Melons and raspberries,
Bloom-down-cheeked peaches,
Swart-headed mulberries,
Wild free-born cranberries,
Crab-apples, dewberries,
Pine-apples, blackberries,
Apricots, strawberries;—
All ripe together

In summer weather,—
Morns that pass by,
Fair eves that fly;
Come buy, come buy:
Our grapes fresh from the vine,
Pomegranates full and fine,
Dates and sharp bullaces,
Rare pears and greengages,
Damsons and bilberries,
Taste them and try:
Currants and gooseberries,
Bright-fire-like barberries,
Figs to fill your mouth,
Citrons from the South,
Sweet to tongue and sound to eye;
Come buy, come buy.'

Evening by evening
Among the brookside rushes,
Laura bowed her head to hear,
Lizzie veiled her blushes:
Crouching close together
In the cooling weather,
With clasping arms and cautioning lips,
With tingling cheeks and finger tips.
'Lie close,' Laura said,
Pricking up her golden head:
'We must not look at goblin men,
We must not buy their fruits:
Who knows upon what soil they fed
Their hungry thirsty roots?'

'Come buy,' call the goblins
Hobbling down the glen.

'Oh,' cried Lizzie, 'Laura, Laura,
You should not peep at goblin men.'
Lizzie covered up her eyes,
Covered close lest they should look;
Laura reared her glossy head,
And whispered like the restless brook:
'Look, Lizzie, look, Lizzie,
Down the glen tramp little men.
One hauls a basket,
One bears a plate,
One lugs a golden dish
Of many pounds weight.
How fair the vine must grow
Whose grapes are so luscious;
How warm the wind must blow
Through those fruit bushes.'
'No,' said Lizzie, 'No, no, no;
Their offers should not charm us,
Their evil gifts would harm us.'
She thrust a dimpled finger
In each ear, shut eyes and ran:
Curious Laura chose to linger
Wondering at each merchant man.
One had a cat's face,
One whisked a tail,
One tramped at a rat's pace,
One crawled like a snail,
One like a wombat prowled obtuse and furry,

One like a ratel tumbled hurry skurry.
She heard a voice like voice of doves
Cooing all together:
They sounded kind and full of loves
In the pleasant weather.

Laura stretched her gleaming neck
Like a rush-imbedded swan,
Like a lily from the beck,
Like a moonlit poplar branch,
Like a vessel at the launch
When its last restraint is gone.

Backwards up the mossy glen
Turned and trooped the goblin men,
With their shrill repeated cry,
'Come buy, come buy.'
When they reached where Laura was
They stood stock still upon the moss,
Leering at each other,
Brother with queer brother;
Signalling each other,
Brother with sly brother.
One set his basket down,
One reared his plate;
One began to weave a crown
Of tendrils, leaves, and rough nuts brown
(Men sell not such in any town);
One heaved the golden weight
Of dish and fruit to offer her:
'Come buy, come buy,' was still their cry.

Laura stared but did not stir,
Longed but had no money:
The whisk-tailed merchant bade her taste
In tones as smooth as honey,
The cat-faced purr'd,
The rat-faced spoke a word
Of welcome, and the snail-paced even was heard;
One parrot-voiced and jolly
Cried 'Pretty Goblin' still for 'Pretty Polly;'—
One whistled like a bird.

But sweet-tooth Laura spoke in haste:
'Good folk, I have no coin;
To take were to purloin:
I have no copper in my purse,
I have no silver either,
And all my gold is on the furze
That shakes in windy weather
Above the rusty heather.'
'You have much gold upon your head,'
They answered all together:
'Buy from us with a golden curl.'
She clipped a precious golden lock,
She dropped a tear more rare than pearl,
Then sucked their fruit globes fair or red:
Sweeter than honey from the rock,
Stronger than man-rejoicing wine,
Clearer than water flowed that juice;
She never tasted such before,
How should it cloy with length of use?
She sucked and sucked and sucked the more

Fruits which that unknown orchard bore;
She sucked until her lips were sore;
Then flung the emptied rinds away
But gathered up one kernel stone,
And knew not was it night or day
As she turned home alone.

Lizzie met her at the gate
Full of wise upbraidings:
'Dear, you should not stay so late,
Twilight is not good for maidens;
Should not loiter in the glen
In the haunts of goblin men.
Do you not remember Jeanie,
How she met them in the moonlight,
Took their gifts both choice and many,
Ate their fruits and wore their flowers
Plucked from bowers
Where summer ripens at all hours?
But ever in the noonlight
She pined and pined away;
Sought them by night and day,
Found them no more, but dwindled and grew grey;
Then fell with the first snow,
While to this day no grass will grow
Where she lies low:
I planted daisies there a year ago
That never blow.
You should not loiter so.'
'Nay, hush,' said Laura:
'Nay, hush, my sister:

I ate and ate my fill,
Yet my mouth waters still;
To-morrow night I will
Buy more:' and kissed her:
'Have done with sorrow;
I'll bring you plums to-morrow
Fresh on their mother twigs,
Cherries worth getting;
You cannot think what figs
My teeth have met in,
What melons icy-cold
Piled on a dish of gold
Too huge for me to hold,
What peaches with a velvet nap,
Pellucid grapes without one seed:
Odorous indeed must be the mead
Whereon they grow, and pure the wave they drink
With lilies at the brink,
And sugar-sweet their sap.'

Golden head by golden head,
Like two pigeons in one nest
Folded in each other's wings,
They lay down in their curtained bed:
Like two blossoms on one stem,
Like two flakes of new-fall'n snow,
Like two wands of ivory
Tipped with gold for awful kings.
Moon and stars gazed in at them,
Wind sang to them lullaby,

Lumbering owls forbore to fly,
Not a bat flapped to and fro
Round their rest:
Cheek to cheek and breast to breast
Locked together in one nest.

Early in the morning
When the first cock crowed his warning,
Neat like bees, as sweet and busy,
Laura rose with Lizzie:
Fetched in honey, milked the cows,
Aired and set to rights the house,
Kneaded cakes of whitest wheat,
Cakes for dainty mouths to eat,
Next churned butter, whipped up cream,
Fed their poultry, sat and sewed;
Talked as modest maidens should:
Lizzie with an open heart,
Laura in an absent dream,
One content, one sick in part;
One warbling for the mere bright day's delight,
One longing for the night.

At length slow evening came:
They went with pitchers to the reedy brook;
Lizzie most placid in her look,
Laura most like a leaping flame.
They drew the gurgling water from its deep;
Lizzie plucked purple and rich golden flags,
Then turning homeward said: 'The sunset flushes

Those furthest loftiest crags;
Come, Laura, not another maiden lags,
No wilful squirrel wags,
The beasts and birds are fast asleep.'
But Laura loitered still among the rushes
And said the bank was steep.

And said the hour was early still
The dew not fall'n, the wind not chill:
Listening ever, but not catching
The customary cry,
'Come buy, come buy,'
With its iterated jingle
Of sugar-baited words:
Not for all her watching
Once discerning even one goblin
Racing, whisking, tumbling, hobbling;
Let alone the herds
That used to tramp along the glen,
In groups or single,
Of brisk fruit-merchant men.

Till Lizzie urged, 'O Laura, come;
I hear the fruit-call but I dare not look:
You should not loiter longer at this brook:
Come with me home.
The stars rise, the moon bends her arc,
Each glowworm winks her spark,
Let us get home before the night grows dark:
For clouds may gather

Though this is summer weather,
Put out the lights and drench us through;
Then if we lost our way what should we do?'

Laura turned cold as stone
To find her sister heard that cry alone,
That goblin cry,
'Come buy our fruits, come buy.'
Must she then buy no more such dainty fruit?
Must she no more such succous pasture find,
Gone deaf and blind?
Her tree of life drooped from the root:
She said not one word in her heart's sore ache;
But peering thro' the dimness, nought discerning,
Trudged home, her pitcher dripping all the way;
So crept to bed, and lay
Silent till Lizzie slept;
Then sat up in a passionate yearning,
And gnashed her teeth for baulked desire, and wept
As if her heart would break.

Day after day, night after night,
Laura kept watch in vain
In sullen silence of exceeding pain.
She never caught again the goblin cry:
'Come buy, come buy;'—
She never spied the goblin men
Hawking their fruits along the glen:
But when the noon waxed bright
Her hair grew thin and grey;

She dwindled, as the fair full moon doth turn
To swift decay and burn
Her fire away.

One day remembering her kernel-stone
She set it by a wall that faced the south;
Dewed it with tears, hoped for a root,
Watched for a waxing shoot,
But there came none;
It never saw the sun,
It never felt the trickling moisture run:
While with sunk eyes and faded mouth
She dreamed of melons, as a traveller sees
False waves in desert drouth
With shade of leaf-crowned trees,
And burns the thirstier in the sandful breeze.

She no more swept the house,
Tended the fowls or cows,
Fetched honey, kneaded cakes of wheat,
Brought water from the brook:
But sat down listless in the chimney-nook
And would not eat.

Tender Lizzie could not bear
To watch her sister's cankerous care
Yet not to share.
She night and morning
Caught the goblins' cry:
'Come buy our orchard fruits,
Come buy, come buy:'—

Beside the brook, along the glen,
She heard the tramp of goblin men,
The voice and stir
Poor Laura could not hear;
Longed to buy fruit to comfort her,
But feared to pay too dear.
She thought of Jeanie in her grave,
Who should have been a bride;
But who for joys brides hope to have
Fell sick and died
In her gay prime,
In earliest Winter time
With the first glazing rime,
With the first snow-fall of crisp Winter time.

Till Laura dwindling
Seemed knocking at Death's door:
Then Lizzie weighed no more
Better and worse;
But put a silver penny in her purse,
Kissed Laura, crossed the heath with clumps of furze
At twilight, halted by the brook:
And for the first time in her life
Began to listen and look.

Laughed every goblin
When they spied her peeping:
Came towards her hobbling,
Flying, running, leaping,
Puffing and blowing,
Chuckling, clapping, crowing,

Clucking and gobbling,
Mopping and mowing,
Full of airs and graces,
Pulling wry faces,
Demure grimaces,
Cat-like and rat-like,
Ratel- and wombat-like,
Snail-paced in a hurry,
Parrot-voiced and whistler,
Helter skelter, hurry skurry,
Chattering like magpies,
Fluttering like pigeons,
Gliding like fishes,—
Hugged her and kissed her:
Squeezed and caressed her:
Stretched up their dishes,
Panniers, and plates:
'Look at our apples
Russet and dun,
Bob at our cherries,
Bite at our peaches,
Citrons and dates,
Grapes for the asking,
Pears red with basking
Out in the sun,
Plums on their twigs;
Pluck them and suck them,
Pomegranates, figs.'—

'Good folk,' said Lizzie,
Mindful of Jeanie:

'Give me much and many:'—
Held out her apron,
Tossed them her penny.
'Nay, take a seat with us,
Honour and eat with us,'
They answered grinning:
'Our feast is but beginning.
Night yet is early,
Warm and dew-pearly,
Wakeful and starry:
Such fruits as these
No man can carry;
Half their bloom would fly,
Half their dew would dry,
Half their flavour would pass by.
Sit down and feast with us,
Be welcome guest with us,
Cheer you and rest with us.'—
'Thank you,' said Lizzie: 'But one waits
At home alone for me:
So without further parleying,
If you will not sell me any
Of your fruits though much and many,
Give me back my silver penny
I tossed you for a fee.'—
They began to scratch their pates,
No longer wagging, purring,
But visibly demurring,
Grunting and snarling.
One called her proud,
Cross-grained, uncivil;

Their tones waxed loud,
Their looks were evil.
Lashing their tails
They trod and hustled her,
Elbowed and jostled her,
Clawed with their nails,
Barking, mewing, hissing, mocking,
Tore her gown and soiled her stocking,
Twitched her hair out by the roots,
Stamped upon her tender feet,
Held her hands and squeezed their fruits
Against her mouth to make her eat.

White and golden Lizzie stood,
Like a lily in a flood,—
Like a rock of blue-veined stone
Lashed by tides obstreperously,—
Like a beacon left alone
In a hoary roaring sea,
Sending up a golden fire,—
Like a fruit-crowned orange-tree
White with blossoms honey-sweet
Sore beset by wasp and bee,—
Like a royal virgin town
Topped with gilded dome and spire
Close beleaguered by a fleet
Mad to tug her standard down.

One may lead a horse to water,
Twenty cannot make him drink.
Though the goblins cuffed and caught her,

Coaxed and fought her,
Bullied and besought her,
Scratched her, pinched her black as ink,
Kicked and knocked her,
Mauled and mocked her,
Lizzie uttered not a word;
Would not open lip from lip
Lest they should cram a mouthful in:
But laughed in heart to feel the drip
Of juice that syrupped all her face,
And lodged in dimples of her chin,
And streaked her neck which quaked like curd.
At last the evil people,
Worn out by her resistance,
Flung back her penny, kicked their fruit
Along whichever road they took,
Not leaving root or stone or shoot;
Some writhed into the ground,
Some dived into the brook
With ring and ripple,
Some scudded on the gale without a sound,
Some vanished in the distance.

In a smart, ache, tingle,
Lizzie went her way;
Knew not was it night or day;
Sprang up the bank, tore thro' the furze,
Threaded copse and dingle,
And heard her penny jingle
Bouncing in her purse,—
Its bounce was music to her ear.

She ran and ran
As if she feared some goblin man
Dogged her with gibe or curse
Or something worse:
But not one goblin skurried after,
Nor was she pricked by fear;
The kind heart made her windy-paced
That urged her home quite out of breath with haste
And inward laughter.

She cried 'Laura,' up the garden,
'Did you miss me?
Come and kiss me.
Never mind my bruises,
Hug me, kiss me, suck my juices
Squeezed from goblin fruits for you,
Goblin pulp and goblin dew.
Eat me, drink me, love me;
Laura, make much of me:
For your sake I have braved the glen
And had to do with goblin merchant men.'

Laura started from her chair,
Flung her arms up in the air,
Clutched her hair:
'Lizzie, Lizzie, have you tasted
For my sake the fruit forbidden?
Must your light like mine be hidden,
Your young life like mine be wasted,
Undone in mine undoing,

And ruined in my ruin,
Thirsty, cankered, goblin-ridden?'—
She clung about her sister,
Kissed and kissed and kissed her:
Tears once again
Refreshed her shrunken eyes,
Dropping like rain
After long sultry drouth;
Shaking with aguish fear, and pain,
She kissed and kissed her with a hungry mouth.

Her lips began to scorch,
That juice was wormwood to her tongue,
She loathed the feast:
Writhing as one possessed she leaped and sung,
Rent all her robe, and wrung
Her hands in lamentable haste,
And beat her breast.
Her locks streamed like the torch
Borne by a racer at full speed,
Or like the mane of horses in their flight,
Or like an eagle when she stems the light
Straight toward the sun,
Or like a caged thing freed,
Or like a flying flag when armies run.

Swift fire spread through her veins,
            knocked at her heart,
Met the fire smouldering there
And overbore its lesser flame;

She gorged on bitterness without a name:
Ah! fool, to choose such part
Of soul-consuming care!
Sense failed in the mortal strife:
Like the watch-tower of a town
Which an earthquake shatters down,
Like a lightning-stricken mast,
Like a wind-uprooted tree
Spun about,
Like a foam-topped waterspout
Cast down headlong in the sea,
She fell at last;
Pleasure past and anguish past,
Is it death or is it life?

Life out of death.
That night long Lizzie watched by her,
Counted her pulse's flagging stir,
Felt for her breath,
Held water to her lips, and cooled her face
With tears and fanning leaves:
But when the first birds chirped about their eaves,
And early reapers plodded to the place
Of golden sheaves,
And dew-wet grass
Bowed in the morning winds so brisk to pass,
And new buds with new day
Opened of cup-like lilies on the stream,
Laura awoke as from a dream,
Laughed in the innocent old way,

Hugged Lizzie but not twice or thrice;
Her gleaming locks showed not one thread of grey,
Her breath was sweet as May
And light danced in her eyes.

Days, weeks, months, years
Afterwards, when both were wives
With children of their own;
Their mother-hearts beset with fears,
Their lives bound up in tender lives;
Laura would call the little ones
And tell them of her early prime,
Those pleasant days long gone
Of not-returning time:
Would talk about the haunted glen,
The wicked, quaint fruit-merchant men,
Their fruits like honey to the throat
But poison in the blood;
(Men sell not such in any town:)
Would tell them how her sister stood
In deadly peril to do her good,
And win the fiery antidote:
Then joining hands to little hands
Would bid them cling together,
'For there is no friend like a sister
In calm or stormy weather;
To cheer one on the tedious way,
To fetch one if one goes astray,
To lift one if one totters down,
To strengthen whilst one stands.'

PART TWO

Byronic Heroes and Sympathetic Monsters

ROGER DODSWORTH: THE REANIMATED ENGLISHMAN

(1826)

MARY SHELLEY

It may be remembered, that on the fourth of July last, a paragraph appeared in the papers importing that Dr. Hotham, of Northumberland, returning from Italy, over Mount St. Gothard, a score or two of years ago, had dug out from under an avalanche, in the neighbourhood of the mountain, a human being whose animation had been suspended by the action of the frost. Upon the application of the usual remedies, the patient was resuscitated, and discovered himself to be Mr. Dodsworth, the son of the antiquary Dodsworth, who perished in the reign of Charles I. He was thirty-seven years of age at the time of his inhumation, which had taken place as he was returning from Italy, in 1654. It was added that as soon as he was sufficiently recovered he would return to England, under the protection of his preserver. We have since heard no more of him, and various plans for public benefit, which have started in philanthropic minds on reading the statement, have already returned to their pristine nothingness. The antiquarian society had eaten their way to several votes for medals, and had already begun, in idea, to consider what prices it could afford to offer for Mr. Dodsworth's old clothes, and to conjecture what treasures in the way of pamphlet, old song, or autographic letter his pockets might contain. Poems from all quarters, of all kinds, elegiac, congratulatory, burlesque and allegoric, were half written. Mr. Godwin had suspended for the sake of such authentic information the history of the Commonwealth he had just begun. It is hard not only that the world should be baulked of these destined gifts from the talents of the country, but also that it should be promised and then deprived of a new subject of romantic wonder and scientific interest. A novel idea is worth much in the commonplace routine of life, but a new fact, an astonishment, a miracle, a palpable wandering from the course of things into apparent impossibilities, is a circumstance to which the imagination must cling with delight, and we say again that it is hard, very hard, that Mr. Dodsworth refuses to appear, and that the believers in his resuscitation are forced to undergo the sarcasms and triumphant arguments of those sceptics who always keep on the safe side of the hedge.

Now we do not believe that any contradiction or impossibility is attached to the adventures of this youthful antique. Animation (I believe physiologists agree) can as easily be suspended for an hundred or two years, as for as many seconds. A body hermetically sealed up by the frost, is of necessity preserved in its pristine entireness. That which is totally secluded from the action of external agency, can neither have any thing added to nor taken away from it: no decay can take place, for something can never become nothing; under the influence of that state of being which we call death, change but not annihilation removes from our sight the corporeal atoma; the earth receives sustenance from them, the air is fed by them, each element takes its own, thus seizing forcible repayment of what it had lent. But the elements that hovered round Mr. Dodsworth's icy shroud had no power to overcome the obstacle it presented. No zephyr could gather a hair from his head, nor could the influence of dewy night or genial morn penetrate his more than adamantine panoply. The story of the Seven Sleepers rests on a miraculous interposition—they slept. Mr. Dodsworth did not sleep; his breast never heaved, his pulses were stopped; death had his finger pressed on his lips which no breath might pass. He has removed it now, the grim shadow is vanquished, and stands wondering. His victim has cast from him the frosty spell, and arises as perfect a man as he had lain down an hundred and fifty years before. We have eagerly desired to be furnished with some particulars of his first conversations, and the mode in which he has learnt to adapt himself to his new scene of life. But since facts are denied to us, let us be permitted to indulge in conjecture. What his first words were may be guessed from the expressions used by people exposed to shorter accidents of the like nature. But as his powers return, the plot thickens. His dress had already excited Dr. Hotham's astonishment—the peaked beard—the love locks—the frill, which, until it was thawed, stood stiff under the mingled influence of starch and frost; his dress fashioned like that of one of Vandyke's portraits, or (a more familiar similitude) Mr. Sapio's costume in Winter's Opera of the Oracle, his pointed shoes—all spoke of other times. The curiosity of his preserver was keenly awake, that of Mr. Dodsworth was about to be roused. But to be enabled to conjecture with any degree of likelihood the tenor of his first inquiries, we must endeavour to make out what part he played in his former life. He lived at the most interesting period of English History—he was lost to the world when Oliver Cromwell had arrived at the summit of his ambition, and in the eyes of all Europe the commonwealth of England appeared so established as to endure for ever. Charles I was dead; Charles II was an outcast, a beggar, bankrupt even in hope. Mr. Dodsworth's father, the antiquary, received a salary from the republican general, Lord Fairfax, who was himself a great lover of antiquities, and died the very year that his son went to his long, but not unending sleep, a curious coincidence this, for it would seem that our frost-preserved friend was returning to England on his father's death, to claim probably his inheritance—how short lived are human views! Where now is Mr. Dodsworth's patrimony? Where his co-heirs, executors, and fellow legatees? His protracted absence has, we should suppose, given the present possessors to his estate—the world's chronology is an hundred and seventy years older since he seceded from the busy scene, hands after hands have tilled his acres, and then become clods beneath them; we may be permitted to doubt whether one single particle of their surface is individually the same as those which were to have been his—the youthful soil would of itself reject the antique clay of its claimant.

Mr. Dodsworth, if we may judge from the circumstance of his being abroad, was no zealous commonwealth's man, yet his having chosen Italy as the country in which to make his tour and his projected return to England on his father's death, renders it probable that he was no violent loyalist. One of those men he seems to be (or to have been) who did not follow

Cato's advice as recorded in the *Pharsalia*; a party, if to be of no party admits of such a term, which Dante recommends us utterly to despise, and which not unseldom falls between the two stools, a seat on either of which is so carefully avoided. Still Mr. Dodsworth could hardly fail to feel anxious for the latest news from his native country at so critical a period; his absence might have put his own property in jeopardy; we may imagine therefore that after his limbs had felt the cheerful return of circulation, and after he had refreshed himself with such of earth's products as from all analogy he never could have hoped to live to eat, after he had been told from what peril he had been rescued, and said a prayer thereon which even appeared enormously long to Dr. Hotham—we may imagine, we say, that his first question would be: "if any news had arrived lately from England?"

"I had letters yesterday," Dr. Hotham may well be supposed to reply.

"Indeed," cries Mr. Dodsworth, "and pray, sir, has any change for better or worse occurred in that poor distracted country?"

Dr. Hotham suspects a Radical, and coldly replies: "Why, sir, it would be difficult to say in what its distraction consists. People talk of starving manufacturers, bankruptcies, and the fall of the Joint Stock Companies—excrescences these, excrescences which will attach themselves to a state of full health. England, in fact, was never in a more prosperous condition."

Mr. Dodsworth now more than suspects the Republican, and, with what we have supposed to be his accustomed caution, sinks for awhile his loyalty, and in a moderate tone asks: "Do our governors look with careless eyes upon the symptoms of over-health?"

"Our governors," answers his preserver, "if you mean our ministry, are only too alive to temporary embarrassment." (We beg Dr. Hotham's pardon if we wrong him in making him a high Tory; such a quality appertains to our pure anticipated cognition of a Doctor, and such is the only cognizance that we have of this gentleman.) "It were to be wished that they showed themselves more firm—the king, God bless him!"

"Sir!" exclaims Mr. Dodsworth.

Dr. Hotham continues, not aware of the excessive astonishment exhibited by his patient: "The king, God bless him, spares immense sums from his privy purse for the relief of his subjects, and his example has been imitated by all the aristocracy and wealth of England."

"The king!" ejaculates Mr. Dodsworth.

"Yes, sir," emphatically rejoins his preserver; "the king, and I am happy to say that the prejudices that so unhappily and unwarrantably possessed the English people with regard to his Majesty are now, with a few" (with added severity) "and I may say contemptible exceptions, exchanged for dutiful love and such reverence as his talents, virtues, and paternal care deserve."

"Dear sir, you delight me," replies Mr. Dodsworth, while his loyalty late a tiny bud suddenly expands into full flower; "yet I hardly understand; the change is so sudden; and the man—Charles Stuart, King Charles, I may now call him, his murder is I trust execrated as it deserves?"

Dr. Hotham put his hand on the pulse of his patient—he feared an access of delirium from such a wandering from the subject. The pulse was calm, and Mr. Dodsworth continued: "That unfortunate martyr looking down from heaven is, I trust, appeased by the reverence paid to his name and the prayers dedicated to his memory. No sentiment, I think I may venture to assert, is so general in England as the compassion and love in which the memory of that hapless monarch is held?"

"And his son, who now reigns?—"

"Surely, sir, you forget; no son; that of course is impossible. No descendant of his fills the English throne, now worthily occupied by the house of Hanover. The despicable race of the Stuarts, long outcast and wandering, is now extinct, and the last days of the last Pretender to the crown of that family justified in the eyes of the world the sentence which ejected it from the kingdom for ever."

Such must have been Mr. Dodsworth's first lesson in politics. Soon, to the wonder of the preserver and preserved, the real state of the case must have been revealed; for a time, the strange and tremendous circumstance of his long trance may have threatened the wits of Mr. Dodsworth with a total overthrow. He had, as he crossed Mount St. Gothard, mourned a father—now every human being he had ever seen is "lapped in lead," is dust, each voice he had ever heard is mute. The very sound of the English tongue is changed, as his experience in conversation with Dr. Hotham assures him. Empires, religions, races of men, have probably sprung up or faded; his own patrimony (the thought is idle, yet, without it, how can he live?) is sunk into the thirsty gulph that gapes ever greedy to swallow the past; his learning, his acquirements, are probably obsolete; with a bitter smile he thinks to himself, I must take to my father's profession, and turn antiquary. The familiar objects, thoughts, and habits of my boyhood, are now antiquities. He wonders where the hundred and sixty folio volumes of MS. that his father had compiled, and which, as a lad, he had regarded with religious reverence, now are—where—ah, where? His favourite play-mate, the friend of his later years, his destined and lovely bride, tears long frozen are uncongealed, and flow down his young old cheeks.

But we do not wish to be pathetic; surely since the days of the patriarchs, no fair lady had her death mourned by her lover so many years after it had taken place. Necessity, tyrant of the world, in some degree reconciles Mr. Dodsworth to his fate. At first he is persuaded that the later generation of man is much deteriorated from his contemporaries; they are neither so tall, so handsome, nor so intelligent. Then by degrees he begins to doubt his first impression. The ideas that had taken possession of his brain before his accident, and which had been frozen up for so many years, begin to thaw and dissolve away, making room for others. He dresses himself in the modern style, and does not object much to anything except the neck-cloth and hard-boarded hat. He admires the texture of his shoes and stockings, and looks with admiration on a small Genevese watch, which he often consults, as if he were not yet assured that time had made progress in its accustomed manner, and as if he should find on its dial plate occular demonstration that he had exchanged his thirty-seventh year for his two hundredth and upwards, and had left A.D. 1654 far behind to find himself suddenly a beholder of the ways of men in this enlightened nineteenth century. His curiosity is insatiable; when he reads, his eyes cannot purvey fast enough to his mind, and every now and then he lights upon some inexplicable passage, some discovery and knowledge familiar to us, but undreamed of in his days, that throws him into wonder and interminable reverie. Indeed, he may be supposed to pass much of his time in that state, now and then interrupting himself with a royalist song against old Noll and the Roundheads, breaking off suddenly, and looking round fearfully to see who were his auditors, and on beholding the modern appearance of his friend the Doctor, sighing to think that it is no longer of import to any, whether he sing a cavalier catch or a puritanic psalm.

It were an endless task to develope all the philosophic ideas to which Mr. Dodsworth's resuscitation naturally gives birth. We should like much to converse with this gentleman, and still more to observe the progress of his mind, and the change of his ideas in his very novel situation. If he be a sprightly youth, fond of the shows of the world, careless of the higher human pursuits, he may proceed summarily to cast into the shade all trace of his former life, and endeavour to merge himself at once into the stream of humanity now flowing. It would be curious enough to observe the mistakes he would make, and the medley of manners which would thus be produced. He may think to enter into active life, become Whig or Tory as his inclinations lead, and get a seat in the, even to him, once-called "chapel" of St. Stephens[1]. He may content himself with turning contemplative philosopher, and find sufficient food for his mind in tracing the march of the human intellect, the changes which have been wrought in the dispositions, desires, and powers of mankind. Will he be an advocate for perfectibility or deterioration? He must admire our manufactures, the progress of science, the diffusion of knowledge, and the fresh spirit of enterprise characteristic of our countrymen. Will he find any individuals to be compared to the glorious spirits of his day? Moderate in his views as we have supposed him to be, he will probably fall at once into the temporising tone of mind now so much in vogue. He will be pleased to find a calm in politics; he

1 After a fire in 1834, St. Stephens Chapel became St. Stephens Hall, now the public entranceway for Parliament.

will greatly admire the ministry who have succeeded in conciliating almost all parties—to find peace where he left feud. The same character which he bore a couple of hundred years ago, will influence him now; he will still be the moderate, peaceful, unenthusiastic Mr. Dodsworth that he was in 1647.

For notwithstanding education and circumstances may suffice to direct and form the rough material of the mind, it cannot create, nor give intellect, noble aspiration, and energetic constancy where dulness, wavering of purpose, and grovelling desires, are stamped by nature. Entertaining this belief we have (to forget Mr. Dodsworth for awhile) often made conjectures how such and such heroes of antiquity would act, if they were reborn in these times: and then awakened fancy has gone on to imagine that some of them are reborn; that according to the theory explained by Virgil in his sixth Æneid, every thousand years the dead return to life, and their souls endued with the same sensibilities and capacities as before, are turned naked of knowledge into this world, again to dress their skeleton powers in such habiliments as situation, education, and experience will furnish. Pythagoras, we are told, remembered many transmigrations of this sort, as having occurred to himself, though for a philosopher he made very little use of his anterior memories. It would prove an instructive school for kings and statesmen, and in fact for all human beings, called on as they are, to play their part on the stage of the world, could they remember what they had been. Thus we might obtain a glimpse of heaven and of hell, as, the secret of our former identity confined to our own bosoms, we winced or exulted in the blame or praise bestowed on our former selves. While the love of glory and posthumous reputation is as natural to man as his attachment to life itself, he must be, under such a state of things, tremblingly alive to the historic records of his honour or shame. The mild spirit of Fox would have been soothed by the recollection that he had played a worthy part as Marcus Antoninus—the former experiences of Alcibiades or even of the emasculated Steeny of James I might have caused Sheridan to have refused to tread over again the same path of dazzling but fleeting brilliancy. The soul of our modern Corinna would have been purified and exalted by a consciousness that once it had given life to the form of Sappho. If at the present moment the witch, memory, were in a freak, to cause all the present generation to recollect that some ten centuries back they had been somebody else, would not several of our free thinking martyrs wonder to find that they had suffered as Christians under Domitian, while the judge as he passed sentence would suddenly become aware, that formerly he had condemned the saints of the early church to the torture, for not renouncing the religion he now upheld—nothing but benevolent actions and real goodness would come pure out of the ordeal. While it would be whimsical to perceive how some great men in parish affairs would strut under the consciousness that their hands had once held a sceptre, an honest artizan or pilfering domestic would find that he was little altered by being transformed into an idle noble or director of a joint stock company; in every way we may suppose that the humble would be exalted, and the noble and the proud would feel their stars and honours dwindle into baubles and child's play when they called to mind the lowly stations they had once occupied. If philosophical novels were in fashion, we conceive an excellent one might be written on the development of the same mind in various stations, in different periods of the world's history.

But to return to Mr. Dodsworth, and indeed with a few more words to bid him farewell. We entreat him no longer to bury himself in obscurity; or, if he modestly decline publicity, we beg him to make himself known personally to us. We have a thousand inquiries to make, doubts to clear up, facts to ascertain. If any fear that old habits and strangeness of appearance will make him ridiculous to those accustomed to associate with modern exquisites, we beg to assure him that we are not given to ridicule mere outward shows, and that worth and intrinsic excellence will always claim our respect.

This we say, if Mr. Dodsworth is alive. Perhaps he is again no more. Perhaps he opened his eyes only to shut them again more obstinately; perhaps his ancient clay could not thrive on the harvests of these latter days. After a little wonder; a little shuddering to find himself the dead alive—finding no affinity between himself and the present state of things—he has bidden once more an eternal farewell to the sun. Followed to his grave by his preserver and the wondering villagers, he may sleep the true death-sleep in the same valley where he so long reposed. Dr. Hotham may have erected a simple tablet over his twice-buried remains, inscribed—

To the Memory of R. Dodsworth,
An Englishman,
Born April 1, 1617; Died July 16, 18;– Aged 187.

An inscription which, if it were preserved during any terrible convulsion that caused the world to begin its life again, would occasion many learned disquisitions and ingenious theories concerning a race which authentic records showed to have secured the privilege of attaining so vast an age.

THE MORTAL IMMORTAL

(1833)

Mary Shelley

July 16, 1833.—This is a memorable anniversary for me; on it I complete my three hundred and twenty-third year!

The Wandering Jew?—certainly not. More than eighteen centuries have passed over his head. In comparison with him, I am a very young Immortal.

Am I, then, immortal? This is a question which I have asked myself, by day and night, for now three hundred and three years, and yet cannot answer it. I detected a grey hair amidst my brown locks this very day—that surely signifies decay. Yet it may have remained concealed there for three hundred years—for some persons have become entirely white-headed before twenty years of age.

I will tell my story, and my reader shall judge for me. I will tell my story, and so contrive to pass some few hours of a long eternity, become so wearisome to me. For ever! Can it be? to live for ever! I have heard of enchantments, in which the victims were plunged into a deep sleep, to wake, after a hundred years, as fresh as ever: I have heard of the Seven Sleepers—thus to be immortal would not be so burthensome: but, oh! the weight of never-ending time—the tedious passage of the still-succeeding hours! How happy was the fabled Nourjahad!—But to my task.

All the world has heard of Cornelius Agrippa. His memory is as immortal as his arts have made me. All the world has also heard of his scholar, who, unawares, raised the foul fiend during his master's absence, and was destroyed by him. The report, true or false, of this accident, was attended with many inconveniences to the renowned philosopher. All his scholars at once deserted him—his servants disappeared. He had no one near him to put coals on his ever-burning fires while he slept, or to attend to the changeful colours of his medicines while he studied. Experiment after experiment failed, because one pair of hands was insufficient to complete them: the dark spirits laughed at him for not being able to retain a single mortal in his service.

I was then very young—very poor—and very much in love. I had been for about a year the pupil of Cornelius, though I was absent when this accident took place. On my return, my friends implored me not to return to the alchymist's abode. I trembled as I listened to the dire tale they told; I required no second warning; and when Cornelius came and offered me a purse of gold if I would remain under his roof, I felt as if Satan himself tempted me. My teeth chattered—my hair stood on end;—I ran off as fast as my trembling knees would permit.

My failing steps were directed whither for two years they had every evening been attracted,—a gently bubbling spring of pure living water, beside which lingered a dark-haired girl, whose beaming eyes were fixed on the path I was accustomed each night to tread. I cannot remember the hour when I did not love Bertha; we had been neighbours and playmates from infancy,—her parents, like mine, were of humble life, yet respectable,—our attachment had been a source of pleasure to them. In an evil hour, a malignant fever carried off both her father and mother, and Bertha became an orphan. She would have found a home beneath my paternal roof, but, unfortunately, the old lady of the near castle, rich, childless, and solitary, declared her intention to adopt her. Henceforth Bertha was clad in silk—inhabited a marble palace—and was looked on as being highly favoured by fortune. But in her new situation among her new associates, Bertha remained true to the friend of her humbler days; she often visited the cottage of my father, and when forbidden to go thither, she would stray towards the neighbouring wood, and meet me beside its shady fountain.

She often declared that she owed no duty to her new protectress equal in sanctity to that which bound us. Yet still I was too poor to marry, and she grew weary of being tormented on my account. She had a haughty but an impatient spirit, and grew angry at the obstacles that prevented our union. We met now after an absence, and she had been sorely beset while I was away; she complained bitterly, and almost reproached me for being poor. I replied hastily,—

"I am honest, if I am poor!—were I not, I might soon become rich!"

This exclamation produced a thousand questions. I feared to shock her by owning the truth, but she drew it from me; and then, casting a look of disdain on me, she said,—

"You pretend to love, and you fear to face the Devil for my sake!"

I protested that I had only dreaded to offend her;—while she dwelt on the magnitude of the reward that I should receive. Thus encouraged—shamed by her—led on by love and hope, laughing at my late fears, with quick steps and a light heart, I returned to accept the offers of the alchymist, and was instantly installed in my office.

A year passed away. I became possessed of no insignificant sum of money. Custom had banished my fears. In spite of the most painful vigilance, I had never detected the trace of a cloven foot; nor was the studious silence of our abode ever disturbed by demoniac howls. I still continued my stolen interviews with Bertha, and Hope dawned on me—Hope—but not perfect joy; for Bertha fancied that love and security were enemies, and her pleasure was to divide them in my bosom. Though true of heart, she was somewhat of a coquette in manner; and I was jealous as a Turk. She slighted me in a thousand ways, yet would never acknowledge herself to be in the wrong. She would drive me mad with anger, and then force me to beg her pardon. Sometimes she fancied that I was not sufficiently submissive, and then she had some story of a rival, favoured by her protectress. She was surrounded by silk-clad youths—the rich and gay. What chance had the sad-robed scholar of Cornelius compared with these?

On one occasion, the philosopher made such large demands upon my time, that I was unable to meet her as I was wont. He was engaged in some mighty work, and I was forced to remain, day and night, feeding his furnaces and watching his chemical preparations. Bertha waited for me in vain at the fountain. Her haughty spirit fired at this neglect; and when at last I stole out during the few short minutes allotted to me for slumber, and hoped to be consoled by her, she received me with disdain, dismissed me in scorn, and vowed that any man should possess her hand rather than he who could not be in two places at once for her sake. She would be revenged! And truly she was. In my dingy retreat I heard that she had been hunting, attended by Albert Hoffer. Albert Hoffer was favoured by her protectress; and the three passed in cavalcade before my smoky window. Methought that they mentioned my name; it was followed by a laugh of derision, as her dark eyes glanced contemptuously towards my abode.

Jealousy, with all its venom and all its misery, entered my breast. Now I shed a torrent of tears, to think that I should never call her mine; and, anon, I imprecated a thousand curses on her inconstancy. Yet, still I must stir the fires of the alchymist, still attend on the changes of his unintelligible medicines.

Cornelius had watched for three days and nights, nor closed his eyes. The progress of his alembics was slower than he expected: in spite of his anxiety, sleep weighed upon his eyelids. Again and again he threw off drowsiness with more than human energy; again and again it stole away his senses. He eyed his crucibles wistfully. "Not ready yet," he murmured; "will another night pass before the work is accomplished? Winzy, you are vigilant—you are faithful—you have slept, my boy—you slept last night. Look at that glass vessel. The liquid it contains is of a soft rose-colour: the moment it begins to change its hue, awaken me—till then I may close my eyes. First, it will turn white, and then emit golden flashes; but wait not till then; when the rose-colour fades, rouse me." I scarcely heard the last words, muttered, as they were, in sleep. Even then he did not quite yield to nature. "Winzy, my boy," he again said, "do not touch the vessel—do not put it to your lips; it is a philter—a philter to cure love; you would not cease to love your Bertha—beware to drink!"

And he slept. His venerable head sunk on his breast, and I scarce heard his regular breathing. For a few minutes I watched the vessel—the rosy hue of the liquid remained unchanged. Then my thoughts wandered—they visited the fountain, and dwelt on a thousand charming scenes never to be renewed—never! Serpents and adders were in my heart as the word "Never!" half formed itself on my lips. False girl!—false and cruel! Never more would she smile on me as that evening she smiled on Albert. Worthless, detested woman! I would not remain unrevenged—she should see Albert expire at her feet—she should die beneath my vengeance. She had smiled in disdain and triumph—she knew my wretchedness and her power. Yet what power had she?—the power of exciting my hate—my utter scorn—my—oh, all but indifference! Could I attain that—could I regard her with careless eyes, transferring my rejected love to one fairer and more true, that were indeed a victory!

A bright flash darted before my eyes. I had forgotten the medicine of the adept; I gazed on it with wonder: flashes of admirable beauty, more bright than those which the diamond emits when the sun's rays are on it, glanced from the surface of the liquid; an odour the most fragrant and grateful stole over my sense; the vessel seemed one globe of living radiance, lovely to the eye, and most inviting to the taste. The first thought, instinctively inspired by the grosser sense, was, I will—I must drink. I raised the vessel to my lips. "It will cure me of love—of torture!" Already I had quaffed half of the most delicious liquor ever tasted by the palate of man, when the philosopher stirred.

I started—I dropped the glass—the fluid flamed and glanced along the floor, while I felt Cornelius's gripe at my throat, as he shrieked aloud, "Wretch! you have destroyed the labour of my life!"

The philosopher was totally unaware that I had drunk any portion of his drug. His idea was, and I gave a tacit assent to it, that I had raised the vessel from curiosity, and that, frighted at its brightness, and the flashes of intense light it gave forth, I had let it fall. I never undeceived him. The fire of the medicine was quenched—the fragrance died away—he grew calm, as a philosopher should under the heaviest trials, and dismissed me to rest.

I will not attempt to describe the sleep of glory and bliss which bathed my soul in paradise during the remaining hours of that memorable night. Words would be faint and shallow types of my enjoyment, or of the gladness that possessed my bosom when I woke. I trod air—my thoughts were in heaven. Earth appeared heaven, and my inheritance upon it was to be one trance of delight. "This it is to be cured of love," I thought; "I will see Bertha this day, and she will find her lover cold and regardless; too happy to be disdainful, yet how utterly indifferent to her!"

The hours danced away. The philosopher, secure that he had once succeeded, and believing that he might again, began to concoct the same medicine once more. He was shut up with his books and drugs, and I had a holiday. I dressed myself with care; I looked in an old but polished shield, which served me for a mirror; methought my good looks had wonderfully improved. I hurried beyond the precincts of the town, joy in my soul, the beauty of heaven and earth around me. I turned my steps towards the castle—I could look on its lofty turrets with lightness of heart, for I was cured of love. My Bertha saw me afar off, as I came up the avenue. I know not what sudden impulse animated her bosom, but at the sight, she sprung with a light fawn-like bound down the marble steps, and was hastening towards me. But I had been perceived by another person. The old high-born hag, who called herself her protectress, and was her tyrant, had seen me also; she hobbled, panting, up the terrace; a page, as ugly as herself, held up her train, and fanned her as she hurried along, and stopped my fair girl with a "How, now, my bold mistress? whither so fast? Back to your cage—hawks are abroad!"

Bertha clasped her hands—her eyes were still bent on my approaching figure. I saw the contest. How I abhorred the old crone who checked the kind impulses of my Bertha's softening heart. Hitherto, respect for her rank had caused me to avoid the lady of the castle; now I disdained such trivial considerations. I was cured of love, and lifted above all human fears; I hastened forwards, and soon reached the terrace. How lovely Bertha looked! her eyes flashing fire, her cheeks glowing with impatience and anger, she was a thousand times more graceful and charming than ever. I no longer loved—Oh no! I adored—worshipped—idolized her!

She had that morning been persecuted, with more than usual vehemence, to consent to an immediate marriage with my rival. She was reproached with the encouragement that she had shown him—she was threatened with being turned out of doors with disgrace and shame. Her proud spirit rose in arms at the threat; but when she remembered the scorn that she had heaped upon me, and how, perhaps, she had thus lost one whom she now regarded as her only friend, she wept with remorse and rage. At that moment I appeared. "Oh, Winzy!" she exclaimed, "take me to your mother's cot; swiftly let me leave the detested luxuries and wretchedness of this noble dwelling—take me to poverty and happiness."

I clasped her in my arms with transport. The old dame was speechless with fury, and broke forth into invective only when we were far on our road to my natal cottage. My mother received the fair fugitive, escaped from a gilt cage to nature and liberty, with tenderness and joy; my father, who loved her, welcomed her heartily; it was a day of rejoicing, which did not need the addition of the celestial potion of the alchymist to steep me in delight.

Soon after this eventful day, I became the husband of Bertha. I ceased to be the scholar of Cornelius, but I continued his friend. I always felt grateful to him for having, unawares, procured me that delicious draught of a divine elixir, which, instead of curing me of love (sad cure! solitary and joyless remedy for evils which seem blessings to the memory), had inspired me with courage and resolution, thus winning for me an inestimable treasure in my Bertha.

I often called to mind that period of trance-like inebriation with wonder. The drink of Cornelius had not fulfilled the task for which he affirmed that it had been prepared, but its effects were more potent and blissful than words can express. They had faded by degrees, yet they lingered long—and painted life in hues of splendour. Bertha often wondered at my lightness of heart and unaccustomed gaiety; for, before, I had been rather serious, or even sad, in my disposition. She loved me the better for my cheerful temper, and our days were winged by joy.

Five years afterwards I was suddenly summoned to the bedside of the dying Cornelius. He had sent for me in haste, conjuring my instant presence. I found him stretched on his pallet, enfeebled even to death; all of life that yet remained animated his piercing eyes, and they were fixed on a glass vessel, full of a roseate liquid.

"Behold," he said, in a broken and inward voice, "the vanity of human wishes! a second time my hopes are about to be crowned, a second time they are destroyed. Look at that liquor—you remember five years ago I had prepared the same, with the same success;—then, as now, my thirsting lips expected to taste the immortal elixir—you dashed it from me! and at present it is too late."

He spoke with difficulty, and fell back on his pillow. I could not help saying,—

"How, revered master, can a cure for love restore you to life?"

A faint smile gleamed across his face as I listened earnestly to his scarcely intelligible answer.

"A cure for love and for all things—the Elixir of Immortality. Ah! if now I might drink, I should live for ever!"

As he spoke, a golden flash gleamed from the fluid; a well-remembered fragrance stole over the air; he raised himself, all weak as he was—strength seemed miraculously to re-enter his frame—he stretched forth his hand—a loud explosion startled me—a ray of fire shot up from the elixir, and the glass vessel which contained it was shivered to atoms! I turned my eyes towards the philosopher; he had fallen back—his eyes were glassy—his features rigid—he was dead!

But I lived, and was to live for ever! So said the unfortunate alchymist, and for a few days I believed his words. I remembered the glorious intoxication that had followed my stolen draught. I reflected on the change I had felt in my frame—in my soul. The bounding elasticity of the one—the buoyant lightness of the other. I surveyed myself in a mirror, and could perceive no change in my features during the space of the five years which had elapsed. I remembered the radiant hues and grateful scent of that delicious beverage—worthy the gift it was capable of bestowing—I was, then, IMMORTAL!

A few days after I laughed at my credulity. The old proverb, that "a prophet is least regarded in his own country," was true with respect to me and my defunct master. I loved him as a man—I respected him as a sage—but I derided the notion that he could command the powers of darkness, and laughed at the superstitious fears with which he was regarded by the vulgar. He was a wise philosopher, but had no acquaintance with any spirits but those clad in flesh and blood. His science was simply human; and human science, I soon persuaded myself, could never conquer nature's laws so far as to imprison the soul for ever within its carnal habitation. Cornelius had brewed a soul-refreshing drink—more inebriating than wine—sweeter and more fragrant than any fruit: it possessed probably strong medicinal powers, imparting gladness to the heart and vigour to the limbs; but its effects would wear out; already were they diminished in my frame. I was a lucky fellow to have quaffed health and joyous spirits, and perhaps long life, at my master's hands; but my good fortune ended there: longevity was far different from immortality.

I continued to entertain this belief for many years. Sometimes a thought stole across me—Was the alchymist indeed deceived? But my habitual credence was, that I should meet the fate of all the children of Adam at my appointed time—a little late, but still at a natural age. Yet it was certain that I retained a wonderfully youthful look. I was laughed at for my vanity in consulting the mirror so often, but I consulted it in vain—my brow was untrenched—my cheeks—my eyes—my whole person continued as untarnished as in my twentieth year.

I was troubled. I looked at the faded beauty of Bertha—I seemed more like her son. By degrees our neighbours began to make similar observations, and I found at last that I went by the name of the Scholar bewitched. Bertha herself grew uneasy. She became jealous and peevish, and at length she began to question me. We had no children; we were all in all to each other; and though, as she grew older, her vivacious spirit became a little allied to ill-temper, and her beauty sadly diminished, I cherished her in my heart as the mistress I had idolized, the wife I had sought and won with such perfect love.

At last our situation became intolerable: Bertha was fifty—I twenty years of age. I had, in very shame, in some measure adopted the habits of a more advanced age; I no longer mingled in the dance among the young and gay, but my heart bounded along with them while I restrained my feet; and a sorry figure I cut among the Nestors of our village. But before the time I mention, things were altered—we were universally shunned; we were—at least, I was—reported to have kept up an iniquitous acquaintance with some of my former master's supposed friends. Poor Bertha was pitied, but deserted. I was regarded with horror and detestation.

What was to be done? we sat by our winter fire—poverty had made itself felt, for none would buy the produce of my farm; and often I had been forced to journey twenty miles, to some place where I was not known, to dispose of our property. It is true, we had saved something for an evil day—that day was come.

We sat by our lone fireside—the old-hearted youth and his antiquated wife. Again Bertha insisted on knowing the truth; she recapitulated all she had ever heard said about me, and added her own observations. She conjured me to cast off the spell; she described how much more comely grey hairs were than my chestnut locks; she descanted on the reverence and respect due to age—how preferable to the slight regard paid to mere children: could I imagine that the despicable gifts of youth and good looks outweighed disgrace, hatred, and scorn? Nay, in the end I should be burnt as a dealer in the black art, while she, to whom I had not deigned to communicate any portion of my good fortune, might be stoned as my accomplice. At length she insinuated that I must share my secret with her, and bestow on her like benefits to those I myself enjoyed, or she would denounce me—and then she burst into tears.

Thus beset, methought it was the best way to tell the truth. I revealed it as tenderly as I could, and spoke only of a *very long life*, not of immortality—which representation, indeed, coincided best with my own ideas. When I ended, I rose and said,—

"And now, my Bertha, will you denounce the lover of your youth?—You will not, I know. But it is too hard, my poor wife, that you should suffer from my ill-luck and the accursed arts of Cornelius. I will leave you—you have wealth enough, and friends will return in my absence. I will go; young as I seem, and strong as I am, I can work and gain my bread among strangers, unsuspected and unknown. I loved you in youth; God is my witness that I would not desert you in age, but that your safety and happiness require it."

I took my cap and moved towards the door; in a moment Bertha's arms were round my neck, and her lips were pressed to mine. "No, my husband, my Winzy," she said, "you shall not go alone—take me with you; we will remove from this place, and, as you say, among strangers we shall be unsuspected and safe. I am not so very old as quite to shame you, my Winzy; and I daresay the charm will soon wear off, and, with the blessing of God, you will become more elderly-looking, as is fitting; you shall not leave me."

I returned the good soul's embrace heartily. "I will not, my Bertha; but for your sake I had not thought of such a thing. I will be your true, faithful husband while you are spared to me, and do my duty by you to the last."

The next day we prepared secretly for our emigration. We were obliged to make great pecuniary sacrifices—it could not be helped. We realized a sum sufficient, at least, to maintain us while Bertha lived; and, without saying adieu to any one, quitted our native country to take refuge in a remote part of western France.

It was a cruel thing to transport poor Bertha from her native village, and the friends of her youth, to a new country, new language, new customs. The strange secret of my destiny rendered this removal immaterial to me; but I compassionated her deeply, and was glad to perceive that she found compensation for her misfortunes in a variety of little ridiculous circumstances. Away from all tell-tale chroniclers, she sought to decrease the apparent disparity of our ages by a thousand feminine arts—rouge, youthful dress, and assumed juvenility of manner. I could not be angry. Did not I myself wear a mask? Why quarrel with hers, because it was less successful? I grieved deeply when I remembered that this was my Bertha, whom I had loved so fondly, and won with such transport—the dark-eyed, dark-haired girl, with smiles of enchanting archness and a step like a fawn—this mincing, simpering, jealous old woman. I should have revered her grey locks and withered cheeks; but thus!—It was my work, I knew; but I did not the less deplore this type of human weakness.

Her jealousy never slept. Her chief occupation was to discover that, in spite of outward appearances, I was myself growing old. I verily believe that the poor soul loved me truly in her heart, but never had woman so tormenting a mode of displaying fondness. She would discern wrinkles in my face and decrepitude in my walk, while I bounded along in youthful vigour, the youngest looking of twenty youths. I never dared address another woman. On one occasion, fancying that the belle of the village regarded me with favouring eyes, she brought me a grey wig. Her constant discourse among her acquaintances was, that though I looked so young, there was ruin at work within my frame; and she affirmed that the worst symptom about me was my apparent health. My youth was a disease, she said, and I ought at all times to prepare, if not for a sudden and awful death, at least to awake some morning white-headed and bowed down with all the marks of advanced years. I let her talk—I often joined in her conjectures. Her warnings chimed in with my never-ceasing speculations concerning my state, and I took an earnest, though painful, interest in listening to all that her quick wit and excited imagination could say on the subject.

Why dwell on these minute circumstances? We lived on for many long years. Bertha became bedrid and paralytic; I nursed her as a mother might a child. She grew peevish, and still harped upon one string—of how long I should survive her. It has ever been a source of consolation to me, that I performed my duty scrupulously towards her. She had been mine in youth, she was mine in age; and at last, when I heaped the sod over her corpse, I wept to feel that I had lost all that really bound me to humanity.

Since then how many have been my cares and woes, how few and empty my enjoyments! I pause here in my history—I will pursue it no further. A sailor without rudder or compass, tossed on a stormy sea—a traveller lost on a widespread heath, without landmark or stone to guide him—such have I been: more lost, more hopeless than either. A nearing ship, a gleam from some far cot, may save them; but I have no beacon except the hope of death.

Death! mysterious, ill-visaged friend of weak humanity! Why alone of all mortals have you cast me from your sheltering fold? Oh, for the peace of the grave! the deep silence of the iron-bound tomb! that thought would cease to work in my brain, and my heart beat no more with emotions varied only by new forms of sadness!

Am I immortal? I return to my first question. In the first place, is it not more probable that the beverage of the alchymist was fraught rather with longevity than eternal life? Such is my hope. And then be it remembered, that I only drank *half* of the potion prepared by him. Was not the whole necessary to complete the charm? To have drained half the Elixir of Immortality is but to be half-immortal—my For-ever is thus truncated and null.

But again, who shall number the years of the half of eternity? I often try to imagine by what rule the infinite may be divided. Sometimes I fancy age advancing upon me. One grey hair I have found. Fool! do I lament? Yes, the fear of age and death often creeps coldly into my heart; and the more I live, the more I dread death, even while I abhor life. Such an enigma is man—born to perish—when he wars, as I do, against the established laws of his nature.

But for this anomaly of feeling surely I might die: the medicine of the alchymist would not be proof against fire—sword—and the strangling waters. I have gazed upon the blue depths of many a placid lake, and the tumultuous rushing of many a mighty river, and have said, peace inhabits those waters; yet I have turned my steps away, to live yet another day. I have asked myself, whether suicide would be a crime in one to whom thus only the portals of the other world could be opened. I have done all, except presenting myself as a soldier or duellist, an object of destruction to my—no, *not* my fellow-mortals, and therefore I have shrunk away. They are not my fellows. The inextinguishable power of life in my frame, and their ephemeral existence, places us wide as the poles asunder. I could not raise a hand against the meanest or the most powerful among them.

Thus I have lived on for many a year—alone, and weary of myself—desirous of death, yet never dying—a mortal immortal. Neither ambition nor avarice can enter my mind, and the ardent love that gnaws at my heart, never to be returned—never to find an equal on which to expend itself—lives there only to torment me.

This very day I conceived a design by which I may end all—without self-slaughter, without making another man a Cain—an expedition, which mortal frame can never survive, even endued with the youth and strength that inhabits mine. Thus I shall put my immortality to the test, and rest for ever—or return, the wonder and benefactor of the human species.

Before I go, a miserable vanity has caused me to pen these pages. I would not die, and leave no name behind. Three centuries have passed since I quaffed the fatal beverage; another year shall not elapse before, encountering gigantic dangers—warring with the powers of frost in their home—beset by famine, toil, and tempest—I yield this body, too tenacious a cage for a soul which thirsts for freedom, to the destructive elements of air and water; or, if I survive, my name shall be recorded as one of the most famous among the sons of men; and, my task achieved, I shall adopt more resolute means, and, by scattering and annihilating the atoms that compose my frame, set at liberty the life imprisoned within, and so cruelly prevented from soaring from this dim earth to a sphere more congenial to its immortal essence.

EXCERPT FROM

WUTHERING HEIGHTS

(1847)

Emily Brontë

Chapter IX

I went into the kitchen, and sat down to lull my little lamb to sleep. Heathcliff, as I thought, walked through to the barn. It turned out afterwards that he only got as far as the other side the settle, when he flung himself on a bench by the wall, removed from the fire and remained silent.

I was rocking Hareton on my knee, and humming a song that began—

> *"It was far in the night, and the bairnies grat,*
> *The mither beneath the mools heard that—"*

when Miss Cathy, who had listened to the hubbub from her room, put her head in, and whispered 'Are you alone, Nelly?'

'Yes, Miss,' I replied.

She entered and approached the hearth. I, supposing she was going to say something, looked up. The expression of her face seemed disturbed and anxious. Her lips were half asunder, as if she meant to speak, and she drew a breath; but it escaped in a sigh instead of a sentence. I resumed my song; not having forgotten her recent behaviour.

'Where's Heathcliff?' she said, interrupting me.

'About his work in the stable,' was my answer.

He did not contradict me; perhaps he had fallen into a doze. There followed another long pause, during which I perceived a drop or two trickle from Catherine's cheek to the flags. Is she sorry for her shameful conduct?—I asked myself. That will be a novelty: but she may come to the point—as she will—I sha'n't help her! No, she felt small trouble regarding any subject, save her own concerns.

'Oh, dear!' she cried at last. 'I'm very unhappy!'

'A pity,' observed I. 'You're hard to please; so many friends and so few cares, and can't make yourself content!'

'Nelly, will you keep a secret for me?' she pursued, kneeling down by me, and lifting her winsome eyes to my face with that sort of look which turns off bad temper, even when one has all the right in the world to indulge it.

'Is it worth keeping?' I inquired, less sulkily.

'Yes, and it worries me, and I must let it out! I want to know what I should do. Today, Edgar Linton has asked me to marry him, and I've given him an answer. Now, before I tell you whether it was a consent or denial, you tell me which it ought to have been.'

'Really, Miss Catherine, how can I know?' I replied. 'To be sure, considering the exhibition you performed in his presence this afternoon, I might say it would be wise to refuse him: since he asked you after that, he must either be hopelessly stupid or a venturesome fool.'

'If you talk so, I won't tell you any more,' she returned, peevishly rising to her feet. 'I accepted him, Nelly. Be quick, and say whether I was wrong!'

'You accepted him! Then what good is it discussing the matter? You have pledged your word, and cannot retract.'

'But say whether I should have done so—do!' she exclaimed in an irritated tone; chafing her hands together, and frowning.

'There are many things to be considered before that question can be answered properly,' I said, sententiously. 'First and foremost, do you love Mr. Edgar?'

'Who can help it? Of course I do,' she answered.

Then I put her through the following catechism: for a girl of twenty-two it was not injudicious.

'Why do you love him, Miss Cathy?'

'Nonsense, I do—that's sufficient.'

'By no means; you must say why?'

'Well, because he is handsome, and pleasant to be with.'

'Bad!' was my commentary.

'And because he is young and cheerful.'

'Bad, still.'

'And because he loves me.'

'Indifferent, coming there.'

'And he will be rich, and I shall like to be the greatest woman of the neighbourhood, and I shall be proud of having such a husband.'

'Worst of all. And now, say how you love him?'

'As everybody loves—you're silly, Nelly.'

'Not at all—answer.'

'I love the ground under his feet, and the air over his head, and everything he touches, and every word he says. I love all his looks, and all his actions, and him entirely and altogether. There now!'

'And why?'

'Nay; you are making a jest of it: it is exceedingly ill-natured! It's no jest to me!' said the young lady, scowling, and turning her face to the fire.

'I'm very far from jesting, Miss Catherine,' I replied. 'You love Mr. Edgar because he is handsome, and young, and cheerful, and rich, and loves you. The last, however, goes for nothing: you would love him without that, probably; and with it you wouldn't, unless he possessed the four former attractions.'

'No, to be sure not: I should only pity him—hate him, perhaps, if he were ugly, and a clown.'

'But there are several other handsome, rich young men in the world: handsomer, possibly, and richer than he is. What should hinder you from loving them?'

'If there be any, they are out of my way: I've seen none like Edgar.'

'You may see some; and he won't always be handsome, and young, and may not always be rich.'

'He is now; and I have only to do with the present. I wish you would speak rationally.'

'Well, that settles it: if you have only to do with the present, marry Mr. Linton.'

'I don't want your permission for that—I *shall* marry him: and yet you have not told me whether I'm right.'

'Perfectly right; if people be right to marry only for the present. And now, let us hear what you are unhappy about. Your brother will be pleased; the old lady and gentleman will not object, I think; you will escape from a disorderly, comfortless home into a wealthy, respectable one; and you love Edgar, and Edgar loves you. All seems smooth and easy: where is the obstacle?'

'*Here!* and *here!*' replied Catherine, striking one hand on her forehead, and the other on her breast: 'in whichever place the soul lives. In my soul and in my heart, I'm convinced I'm wrong!'

'That's very strange! I cannot make it out.'

'It's my secret. But if you will not mock at me, I'll explain it: I can't do it distinctly; but I'll give you a feeling of how I feel.'

She seated herself by me again: her countenance grew sadder and graver, and her clasped hands trembled.

'Nelly, do you never dream queer dreams?' she said, suddenly, after some minutes' reflection.

'Yes, now and then,' I answered.

'And so do I. I've dreamt in my life dreams that have stayed with me ever after, and changed my ideas: they've gone through and through me, like wine through water, and altered the colour of my mind. And this is one: I'm going to tell it—but take care not to smile at any part of it.'

'Oh! don't, Miss Catherine!' I cried. 'We're dismal enough without conjuring up ghosts and visions to perplex us. Come, come, be merry and like yourself! Look at little Hareton! *He's* dreaming nothing dreary. How sweetly he smiles in his sleep!'

'Yes; and how sweetly his father curses in his solitude! You remember him, I daresay, when he was just such another as that chubby thing: nearly as young and innocent. However, Nelly, I shall oblige you to listen: it's not long; and I've no power to be merry tonight.'

'I won't hear it, I won't hear it!' I repeated, hastily.

I was superstitious about dreams then, and am still; and Catherine had an unusual gloom in her aspect, that made me dread something from which I might shape a prophecy, and foresee a fearful catastrophe. She was vexed, but she did not proceed. Apparently taking up another subject, she recommenced in a short time.

'If I were in heaven, Nelly, I should be extremely miserable.'

'Because you are not fit to go there,' I answered. 'All sinners would be miserable in heaven.'

'But it is not for that. I dreamt once that I was there.'

'I tell you I won't hearken to your dreams, Miss Catherine! I'll go to bed,' I interrupted again.

She laughed, and held me down; for I made a motion to leave my chair.

'This is nothing,' cried she: 'I was only going to say that heaven did not seem to be my home; and I broke my heart with weeping to come back to earth; and the angels were so angry that they flung me out into the middle of the heath on the top of Wuthering Heights; where I woke sobbing for joy. That will do to explain my secret, as well as the other. I've no more business to marry Edgar Linton than I have to be in heaven; and if the wicked man in there had not brought Heathcliff so low, I shouldn't have thought of it. It would degrade me to marry Heathcliff now; so he shall never know how I love him: and that, not because he's handsome, Nelly, but because he's more myself than I am. Whatever our souls are made of, his and mine are the same; and Linton's is as different as a moonbeam from lightning, or frost from fire.'

Ere this speech ended I became sensible of Heathcliff's presence. Having noticed a slight movement, I turned my head, and saw him rise from the bench, and steal out noiselessly. He had listened till he heard Catherine say it would degrade her to marry him, and then he stayed to hear no further. My companion, sitting on the ground, was prevented by the back of the settle from remarking his presence or departure; but I started, and bade her hush!

'Why?' she asked, gazing nervously round.

'Joseph is here,' I answered, catching opportunely the roll of his cartwheels up the road; 'and Heathcliff will come in with him. I'm not sure whether he were not at the door this moment.'

'Oh, he couldn't overhear me at the door!' said she. 'Give me Hareton, while you get the supper, and when it is ready ask me to sup with you. I want to cheat my uncomfortable conscience, and be convinced that Heathcliff has no notion of these things. He has not, has he? He does not know what being in love is!'

'I see no reason that he should not know, as well as you,' I returned; 'and if you are his choice, he'll be the most unfortunate creature that ever was born! As soon as you become Mrs. Linton, he loses friend, and love, and all! Have you considered how you'll bear the separation, and how he'll bear to be quite deserted in the world? Because, Miss Catherine—'

'He quite deserted! we separated!' she exclaimed, with an accent of indignation. 'Who is to separate us, pray? They'll meet the fate of Milo! Not as long as I live, Ellen: for no mortal creature. Every Linton on the face of the earth might melt into nothing before I could consent to forsake Heathcliff. Oh, that's not what I intend—that's not what I mean! I shouldn't be Mrs. Linton were such a price demanded! He'll be as much to me as he has been all his lifetime. Edgar must shake off his antipathy, and tolerate him, at least. He will, when he learns my true feelings towards him. Nelly, I see now you think me a selfish wretch; but did it never strike you that if Heathcliff and I married, we should be beggars? whereas, if I marry Linton I can aid Heathcliff to rise, and place him out of my brother's power.'

'With your husband's money, Miss Catherine?' I asked. 'You'll find him not so pliable as you calculate upon: and, though I'm hardly a judge, I think that's the worst motive you've given yet for being the wife of young Linton.'

'It is not,' retorted she; 'it is the best! The others were the satisfaction of my whims: and for Edgar's sake, too, to satisfy him. This is for the sake of one who comprehends in his person my feelings to Edgar and myself. I cannot express it; but surely you and everybody have a notion that there is or should be an existence of yours beyond you. What were the use of my creation, if I were entirely contained here? My great miseries in this world have been Heathcliff's miseries, and I watched and felt each from the beginning: my great thought in living is himself. If all else perished, and *he* remained, I should still continue to be; and if all else remained, and he were annihilated, the universe would turn to a mighty stranger: I should not seem a part of it.—My love for Linton is like the foliage in the woods: time will change it, I'm well aware, as winter changes the trees. My love for Heathcliff resembles the eternal rocks beneath: a source of little visible delight, but necessary. Nelly, I *am* Heathcliff! He's always, always in my mind: not as a pleasure, any more than I am always a pleasure to myself, but as my own being.'

EXCERPT FROM

MARY BARTON: A TALE OF MANCHESTER LIFE

(1848)

Elizabeth Gaskell

[John Barton had been part of a workers delegation sent from Manchester to London to join in presenting a petition for relief to the House of Commons signed by 1.3 million working people. This historical event occurred in 1839. The MPs voted by an overwhelming margin not to hear the petition. Gaskell relates how capitalism creates what she calls "Frankenstein, that monster of many human qualities, ungifted with a soul, a knowledge of good and evil."]

Chapter XV

A VIOLENT MEETING BETWEEN THE RIVALS

What thoughtful heart can look into this gulf
That darkly yawns 'twixt rich and poor,
And not find food for saddest meditation!
Can see, without a pang of keenest grief,
Them fiercely battling (like some natural foes)
Whom God hath made, with help and sympathy,
To stand as brothers, side by side, united!
Where is the wisdom that shall bridge this gulf,
And bind them once again in trust and love?

—*Love-Truths.*

We must return to John Barton. Poor John! He never got over his disappointing journey to London. The deep mortification he then experienced (with, perhaps, as little selfishness for its cause as mortification ever bad) was of no temporary nature; indeed few of his feelings were.

Then came a long period of bodily privation; of daily hunger after food; and though he tried to persuade himself he could bear want himself with stoical indifference, and did care about it as little as most men, yet the body took its revenge for its uneasy feelings. The mind became soured and morose, and lost much of its equipoise. It was no longer elastic, as in the days of youth, or in times of comparative happiness; it ceased to hope. And it is hard to live on when one can no longer hope.

The same state of feeling which John Barton entertained, if belonging to one who had had leisure to think of such things, and physicians to give names to them would have been called monomania; so haunting, so incessant, were the thoughts that pressed upon him. I have somewhere read a forcibly described punishment among the Italians, worthy of a Borgia. The supposed or real criminal was shut up in a room, supplied with every convenience and luxury; and at first mourned little over his imprisonment. But day by day he became aware that the space between the walls of his apartment was narrowing, and then he understood the end. Those painted walls would come into hideous nearness, and at last crush the life out of him.

And so day by day, nearer and nearer, came the diseased thoughts of John Barton. They excluded the light of heaven, the cheering sounds of earth. They were preparing his death.

It is true much of their morbid power might be ascribed to the use of opium. But before you blame too harshly this use, or rather abuse, try a hopeless life, with daily cravings of the body for food. Try, not alone being without hope yourself, but seeing all around you reduced to the same despair, arising from the same circumstances; all around you telling (though they use no words or language), by their looks and feeble actions, that they are suffering and sinking under the pressure of want. Would you not be glad to forget life, and its burdens? And opium gives forgetfulness for a time.

It is true they who thus purchase it pay dearly for their oblivion; but can you expect the uneducated to count the cost of their whistle? Poor wretches! They pay a heavy price. Days of oppressive weariness and languor, whose realities have the feeble sickliness of dreams; nights, whose dreams are fierce realities of agony; sinking health, tottering frames, incipient madness, and worse, the *consciousness* of incipient madness; this is the price of their whistle. But have you taught them the science of consequences?

John Barton's overpowering thought, which was to work out his fate on earth, was rich and poor; why are they so separate, so distinct, when God has made them all? It is not His will that their interests are so far apart. Whose doing is it?

And so on into the problems and mysteries of life, until, bewildered and lost, unhappy and suffering, the only feeling that remained clear and undisturbed in the tumult of his heart, was hatred to the one class, and keen sympathy with the other.

But what availed his sympathy? No education had given him wisdom; and without wisdom, even love, with all its effects, too often works but harm. He acted to the best of his judgement, but it was a widely erring judgement.

The actions of the uneducated seem to me typified in those of Frankenstein, that monster of many human qualities, ungifted with a soul, a knowledge of the difference between good and evil.

The people rise up to life; they irritate us, they terrify us, and we become their enemies. Then, in the sorrowful moment of our triumphant power, their eyes gaze on us with mute reproach. Why have we made them what they are; a powerful monster, yet without the inner means for peace and happiness?

John Barton became a Chartist, a Communist; all that is commonly called wild and visionary. Aye! but being visionary is something. It shows a soul, a being not altogether sensual; a creature who looks forward for others, if not for himself.

And with all his weakness he had a sort of practical power, which made him useful to the bodies of men to whom he belonged. He had a ready kind of rough Lancashire eloquence, arising out of the fulness of his heart, which was very stirring to men similarly circumstanced, who liked to hear their feelings put into words. He had a pretty clear head at times, for method and arrangement; a necessary talent to large combinations of men. And what perhaps more than all made him relied upon and valued, was the consciousness which every one who came in contact with him felt, that he was actuated by no selfish motives; that his class, his order, was what he stood by, not the rights of his own paltry self. For even in great and noble men, as soon as self comes into prominent existence, it becomes a mean and paltry thing.

A little time before this, there had come one of those occasions for deliberation among the employed, which deeply interested John Barton, and the discussions concerning which bad caused his frequent absence from home of late.

I am not sure if I can express myself in the technical terms of either masters or workmen, but I will try simply to state the case on which the latter deliberated.

An order for coarse goods came in from a new foreign market. It was a large order, giving employment to all the mills engaged in that species of manufacture; but it was necessary to execute it speedily, and at as low prices as possible, as the masters had reason to believe that a duplicate order had been sent to one of the continental manufacturing towns, where there were no restrictions on food, no taxes on building or machinery, and where consequently they dreaded that the goods could be made at a much lower price than they could afford them for; and that, by so acting and charging, the rival manufacturers would obtain undivided possession of the market. It was clearly their interest to buy cotton as cheaply, and to beat down wages as low as possible. And in the long run the interests of the workmen would have been thereby benefited. Distrust each other as they may, the employers and the employed must rise or fall together. There may be some difference as to chronology, none as to fact.

But the masters did not choose to make all these facts known. They stood upon being the masters, and that they had a right to order work at their own prices, and they believed that in the present depression of trade, and unemployment of hands, there would be no difficulty in getting it done.

Now let us turn to the workmen's view of the question. The masters (of the tottering foundation of whose prosperity they were ignorant) seemed doing well, and, like gentlemen, "lived at home in ease," while they were starving, gasping on from day to day; and there was a foreign order to be executed, the extent of which, large as it was, was greatly exaggerated; and it was to be done speedily. Why were the masters offering such low wages under these circumstances? Shame upon them! It was taking advantage of their workpeople being almost starved; but they would starve entirely rather than come into such terms. It was bad enough to be poor, while by the labour of their thin hands, the sweat of their brows, the masters were made rich; but they would not be utterly ground down to dust. No! they would fold their hands and sit idle, and smile at the masters, whom even in death they could baffle. With Spartan endurance they determined to let the employers know their power, by refusing to work.

So class distrusted class, and their want of mutual confidence wrought sorrow to both. The masters would not be bullied, and compelled to reveal why they felt it wisest and best to offer only such low wages; they would not be made to tell that they were even sacrificing capital to obtain a decisive victory over the continental manufacturers. And the workmen sat silent and stern with folded hands refusing to work for such pay. There was a strike in Manchester.

Of course it was succeeded by the usual consequences. Many other Trades' Unions, connected with different branches of business, supported with money, countenance, and encouragement of every kind, the stand which the Manchester power-loom weavers were making against their masters. Delegates from Glasgow, from Nottingham, and other towns, were sent to Manchester, to keep up the spirit of resistance; a committee was formed, and all the requisite officers elected; chairman, treasurer, honorary secretary:—among them was John Barton.

The masters, meanwhile, took their measures. They placarded the walls with advertisements for power-loom weavers. The workmen replied by a placard in still larger letters, stating their grievances. The masters met daily in town, to mourn over the time (so fast slipping away) for the fulfilment of the foreign orders; and to strengthen each other in their resolution not to yield. If they gave up now, they might give up always. It would never do. And amongst the most energetic of the masters, the Carsons, father and son, took their places. It is well known, that there is no religionist so zealous as a convert; no masters so stern, and regardless of the interests of their workpeople, as those who have risen from such a station themselves. This would account for the elder Mr. Carson's determination not to be bullied into yielding; not even to be bullied into giving reasons for acting as the masters did. It was the employers' will, and that should be enough for the employed. Harry Carson did not trouble himself much about the grounds for his conduct.

He liked the excitement of the affair. He liked the attitude of resistance. He was brave, and he liked the idea of personal danger, with which some of the more cautious tried to intimidate the violent among the masters.

Meanwhile, the power-loom weavers living in the more remote parts of Lancashire, and the neighbouring counties, heard of the masters' advertisements for workmen; and in their solitary dwellings grew weary of starvation, and resolved to come to Manchester. Foot-sore, way-worn, half-starved looking men they were, as they tried to steal into town in the early dawn, before people were astir, or in the dusk of the evening. And now began the real wrong-doing of the Trades' Unions. As to their decision to work, or not, at such a particular rate of wages, that was either wise or unwise; all error of judgement at the worst. But they had no right to tyrannize over others, and tie them down to their own Procrustean bed. Abhorring what they considered oppression in the masters, why did they oppress others? Because, when men get excited, they know not what they do. Judge, then, with something of the mercy of the Holy One, whom we all love.

In spite of policemen, set to watch over the safety of the poor country weavers—in spite of magistrates, and prisons, and severe punishments—the poor depressed men tramping in from Burnley, Padiham, and other places, to work at the condemned "Starvation Prices," were waylaid, and beaten, and left almost for dead by the road-side. The police broke up every lounging knot of men:—they separated quietly, to reunite half-a-mile further out of town.

Of course the feeling between the masters and workmen did not improve under these circumstances.

Combination is an awful power. It is like the equally

mighty agency of steam; capable of almost unlimited good or evil. But to obtain a blessing on its labours, it must work under the direction of a high and intelligent will; incapable of being misled by passion or excitement. The will of the operatives had not been guided to the calmness of wisdom.

So much for generalities. Let us now return to individuals.

A note, respectfully worded, although its tone of determination was strong, had been sent by the power-loom weavers, requesting that a "deputation" of them might have a meeting with the masters, to state the conditions they must have fulfilled before they would end the turn-out. They thought they had attained a sufficiently commanding position to dictate. John Barton was appointed one of the deputation.

The masters agreed to this meeting, being anxious to end the strife, although undetermined among themselves how far they should yield, or whether they should yield at all. Some of the old, whose experience had taught them sympathy, were for concession. Others, white-headed men too, had only learnt hardness and obstinacy from the days of the years of their lives, and sneered at the more gentle and yielding. The younger men were one and all for an unflinching resistance to claims urged with so much violence. Of this party Harry Carson was the leader.

[John Barton completes his transformation from Chartist to monster when he murders Harry Carson. In the end, Barton confesses and dies in the arms of the elder Carson, who, turning away from his ledgers to his Bible, forgives him. For Gaskell, the Bible is a balm for finding yourself a soulless "Frankenstein."]

EXCERPT FROM

GREAT EXPECTATIONS

(1861)

Charles Dickens

[Pip, born poor, has an unknown benefactor who has made him a gentleman. Only late in the novel does he discover his benefactor to be what he describes, in an allusion to Shelley's story, as "a misshapen creature"—the escaped convict Magwitch whom he had met—and been terrified of—as a boy wandering in the marshes near his childhood home.]

Chapter 40

It was fortunate for me that I had to take precautions to ensure (so far as I could) the safety of my dreaded visitor; for, this thought pressing on me when I awoke, held other thoughts in a confused concourse at a distance.

The impossibility of keeping him concealed in the chambers was self-evident. It could not be done, and the attempt to do it would inevitably engender suspicion. True, I had no Avenger in my service now, but I was looked after by an inflammatory old female, assisted by an animated rag-bag whom she called her niece, and to keep a room secret from them would be to invite curiosity and exaggeration. They both had weak eyes, which I had long attributed to their chronically looking in at keyholes, and they were always at hand when not wanted; indeed that was their only reliable quality besides larceny. Not to get up a mystery with these people, I resolved to announce in the morning that my uncle had unexpectedly come from the country.

This course I decided on while I was yet groping about in the darkness for the means of getting a light. Not stumbling on the means after all, I was fain to go out to the adjacent Lodge and get the watchman there to come with his lantern. Now, in groping my way down the black staircase I fell over something, and that something was a man crouching in a corner.

As the man made no answer when I asked him what he did there, but eluded my touch in silence, I ran to the Lodge and urged the watchman to come quickly: telling him of the incident on the way back. The wind being as fierce as ever, we did not care to endanger the light in the lantern by rekindling the extinguished lamps on the staircase, but we examined the staircase from the bottom to the top and found no one there. It then occurred to me as possible that the man might have slipped into my rooms; so, lighting my candle at the watchman's, and leaving him standing at the door, I examined them carefully, including the room in which my dreaded guest lay asleep. All was quiet, and assuredly no other man was in those chambers.

It troubled me that there should have been a lurker on the stairs, on that night of all nights in the year, and I asked the watchman, on the chance of eliciting some hopeful explanation as I handed him a dram at the door, whether he had admitted at his gate any gentleman who had perceptibly been dining out? Yes, he said; at different times of the night, three. One lived in Fountain Court, and the other two lived in the Lane, and he had seen them all go home. Again, the only other man who dwelt in the house of which my chambers formed a part, had been in the country for some weeks; and he certainly had not returned in the night, because we had seen his door with his seal on it as we came up-stairs.

"The night being so bad, sir," said the watchman, as he gave me back my glass, "uncommon few have come in at my gate. Besides them three gentlemen that I have named, I don't call to mind another since about eleven o'clock, when a stranger asked for you."

"My uncle," I muttered. "Yes."

"You saw him, sir?"

"Yes. Oh yes."

"Likewise the person with him?"

"Person with him!" I repeated.

"I judged the person to be with him," returned the watchman. "The person stopped, when he stopped to make inquiry of me, and the person took this way when he took this way."

"What sort of person?"

The watchman had not particularly noticed; he should say a working person; to the best of his belief, he had a dust-coloured kind of clothes on, under a dark coat. The watchman made more light of the matter than I did, and naturally; not having my reason for attaching weight to it.

When I had got rid of him, which I thought it well to do without prolonging explanations, my mind was much troubled by these two circumstances taken together. Whereas they were easy of innocent solution apart—as, for instance, some diner-out or diner-at-home, who had not gone near this watchman's gate, might have strayed to my staircase and dropped asleep there—and my nameless visitor might have brought some one with him to show him the way—still, joined, they had an ugly look to one as prone to distrust and fear as the changes of a few hours had made me.

I lighted my fire, which burnt with a raw pale flare at that time of the morning, and fell into a doze before it. I seemed to have been dozing a whole night when the clocks struck six. As there was full an hour and a half between me and daylight, I dozed again; now, waking up uneasily, with prolix conversations about nothing, in my ears; now, making thunder of the wind in the chimney; at length, falling off into a profound sleep from which the daylight woke me with a start.

All this time I had never been able to consider my own situation, nor could I do so yet. I had not the power to attend to it. I was greatly dejected and distressed, but in an incoherent wholesale sort of way. As to forming any plan for the future, I could as soon have formed an elephant. When I opened the shutters and looked out at the wet wild morning, all of a leaden hue; when I walked from room to room; when I sat down again shivering, before the fire, waiting for my laundress to appear; I thought how miserable I was, but hardly knew why, or how long I had been so, or on what day of the week I made the reflection, or even who I was that made it.

At last, the old woman and the niece came in—the latter with a head not easily distinguishable from her dusty broom—and testified surprise at sight of me and the fire. To whom I imparted how my uncle had come in the night and was then asleep, and how the breakfast preparations were to be modified accordingly. Then, I washed and dressed while they knocked the furniture about and made a dust; and so, in a sort of dream or sleep-waking, I found myself sitting by the fire again, waiting for—Him—to come to breakfast.

By-and-by, his door opened and he came out. I could not bring myself to bear the sight of him, and I thought he had a worse look by daylight.

"I do not even know," said I, speaking low as he took his seat at the table, "by what name to call you. I have given out that you are my uncle."

"That's it, dear boy! Call me uncle."

"You assumed some name, I suppose, on board ship?"

"Yes, dear boy. I took the name of Provis."

"Do you mean to keep that name?"

"Why, yes, dear boy, it's as good as another—unless you'd like another."

"What is your real name?" I asked him in a whisper.

"Magwitch," he answered, in the same tone; "chrisen'd Abel."

"What were you brought up to be?"

"A warmint, dear boy."

He answered quite seriously, and used the word as if it denoted some profession.

"When you came into the Temple last night—" said I, pausing to wonder whether that could really have been last night, which seemed so long ago.

"Yes, dear boy?"

"When you came in at the gate and asked the watchman the way here, had you any one with you?"

"With me? No, dear boy."

"But there was some one there?"

"I didn't take particular notice," he said, dubiously, "not knowing the ways of the place. But I think there was a person, too, come in alonger me."

"Are you known in London?"

"I hope not!" said he, giving his neck a jerk with his forefinger that made me turn hot and sick.

"Were you known in London, once?"

"Not over and above, dear boy. I was in the provinces mostly."

"Were you—tried—in London?"

"Which time?" said he, with a sharp look.

"The last time."

He nodded. "First knowed Mr. Jaggers that way. Jaggers was for me."

It was on my lips to ask him what he was tried for, but he took up a knife, gave it a flourish, and with the words, "And what I done is worked out and paid for!" fell to at his breakfast.

He ate in a ravenous way that was very disagreeable, and all his actions were uncouth, noisy, and greedy. Some of his teeth had failed him since I saw him eat on the marshes, and as he turned his food in his mouth, and turned his head sideways to bring his strongest fangs to bear upon it, he looked terribly like a hungry old dog. If I had begun with any appetite, he would have taken it away, and I should have sat much as I did—repelled from him by an insurmountable aversion, and gloomily looking at the cloth.

"I'm a heavy grubber, dear boy," he said, as a polite kind of apology when he made an end of his meal, "but I always was. If it had been in my constitution to be a lighter grubber, I might ha' got into lighter trouble. Similarly, I must have my smoke. When I was first hired out as shepherd t'other side the world, it's my belief I should ha' turned into a molloncolly-mad sheep myself, if I hadn't a had my smoke."

As he said so, he got up from the table, and putting his hand into the breast of the pea-coat he wore, brought out a short black pipe, and a handful of loose tobacco of the kind that is called Negro-head. Having filled his pipe, he put the surplus tobacco back again, as if his pocket were a drawer. Then, he took a live coal from the fire with the tongs, and lighted his pipe at it, and then turned round on the hearth-rug with his back to the fire, and went through his favourite action of holding out both his hands for mine.

"And this," said he, dandling my hands up and down in his, as he puffed at his pipe; "and this is the gentleman what I made! The real genuine One! It does me good fur to look at you, Pip. All I stip'late, is, to stand by and look at you, dear boy!"

I released my hands as soon as I could, and found that I was beginning slowly to settle down to the contemplation of my condition. What I was chained to, and how heavily, became intelligible to me, as I heard his hoarse voice, and sat looking up at his furrowed bald head with its iron grey hair at the sides.

"I mustn't see my gentleman a footing it in the mire of the streets; there mustn't be no mud on his boots. My gentleman must have horses, Pip! Horses to ride, and horses to drive, and horses for his servant to ride and drive as well. Shall colonists have their horses (and blood 'uns, if you please, good Lord!) and not my London gentleman? No, no. We'll show 'em another pair of shoes than that, Pip; won't us?"

He took out of his pocket a great thick pocket-book, bursting with papers, and tossed it on the table.

"There's something worth spending in that there book, dear boy. It's yourn. All I've got ain't mine; it's yourn. Don't you be afeerd on it. There's more where that come from. I've come to the old country fur to see my gentleman spend his money like a gentleman. That'll be my pleasure. My pleasure 'ull be fur to see him do it. And blast you all!" he wound up, looking round the room and snapping his fingers once with a loud snap, "blast you every one, from the judge in his wig, to the colonist a stirring up the dust, I'll show a better gentleman than the whole kit on you put together!"

"Stop!" said I, almost in a frenzy of fear and dislike, "I want to speak to you. I want to know what is to be done. I want to know how you are to be kept out of danger, how long you are going to stay, what projects you have."

"Look'ee here, Pip," said he, laying his hand on my arm in a suddenly altered and subdued manner; "first of all, look'ee here. I forgot myself half a minute ago. What I said was low; that's what it was; low. Look'ee here, Pip. Look over it. I ain't a-going to be low."

"First," I resumed, half-groaning, "what precautions can be taken against your being recognized and seized?"

"No, dear boy," he said, in the same tone as before, "that don't go first. Lowness goes first. I ain't took so many years to make a gentleman, not without knowing what's due to him. Look'ee here, Pip. I was low; that's what I was; low. Look over it, dear boy."

Some sense of the grimly-ludicrous moved me to a fretful laugh, as I replied, "I have looked over it. In Heaven's name, don't harp upon it!"

"Yes, but look'ee here," he persisted. "Dear boy, I ain't come so fur, not fur to be low. Now, go on, dear boy. You was a-saying—"

"How are you to be guarded from the danger you have incurred?"

"Well, dear boy, the danger ain't so great. Without I was informed agen, the danger ain't so much to signify. There's Jaggers, and there's Wemmick, and there's you. Who else is there to inform?"

"Is there no chance person who might identify you in the street?" said I.

"Well," he returned, "there ain't many. Nor yet I don't intend to advertise myself in the newspapers by the name of A. M. come back from Botany Bay; and years have rolled away, and who's to gain by it? Still, look'ee here, Pip. If the danger had been fifty times as great, I should ha' come to see you, mind you, just the same."

"And how long do you remain?"

"How long?" said he, taking his black pipe from his mouth, and dropping his jaw as he stared at me. "I'm not a-going back. I've come for good."

"Where are you to live?" said I. "What is to be done with you? Where will you be safe?"

"Dear boy," he returned, "there's disguising wigs can be bought for money, and there's hair powder, and spectacles, and black clothes—shorts and what not. Others has done it safe afore, and what others has done afore, others can do agen. As to the where and how of living, dear boy, give me your own opinions on it."

"You take it smoothly now," said I, "but you were very serious last night, when you swore it was Death."

"And so I swear it is Death," said he, putting his pipe back in his mouth, "and Death by the rope, in the open street not fur from this, and it's serious that you should fully understand it to be so. What then, when that's once done? Here I am. To go back now, 'ud be as bad as to stand ground—worse. Besides, Pip, I'm here, because I've meant it by you, years and years. As to what I dare, I'm a old bird now, as has dared all manner of traps since first he was fledged, and I'm not afeerd to perch upon a scarecrow. If there's Death hid inside of it, there is, and let him come out, and I'll face him, and then I'll believe in him and not afore. And now let me have a look at my gentleman agen."

Once more, he took me by both hands and surveyed me with an air of admiring proprietorship: smoking with great complacency all the while.

It appeared to me that I could do no better than secure him some quiet lodging hard by, of which he might take possession when Herbert returned: whom I expected in two or three days. That the secret must be confided to Herbert as a matter of unavoidable necessity, even if I could have put the immense relief I should derive from sharing it with him out of the question, was plain to me. But it was by no means so plain to Mr. Provis (I resolved to call him by that name), who reserved his consent to Herbert's participation until he should have seen him and formed a favourable judgment of his physiognomy. "And even then, dear boy," said he, pulling a greasy little clasped black Testament out of his pocket, "we'll have him on his oath."

To state that my terrible patron carried this little black book about the world solely to swear people on in cases of emergency, would be to state what I never quite established—but this I can say, that I never knew him put it to any other use. The book itself had the appearance of having been stolen from some court of justice, and perhaps his knowledge of its antecedents, combined with his own experience in that wise, gave him a reliance on its powers as a sort of legal spell or charm. On this first occasion of his producing it, I recalled how he had made me swear fidelity in the churchyard long ago, and how he had described himself last night as always swearing to his resolutions in his solitude.

As he was at present dressed in a seafaring slop suit, in which he looked as if he had some parrots and cigars to dispose of, I next discussed with him what dress he should wear. He cherished an extraordinary belief in the virtues of "shorts" as a disguise, and had in his own mind sketched a dress for himself that would have made him something between a dean and a dentist. It was with considerable difficulty that I won him over to the assumption of a dress more like a prosperous farmer's; and we arranged that he should cut his hair close, and wear a little powder. Lastly, as he had not yet been seen by the laundress or her niece, he was to keep himself out of their view until his change of dress was made.

It would seem a simple matter to decide on these precautions; but in my dazed, not to say distracted, state, it took so long, that I did not get out to further them, until two or three in the afternoon. He was to remain shut up in the chambers while I was gone, and was on no account to open the door.

There being to my knowledge a respectable lodging-house in Essex-street, the back of which looked into the Temple, and was almost within hail of my windows, I first of all repaired to that house, and was so fortunate as to secure the second floor for my uncle, Mr. Provis. I then went from shop to shop, making such purchases as were necessary to the change in his appearance. This business transacted, I turned my face, on my own account, to Little Britain. Mr. Jaggers was at his desk, but, seeing me enter, got up immediately and stood before his fire.

"Now, Pip," said he, "be careful."

"I will, sir," I returned. For, coming along I had thought well of what I was going to say.

"Don't commit yourself," said Mr. Jaggers, "and don't commit any one. You understand—any one. Don't tell me anything: I don't want to know anything; I am not curious."

Of course I saw that he knew the man was come.

"I merely want, Mr. Jaggers," said I, "to assure myself that what I have been told, is true. I have no hope of its being untrue, but at least I may verify it."

Mr. Jaggers nodded. "But did you say 'told' or 'informed'?" he asked me, with his head on one side, and not looking at me, but looking in a listening way at the floor. "Told would seem to imply verbal communication. You can't have verbal communication with a man in New South Wales, you know."

"I will say, informed, Mr. Jaggers."

"Good."

"I have been informed by a person named Abel Magwitch, that he is the benefactor so long unknown to me."

"That is the man," said Mr. Jaggers, "—in New South Wales."

"And only he?" said I.

"And only he," said Mr. Jaggers.

"I am not so unreasonable, sir, as to think you at all responsible for my mistakes and wrong conclusions; but I always supposed it was Miss Havisham."

"As you say, Pip," returned Mr. Jaggers, turning his eyes upon me coolly, and taking a bite at his forefinger, "I am not at all responsible for that."

"And yet it looked so like it, sir," I pleaded with a downcast heart.

"Not a particle of evidence, Pip," said Mr. Jaggers, shaking his head and gathering up his skirts. "Take nothing on its looks; take everything on evidence. There's no better rule."

"I have no more to say," said I, with a sigh, after standing silent for a little while. "I have verified my information, and there's an end."

"And Magwitch—in New South Wales—having at last disclosed himself," said Mr. Jaggers, "you will comprehend, Pip, how rigidly throughout my communication with you, I have always adhered to the strict line of fact. There has never been the least departure from the strict line of fact. You are quite aware of that?"

"Quite, sir."

"I communicated to Magwitch—in New South Wales—when he first wrote to me—from New South Wales—the caution that he must not expect me ever to deviate from the strict line of fact. I also communicated to him another caution. He appeared to me to have obscurely hinted in his letter at some distant idea he had of seeing you in England here. I cautioned him that I must hear no more of that; that he was not at all likely to obtain a pardon; that he was expatriated for the term of his natural life; and that his presenting himself in this country would be an act of felony, rendering him liable to the extreme penalty of the law. I gave Magwitch that caution," said Mr. Jaggers, looking hard at me; "I wrote it to New South Wales. He guided himself by it, no doubt."

"No doubt," said I.

"I have been informed by Wemmick," pursued Mr. Jaggers, still looking hard at me, "that he has received a letter, under date Portsmouth, from a colonist of the name of Purvis, or—"

"Or Provis," I suggested.

"Or Provis—thank you, Pip. Perhaps it is Provis? Perhaps you know it's Provis?"

"Yes," said I.

"You know it's Provis. A letter, under date Portsmouth, from a colonist of the name of Provis, asking for the particulars of your address, on behalf of Magwitch. Wemmick sent him the particulars, I understand, by return of post. Probably it is through Provis that you have received the explanation of Magwitch—in New South Wales?"

"It came through Provis," I replied.

"Good day, Pip," said Mr. Jaggers, offering his hand; "glad to have seen you. In writing by post to Magwitch—in New South Wales—or in communicating with him through Provis, have the goodness to mention that the particulars and vouchers of our long account shall be sent to you, together with the balance; for there is still a balance remaining. Good day, Pip!"

We shook hands, and he looked hard at me as long as he could see me. I turned at the door, and he was still looking hard at me, while the two vile casts on the shelf seemed to be trying to get their eyelids open, and to force out of their swollen throats, "O, what a man he is!"

Wemmick was out, and though he had been at his desk he could have done nothing for me. I went straight back to the Temple, where I found the terrible Provis drinking rum-and-water and smoking Negro-head, in safety.

Next day the clothes I had ordered all came home, and he put them on. Whatever he put on, became him less (it dismally seemed to me) than what he had worn before. To my thinking, there was something in him that made it hopeless to attempt to disguise him. The more I dressed him and the better I dressed him, the more he looked like the slouching fugitive on the marshes. This effect on my anxious fancy was partly referable, no doubt, to his old face and manner growing more familiar to me; but I believe too that he dragged one of his legs as if there were still a weight of iron on it, and that from head to foot there was Convict in the very grain of the man.

The influences of his solitary hut-life were upon him besides, and gave him a savage air that no dress could tame; added to these, were the influences of his subsequent branded life among men, and, crowning all, his consciousness that he was dodging and hiding now. In all his ways of sitting and standing, and eating and drinking—of brooding about, in a high-shouldered reluctant style—of taking out his great horn-handled jack-knife and wiping it on his legs and cutting his food—of lifting light glasses and cups to his lips, as if they were clumsy pannikins—of chopping a wedge off his bread, and soaking up with it the last fragments of gravy round and round his plate, as if to make the most of an allowance, and then drying his finger-ends on it, and then swallowing it—in these ways and a thousand other small nameless instances arising every minute in the day, there was Prisoner, Felon, Bondsman, plain as plain could be.

It had been his own idea to wear that touch of powder, and I had conceded the powder after overcoming the shorts. But I can compare the effect of it, when on, to nothing but the probable effect of rouge upon the dead; so awful was the manner in which everything in him that it was most desirable to repress, started through that thin layer of pretence, and seemed to come blazing out at the crown of his head. It was abandoned as soon as tried, and he wore his grizzled hair cut short.

Words cannot tell what a sense I had, at the same time, of the dreadful mystery that he was to me. When he fell asleep of an evening, with his knotted hands clenching the sides of the easy-chair, and his bald head tattooed with deep wrinkles falling forward on his breast, I would sit and look at him, wondering what he had done, and loading him with all the crimes in the Calendar, until the impulse was powerful on me to start up and fly from him. Every hour so increased my abhorrence of him, that I even think I might have yielded to this impulse in the first agonies of being so haunted, notwithstanding all he had done for me, and the risk he ran, but for the knowledge that Herbert must soon come back. Once, I actually did start out of bed in the night, and begin to dress myself in my worst clothes, hurriedly intending to leave him there with everything else I possessed, and enlist for India as a private soldier.

I doubt if a ghost could have been more terrible to me, up in those lonely rooms in the long evenings and long nights, with the wind and the rain always rushing by. A ghost could not have been taken and hanged on my account, and the consideration that he could be, and the dread that he would be, were no small addition to my horrors. When he was not asleep, or playing a complicated kind of patience with a ragged pack of cards of his own—a game that I never saw before or since, and in which he recorded his winnings by sticking his jack-knife into the table—when he was not engaged in either of these pursuits, he would ask me to read to him—"Foreign language, dear boy!" While I complied, he, not comprehending a single word, would stand before the fire surveying me with the air of an Exhibitor, and I would see him, between the fingers of the hand with which I shaded my face, appealing in dumb show to the furniture to take notice of my proficiency. The imaginary student pursued by the misshapen creature he had impiously made, was not more wretched than I, pursued by the creature who had made me, and recoiling from him with a stronger repulsion, the more he admired me and the fonder he was of me.

This is written of, I am sensible, as if it had lasted a year. It lasted about five days. Expecting Herbert all the time, I dared not go out, except when I took Provis for an airing after dark. At length, one evening when dinner was over and I had dropped into a slumber quite worn out—for my nights had been agitated and my rest broken by fearful dreams—I was roused by the welcome footstep on the staircase. Provis, who had been asleep too, staggered up at the noise I made, and in an instant I saw his jack-knife shining in his hand.

"Quiet! It's Herbert!" I said; and Herbert came bursting in, with the airy freshness of six hundred miles of France upon him.

"Handel, my dear fellow, how are you, and again how are you, and again how are you? I seem to have been gone a twelvemonth! Why, so I must have been, for you have grown quite thin and pale! Handel, my—Halloa! I beg your pardon."

He was stopped in his running on and in his shaking hands with me, by seeing Provis. Provis, regarding him with a fixed attention, was slowly putting up his jack-knife, and groping in another pocket for something else.

"Herbert, my dear friend," said I, shutting the double doors, while Herbert stood staring and wondering, "something very strange has happened. This is—a visitor of mine."

"It's all right, dear boy!" said Provis coming forward, with his little clasped black book, and then addressing himself to Herbert. "Take it in your right hand. Lord strike you dead on the spot, if ever you split in any way sumever! Kiss it!"

"Do so, as he wishes it," I said to Herbert. So, Herbert, looking at me with a friendly uneasiness and amazement, complied, and Provis immediately shaking hands with him, said, "Now you're on your oath, you know. And never believe me on mine, if Pip shan't make a gentleman on you!"

> [As "the imaginary student" is "pursued by the misshapen creature," so the misshapen creator haunts the thing he made—his gentleman; instead of raising the dead, ill-gotten money raises a boy from poverty; yet still, creator and created are bound by shameful secrets.]

EXCERPT FROM

SPORT OF THE GODS

(1902)

PAUL LAURENCE DUNBAR

[The chapter title, "Frankenstein," is Dunbar's only direct allusion to Shelley's novel. The connection between Joe Hamilton's fall and Shelley's wretched Creature are assumed to be obvious enough. Joe's father is an emancipated Black man in the American South wrongfully imprisoned for theft because of racism. His family is expelled and moves in poverty to the North, to New York, where Joe takes up with a club entertainer, Hattie Sterling, and declines into alcoholism until Hattie throws him out. In the end, she realizes, just before he strangles her to death, that he is "a terrible, terrible man or a monster." Joe tells her, "you made me what I am." But the reader can see a larger context: how racism acted to destroy a family.]

XIV. Frankenstein

Five years is but a short time in the life of a man, and yet many things may happen therein. For instance, the whole way of a family's life may be changed. Good natures may be made into bad ones and out of a soul of faith grow a spirit of unbelief. The independence of respectability may harden into the insolence of defiance, and the sensitive cheek of modesty into the brazen face of shamelessness. It may be true that the habits of years are hard to change, but this is not true of the first sixteen or seventeen years of a young person's life, else Kitty Hamilton and Joe could not so easily have become what they were. It had taken barely five years to accomplish an entire metamorphosis of their characters. In Joe's case even a shorter time was needed. He was so ready to go down that it needed but a gentle push to start him, and once started, there was nothing within him to hold him back from the depths. For his will was as flabby as his conscience, and his pride, which stands to some men for conscience, had no definite aim or direction.

Hattie Sterling had given him both his greatest impulse for evil and for good. She had at first given him his gentle push, but when she saw that his collapse would lose her a faithful and useful slave she had sought to check his course. Her threat of the severance of their relations had held him up for a little time, and she began to believe that he was safe again. He went back to the work he had neglected, drank moderately, and acted in most things as a sound, sensible being. Then, all of a sudden, he went down again, and went down badly. She kept her promise and threw him over. Then he became a hanger-on at the clubs, a genteel loafer. He used to say in his sober moments that at last he was one of the boys that Sadness had spoken of. He did not work, and yet he lived and ate and was proud of his degradation. But he soon tired of being separated from Hattie, and straightened up again. After some demur she received him upon his former footing. It was only for a few months. He fell again. For almost four years this had happened intermittently. Finally he took a turn for the better that endured so long that Hattie Sterling again gave him her faith. Then the woman made her mistake. She warmed to him. She showed him that she was proud of him. He went forth at once to celebrate his victory. He did not return to her for three days. Then he was battered, unkempt, and thick of speech.

She looked at him in silent contempt for a while as he sat nursing his aching head.

"Well, you're a beauty," she said finally with cutting scorn. "You ought to be put under a glass case and placed on exhibition."

He groaned and his head sunk lower. A drunken man is always disarmed.

His helplessness, instead of inspiring her with pity, inflamed her with an unfeeling anger that burst forth in a volume of taunts.

"You're the thing I've given up all my chances for—you, a miserable, drunken jay, without a jay's decency. No one had ever looked at you until I picked you up and you've been strutting around ever since, showing off because I was kind to you, and now this is the way you pay me back. Drunk half the time and half drunk the rest. Well, you know what I told you the last time you got 'loaded'? I mean it too. You're not the only star in sight, see?"

She laughed meanly and began to sing, "You'll have to find another baby now."

For the first time he looked up, and his eyes were full of tears—tears both of grief and intoxication. There was an expression of a whipped dog on his face.

"Do'—Ha'ie, do'—" he pleaded, stretching out his hands to her.

Her eyes blazed back at him, but she sang on insolently, tauntingly.

The very inanity of the man disgusted her, and on a sudden impulse she sprang up and struck him full in the face with the flat of her hand. He was too weak to resist the blow, and, tumbling from the chair, fell limply to the floor, where he lay at her feet, alternately weeping aloud and quivering with drunken, hiccoughing sobs.

"Get up!" she cried; "get up and get out o' here. You sha'n't lay around my house."

He had already begun to fall into a drunken sleep, but she shook him, got him to his feet, and pushed him outside the door. "Now, go, you drunken dog, and never put your foot inside this house again."

He stood outside, swaying dizzily upon his feet and looking back with dazed eyes at the door, then he muttered: "Pu' me out, wi' you? Pu' me out, damn you! Well, I ki' you. See 'f I don't;" and he half walked, half fell down the street.

Sadness and Skaggsy were together at the club that night. Five years had not changed the latter as to wealth or position or inclination, and he was still a frequent visitor at the Banner. He always came in alone now, for Maudie had gone the way of all the half-world, and reached depths to which Mr. Skaggs's job prevented him from following her. However, he mourned truly for his lost companion, and to-night he was in a particularly pensive mood.

Some one was playing rag-time on the piano, and the dancers were wheeling in time to the music. Skaggsy looked at them regretfully as he sipped his liquor. It made him think of Maudie. He sighed and turned away.

"I tell you, Sadness," he said impulsively, "dancing is the poetry of motion."

"Yes," replied Sadness, "and dancing in rag-time is the dialect poetry."

The reporter did not like this. It savoured of flippancy, and he was about entering upon a discussion to prove that Sadness had no soul, when Joe, with blood-shot eyes and dishevelled clothes, staggered in and reeled towards them.

"Drunk again," said Sadness. "Really, it's a waste of time for Joe to sober up. Hullo there!" as the young man brought up against him; "take a seat." He put him in a chair at the table. "Been lushin' a bit, eh?"

"Gi' me some'n' drink."

"Oh, a hair of the dog. Some men shave their dogs clean, and then have hydrophobia. Here, Jack!"

They drank, and then, as if the whiskey had done him good, Joe sat up in his chair.

"Ha'ie's throwed me down."

"Lucky dog! You might have known it would have happened sooner or later. Better sooner than never."

Skaggs smoked in silence and looked at Joe.

"I'm goin' to kill her."

"I wouldn't if I were you. Take old Sadness's advice and thank your stars that you're rid of her."

"I'm goin' to kill her." He paused and looked at them drowsily. Then, bracing himself up again, he broke out suddenly, "Say, d' ever tell y' 'bout the ol' man? He never stole that money. Know he di' n'."

He threatened to fall asleep now, but the reporter was all alert. He scented a story.

"By Jove!" he exclaimed, "did you hear that? Bet the chap stole it himself and 's letting the old man suffer for it. Great story, ain't it? Come, come, wake up here. Three more, Jack. What about your father?"

"Father? Who's father. Oh, do' bother me. What?"

"Here, here, tell us about your father and the money. If he didn't steal it, who did?"

"Who did? Tha' 's it, who did? Ol' man di' n' steal it, know he di' n'."

"Oh, let him alone, Skaggsy, he don't know what he's saying."

"Yes, he does, a drunken man tells the truth."

"In some cases," said Sadness.

"Oh, let me alone, man. I've been trying for years to get a big sensation for my paper, and if this story is one, I'm a made man."

The drink seemed to revive the young man again, and by bits Skaggs was able to pick out of him the story of his father's arrest and conviction. At its close he relapsed into stupidity, murmuring, "She throwed me down."

"Well," sneered Sadness, "you see drunken men tell the truth, and you don't seem to get much guilt out of our young friend. You're disappointed, aren't you?"

"I confess I am disappointed, but I've got an idea, just the same."

"Oh, you have? Well, don't handle it carelessly; it might go off." And Sadness rose. The reporter sat thinking for a time and then followed him, leaving Joe in a drunken sleep at the table. There he lay for more than two hours. When he finally awoke, he started up as if some determination had come to him in his sleep. A part of the helplessness of his intoxication had gone, but his first act was to call for more whiskey. This he gulped down, and followed with another and another. For a while he stood still, brooding silently, his red eyes blinking at the light. Then he turned abruptly and left the club.

It was very late when he reached Hattie's door, but he opened it with his latch-key, as he had been used to do. He stopped to help himself to a glass of brandy, as he had so often done before. Then he went directly to her room. She was a light sleeper, and his step awakened her.

"Who is it?" she cried in affright.

"It's me." His voice was steadier now, but grim.

"What do you want? Didn't I tell you never to come here again? Get out or I'll have you taken out."

She sprang up in bed, glaring angrily at him.

His hands twitched nervously, as if her will were conquering him and he were uneasy, but he held her eye with his own.

"You put me out to-night," he said.

"Yes, and I'm going to do it again. You're drunk."

She started to rise, but he took a step towards her and she paused. He looked as she had never seen him look before. His face was ashen and his eyes like fire and blood. She quailed beneath the look. He took another step towards her.

"You put me out to-night," he repeated, "like a dog."

His step was steady and his tone was clear, menacingly clear. She shrank back from him, back to the wall.

Still his hands twitched and his eye held her. Still he crept slowly towards her, his lips working and his hands moving convulsively.

"Joe, Joe!" she said hoarsely, "what's the matter? Oh, don't look at me like that."

The gown had fallen away from her breast and showed the convulsive fluttering of her heart.

He broke into a laugh, a dry, murderous laugh, and his hands sought each other while the fingers twitched over one another like coiling serpents.

"You put me out—you—you, and you made me what I am." The realisation of what he was, of his foulness and degradation, seemed just to have come to him fully. "You made me what I am, and then you sent me away. You let me come back, and now you put me out."

She gazed at him fascinated. She tried to scream and she could not. This was not Joe. This was not the boy that she had turned and twisted about her little finger. This was a terrible, terrible man or a monster.

He moved a step nearer her. His eyes fell to her throat. For an instant she lost their steady glare and then she found her voice. The scream was checked as it began. His fingers had closed over her throat just where the gown had left it temptingly bare. They gave it the caress of death. She struggled. They held her. Her eyes prayed to his. But his were the fire of hell. She fell back upon her pillow in silence. He had not uttered a word. He held her. Finally he flung her from him like a rag, and sank into a chair. And there the officers found him when Hattie Sterling's disappearance had become a strange thing.

PART THREE

Mad Science!!!

THE FACTS IN THE CASE OF M. VALDEMAR

(1845)

EDGAR ALLEN POE

Of course I shall not pretend to consider it any matter for wonder, that the extraordinary case of M. Valdemar has excited discussion. It would have been a miracle had it not—especially under the circumstances. Through the desire of all parties concerned, to keep the affair from the public, at least for the present, or until we had farther opportunities for investigation—through our endeavors to effect this—a garbled or exaggerated account made its way into society, and became the source of many unpleasant misrepresentations; and, very naturally, of a great deal of disbelief.

It is now rendered necessary that I give the *facts*—as far as I comprehend them myself. They are, succinctly, these:

My attention, for the last three years, had been repeatedly drawn to the subject of Mesmerism; and, about nine months ago, it occurred to me, quite suddenly, that in the series of experiments made hitherto, there had been a very remarkable and most unaccountable omission:—no person had as yet been mesmerized *in articulo mortis*. It remained to be seen, first, whether, in such condition, there existed in the patient any susceptibility to the magnetic influence; secondly, whether, if any existed, it was impaired or increased by the condition; thirdly, to what extent, or for how long a period, the encroachments of Death might be arrested by the process. There were other points to be ascertained, but these most excited my curiosity—the last in especial, from the immensely important character of its consequences.

In looking around me for some subject by whose means I might test these particulars, I was brought to think of my friend, M. Ernest Valdemar, the well-known compiler of the "Bibliotheca Forensica," and author (under the *nom de plume* of Issachar Marx) of the Polish versions of "Wallenstein" and "Gargantua." M. Valdemar, who has resided principally at Harlem, N. Y., since the year 1839, is (or was) particularly noticeable for the extreme spareness of his person—his lower limbs much resembling those of John Randolph; and, also, for the whiteness of his whiskers, in violent contrast to the blackness of his hair—the latter, in consequence, being very generally mistaken for a wig. His temperament was markedly nervous, and rendered him a good subject for mesmeric experiment. On two or three occasions I had put him to sleep with little difficulty, but was disappointed in other results which his peculiar constitution had naturally led me to anticipate. His will was at no period positively, or thoroughly, under my control, and in regard to *clairvoyance*,

I could accomplish with him nothing to be relied upon. I always attributed my failure at these points to the disordered state of his health. For some months previous to my becoming acquainted with him, his physicians had declared him in a confirmed phthisis. It was his custom, indeed, to speak calmly of his approaching dissolution, as of a matter neither to be avoided nor regretted.

When the ideas to which I have alluded first occurred to me, it was of course very natural that I should think of M. Valdemar. I knew the steady philosophy of the man too well to apprehend any scruples from *him*; and he had no relatives in America who would be likely to interfere. I spoke to him frankly upon the subject; and, to my surprise, his interest seemed vividly excited. I say to my surprise; for, although he had always yielded his person freely to my experiments, he had never before given me any tokens of sympathy with what I did. His disease was of that character which would admit of exact calculation in respect to the epoch of its termination in death; and it was finally arranged between us that he would send for me about twenty-four hours before the period announced by his physicians as that of his decease.

It is now rather more than seven months since I received, from M. Valdemar himself, the subjoined note:

> "MY DEAR P——,
>
> "You may as well come *now*. D—— and F—— are agreed that I cannot hold out beyond to-morrow midnight; and I think they have hit the time very nearly.
>
> "VALDEMAR."

I received this note within half an hour after it was written, and in fifteen minutes more I was in the dying man's chamber. I had not seen him for ten days, and was appalled by the fearful alteration which the brief interval had wrought in him. His face wore a leaden hue; the eyes were utterly lustreless; and the emaciation was so extreme, that the skin had been broken through by the cheek-bones. His expectoration was excessive. The pulse was barely perceptible. He retained, nevertheless, in a very remarkable manner, both his mental power and a certain degree of physical strength. He spoke with distinctness—took some palliative medicines without aid—and, when I entered the room, was occupied in penciling memoranda in a pocket-book. He was propped up in the bed by pillows. Doctors D—— and F—— were in attendance.

After pressing Valdemar's hand, I took these gentlemen aside, and obtained from them a minute account of the patient's condition. The left lung had been for eighteen months in a semi-osseous or cartilaginous state, and was, of course, entirely useless for all purposes of vitality. The right, in its upper portion, was also partially, if not thoroughly, ossified, while the lower region was merely a mass of purulent tubercles, running one into another. Several extensive perforations existed; and, at one point, permanent adhesion to the ribs had taken place. These appearances in the right lobe were of comparatively recent date. The ossification had proceeded with very unusual rapidity; no sign of it had been discovered a month before, and the adhesion had only been observed during the three previous days. Independently of the phthisis, the patient was suspected of aneurism of the aorta; but on this point the osseous symptoms rendered an exact diagnosis impossible. It was the opinion of both physicians that M. Valdemar would die about midnight on the morrow (Sunday). It was then seven o'clock on Saturday evening.

On quitting the invalid's bed-side to hold conversation with myself, Doctors D—— and F—— had bidden him a final farewell. It had not been their intention to return; but, at my request, they agreed to look in upon the patient about ten the next night.

When they had gone, I spoke freely with M. Valdemar on the subject of his approaching dissolution, as well as, more particularly, of the experiment proposed. He still professed himself quite willing and even anxious to have it made, and urged me to commence it at once. A male and a female nurse were in attendance; but I did not feel myself altogether at liberty to engage in a task of this character with no more reliable witnesses than these people, in case of sudden accident, might prove. I therefore postponed operations until about eight the next night, when the arrival of a medical student, with whom I had some acquaintance, (Mr. Theodore L——l), relieved me from farther embarrassment. It had been my design, originally, to wait for the physicians; but I was induced to proceed, first, by the urgent entreaties of M. Valdemar, and secondly, by my conviction that I had not a moment to lose, as he was evidently sinking fast.

Mr. L——l was so kind as to accede to my desire that he would take notes of all that occurred; and it is from his memoranda that what I now have to relate is, for the most part, either condensed or copied *verbatim*.

It wanted about five minutes of eight when, taking the patient's hand, I begged him to state, as distinctly as he could, to Mr. L——l, whether he (M. Valdemar), was entirely willing that I should make the experiment of mesmerizing him in his then condition.

He replied feebly, yet quite audibly, "Yes, I wish to be mesmerized"—adding immediately afterwards, "I fear you have deferred it too long."

While he spoke thus, I commenced the passes which I had already found most effectual in subduing him. He was evidently influenced with the first lateral stroke of my hand across his forehead; but although I exerted all my powers, no farther perceptible effect was induced until some minutes after ten o'clock, when Doctors D—— and F—— called, according to appointment. I explained to them, in a few words, what I designed, and as they opposed no objection, saying that the patient was already in the death agony, I proceeded without hesitation—exchanging, however, the lateral passes for downward ones, and directing my gaze entirely into the right eye of the sufferer.

By this time his pulse was imperceptible and his breathing was stertorous, and at intervals of half a minute.

This condition was nearly unaltered for a quarter of an hour. At the expiration of this period, however, a natural although a very deep sigh escaped the bosom of the dying man, and the stertorous breathing ceased—that is to say, its stertorousness was no longer apparent; the intervals were undiminished. The patient's extremities were of an icy coldness.

At five minutes before eleven, I perceived unequivocal signs of the mesmeric influence. The glassy roll of the eye was changed for that expression of uneasy *inward* examination which is never seen except in cases of sleep-waking, and which it is quite impossible to mistake. With a few rapid lateral passes

I made the lids quiver, as in incipient sleep, and with a few more I closed them altogether. I was not satisfied, however, with this, but continued the manipulations vigorously, and with the fullest exertion of the will, until I had completely stiffened the limbs of the slumberer, after placing them in a seemingly easy position. The legs were at full length; the arms were nearly so, and reposed on the bed at a moderate distance from the loins. The head was very slightly elevated.

When I had accomplished this, it was fully midnight, and I requested the gentlemen present to examine M. Valdemar's condition. After a few experiments, they admitted him to be in an unusually perfect state of mesmeric trance. The curiosity of both the physicians was greatly excited. Dr. D—— resolved at once to remain with the patient all night, while Dr. F—— took leave with a promise to return at daybreak. Mr. L——l and the nurses remained.

We left M. Valdemar entirely undisturbed until about three o'clock in the morning, when I approached him and found him in precisely the same condition as when Dr. F—— went away—that is to say, he lay in the same position; the pulse was imperceptible; the breathing was gentle (scarcely noticeable, unless through the application of a mirror to the lips;) the eyes were closed naturally; and the limbs were as rigid and as cold as marble. Still, the general appearance was certainly not that of death.

As I approached M. Valdemar I made a kind of half effort to influence his right arm into pursuit of my own, as I passed the latter gently to and fro above his person. In such experiments with this patient, I had never perfectly succeeded before, and assuredly I had little thought of succeeding now; but to my astonishment, his arm very readily, although feebly, followed every direction I assigned it with mine. I determined to hazard a few words of conversation.

"M. Valdemar," I said, "are you asleep?" He made no answer, but I perceived a tremor about the lips, and was thus induced to repeat the question, again and again. At its third repetition, his whole frame was agitated by a very slight shivering; the eye-lids unclosed themselves so far as to display a white line of a ball; the lips moved sluggishly, and from between them, in a barely audible whisper, issued the words:

"Yes;—asleep now. Do not wake me!—let me die so!"

I here felt the limbs and found them as rigid as ever. The right arm, as before, obeyed the direction of my hand. I questioned the sleep-waker again:

"Do you still feel pain in the breast, M. Valdemar?"

The answer now was immediate, but even less audible than before:

"No pain—I am dying."

I did not think it advisable to disturb him farther just then, and nothing more was said or done until the arrival of Dr. F——, who came a little before sunrise, and expressed unbounded astonishment at finding the patient still alive. After feeling the pulse and applying a mirror to the lips, he requested me to speak to the sleep-waker again. I did so, saying:

"M. Valdemar, do you still sleep?"

As before, some minutes elapsed ere a reply was made; and during the interval the dying man seemed to be collecting his energies to speak. At my fourth repetition of the question, he said very faintly, almost inaudibly:

"Yes; still asleep—dying."

It was now the opinion, or rather the wish, of the physicians, that M. Valdemar should be suffered to remain undisturbed in his present apparently tranquil condition, until death should supervene—and this, it was generally agreed, must now take place within a few minutes. I concluded, however, to speak to him once more, and merely repeated my previous question.

While I spoke, there came a marked change over the countenance of the sleep-waker. The eyes rolled themselves slowly open, the pupils disappearing upwardly; the skin generally assumed a cadaverous hue, resembling not so much parchment as white paper; and the circular hectic spots which, hitherto, had been strongly defined in the centre of each cheek, *went out* at once. I use this expression, because the suddenness of their departure put me in mind of nothing so much as the extinguishment of a candle by a puff of the breath. The upper lip, at the same time, writhed itself away from the teeth, which it had previously covered completely; while the lower jaw fell with an audible jerk, leaving the mouth widely extended, and disclosing in full view the swollen and blackened tongue. I presume that no member of the party then present had been unaccustomed to death-bed horrors; but so hideous beyond conception was the appearance of M. Valdemar at this moment, that there was a general shrinking back from the region of the bed.

I now feel that I have reached a point of this narrative at which every reader will be startled into positive disbelief. It is my business, however, simply to proceed.

There was no longer the faintest sign of vitality in M. Valdemar; and concluding him to be dead, we were consigning him to the charge of the nurses, when a strong vibratory motion was observable in the tongue. This continued for perhaps a minute. At the expiration of this period, there issued from the distended and motionless jaws a voice—such as it would be madness in me to attempt describing. There are, indeed, two or three epithets which might be considered as applicable to it in part; I might say, for example, that the sound was harsh, and broken and hollow; but the hideous whole is indescribable, for the simple reason that no similar sounds have ever jarred upon the ear of humanity. There were two particulars, nevertheless, which I thought then, and still think, might fairly be stated as characteriztic of the intonation—as well adapted to convey some idea of its unearthly peculiarity. In the first place, the voice seemed to reach our ears—at least mine—from a vast distance, or from some deep cavern within the earth. In the second place, it impressed me (I fear, indeed, that it will be impossible to make myself comprehended) as gelatinous or glutinous matters impress the sense of touch.

I have spoken both of "sound" and of "voice." I mean to say that the sound was one of distinct—of even wonderfully, thrillingly distinct—syllabification. M. Valdemar *spoke*—obviously in reply to the question I had propounded to him a few minutes before. I had asked him, it will be remembered, if he still slept. He now said:

"Yes;—no;—I *have been* sleeping—and now—now—*I am dead*."

No person present even affected to deny, or attempted to repress, the unutterable, shuddering horror which these few words, thus uttered, were so well calculated to convey. Mr. L——l (the student) swooned. The nurses immediately left the chamber, and could not be induced to return. My own impressions I would not pretend to render intelligible to the reader. For nearly an hour, we busied ourselves, silently—without the utterance of a word—in endeavors to revive Mr.L——l. When he came to himself, we addressed ourselves again to an investigation of M. Valdemar's condition.

It remained in all respects as I have last described it, with the exception that the mirror no longer afforded evidence of respiration. An attempt to draw blood from the arm failed. I should mention, too, that this limb was no farther subject to my will. I endeavored in vain to make it follow the direction of my hand. The only real indication, indeed, of the mesmeric influence, was now found in the vibratory movement of the tongue, whenever I addressed M. Valdemar a question. He seemed to be making an effort to reply, but had no longer sufficient volition. To queries put to him by any other person than myself he seemed utterly insensible—although I endeavored to place each member of the company in mesmeric *rapport* with him. I believe that I have now related all that is necessary to an understanding of the sleep-waker's state at this epoch. Other nurses were procured; and at ten o'clock I left the house in company with the two physicians and Mr. L——l.

In the afternoon we all called again to see the patient. His condition remained precisely the same. We had now some discussion as to the propriety and feasibility of awakening him; but we had little difficulty in agreeing that no good purpose would be served by so doing. It was evident that, so far, death (or what is usually termed death) had been arrested by the mesmeric process. It seemed clear to us all that to awaken M. Valdemar would be merely to insure his instant, or at least his speedy dissolution.

From this period until the close of last week—*an interval of nearly seven months*—we continued to make daily calls at M. Valdemar's house, accompanied, now and then, by medical and other friends. All this time the sleeper-waker remained *exactly* as I have last described him. The nurses' attentions were continual.

It was on Friday last that we finally resolved to make the experiment of awakening, or attempting to awaken him; and it is the (perhaps) unfortunate result of this latter experiment which has given rise to so much discussion in private circles—to so much of what I cannot help thinking unwarranted popular feeling.

For the purpose of relieving M. Valdemar from the mesmeric trance, I made use of the customary passes. These, for a time, were unsuccessful. The first indication of revival was afforded by a partial descent of the iris. It was observed, as especially remarkable, that this lowering of the pupil was accompanied by the profuse out-flowing of a yellowish ichor (from beneath the lids) of a pungent and highly offensive odor.

It was now suggested that I should attempt to influence the patient's arm, as heretofore. I made the attempt and failed. Dr. F—— then intimated a desire to have me put a question. I did so, as follows:

"M. Valdemar, can you explain to us what are your feelings or wishes now?"

There was an instant return of the hectic circles on the cheeks; the tongue quivered, or rather rolled violently in the mouth (although the jaws and lips remained rigid as before;) and at length the same hideous voice which I have already described, broke forth:

"For God's sake!—quick!—quick!—put me to sleep—or, quick!—waken me!—quick!—*I say to you that I am dead!*"

I was thoroughly unnerved, and for an instant remained undecided what to do. At first I made an endeavor to re-compose the patient; but, failing in this through total abeyance of the will, I retraced my steps and as earnestly struggled to awaken him. In this attempt I soon saw that I should be successful—or at least I soon fancied that my success would be complete—and I am sure that all in the room were prepared to see the patient awaken.

For what really occurred, however, it is quite impossible that any human being could have been prepared.

As I rapidly made the mesmeric passes, amid ejaculations of "dead! dead!" absolutely *bursting* from the tongue and not from the lips of the sufferer, his whole frame at once—within the space of a single minute, or even less, shrunk—crumbled—absolutely *rotted* away beneath my hands. Upon the bed, before that whole company, there lay a nearly liquid mass of loathsome—of detestable putridity.

EXCERPT FROM

THE STRANGE CASE OF DR. JEKYLL AND MR. HYDE

(1886)

Robert Louis Stevenson

HENRY JEKYLL'S FULL STATEMENT OF THE CASE

I was born in the year 18— to a large fortune, endowed besides with excellent parts, inclined by nature to industry, fond of the respect of the wise and good among my fellow men, and thus, as might have been supposed, with every guarantee of an honourable and distinguished future. And indeed the worst of my faults was a certain impatient gaiety of disposition, such as has made the happiness of many, but such as I found it hard to reconcile with my imperious desire to carry my head high, and wear a more than commonly grave countenance before the public. Hence it came about that I concealed my pleasures; and that when I reached years of reflection, and began to look round me and take stock of my progress and position in the world, I stood already committed to a profound duplicity of life. Many a man would have even blazoned such irregularities as I was guilty of; but from the high views that I had set before me, I regarded and hid them with an almost morbid sense of shame. It was thus rather the exacting nature of my aspirations than any particular degradation in my faults, that made me what I was, and, with even a deeper trench than in the majority of men, severed in me those provinces of good and ill which divide and compound man's dual nature. In this case, I was driven to reflect deeply and inveterately on that hard law of life, which lies at the root of religion and is one of the most plentiful springs of distress. Though so profound a double-dealer, I was in no sense a hypocrite; both sides of me were in dead earnest; I was no more myself when I laid aside restraint and plunged in shame, than when I laboured, in the eye of day, at the furtherance of knowledge or the relief of sorrow and suffering. And it chanced that the direction of my scientific studies, which led wholly towards the mystic and the transcendental, reacted and shed a strong light on this consciousness of the perennial war among my members. With every day, and from both sides of my intelligence, the moral and the intellectual, I thus drew steadily nearer to that truth, by whose partial discovery I have been doomed to such a dreadful shipwreck: that man is not truly one, but truly two. I say two, because the state of my own knowledge does not pass beyond that point. Others will follow, others will outstrip me on the same lines; and I hazard the guess that man will be ultimately known for a mere polity of multifarious, incongruous and independent denizens.

I, for my part, from the nature of my life, advanced infallibly in one direction and in one direction only. It was on the moral side, and in my own person, that I learned to recognise the thorough and primitive duality of man; I saw that, of the two natures that contended in the field of my consciousness, even if I could rightly be said to be either, it was only because I was radically both; and from an early date, even before the course of my scientific discoveries had begun to suggest the most naked possibility of such a miracle, I had learned to dwell with pleasure, as a beloved daydream, on the thought of the separation of these elements. If each, I told myself, could be housed in separate identities, life would be relieved of all that was unbearable; the unjust might go his way, delivered from the aspirations and remorse of his more upright twin; and the just could walk steadfastly and securely on his upward path, doing the good things in which he found his pleasure, and no longer exposed to disgrace and penitence by the hands of this extraneous evil. It was the curse of mankind that these incongruous faggots were thus bound together—that in the agonised womb of consciousness, these polar twins should be continuously struggling. How, then were they dissociated?

I was so far in my reflections when, as I have said, a side light began to shine upon the subject from the laboratory table. I began to perceive more deeply than it has ever yet been stated, the trembling immateriality, the mistlike transience, of this seemingly so solid body in which we walk attired. Certain agents I found to have the power to shake and pluck back that fleshly vestment, even as a wind might toss the curtains of a pavilion. For two good reasons, I will not enter deeply into this scientific branch of my confession. First, because I have been made to learn that the doom and burthen of our life is bound for ever on man's shoulders, and when the attempt is made to cast it off, it but returns upon us with more unfamiliar and more awful pressure. Second, because, as my narrative will make, alas! too evident, my discoveries were incomplete. Enough then, that I not only recognised my natural body from the mere aura and effulgence of certain of the powers that made up my spirit, but managed to compound a drug by which these powers should be dethroned from their supremacy, and a second form and countenance substituted, none the less natural to me because they were the expression, and bore the stamp of lower elements in my soul.

I hesitated long before I put this theory to the test of practice. I knew well that I risked death; for any drug that so potently controlled and shook the very fortress of identity, might, by the least scruple of an overdose or at the least inopportunity in the moment of exhibition, utterly blot out that immaterial tabernacle which I looked to it to change. But the temptation of a discovery so singular and profound at last overcame the suggestions of alarm. I had long since prepared my tincture; I purchased at once, from a firm of wholesale chemists, a large quantity of a particular salt which I knew, from my experiments, to be the last ingredient required; and late one accursed night, I compounded the elements, watched them boil and smoke together in the glass, and when the ebullition had subsided, with a strong glow of courage, drank off the potion.

The most racking pangs succeeded: a grinding in the bones, deadly nausea, and a horror of the spirit that cannot be exceeded at the hour of birth or death. Then these agonies began swiftly to subside, and I came to myself as if out of a great sickness. There was something strange in my sensations, something indescribably new and, from its very novelty, incredibly sweet. I felt younger, lighter, happier in body; within I was conscious of a heady recklessness, a current of disordered sensual images running like a millrace in my fancy, a solution of the bonds of obligation, an unknown but not an innocent freedom of the soul. I knew myself, at the first breath of this new life, to be more wicked, tenfold more wicked, sold a slave to my original evil; and the thought, in that moment, braced and delighted me like wine. I stretched out my hands, exulting in the freshness of these sensations; and in the act, I was suddenly aware that I had lost in stature.

There was no mirror, at that date, in my room; that which stands beside me as I write, was brought there later on and for the very purpose of these transformations. The night however, was far gone into the morning—the morning, black as it was, was nearly ripe for the conception of the day—the inmates of my house were locked in the most rigorous hours of slumber; and I determined, flushed as I was with hope and triumph, to venture in my new shape as far as to my bedroom. I crossed the yard, wherein the constellations looked down upon me, I could have thought, with wonder, the first creature of that sort that their unsleeping vigilance had yet disclosed to them; I stole through the corridors, a stranger in my own house; and coming to my room, I saw for the first time the appearance of Edward Hyde.

I must here speak by theory alone, saying not that which I know, but that which I suppose to be most probable. The evil side of my nature, to which I had now transferred the stamping efficacy, was less robust and less developed than the good which I had just deposed. Again, in the course of my life, which had been, after all, nine tenths a life of effort, virtue and control, it had been much less exercised and much less exhausted. And hence, as I think, it came about that Edward Hyde was so much smaller, slighter and younger than Henry Jekyll. Even as good shone upon the countenance of the one, evil was written broadly and plainly on the face of the other. Evil besides (which I must still believe to be the lethal side of man) had left on that body an imprint of deformity and decay. And yet when I looked upon that ugly idol in the glass, I was conscious of no repugnance, rather of a leap of welcome. This, too, was myself. It seemed natural and human. In my eyes it bore a livelier image of the spirit, it seemed more express and single, than the imperfect and divided countenance I had been hitherto accustomed to call mine. And in so far I was doubtless right. I have observed that when I wore the semblance of Edward Hyde, none could come near to me at first without a visible misgiving of the flesh. This, as I take it, was because all human beings, as we meet them, are commingled out of good and evil: and Edward Hyde, alone in the ranks of mankind, was pure evil.

I lingered but a moment at the mirror: the second and conclusive experiment had yet to be attempted; it yet remained to be seen if I had lost my identity beyond redemption and must flee before daylight from a house that was no longer mine; and hurrying back to my cabinet, I once more prepared and drank the cup, once more suffered the pangs of dissolution, and came to myself once more with the character, the stature and the face of Henry Jekyll.

That night I had come to the fatal cross-roads. Had I approached my discovery in a more noble spirit, had I risked the experiment while under the empire of generous or pious aspirations, all must have been otherwise, and from these agonies of death and birth, I had come forth an angel instead of a fiend. The drug had no discriminating action; it was neither diabolical nor divine; it but shook the doors of the prisonhouse of my disposition; and like the captives of Philippi, that which stood within ran forth. At that time my virtue slumbered; my evil, kept awake by ambition, was alert and swift to seize the occasion; and the thing that was projected was Edward Hyde. Hence, although I had now two characters as well as two appearances, one was wholly evil, and the other was still the old Henry Jekyll, that incongruous compound of whose reformation and improvement I had already learned to despair. The movement was thus wholly toward the worse.

Even at that time, I had not conquered my aversions to the dryness of a life of study. I would still be merrily disposed at times; and as my pleasures were (to say the least) undignified, and I was not only well known and highly considered, but growing towards the elderly man, this incoherency of my life was daily growing more unwelcome. It was on this side that my new power tempted me until I fell in slavery. I had but to drink the cup, to doff at once the body of the noted professor, and to assume, like a thick cloak, that of Edward Hyde. I smiled at the notion; it seemed to me at the time to be humourous; and I made my preparations with the most studious care. I took and furnished that house in Soho, to which Hyde was tracked by the police; and engaged as a housekeeper a creature whom I knew well to be silent and unscrupulous. On the other side, I announced to my servants that a Mr. Hyde (whom I described) was to have full liberty and power about my house in the square; and to parry mishaps, I even called and made myself a familiar object, in my second character. I next drew up that will to which you so much objected; so that if anything befell me in the person of Dr. Jekyll, I could enter on that of Edward Hyde without pecuniary loss. And thus fortified, as I supposed, on every side, I began to profit by the strange immunities of my position.

Men have before hired bravos to transact their crimes, while their own person and reputation sat under shelter. I was the first that ever did so for his pleasures. I was the first that could plod in the public eye with a load of genial respectability, and in a moment, like a schoolboy, strip off these lendings and spring headlong into the sea of liberty. But for me, in my impenetrable mantle, the safety was complete. Think of it—I did not even exist! Let me but escape into my laboratory door, give me but a second or two to mix and swallow the draught that I had always standing ready; and whatever he had done, Edward Hyde would pass away like the stain of breath upon a mirror; and there in his stead, quietly at home, trimming the midnight lamp in his study, a man who could afford to laugh at suspicion, would be Henry Jekyll.

The pleasures which I made haste to seek in my disguise were, as I have said, undignified; I would scarce use a harder term. But in the hands of Edward Hyde, they soon began to turn toward the monstrous. When I would come back from these excursions, I was often plunged into a kind of wonder at my vicarious depravity. This familiar that I called out of my own soul, and sent forth alone to do his good pleasure, was a being inherently malign and villainous; his every act and thought centered on self; drinking pleasure with bestial avidity from any degree of torture to another; relentless like a man of stone. Henry Jekyll stood at times aghast before the acts of Edward Hyde; but the situation was apart from ordinary laws, and insidiously relaxed the grasp of conscience. It was Hyde, after all, and Hyde alone, that was guilty. Jekyll was no worse; he woke again to his good qualities seemingly unimpaired; he would even make haste, where it was possible, to undo the evil done by Hyde. And thus his conscience slumbered.

Into the details of the infamy at which I thus connived (for even now I can scarce grant that I committed it) I have no design of entering; I mean but to point out the warnings and the successive steps with which my chastisement approached. I met with one accident which, as it brought on no consequence, I shall no more than mention. An act of cruelty to a child aroused against me the anger of a passer-by, whom I recognised the other day in the person of your kinsman; the doctor and the child's family joined him; there were moments when I feared for my life; and at last, in order to pacify their too just resentment, Edward Hyde had to bring them to the door, and pay them in a cheque drawn in the name of Henry Jekyll. But this danger was easily eliminated from the future, by opening an account at another bank in the name of Edward Hyde himself; and when, by sloping my own hand backward, I had supplied my double with a signature, I thought I sat beyond the reach of fate.

Some two months before the murder of Sir Danvers, I had been out for one of my adventures, had returned at a late hour, and woke the next day in bed with somewhat odd sensations. It was in vain I looked about me; in vain I saw the decent furniture and tall proportions of my room in the square; in vain that I recognised the pattern of the bed curtains and the design of the mahogany frame; something still kept insisting that I was not where I was, that I had not wakened where I seemed to be, but in the little room in Soho where I was accustomed to sleep in the body of Edward Hyde. I smiled to myself, and in my psychological way, began lazily to inquire into the elements of this illusion, occasionally, even as I did so, dropping back into a comfortable morning doze. I was still so engaged when, in one of my more wakeful moments, my eyes fell upon my hand. Now the hand of Henry Jekyll (as you have often remarked) was professional in shape and size; it was large, firm, white and comely. But the hand which I now saw, clearly enough, in the yellow light of a mid-London morning, lying half shut on the bedclothes, was lean, corded, knuckly, of a dusky pallor and thickly shaded with a swart growth of hair. It was the hand of Edward Hyde.

I must have stared upon it for near half a minute, sunk as I was in the mere stupidity of wonder, before terror woke up in my breast as sudden and startling as the crash of cymbals; and bounding from my bed I rushed to the mirror. At the sight that met my eyes, my blood was changed into something exquisitely thin and icy. Yes, I had gone to bed Henry Jekyll, I had awakened Edward Hyde. How was this to be explained? I asked myself; and then, with another bound of terror—how was it to be remedied? It was well on in the morning; the servants were up; all my drugs were in the cabinet—a long journey down two pairs of stairs, through the back passage, across the open court and through the anatomical theatre, from where I was then standing horror-struck. It might indeed be possible to cover my face; but of what use was that, when I was unable to conceal the alteration in my stature? And then with an overpowering sweetness of relief, it came back upon my mind that the servants were already used to the coming and going of my second self. I had soon dressed, as well as I was able, in clothes of my own size: had soon passed through the house, where Bradshaw stared and drew back at seeing Mr. Hyde at such an hour and in such a strange array; and ten minutes later, Dr. Jekyll had returned to his own shape and was sitting down, with a darkened brow, to make a feint of breakfasting.

Small indeed was my appetite. This inexplicable incident, this reversal of my previous experience, seemed, like the Babylonian finger on the wall, to be spelling out the letters of my judgment; and I began to reflect more seriously than ever before on the issues and possibilities of my double existence. That part of me which I had the power of projecting, had lately been much exercised and nourished; it had seemed to me of late as though the body of Edward Hyde had grown in stature, as though (when I wore that form) I were conscious of a more generous tide of blood; and I began to spy a danger that, if this were much prolonged, the balance of my nature might be permanently overthrown, the power of voluntary change be forfeited, and the character of Edward Hyde become irrevocably mine. The power of the drug had not been always equally displayed. Once, very early in my career, it had totally failed me; since then I had been obliged on more than one occasion to double, and once, with infinite risk of death, to treble the amount; and these rare uncertainties had cast hitherto the sole shadow on my contentment. Now, however, and in the light of that morning's accident, I was led to remark that whereas, in the beginning, the difficulty had been to throw off the body of Jekyll, it had of late gradually but decidedly transferred itself to the other side. All things therefore seemed to point to this; that I was slowly losing hold of my original and better self, and becoming slowly incorporated with my second and worse.

Between these two, I now felt I had to choose. My two natures had memory in common, but all other faculties were most unequally shared between them. Jekyll (who was composite) now with the most sensitive apprehensions, now with a greedy gusto, projected and shared in the pleasures and adventures of Hyde; but Hyde was indifferent to Jekyll, or but remembered him as the mountain bandit remembers the cavern in which he conceals himself from pursuit. Jekyll had more than a father's interest; Hyde had more than a son's indifference. To cast in my lot with Jekyll, was to die to those appetites which I had long secretly indulged and had of late begun to pamper. To cast it in with Hyde, was to die to a thousand interests and aspirations, and to become, at a blow and forever, despised and friendless. The bargain might appear unequal; but there was still another consideration in the scales; for while Jekyll would suffer smartingly in the fires of abstinence, Hyde would be not even conscious of all that he had lost. Strange as my circumstances were, the terms of this debate are as old and commonplace as man; much the same inducements and alarms cast the die for any tempted and trembling sinner; and it fell out with me, as it falls with so vast a majority of my fellows, that I chose the better part and was found wanting in the strength to keep to it.

THE MONSTER-MAKER

(1887)

W. C. Morrow

A young man of refined appearance, but evidently suffering great mental distress, presented himself one morning at the residence of a singular old man, who was known as a surgeon of remarkable skill. The house was a queer and primitive brick affair, entirely out of date, and tolerable only in the decayed part of the city in which it stood. It was large, gloomy, and dark, and had long corridors and dismal rooms; and it was absurdly large for the small family—man and wife—that occupied it. The house described, the man is portrayed—but not the woman. He could be agreeable on occasion, but, for all that, he was but animated mystery. His wife was weak, wan, reticent, evidently miserable, and possibly living a life of dread or horror—perhaps witness of repulsive things, subject of anxieties, and victim of fear and tyranny; but there is a great deal of guessing in these assumptions. He was about sixty-five years of age and she about forty. He was lean, tall, and bald, with a thin, smooth-shaven face, and very keen eyes; kept always at home, and was slovenly. The man was strong, the woman weak; he dominated, she suffered.

Although he was a surgeon of rare skill, his practice was almost nothing, for it was a rare occurrence that the few who knew of his great ability were brave enough to penetrate the gloom of his house, and when they did so it was with deaf ear turned to sundry ghoulish stories that were whispered concerning him. These were, in great part, but exaggerations of his experiments in vivisection; he was devoted to the science of surgery.

The young man who presented himself on the morning just mentioned was a handsome fellow, yet of evident weak character and unhealthy temperament—sensitive, and easily exalted or depressed. A single glance convinced the surgeon that his visitor was seriously affected in mind, for there was never a bolder skull-grin of melancholia, fixed and irremediable.

A stranger would not have suspected any occupancy of the house. The street door—old, warped, and blistered by the sun—was locked, and the small, faded-green window-blinds were closed. The young man rapped at the door. No answer. He rapped again. Still no sign. He examined a slip of paper, glanced at the number on the house, and then, with the impatience of a child, he furiously kicked the door. There were signs of numerous other such kicks. A response came in the shape of a shuffling footstep in the hall, a turning of the rusty key, and a sharp face that peered through a cautious opening in the door.

"Are you the doctor?" asked the young man.

"Yes, yes! Come in," briskly replied the master of the house.

The young man entered. The old surgeon closed the door and carefully locked it. "This way," he said, advancing to a rickety flight of stairs. The young man followed. The surgeon led the way up the stairs, turned into a narrow, musty-smelling corridor at the left, traversed it, rattling the loose boards under his feet, at the farther end opened a door at the right, and beckoned his visitor to enter. The young man found himself in a pleasant room, furnished in antique fashion and with hard simplicity.

"Sit down," said the old man, placing a chair so that its occupant should face a window that looked out upon a dead wall about six feet from the house. He threw open the blind, and a pale light entered. He then seated himself near his visitor and directly facing him, and with a searching look, that had all the power of a microscope, he proceeded to diagnosticate the case.

"Well?" he presently asked.

The young man shifted uneasily in his seat.

"I—I have come to see you," he finally stammered, "because I'm in trouble."

"Ah!"

"Yes; you see, I—that is—I have given it up."

"Ah!" There was pity added to sympathy in the ejaculation.

"That's it. Given it up," added the visitor. He took from his pocket a roll of banknotes, and with the utmost deliberation he counted them out upon his knee. "Five thousand dollars," he calmly remarked. "That is for you. It's all I have; but I presume—I imagine—no; that is not the word—assume—yes; that's the word—assume that five thousand—is it really that much? Let me count." He counted again. "That five thousand dollars is a sufficient fee for what I want you to do."

The surgeon's lips curled pityingly—perhaps disdainfully also. "What do you want me to do?" he carelessly inquired.

The young man rose, looked around with a mysterious air, approached the surgeon, and laid the money across his knee. Then he stooped and whispered two words in the surgeon's ear.

These words produced an electric effect. The old man started violently; then, springing to his feet, he caught his visitor angrily, and transfixed him with a look that was as sharp as a knife. His eyes flashed, and he opened his mouth to give utterance to some harsh imprecation, when he suddenly checked himself. The anger left his face, and only pity remained. He relinquished his grasp, picked up the scattered notes, and, offering them to the visitor, slowly said:

"I do not want your money. You are simply foolish. You think you are in trouble. Well, you do not know what trouble is. Your only trouble is that you have not a trace of manhood in your nature. You are merely insane—I shall not say pusillanimous. You should surrender yourself to the authorities, and be sent to a lunatic asylum for proper treatment."

The young man keenly felt the intended insult, and his eyes flashed dangerously.

"You old dog—you insult me thus!" he cried. "Grand airs, these, you give yourself! Virtuously indignant, old murderer, you! Don't want my money, eh? When a man comes to you himself and wants it done, you fly into a passion and spurn his money; but let an enemy of his come and pay you, and you are only too willing. How many such jobs have you done in this miserable old hole? It is a good thing for you that the police have not run you down, and brought spade and shovel with them. Do you know what is said of you? Do you think you have kept your windows so closely shut that no sound has ever penetrated beyond them? Where do you keep your infernal implements?"

He had worked himself into a high passion. His voice was hoarse, loud, and rasping. His eyes, bloodshot, started from their sockets. His whole frame twitched, and his fingers writhed. But he was in the presence of a man infinitely his superior. Two eyes, like those of a snake, burned two holes through him. An overmastering, inflexible presence confronted one weak and passionate. The result came.

"Sit down," commanded the stern voice of the surgeon.

It was the voice of father to child, of master to slave. The fury left the visitor, who, weak and overcome, fell upon a chair.

Meanwhile, a peculiar light had appeared in the old surgeon's face, the dawn of a strange idea; a gloomy ray, strayed from the fires of the bottomless pit; the baleful light that illumines the way of the enthusiast. The old man remained a moment in profound abstraction, gleams of eager intelligence bursting momentarily through the cloud of sombre meditation that covered his face. Then broke the broad light of a deep, impenetrable determination. There was something sinister in it, suggesting the sacrifice of something held sacred. After a struggle, mind had vanquished conscience.

Taking a piece of paper and a pencil, the surgeon carefully wrote answers to questions which he peremptorily addressed to his visitor, such as his name, age, place of residence, occupation, and the like, and the same inquiries concerning his parents, together with other particular matters.

"Does any one know you came to this house?" he asked.

"No."

"You swear it?"

"Yes."

"But your prolonged absence will cause alarm and lead to search."

"I have provided against that."

"How?"

"By depositing a note in the post, as I came along, announcing my intention to drown myself."

"The river will be dragged."

"What then?" asked the young man, shrugging his shoulders with careless indifference. "Rapid undercurrent, you know. A good many are never found."

There was a pause.

"Are you ready?" finally asked the surgeon.

"Perfectly." The answer was cool and determined.

The manner of the surgeon, however, showed much perturbation. The pallor that had come into his face at the moment his decision was formed became intense. A nervous tremulousness came over his frame. Above it all shone the light of enthusiasm.

"Have you a choice in the method?" he asked.

"Yes; extreme anæsthesia."

"With what agent?"

"The surest and quickest."

"Do you desire any—any subsequent disposition?"

"No; only nullification; simply a blowing out, as of a candle in the wind; a puff—then darkness, without a trace. A sense of your own safety may suggest the method. I leave it to you."

"No delivery to your friends?"

"None whatever."

Another pause.

"Did you say you are quite ready?" asked the surgeon.

"Quite ready."

"And perfectly willing?"

"Anxious."

"Then wait a moment."

With this request the old surgeon rose to his feet and stretched himself. Then with the stealthiness of a cat he opened the door and peered into the hall, listening intently. There was no sound. He softly closed the door and locked it. Then he closed the window-blinds and locked them. This done, he opened a door leading into an adjoining room, which, though it had no window, was lighted by means of a small skylight. The young man watched closely. A strange change had come over him. While his determination had not one whit lessened, a look of great relief came into his face, displacing the haggard, despairing look of a half-hour before. Melancholic then, he was ecstatic now.

The opening of the second door disclosed a curious sight. In the centre of the room, directly under the skylight, was an operating-table, such as is used by demonstrators of anatomy. A glass case against the wall held surgical instruments of every kind. Hanging in another case were human skeletons of various sizes. In sealed jars, arranged on shelves, were monstrosities of divers kinds preserved in alcohol. There were also, among innumerable other articles scattered about the room, a manikin, a stuffed cat, a desiccated human heart, plaster casts of various parts of the body, numerous charts, and a large assortment of drugs and chemicals. There was also a lounge, which could be opened to form a couch. The surgeon opened it and moved the operating-table aside, giving its place to the lounge.

"Come in," he called to his visitor.

The young man obeyed without the least hesitation.

"Take off your coat."

Hc complied.

"Lie down on that lounge."

In a moment the young man was stretched at full length, eyeing the surgeon. The latter undoubtedly was suffering under great excitement, but he did not waver; his movements were sure and quick. Selecting a bottle containing a liquid, he carefully measured out a certain quantity. While doing this he asked:

"Have you ever had any irregularity of the heart?"

"No."

The answer was prompt, but it was immediately followed by a quizzical look in the speaker's face.

"I presume," he added, "you mean by your question that it might be dangerous to give me a certain drug. Under the circumstances, however, I fail to see any relevancy in your question."

This took the surgeon aback; but he hastened to explain that he did not wish to inflict unnecessary pain, and hence his question.

He placed the glass on a stand, approached his visitor, and carefully examined his pulse.

"Wonderful!" he exclaimed.

"Why?"

"It is perfectly normal."

"Because I am wholly resigned. Indeed, it has been long since I knew such happiness. It is not active, but infinitely sweet."

"You have no lingering desire to retract?"

"None whatever."

The surgeon went to the stand and returned with the draught.

"Take this," he said, kindly.

The young man partially raised himself and took the glass in his hand. He did not show the vibration of a single nerve. He drank the liquid, draining the last drop. Then he returned the glass with a smile.

"Thank you," he said; "you are the noblest man that lives. May you always prosper and be happy! You are my benefactor, my liberator. Bless you, bless you! You reach down from your seat with the gods and lift me up into glorious peace and rest. I love you—I love you with all my heart!"

These words, spoken earnestly, in a musical, low voice, and accompanied with a smile of ineffable tenderness, pierced the old man's heart. A suppressed convulsion swept over him; intense anguish wrung his vitals; perspiration trickled down his face. The young man continued to smile.

"Ah, it does me good!" said he.

The surgeon, with a strong effort to control himself, sat down upon the edge of the lounge and took his visitor's wrist, counting the pulse.

"How long will it take?" the young man asked.

"Ten minutes. Two have passed." The voice was hoarse.

"Ah, only eight minutes more!... Delicious, delicious! I feel it coming.... What was that?... Ah, I understand. Music.... Beautiful!... Coming, coming.... Is that—that—water?... Trickling? Dripping? Doctor!"

"Well?"

"Thank you,... thank you.... Noble man,... my saviour,... my bene... bene... factor.... Trickling,... trickling.... Dripping, dripping.... Doctor!"

"Well?"

"Doctor!"

"Past hearing," muttered the surgeon.

"Doctor!"

"And blind."

Response was made by a firm grasp of the hand.

"Doctor!"

"And numb."

"Doctor!"

The old man watched and waited.

"Dripping,... dripping."

The last drop had run. There was a sigh, and nothing more.

The surgeon laid down the hand.

"The first step," he groaned, rising to his feet; then his whole frame dilated. "The first step—the most difficult, yet the simplest. A providential delivery into my hands of that for which I have hungered for forty years. No withdrawal now! It is possible, because scientific; rational, but perilous. If I succeed—*if?* I *shall* succeed. I *will* succeed.... And after success—what?... Yes; what? Publish the plan and the result? The gallows.... So long as *it* shall exist,... and *I* exist, the gallows. That much.... But how account for its presence? Ah, that pinches hard! I must trust to the future."

He tore himself from the revery and started.

"I wonder if *she* heard or saw anything."

With that reflection he cast a glance upon the form on the lounge, and then left the room, locked the door, locked also the door of the outer room, walked down two or three corridors, penetrated to a remote part of the house, and rapped at a door. It was opened by his wife. He, by this time, had regained complete mastery over himself.

"I thought I heard some one in the house just now," he said, "but I can find no one."

"I heard nothing."

He was greatly relieved.

"I did hear some one knock at the door less than an hour ago," she resumed, "and heard you speak, I think. Did he come in?"

"No."

The woman glanced at his feet and seemed perplexed.

"I am almost certain," she said, "that I heard foot-falls in the house, and yet I see that you are wearing slippers."

"Oh, I had on my shoes then!"

"That explains it," said the woman, satisfied; "I think the sound you heard must have been caused by rats."

"Ah, that was it!" exclaimed the surgeon. Leaving, he closed the door, reopened it, and said, "I do not wish to be disturbed to-day." He said to himself, as he went down the hall, "All is clear there."

He returned to the room in which his visitor lay, and made a careful examination.

"Splendid specimen!" he softly exclaimed; "every organ sound, every function perfect; fine, large frame; well-shaped muscles, strong and sinewy; capable of wonderful development—if given opportunity.... I have no doubt it can be done. Already I have succeeded with a dog,—a task less difficult than this, for in a man the cerebrum overlaps the cerebellum, which is not the case with a dog. This gives a wide range for accident, with but one opportunity in a lifetime! In the cerebrum, the intellect and the affections; in the cerebellum, the senses and the motor forces; in the medulla oblongata, control of the diaphragm. In these two latter lie all the essentials of simple existence. The cerebrum is merely an adornment; that is to say, reason and the affections are almost purely ornamental. I have already proved it. My dog, with its cerebrum removed, was idiotic, but it retained its physical senses to a certain degree."

While thus ruminating he made careful preparations. He moved the couch, replaced the operating-table under the skylight, selected a number of surgical instruments, prepared certain drug-mixtures, and arranged water, towels, and all the accessories of a tedious surgical operation. Suddenly he burst into laughter.

"Poor fool!" he exclaimed. "Paid me five thousand dollars to kill him! Didn't have the courage to snuff his own candle! Singular, singular, the queer freaks these madmen have! You thought you were dying, poor idiot! Allow me to inform you, sir, that you are as much alive at this moment as ever you were in your life. But it will be all the same to you. You shall never be more conscious than you are now; and for all practical purposes, so far as they concern you, you are dead henceforth, though you shall live. By the way, how should you feel *without a head*? Ha, ha, ha!... But that's a sorry joke."

He lifted the unconscious form from the lounge and laid it upon the operating-table.

About three years afterwards the following conversation was held between a captain of police and a detective:

"She may be insane," suggested the captain.

"I think she is."

"And yet you credit her story!"

"I do."

"Singular!"

"Not at all. I myself have learned something."

"What!"

"Much, in one sense; little, in another. You have heard those queer stories of her husband. Well, they are all nonsensical—probably with one exception. He is generally a harmless old fellow, but peculiar. He has performed some wonderful surgical operations. The people in his neighborhood are ignorant, and they fear him and wish to be rid of him; hence they tell a great many lies about him, and they come to believe their own stories. The one important thing that I have learned is that he is almost insanely enthusiastic on the subject of surgery—especially experimental surgery; and with an enthusiast there is hardly such a thing as a scruple. It is this that gives me confidence in the woman's story."

"You say she appeared to be frightened?"

"Doubly so—first, she feared that her husband would learn of her betrayal of him; second, the discovery itself had terrified her."

"But her report of this discovery is very vague," argued the captain. "He conceals everything from her. She is merely guessing."

"In part—yes; in other part—no. She heard the sounds distinctly, though she did not see clearly. Horror closed her eyes. What she thinks she saw is, I admit, preposterous; but she undoubtedly saw something extremely frightful. There are many peculiar little circumstances. He has eaten with her but few times during the last three years, and nearly always carries his food to his private rooms. She says that he either consumes an enormous quantity, throws much away, or is feeding something that eats prodigiously. He explains this to her by saying that he has animals with which he experiments. This is not true. Again, he always keeps the door to these rooms carefully locked; and not only that, but he has had the doors doubled and otherwise strengthened, and has heavily barred a window that looks from one of the rooms upon a dead wall a few feet distant."

"What does it mean?" asked the captain.

"A prison."

"For animals, perhaps."

"Certainly not."

"Why!"

"Because, in the first place, cages would have been better; in the second place, the security that he has provided is infinitely greater than that required for the confinement of ordinary animals."

"All this is easily explained: he has a violent lunatic under treatment."

"I had thought of that, but such is not the fact."

"How do you know?"

"By reasoning thus: He has always refused to treat cases of lunacy; he confines himself to surgery; the walls are not padded, for the woman has heard sharp blows upon them; no human strength, however morbid, could possibly require such resisting strength as has been provided; he would not be likely to conceal a lunatic's confinement from the woman; no lunatic could consume all the food that he provides; so extremely violent mania as these precautions indicate could not continue three years; if there is a lunatic in the case it is very probable that there should have been communication with some one outside concerning the patient, and there has been none; the woman has listened at the keyhole and has heard no human voice within; and last, we have heard the woman's vague description of what she saw."

"You have destroyed every possible theory," said the captain, deeply interested, "and have suggested nothing new."

"Unfortunately, I cannot; but the truth may be very simple, after all. The old surgeon is so peculiar that I am prepared to discover something remarkable."

"Have you suspicions?"

"I have."

"Of what?"

"A crime. The woman suspects it."

"And betrays it?"

"Certainly, because it is so horrible that her humanity revolts; so terrible that her whole nature demands of her that she hand over the criminal to the law; so frightful that she is in mortal terror; so awful that it has shaken her mind."

"What do you propose to do?" asked the captain.

"Secure evidence. I may need help."

"You shall have all the men you require. Go ahead, but be careful. You are on dangerous ground. You would be a mere plaything in the hands of that man."

Two days afterwards the detective again sought the captain.

"I have a queer document," he said, exhibiting torn fragments of paper, on which there was writing. "The woman stole it and brought it to me. She snatched a handful out of a book, getting only a part of each of a few leaves."

These fragments, which the men arranged as best they could, were (the detective explained) torn by the surgeon's wife from the first volume of a number of manuscript books which her husband had written on one subject,—the very one that was the cause of her excitement. "About the time that he began a certain experiment three years ago," continued the detective, "he removed everything from the suite of two rooms containing his study and his operating-room. In one of the bookcases that he removed to a room across the passage was a drawer, which he kept locked, but which he opened from time to time. As is quite common with such pieces of furniture, the lock of the drawer is a very poor one; and so the woman, while making a thorough search yesterday, found a key on her bunch that fitted this lock. She opened the drawer, drew out the bottom book of a pile (so that its mutilation would more likely escape discovery), saw that it might contain a clew, and tore out a handful of the leaves. She had barely replaced the book, locked the drawer, and made her escape when her husband appeared. He hardly ever allows her to be out of his sight when she is in that part of the house."

The fragments read as follows: "...the motory nerves. I had hardly dared to hope for such a result, although inductive reasoning had convinced me of its possibility, my only doubt having been on the score of my lack of skill. Their operation has been only slightly impaired, and even this would not have been the case had the operation been performed in infancy, before the intellect had sought and obtained recognition as an essential part of the whole. Therefore I state, as a proved fact, that the cells of the motory nerves have inherent forces sufficient to the purposes of those nerves. But hardly so with the sensory nerves. These latter are, in fact, an offshoot of the former, evolved from them by natural (though not essential) heterogeneity, and to a certain extent are dependent on the evolution and expansion of a contemporaneous tendency, that developed into mentality, or mental function. Both of these latter tendencies, these evolvements, are merely refinements of the motory system, and not independent entities; that is to say, they are the blossoms of a plant that propagates from its roots. The motory system is the first...nor am I surprised that such prodigious muscular energy is developing. It promises yet to surpass the wildest dreams of human strength. I account for it thus: The powers of assimilation had reached their full development. They had formed the habit of doing a certain amount of work. They sent their products to all parts of the system. As a result of my operation the consumption of these products was reduced fully one-half; that is to say, about one-half of the demand for them was withdrawn. But force of habit required the production to proceed. This production was strength, vitality, energy. Thus double the usual quantity of this strength, this energy, was stored in the remaining...developed a tendency that did surprise me. Nature, no longer suffering the distraction of extraneous interferences, and at the same time being cut in two (as it were), with reference to this case, did not fully adjust herself to the new situation, as does a magnet, which, when divided at the point of equilibrium, renews itself in its two fragments by investing each with opposite poles; but, on the contrary, being severed from laws that theretofore had controlled her, and possessing still that mysterious tendency to develop into something more potential and complex, she blindly (having lost her lantern) pushed her demands for material that would secure this development, and as blindly used it when it was given her. Hence this marvellous voracity, this insatiable hunger, this wonderful ravenousness; and hence also (there being nothing but the physical part to receive this vast storing of energy) this strength that is becoming almost hourly herculean, almost daily appalling. It is becoming a serious... narrow escape to-day. By some means, while I was absent, it unscrewed the stopper of the silver feeding-pipe (which I have already herein termed 'the artificial mouth'), and, in one of its curious antics, allowed all the chyle to escape from its stomach through the tube. Its hunger then became intense—I may say furious. I placed my hands upon it to push it into a chair, when, feeling my touch, it caught me, clasped me around the neck, and would have crushed me to death instantly had I not slipped from its powerful grasp. Thus I always had to be on my guard. I have provided the screw stopper with a spring catch, and... usually docile when not hungry; slow and heavy in its movements, which are, of course, purely unconscious; any apparent excitement in movement being due to local irregularities in the blood-supply of the cerebellum, which, if I did not have it enclosed in a silver case that is immovable, I should expose and..."

The captain looked at the detective with a puzzled air.

"I don't understand it at all," said he.

"Nor I," agreed the detective.

"What do you propose to do?"

"Make a raid."

"Do you want a man?"

"Three. The strongest men in your district."

"Why, the surgeon is old and weak!"

"Nevertheless, I want three strong men; and for that matter, prudence really advises me to take twenty."

At one o'clock the next morning a cautious, scratching sound might have been heard in the ceiling of the surgeon's operating-room. Shortly afterwards the skylight sash was carefully raised and laid aside. A man peered into the opening. Nothing could be heard.

"That is singular," thought the detective.

He cautiously lowered himself to the floor by a rope, and then stood for some moments listening intently. There was a dead silence. He shot the slide of a dark-lantern, and rapidly swept the room with the light. It was bare, with the exception of a strong iron staple and ring, screwed to the floor in the centre of the room, with a heavy chain attached. The detective then turned his attention to the outer room; it was perfectly bare. He was deeply perplexed. Returning to the inner room, he called softly to the men to descend. While they were thus occupied he re-entered the outer room and examined the door. A glance sufficed. It was kept closed by a spring attachment, and was locked with a strong spring-lock that could be drawn from the inside.

"The bird has just flown," mused the detective. "A singular accident! The discovery and proper use of this thumb-bolt might not have happened once in fifty years, if my theory is correct."

By this time the men were behind him. He noiselessly drew the spring-bolt, opened the door, and looked out into the hall. He heard a peculiar sound. It was as though a gigantic lobster was floundering and scrambling in some distant part of the old house. Accompanying this sound was a loud, whistling breathing, and frequent rasping gasps.

These sounds were heard by still another person—the surgeon's wife; for they originated very near her rooms, which were a considerable distance from her husband's. She had been sleeping lightly, tortured by fear and harassed by frightful dreams. The conspiracy into which she had recently entered, for the destruction of her husband, was a source of great anxiety. She constantly suffered from the most gloomy forebodings, and lived in an atmosphere of terror. Added to the natural horror of her situation were those countless sources of fear which a fright-shaken mind creates and then magnifies. She was, indeed, in a pitiable state, having been driven first by terror to desperation, and then to madness.

Startled thus out of fitful slumber by the noise at her door, she sprang from her bed to the floor, every terror that lurked in her acutely tense mind and diseased imagination starting up and almost overwhelming her. The idea of flight—one of the strongest of all instincts—seized upon her, and she ran to the door, beyond all control of reason. She drew the bolt and flung the door wide open, and then fled wildly down the passage, the appalling hissing and rasping gurgle ringing in her ears apparently with a thousandfold intensity. But the passage was in absolute darkness, and she had not taken a half-dozen steps when she tripped upon an unseen object on the floor. She fell headlong upon it, encountering in it a large, soft, warm substance that writhed and squirmed, and from which came the sounds that had awakened her. Instantly realizing her situation, she uttered a shriek such as only an unnamable terror can inspire. But hardly had her cry started the echoes in the empty corridor when it was suddenly stifled. Two prodigious arms had closed upon her and crushed the life out of her.

The cry performed the office of directing the detective and his assistants, and it also aroused the old surgeon, who occupied rooms between the officers and the object of their search. The cry of agony pierced him to the marrow, and a realization of the cause of it burst upon him with frightful force.

"It has come at last!" he gasped, springing from his bed.

Snatching from a table a dimly-burning lamp and a long knife which he had kept at hand for three years, he dashed into the corridor. The four officers had already started forward, but when they saw him emerge they halted in silence. In that moment of stillness the surgeon paused to listen. He heard the hissing sound and the clumsy floundering of a bulky, living object in the direction of his wife's apartments. It evidently was advancing towards him. A turn in the corridor shut out the view. He turned up the light, which revealed a ghastly pallor in his face.

"Wife!" he called.

There was no response. He hurriedly advanced, the four men following quietly. He turned the angle of the corridor, and ran so rapidly that by the time the officers had come in sight of him again he was twenty steps away. He ran past a huge, shapeless object, sprawling, crawling, and floundering along, and arrived at the body of his wife.

He gave one horrified glance at her face, and staggered away. Then a fury seized him. Clutching the knife firmly, and holding the lamp aloft, he sprang toward the ungainly object in the corridor. It was then that the officers, still advancing cautiously, saw a little more clearly, though still indistinctly, the object of the surgeon's fury, and the cause of the look of unutterable anguish in his face. The hideous sight caused them to pause. They saw what appeared to be a man, yet evidently was not a man; huge, awkward, shapeless; a squirming, lurching, stumbling mass, completely naked. It raised its broad shoulders. *It had no head*, but instead of it a small metallic ball surmounting its massive neck.

"Devil!" exclaimed the surgeon, raising the knife.

"Hold, there!" commanded a stern voice.

The surgeon quickly raised his eyes and saw the four officers, and for a moment fear paralyzed his arm.

"The police!" he gasped.

Then, with a look of redoubled fury, he sent the knife to the hilt into the squirming mass before him. The wounded monster sprang to its feet and wildly threw its arms about, meanwhile emitting fearful sounds from a silver tube through which it breathed. The surgeon aimed another blow, but never gave it. In his blind fury he lost his caution, and was caught in an iron grasp. The struggling threw the lamp some feet toward the officers, and it fell to the floor, shattered to pieces. Simultaneously with the crash the oil took fire, and the corridor was filled with flame. The officers could not approach. Before them was the spreading blaze, and secure behind it were two forms struggling in a fearful embrace. They heard cries and gasps, and saw the gleaming of a knife.

The wood in the house was old and dry. It took fire at once, and the flames spread with great rapidity. The four officers turned and fled, barely escaping with their lives. In an hour nothing remained of the mysterious old house and its inmates but a blackened ruin.

EXCERPT FROM

THE ISLAND OF DR. MOREAU

(1896)

H. G. Wells

XIV. DOCTOR MOREAU EXPLAINS

"And now, Prendick, I will explain," said Doctor Moreau, so soon as we had eaten and drunk. "I must confess that you are the most dictatorial guest I ever entertained. I warn you that this is the last I shall do to oblige you. The next thing you threaten to commit suicide about, I shan't do,—even at some personal inconvenience."

He sat in my deck chair, a cigar half consumed in his white, dexterous-looking fingers. The light of the swinging lamp fell on his white hair; he stared through the little window out at the starlight. I sat as far away from him as possible, the table between us and the revolvers to hand. Montgomery was not present. I did not care to be with the two of them in such a little room.

"You admit that the vivisected human being, as you called it, is, after all, only the puma?" said Moreau. He had made me visit that horror in the inner room, to assure myself of its inhumanity.

"It is the puma," I said, "still alive, but so cut and mutilated as I pray I may never see living flesh again. Of all vile—"

"Never mind that," said Moreau; "at least, spare me those youthful horrors. Montgomery used to be just the same. You admit that it is the puma. Now be quiet, while I reel off my physiological lecture to you."

And forthwith, beginning in the tone of a man supremely bored, but presently warming a little, he explained his work to me. He was very simple and convincing. Now and then there was a touch of sarcasm in his voice. Presently I found myself hot with shame at our mutual positions.

The creatures I had seen were not men, had never been men. They were animals, humanised animals,—triumphs of vivisection.

"You forget all that a skilled vivisector can do with living things," said Moreau. "For my own part, I'm puzzled why the things I have done here have not been done before. Small efforts, of course, have been made,—amputation, tongue-cutting, excisions. Of course you know a squint may be induced or cured by surgery? Then in the case of excisions you have all kinds of secondary changes, pigmentary disturbances, modifications of the passions, alterations in the secretion of fatty tissue. I have no doubt you have heard of these things?"

"Of course," said I. "But these foul creatures of yours—"

"All in good time," said he, waving his hand at me; "I am only beginning. Those are trivial cases of alteration. Surgery can do better things than that. There is building up as well as breaking down and changing. You have heard, perhaps, of a common surgical operation resorted to in cases where the nose has been destroyed: a flap of skin is cut from the forehead, turned down on the nose, and heals in the new position. This is a kind of grafting in a new position of part of an animal upon itself. Grafting of freshly obtained material from another animal is also possible,—the case of teeth, for example. The grafting of skin and bone is done to facilitate healing: the surgeon places in the middle of the wound pieces of skin snipped from another animal, or fragments of bone from a victim freshly killed. Hunter's cock-spur—possibly you have heard of that—flourished on the bull's neck; and the rhinoceros rats of the Algerian Zouaves are also to be thought of,—monsters manufactured by transferring a slip from the tail of an ordinary rat to its snout, and allowing it to heal in that position."

"Monsters manufactured!" said I. "Then you mean to tell me—"

"Yes. These creatures you have seen are animals carven and wrought into new shapes. To that, to the study of the plasticity of living forms, my life has been devoted. I have studied for years, gaining in knowledge as I go. I see you look horrified, and yet I am telling you nothing new. It all lay in the surface of practical anatomy years ago, but no one had the temerity to touch it. It is not simply the outward form of an animal which I can change. The physiology, the chemical rhythm of the creature, may also be made to undergo an enduring modification,—of which vaccination and other methods of inoculation with living or dead matter are examples that will, no doubt, be familiar to you. A similar operation is the transfusion of blood,—with which subject, indeed, I began. These are all familiar cases. Less so, and probably far more extensive, were the operations of those mediaeval practitioners who made dwarfs and beggar-cripples, show-monsters,—some vestiges of whose art still remain in the preliminary manipulation of the young mountebank or contortionist. Victor Hugo gives an account of them in 'L'Homme qui Rit.'—But perhaps my meaning grows plain now. You begin to see that it is a possible thing to transplant tissue from one part of an animal to another, or from one animal to another; to alter its chemical reactions and methods of growth; to modify the articulations of its limbs; and, indeed, to change it in its most intimate structure.

"And yet this extraordinary branch of knowledge has never been sought as an end, and systematically, by modern investigators until I took it up! Some such things have been hit upon in the last resort of surgery; most of the kindred evidence that will recur to your mind has been demonstrated as it were by accident,—by tyrants, by criminals, by the breeders of horses and dogs, by all kinds of untrained clumsy-handed men working for their own immediate ends. I was the first man to take up this question armed with antiseptic surgery, and with a really scientific knowledge of the laws of growth. Yet one would imagine it must have been practised in secret before. Such creatures as the Siamese Twins—And in the vaults of the Inquisition. No doubt their chief aim was artistic torture, but some at least of the inquisitors must have had a touch of scientific curiosity."

"But," said I, "these things—these animals talk!"

He said that was so, and proceeded to point out that the possibility of vivisection does not stop at a mere physical metamorphosis. A pig may be educated. The mental structure is even less determinate than the bodily. In our growing science of hypnotism we find the promise of a possibility of superseding old inherent instincts by new suggestions, grafting upon or replacing the inherited fixed ideas. Very much indeed of what we call moral education, he said, is such an artificial modification and perversion of instinct; pugnacity is trained into courageous self-sacrifice, and suppressed sexuality into religious emotion. And the great difference between man and monkey is in the larynx, he continued,—in the incapacity to frame delicately different sound-symbols by which thought could be sustained. In this I failed to agree with him, but with a certain incivility he declined to notice my objection. He repeated that the thing was so, and continued his account of his work.

I asked him why he had taken the human form as a model. There seemed to me then, and there still seems to me now, a strange wickedness for that choice.

He confessed that he had chosen that form by chance. "I might just as well have worked to form sheep into llamas and llamas into sheep. I suppose there is something in the human form that appeals to the artistic turn of mind more powerfully than any animal shape can. But I've not confined myself to man-making. Once or twice—" He was silent, for a minute perhaps. "These years! How they have slipped by! And here I have wasted a day saving your life, and am now wasting an hour explaining myself!"

"But," said I, "I still do not understand. Where is your justification for inflicting all this pain? The only thing that could excuse vivisection to me would be some application—"

"Precisely," said he. "But, you see, I am differently constituted. We are on different platforms. You are a materialist."

"I am *not* a materialist," I began hotly.

"In my view—in my view. For it is just this question of pain that parts us. So long as visible or audible pain turns you sick; so long as your own pains drive you; so long as pain underlies your propositions about sin,—so long, I tell you, you are an animal, thinking a little less obscurely what an animal feels. This pain—"

I gave an impatient shrug at such sophistry.

"Oh, but it is such a little thing! A mind truly opened to what science has to teach must see that it is a little thing. It may be that save in this little planet, this speck of cosmic dust, invisible long before the nearest star could be attained—it may be, I say, that nowhere else does this thing called pain occur. But the laws we feel our way towards—Why, even on this earth, even among living things, what pain is there?"

As he spoke he drew a little penknife from his pocket, opened the smaller blade, and moved his chair so that I could see his thigh. Then, choosing the place deliberately, he drove the blade into his leg and withdrew it.

"No doubt," he said, "you have seen that before. It does not hurt a pin-prick. But what does it show? The capacity for pain is not needed in the muscle, and it is not placed there,—is but little needed in the skin, and only here and there over the thigh is a spot capable of feeling pain. Pain is simply our intrinsic medical adviser to warn us and stimulate us. Not all living flesh is painful; nor is all nerve, not even all sensory nerve. There's no taint of pain, real pain, in the sensations of the optic nerve. If you wound the optic nerve, you merely see flashes of light,—just as disease of the auditory nerve merely means a humming in our ears. Plants do not feel pain, nor the lower animals; it's possible that such animals as the starfish and crayfish do not feel pain at all. Then with men, the more intelligent they become, the more intelligently they will see after their own welfare, and the less they will need the goad to keep them out of danger. I never yet heard of a useless thing that was not ground out of existence by evolution sooner or later. Did you? And pain gets needless.

"Then I am a religious man, Prendick, as every sane man must be. It may be, I fancy, that I have seen more of the ways of this world's Maker than you,—for I have sought his laws, in my way, all my life, while you, I understand, have been collecting butterflies. And I tell you, pleasure and pain have nothing to do with heaven or hell. Pleasure and pain—bah! What is your theologian's ecstasy but Mahomet's houri in the dark? This store which men and women set on pleasure and pain, Prendick, is the mark of the beast upon them,—the mark of the beast from which they came! Pain, pain and pleasure, they are for us only so long as we wriggle in the dust.

"You see, I went on with this research just the way it led me. That is the only way I ever heard of true research going. I asked a question, devised some method of obtaining an answer, and got a fresh question. Was this possible or that possible? You cannot imagine what this means to an investigator, what an intellectual passion grows upon him! You cannot imagine the strange, colourless delight of these intellectual desires! The thing before you is no longer an animal, a fellow-creature, but a problem! Sympathetic pain,—all I know of it I remember as a thing I used to suffer from years ago. I wanted—it was the one thing I wanted—to find out the extreme limit of plasticity in a living shape."

"But," said I, "the thing is an abomination—"

"To this day I have never troubled about the ethics of the matter," he continued. "The study of Nature makes a man at last as remorseless as Nature. I have gone on, not heeding anything but the question I was pursuing; and the material has—dripped into the huts yonder. It is nearly eleven years since we came here, I and Montgomery and six Kanakas. I remember the green stillness of the island and the empty ocean about us, as though it was yesterday. The place seemed waiting for me.

"The stores were landed and the house was built. The Kanakas founded some huts near the ravine. I went to work here upon what I had brought with me. There were some disagreeable things happened at first. I began with a sheep, and killed it after a day and a half by a slip of the scalpel. I took another sheep, and made a thing of pain and fear and left it bound up to heal. It looked quite human to me when I had finished it; but when I went to it I was discontented with it. It remembered me, and was terrified beyond imagination; and it had no more than the wits of a sheep. The more I looked at it the clumsier it seemed, until at last I put the monster out of its misery. These animals without courage, these fear-haunted, pain-driven things, without a spark of pugnacious energy to face torment,—they are no good for man-making.

"Then I took a gorilla I had; and upon that, working with infinite care and mastering difficulty after difficulty, I made my first man. All the week, night and day, I moulded him. With him it was chiefly the brain that needed moulding; much had to be added, much changed. I thought him a fair specimen of the negroid type when I had finished him, and he lay bandaged, bound, and motionless before me. It was only when his life was assured that I left him and came into this room again, and found Montgomery much as you are. He had heard some of the cries as the thing grew human,—cries like those that disturbed *you* so. I didn't take him completely into my confidence at first. And the Kanakas too, had realised something of it. They were scared out of their wits by the sight of me. I got Montgomery over to me—in a way; but I and he had the hardest job to prevent the Kanakas deserting. Finally they did; and so we lost the yacht. I spent many days educating the brute,—altogether I had him for three or four months. I taught him the rudiments of English; gave him ideas of counting; even made the thing read the alphabet. But at that he was slow, though I've met with idiots slower. He began with a clean sheet, mentally; had no memories left in his mind of what he had been. When his scars were quite healed, and he was no longer anything but painful and stiff, and able to converse a little, I took him yonder and introduced him to the Kanakas as an interesting stowaway.

"They were horribly afraid of him at first, somehow,—which offended me rather, for I was conceited about him; but his ways seemed so mild, and he was so abject, that after a time they received him and took his education in hand. He was quick to learn, very imitative and adaptive, and built himself a hovel rather better, it seemed to me, than their own shanties. There was one among the boys a bit of a missionary, and he taught the thing to read, or at least to pick out letters, and gave him some rudimentary ideas of morality; but it seems the beast's habits were not all that is desirable.

"I rested from work for some days after this, and was in a mind to write an account of the whole affair to wake up English physiology. Then I came upon the creature squatting up in a tree and gibbering at two of the Kanakas who had been teasing him. I threatened him, told him the inhumanity of such a proceeding, aroused his sense of shame, and came home resolved to do better before I took my work back to England. I have been doing better. But somehow the things drift back again: the stubborn beast-flesh grows day by day back again. But I mean to do better things still. I mean to conquer that. This puma—

"But that's the story. All the Kanaka boys are dead now; one fell overboard of the launch, and one died of a wounded heel that he poisoned in some way with plant-juice. Three went away in the yacht, and I suppose and hope were drowned. The other one—was killed. Well, I have replaced them. Montgomery went on much as you are disposed to do at first, and then—

"What became of the other one?" said I, sharply,—"the other Kanaka who was killed?"

"The fact is, after I had made a number of human creatures I made a Thing—" He hesitated.

"Yes?" said I.

"It was killed."

"I don't understand," said I; "do you mean to say—"

"It killed the Kanaka—yes. It killed several other things that it caught. We chased it for a couple of days. It only got loose by accident—I never meant it to get away. It wasn't finished. It was purely an experiment. It was a limbless thing, with a horrible face, that writhed along the ground in a serpentine fashion. It was immensely strong, and in infuriating pain. It lurked in the woods for some days, until we hunted it; and then it wriggled into the northern part of the island, and we divided the party to close in upon it. Montgomery insisted upon coming with me. The man had a rifle; and when his body was found, one of the barrels was curved into the shape of an S and very nearly bitten through. Montgomery shot the thing. After that I stuck to the ideal of humanity—except for little things."

He became silent. I sat in silence watching his face.

"So for twenty years altogether—counting nine years in England—I have been going on; and there is still something in everything I do that defeats me, makes me dissatisfied, challenges me to further effort. Sometimes I rise above my level, sometimes I fall below it; but always I fall short of the things I dream. The human shape I can get now, almost with ease, so that it is lithe and graceful, or thick and strong; but often there is trouble with the hands and the claws,—painful things, that I dare not shape too freely. But it is in the subtle grafting and reshaping one must needs do to the brain that my trouble lies. The intelligence is often oddly low, with unaccountable blank ends, unexpected gaps. And least satisfactory of all is something that I cannot touch, somewhere—I cannot determine where—in the seat of the emotions. Cravings, instincts, desires that harm humanity, a strange hidden reservoir to burst forth suddenly and inundate the whole being of the creature with anger, hate, or fear. These creatures of mine seemed strange and uncanny to you so soon as you began to observe them; but to me, just after I make them, they seem to be indisputably human beings. It's afterwards, as I observe them, that the persuasion fades. First one animal trait, then another, creeps to the surface and stares out at me. But I will conquer yet! Each time I dip a living creature into the bath of burning pain, I say, 'This time I will burn out all the animal; this time I will make a rational creature of my own!' After all, what is ten years? Men have been a hundred thousand in the making." He thought darkly. "But I am drawing near the fastness. This puma of mine—" After a silence, "And they revert. As soon as my hand is taken from them the beast begins to creep back, begins to assert itself again." Another long silence.

"Then you take the things you make into those dens?" said I.

"They go. I turn them out when I begin to feel the beast in them, and presently they wander there. They all dread this house and me. There is a kind of travesty of humanity over there. Montgomery knows about it, for he interferes in their affairs. He has trained one or two of them to our service. He's ashamed of it, but I believe he half likes some of those beasts. It's his business, not mine. They only sicken me with a sense of failure. I take no interest in them. I fancy they follow in the lines the Kanaka missionary marked out, and have a kind of mockery of a rational life, poor beasts! There's something they call the Law. Sing hymns about 'all thine.' They build themselves their dens, gather fruit, and pull herbs—marry even. But I can see through it all, see into their very souls, and see there nothing but the souls of beasts, beasts that perish, anger and the lusts to live and gratify themselves.—Yet they're odd; complex, like everything else alive. There is a kind of upward striving in them, part vanity, part waste sexual emotion, part waste curiosity. It only mocks me. I have some hope of this puma. I have worked hard at her head and brain—

"And now," said he, standing up after a long gap of silence, during which we had each pursued our own thoughts, "what do you think? Are you in fear of me still?"

I looked at him, and saw but a white-faced, white-haired man, with calm eyes. Save for his serenity, the touch almost of beauty that resulted from his set tranquillity and his magnificent build, he might have passed muster among a hundred other comfortable old gentlemen. Then I shivered. By way of answer to his second question, I handed him a revolver with either hand.

"Keep them," he said, and snatched at a yawn. He stood up, stared at me for a moment, and smiled. "You have had two eventful days," said he. "I should advise some sleep. I'm glad it's all clear. Good-night." He thought me over for a moment, then went out by the inner door.

I immediately turned the key in the outer one. I sat down again; sat for a time in a kind of stagnant mood, so weary, emotionally, mentally, and physically, that I could not think beyond the point at which he had left me. The black window stared at me like an eye. At last with an effort I put out the light and got into the hammock. Very soon I was asleep.

A THOUSAND DEATHS

(1899)

Jack London

I had been in the water about an hour, and cold, exhausted, with a terrible cramp in my right calf, it seemed as though my hour had come. Fruitlessly struggling against the strong ebb tide, I had beheld the maddening procession of the water-front lights slip by; but now I gave up attempting to breast the stream and contented myself with the bitter thoughts of a wasted career, now drawing to a close.

It had been my luck to come of good, English stock, but of parents whose account with the bankers far exceeded their knowledge of child-nature and the rearing of children. While born with a silver spoon in my mouth, the blessed atmosphere of the home circle was to me unknown. My father, a very learned man and a celebrated antiquarian, gave no thought to his family, being constantly lost in the abstractions of his study;

while my mother, noted far more for her good looks than her good sense, sated herself with the adulation of the society in which she was perpetually plunged. I went through the regular school and college routine of a boy of the English bourgeois, and as the years brought me increasing strength and passions, my parents suddenly became aware that I was possessed of an immortal soul, and endeavored to draw the curb. But it was too late; I perpetrated the wildest and most audacious folly, and was disowned by my people, ostracized by the society I had so long outraged, and with the thousand pounds my father gave me, with the declaration that he would neither see me again nor give me more, I took a first-class passage to Australia.

Since then my life had been one long peregrination—from the Orient to the Occident, from the Arctic to the Antarctic—to find myself at last, an able seaman at thirty, in the full vigor of my manhood, drowning in San Francisco bay because of a disastrously successful attempt to desert my ship.

My right leg was drawn up by the cramp, and I was suffering the keenest agony. A slight breeze stirred up a choppy sea, which washed into my mouth and down my throat, nor could I prevent it. Though I still contrived to keep afloat, it was merely mechanical, for I was rapidly becoming unconscious. I have a dim recollection of drifting past the sea-wall, and of catching a glimpse of an up-river steamer's star-board light; then everything became a blank.

I heard the low hum of insect life, and felt the balmy air of a spring morning fanning my cheek. Gradually it assumed a rhythmic flow, to whose soft pulsations my body seemed to respond. I floated on the gentle bosom of a summer's sea, rising and falling with dreamy pleasure on each crooning wave. But the pulsations grew stronger; the humming, louder; the waves, larger, fiercer—I was dashed about on a stormy sea. A great agony fastened upon me. Brilliant, intermittent sparks of light flashed athwart my inner consciousness; in my ears there was the sound of many waters; then a sudden snapping of an intangible something, and I awoke.

The scene, of which I was protagonist, was a curious one. A glance sufficed to inform me that I lay on the cabin floor of some gentleman's yacht, in a most uncomfortable posture. On either side, grasping my arms and working them up and down like pump handles, were two peculiarly clad, dark-skinned creatures. Though conversant with most aboriginal types, I could not conjecture their nationality. Some attachment had been fastened about my head, which connected my respiratory organs with the machine I shall next describe. My nostrils, however, had been closed, forcing me to breathe through the mouth. Foreshortened by the obliquity of my line of vision, I beheld two tubes, similar to small hosing but of different composition, which emerged from my mouth and went off at an acute angle from each other. The first came to an abrupt termination and lay on the floor beside me; the second traversed the floor in numerous coils, connecting with the apparatus I have promised to describe.

In the days before my life had become tangential, I had dabbled not a little in science, and, conversant with the appurtenances and general paraphernalia of the laboratory, I appreciated the machine I now beheld. It was composed chiefly of glass, the construction being of that crude sort which is employed for experimentative purpose. A vessel of water was surrounded by an air chamber, to which was fixed a vertical tube, surmounted by a globe. In the center of this was a vacuum gauge. The water in the tube moved upward and downward, creating alternate inhalations and exhalations, which were in turn communicated to me through the hose. With this, and the aid of the men who pumped my arms so vigorously, had the process of breathing been artificially carried on, my chest rising and falling and my lungs expanding and contracting, till nature could be persuaded to again take up her wonted labor.

As I opened my eyes the appliance about my head, nostrils and mouth was removed. Draining a stiff three fingers of brandy, I staggered to my feet to thank my preserver, and confronted—my father. But long years of fellowship with danger had taught me self-control, and I waited to see if he would recognize me. Not so; he saw in me no more than a runaway sailor and treated me accordingly.

Leaving me to the care of the blackies, he fell to revising the notes he had made on my resuscitation. As I ate of the handsome fare served up to me, confusion began on deck, and from the chanteys of the sailors and the rattling of blocks and tackles I surmised that we were getting under way. What a lark! Off on a cruise with my recluse father into the wide Pacific! Little did I realize, as I laughed to myself, which side the joke was to be on. Aye, had I known, I would have plunged overboard and welcomed the dirty fo'c'sle from which I had just escaped.

I was not allowed on deck till we had sunk the Farallones and the last pilot boat. I appreciated this forethought on the part of my father and made it a point to thank him heartily, in my bluff seaman's manner. I could not suspect that he had his own ends in view, in thus keeping my presence secret to all save the crew. He told me briefly of my rescue by his sailors, assuring me that the obligation was on his side, as my appearance had been most opportune. He had constructed the apparatus for the vindication of a theory concerning certain biological phenomena, and had been waiting for an opportunity to use it.

"You have proved it beyond all doubt," he said; then added with a sigh, "but only in the small matter of drowning."

But, to take a reef in my yarn—he offered me an advance of two pounds on my previous wages to sail with him, and this I considered handsome, for he really did not need me. Contrary to my expectations, I did not join the sailors' mess, for'ard, being assigned to a comfortable stateroom and eating at the captain's table. He had perceived that I was no common sailor, and I resolved to take this chance for reinstating myself in his good graces. I wove a fictitious past to account for my education and present position, and did my best to come in touch with him. I was not long in disclosing a predilection for scientific pursuits, nor he in appreciating my aptitude. I became his assistant, with a corresponding increase in wages, and before long, as he grew confidential and expounded his theories, I was as enthusiastic as himself.

The days flew quickly by, for I was deeply interested in my new studies, passing my waking hours in his well-stocked library, or listening to his plans and aiding him in his laboratory work. But we were forced to forego many enticing experiments, a rolling ship not being exactly the proper place for delicate or intricate work. He promised me, however, many delightful hours in the magnificent laboratory for which we were bound. He had taken possession of an uncharted South Sea island, as he said, and turned it into a scientific paradise.

We had not been on the island long, before I discovered the horrible mare's nest I had fallen into. But before I describe the strange things which came to pass, I must briefly outline the causes which culminated in as startling an experience as ever fell to the lot of man.

Late in life, my father had abandoned the musty charms of antiquity and succumbed to the more fascinating ones embraced under the general head of biology. Having been thoroughly grounded during his youth in the fundamentals, he rapidly explored all the higher branches as far as the scientific world had gone, and found himself on the no man's land of the unknowable. It was his intention to preempt some of this unclaimed territory, and it was at this stage of his investigations that we had been thrown together. Having a good brain, though I say it myself, I had mastered his speculations and methods of reasoning, becoming almost as mad as himself. But I should not say this. The marvelous results we afterward obtained can only go to prove his sanity. I can but say that he was the most abnormal specimen of cold-blooded cruelty I have ever seen.

After having penetrated the dual mysteries of physiology and psychology, his thought had led him to the verge of a great field, for which, the better to explore, he began studies in higher organic chemistry, pathology, toxicology and other sciences and sub-sciences rendered kindred as accessories to his speculative hypotheses. Starting from the proposition that the direct cause of the temporary and permanent arrest of vitality was due to the coagulation of certain elements and compounds in the protoplasm, he had isolated and subjected these various substances to innumerable experiments. Since the temporary arrest of vitality in an organism brought coma, and a permanent arrest death, he held that by artificial means this coagulation of the protoplasm could be retarded, prevented, and even overcome in the extreme states of solidification. Or, to do away with the technical nomenclature, he argued that death, when not violent and in which none of the organs had suffered injury, was merely suspended vitality; and that, in such instances, life could be induced to resume its functions by the use of proper methods. This, then, was his idea: To discover the method—and by practical experimentation prove the possibility—of renewing vitality in a structure from which life had seemingly fled. Of course, he recognized the futility of such endeavor after decomposition had set in; he must have organisms which but the moment, the hour, or the day before, had been quick with life. With me, in a crude way, he had proved this theory. I was really drowned, really dead, when picked from the water of San Francisco bay—but the vital spark had been renewed by means of his aerotherapeutical apparatus, as he called it.

Now to his dark purpose concerning me. He first showed me how completely I was in his power. He had sent the yacht away for a year, retaining only his two blackies, who were utterly devoted to him. He then made an exhaustive review of his theory and outlined the method of proof he had adopted, concluding with the startling announcement that I was to be his subject.

I had faced death and weighed my chances in many a desperate venture, but never in one of this nature. I can swear I am no coward, yet this proposition of journeying back and forth across the borderland of death put the yellow fear upon me. I asked for time, which he granted, at the same time assuring me that but one course was open—I must submit. Escape from the island was out of the question; escape by suicide was not to be entertained, though really preferable to what it seemed I must undergo; my only hope was to destroy my captors. But this latter was frustrated through the precautions taken by my father. I was subjected to a constant surveillance, even in my sleep being guarded by one or the other of the blacks.

Having pleaded in vain, I announced and proved that I was his son. It was my last card, and I had placed all my hopes upon it. But he was inexorable; he was not a father but a scientific machine. I wonder yet how it ever came to pass that he married my mother or begat me, for there was not the slightest grain of emotion in his make-up. Reason was all in all to him, nor could he understand such things as love or sympathy in others, except as petty weaknesses which should be overcome. So he informed me that in the beginning he had given me life, and who had better right to take it away than he? Such, he said, was not his desire, however; he merely wished to borrow it occasionally, promising to return it at the appointed time. Of course, there was a liability of mishaps, but I could do no more than take the chances, since the affairs of men were full of such.

The better to insure success, he wished me to be in the best possible condition, so I was dieted and trained like a great athlete before a decisive contest. What could I do? If I had to undergo the peril, it were best to be in good shape. In my intervals of relaxation he allowed me to assist in the arranging of the apparatus and in the various subsidiary experiments. The interest I took in all such operations can be imagined. I mastered the work as thoroughly as he, and often had the pleasure of seeing some of my suggestions or alterations put into effect. After such events I would smile grimly, conscious of officiating at my own funeral.

He began by inaugurating a series of experiments in toxicology. When all was ready, I was killed by a stiff dose of strychnine and allowed to lie dead for some twenty hours.

During that period my body was dead, absolutely dead. All respiration and circulation ceased; but the frightful part of it was, that while the protoplasmic coagulation proceeded, I retained consciousness and was enabled to study it in all its ghastly details.

The apparatus to bring me back to life was an air-tight chamber, fitted to receive my body. The mechanism was simple—a few valves, a rotary shaft and crank, and an electric motor. When in operation, the interior atmosphere was alternately condensed and rarefied, thus communicating to my lungs an artificial respiration without the agency of the hosing previously used. Though my body was inert, and, for all I knew, in the first stages of decomposition, I was cognizant of everything that transpired. I knew when they placed me in the chamber, and though all my senses were quiescent, I was aware of hypodermic injections of a compound to react upon the coagulatory process. Then the chamber was closed and the machinery started. My anxiety was terrible; but the circulation became gradually restored, the different organs began to carry on their respective functions, and in an hour's time I was eating a hearty dinner.

It cannot be said that I participated in this series, nor in the subsequent ones, with much verve; but after two ineffectual attempts at escape, I began to take quite an interest. Besides, I was becoming accustomed. My father was beside himself at his success, and as the months rolled by his speculations took wilder and yet wilder flights. We ranged through the three great classes of poisons—the neurotics, the gaseous, and the irritants—but carefully avoided some of the mineral irritants and passed the whole group of corrosives. During the poison régime I became quite accustomed to dying, and had but one mishap to shake my growing confidence. Scarifying a number of lesser blood vessels in my arm, he introduced a minute quantity of that most frightful of poisons, the arrow poison, or curare. I lost consciousness at the start, quickly followed by the cessation of respiration and circulation, and so far had the solidification of the protoplasm advanced, that he gave up all hope. But at the last moment he applied a discovery he had been working upon, receiving such encouragement as to redouble his efforts.

In a glass vacuum, similar but not exactly like a Crookes' tube, was placed a magnetic field. When penetrated by polarized light it gave no phenomena of phosphorescence nor of rectilinear projection of atoms, but emitted non-luminous rays, similar to the X ray. While the X ray could reveal opaque objects hidden in dense mediums, this was possessed of far subtler penetrations. By this he photographed my body, and found on the negative an infinite number of blurred shadows, due to the chemical and electric motions still going on. This was an infallible proof that the rigor mortis in which I lay was not genuine; that is, those mysterious forces, those delicate bonds which held my soul to my body, were still in action. The resultants of all other poisons were unapparent, save those of mercurial compounds, which usually left me languid for several days.

Another series of delightful experiments was with electricity. We verified Tesla's assertion that high currents were utterly harmless by passing 100,000 volts through my body. As this did not affect me, the current was reduced to 2,500, and I was quickly electrocuted. This time he ventured so far as to allow me to remain dead, or in a state of suspended vitality, for three days. It took four hours to bring me back.

Once, he superinduced lockjaw; but the agony of dying was so great that I positively refused to undergo similar experiments. The easiest deaths were by asphyxiation, such as drowning, strangling, and suffocation by gas; while those by morphine, opium, cocaine and chloroform, were not at all hard.

Another time, after being suffocated, he kept me in cold storage for three months, not permitting me to freeze or decay. This was without my knowledge, and I was in a great fright on discovering the lapse of time. I became afraid of what he might do with me when I lay dead, my alarm being increased by the predilection he was beginning to betray toward vivisection. The last time I was resurrected, I discovered that he had been tampering with my breast. Though he had carefully dressed and sewed the incisions up, they were so severe that I had to take to my bed for some time. It was during this convalescence that I evolved the plan by which I ultimately escaped.

While feigning unbounded enthusiasm in the work, I asked and received a vacation for my moribund occupation. During this period I devoted myself to laboratory work, while he was too deep in the vivisection of the many animals captured by the blacks to take notice of my work.

It was on these two propositions that I constructed my theory: First, electrolysis, or the decomposition of water into its constituent gases by means of electricity; and, second, by the hypothetical existence of a force, the converse of gravitation, which Astor has named "apergy." Terrestrial attraction, for instance, merely draws objects together but does not combine them; hence, apergy is merely repulsion. Now, atomic or molecular attraction not only draws objects together but integrates them; and it was the converse of this, or a disintegrative force, which I wished to not only discover and produce, but to direct at will. Thus the molecules of hydrogen and oxygen reacting on each other, separate and create new molecules, containing both elements and forming water. Electrolysis causes these molecules to split up and resume their original condition, producing the two gases separately. The force I wished to find must not only do this with two, but with all elements, no matter in what compounds they exist. If I could then entice my father within its radius, he would be instantly disintegrated and sent flying to the four quarters, a mass of isolated elements.

It must not be understood that this force, which I finally came to control, annihilated matter; it merely annihilated form. Nor, as I soon discovered, had it any effect on inorganic structure; but to all organic form it was absolutely fatal. This partiality puzzled me at first, though had I stopped to think deeper I would have seen through it. Since the number of atoms in organic molecules is far greater than in the most complex mineral molecules, organic compounds are characterized by their instability and the ease with which they are split up by physical forces and chemical reagents.

By two powerful batteries, connected with magnets constructed specially for this purpose, two tremendous forces were projected. Considered apart from each other, they were perfectly harmless; but they accomplished their purpose by focusing at an invisible point in mid-air. After practically demonstrating its success, besides narrowly escaping being blown into nothingness, I laid my trap. Concealing the magnets, so that their force made the whole space of my chamber doorway a field of death, and placing by my couch a button by which I could throw on the current from the storage batteries, I climbed into bed.

The blackies still guarded my sleeping quarters, one relieving the other at midnight. I turned on the current as soon as the first man arrived. Hardly had I begun to doze, when I was aroused by a sharp, metallic tinkle. There, on the mid-threshold, lay the collar of Dan, my father's St. Bernard. My keeper ran to pick it up. He disappeared like a gust of wind, his clothes falling to the floor in a heap. There was a slight whiff of ozone in the air, but since the principal gaseous components of his body were hydrogen, oxygen and nitrogen, which are equally colorless and odorless, there was no other manifestation of his departure. Yet when I shut off the current and removed the garments, I found a deposit of carbon in the form of animal charcoal; also other powders, the isolated, solid elements of his organism, such as sulphur, potassium and iron. Resetting the trap, I crawled back to bed. At midnight I got up and removed the remains of the second blacky, and then slept peacefully till morning.

I was awakened by the strident voice of my father, who was calling to me from across the laboratory. I laughed to myself. There had been no one to call him and he had overslept. I could hear him as he approached my room with the intention of rousing me, and so I sat up in bed, the better to observe his translation—perhaps apotheosis were a better term. He paused a moment at the threshold, then took the fatal step. Puff! It was like the wind sighing among the pines. He was gone. His clothes fell in a fantastic heap on the floor. Besides ozone, I noticed the faint, garlic-like odor of phosphorous. A little pile of elementary solids lay among his garments. That was all. The wide world lay before me. My captors were not.

THE THIRD DRUG

(1908)

Edith Nesbit (as E. Bland)

I

Roger Wroxham looked round his studio before he blew out the candle, and wondered whether, perhaps, he looked for the last time. It was large and empty, yet his trouble had filled it and, pressing against him in the prison of those four walls, forced him out into the world, where lights and voices and the presence of other men should give him room to draw back, to set a space between it and him, to decide whether he would ever face it again—he and it alone together. The nature of his trouble is not germane to this story. There was a woman in it, of course, and money, and a friend, and regrets and embarrassments—and all of these reached out tendrils that wove and interwove till they made a puzzle problem of which heart and brain were now weary.

He blew out the candle and went quietly downstairs. It was nine at night, a soft night of May in Paris. Where should he go? He thought of the Seine, and took—an omnibus. When at last it stopped he got off, and so strange was the place to him that it almost seemed as though the trouble itself had been left behind. He did not feel it in the length of three or four streets that he traversed slowly. But in the open space, very light and lively, where he recognised the Taverne de Paris and knew himself in Montmartre, the trouble set its teeth in his heart again, and he broke away from the lamps and the talk to struggle with it in the dark, quiet streets beyond.

A man braced for such a fight has little thought to spare for the details of his surroundings. The next thing that Wroxham knew of the outside world was the fact which he had known for some time that he was not alone in the street. There was someone on the other side of the road keeping pace with him—yes, certainly keeping pace, for, as he slackened his own, the feet on the other pavement also went more slowly. And now they were four feet, not two. Where had the other man sprung from? He had not been there a moment ago. And now, from an archway a little ahead of him, a third man came.

Wroxham stopped. Then three men converged upon him, and, like a sudden magic-lantern picture on a sheet prepared, there came to him all that he had heard and read of Montmartre—dark archways, knives, Apaches, and men who went away from homes where they were beloved and never again returned. He, too—well, if he never returned again, it would be quicker than the Seine, and, in the event of ultramundane possibilities, safer.

He stood still and laughed in the face of the man who first reached him.

"Well, my friend?" said he; and at that the other two drew close.

"Monsieur walks late," said the first, a little confused, as it seemed, by that laugh.

"And will walk still later if it pleases him," said Roger. "Good night, my friends."

"Ah!" said the second, "friends do not say adieu so quickly. Monsieur will tell us the hour."

"I have not a watch," said Roger, quite truthfully.

"I will assist you to search for it," said the third man, and laid a hand on his arm.

Roger threw it off. The man with the hand staggered back.

"The knife searches more surely," said the second.

"No, no," said the third, quickly; "he is too heavy. I for one will not carry him afterwards."

They closed round him, hustling him between them. Their pale, degenerate faces spun and swung round him in the struggle. For there was a struggle. He had not meant that there should be a struggle. Someone would hear—someone would come.

But if any heard none came. The street retained its empty silence; the houses, masked in close shutters, kept their reserve. The four were wrestling, all pressed close together in a writhing bunch, drawing breath hardly through set teeth, their feet slipping and not slipping on the rounded cobble-stones.

It was then that Roger felt the knife. Its point glanced off the cigarette-case in his breast pocket and bit sharply at his inner arm. And at the sting of it Roger knew, suddenly and quite surely, that he did not desire to die. He feigned a reeling weakness, relaxed his grip, swayed sideways, and then suddenly caught the other two in a new grip, crushed their faces together, flung them off, and ran. It was but for an instant that his feet were the only ones that echoed in the street. Then he knew that the others too were running.

He ran more swiftly—he was running now for his life—the life that he had held so cheap three minutes before. And all the streets were empty—empty like dream-streets, with all their windows dark and unhelpful, their doors fast closed against his need. Only now and again he glanced to right or left, if perchance some window might show light to justify a cry for help, some door advance the welcome of an open inch.

There was at last such a door. He did not see it till it was almost behind him. Then there was the drag of the sudden stop—the eternal instant of indecision. Was there time? There must be. He dashed his fingers through the inch-crack, grazing the backs of them, leapt within, drew the door after him, felt madly for a lock or bolt, found a key, and, hanging his whole weight on it, managed to get the door home and turned the key. Then someone cursed breathlessly outside; there was the sound of feet that went away.

He found himself listening, listening, and there was nothing to hear but the silence, and once, before he thought to twist his handkerchief round it, the drip of blood from his hand.

By and by he knew that he was not alone in this house, for from far away there came the faint sound of a footstep, and, quite near, the faint answering echo of it. And at a window high up on the other side of the courtyard a light showed. Light and sound and echo intensified, the light passing window after window, till at last it moved across the courtyard and the little trees threw black shifting shadows as it came towards him—a lamp in the hand of a man.

It was a short, bald man, with pointed beard and bright, friendly eyes. He held the lamp high as he came, and when he saw Roger he drew his breath in an inspiration that spoke of surprise, sympathy, pity.

"Hold! hold!" he said, in a singularly pleasant voice; "there has been a misfortune? You are wounded, monsieur?"

"Apaches," said Roger, and was surprised at the weakness of his own voice.

"Fortunately," said the other, "I am a surgeon. Allow me."

He set the lamp on the step of a closed door, took off Roger's coat, and quickly tied his own handkerchief round the wounded arm.

"Now," he said, "courage! I am alone in the house. No one comes here but me. If you can walk up to my rooms you will save us both much trouble. If you cannot, sit here and I will fetch you a cordial. But I advise you to try to walk. That *porte cochére* is, unfortunately, not very strong, and the lock is a common spring lock, and your friends may return with their friends; whereas the door across the courtyard is heavy, and the bolts are new."

Roger moved towards the heavy door whose bolts were new. The stairs seemed to go on for ever. The doctor lent his arm, but the carved banisters and their lively shadows whirled before Roger's eyes. Also he seemed to be shod with lead, and to have in his legs bones that were red-hot. Then the stairs ceased, and there was light, and a cessation of the dragging of those leaden feet. He was on a couch, and his eyes might close.

When next he saw and heard he was lying at ease, the close intimacy of a bandage clasping his arm, and in his mouth the vivid taste of some cordial.

The doctor was sitting in an arm-chair near a table, looking benevolent through gold-rimmed pince-nez.

"Better?" he said. "No; lie still, you'll be a new man soon."

"I am desolated," said Roger, "to have occasioned you all this trouble."

"In a big house like this," said the doctor, as it seemed a little sadly, "there are many empty rooms, and some rooms which are not empty. There is a bed altogether at your service, monsieur, and I counsel you not to delay in seeking it. You can walk?"

Wroxham stood up. "Why, yes," he said, stretching himself. "I feel, as you say, a new man."

A narrow bed and rush-bottomed chair showed like doll's-house furniture in the large, high, gaunt room to which the doctor led him.

"You are too tired to undress yourself," said the doctor; "rest—only rest," and covered him with a rug, snugly tucked him up, and left him.

"I leave the door open," he said, "in case you should have any fever. Good night. Do not torment yourself. All goes well."

Then he took away the lamp, and Wroxham lay on his back and saw the shadows of the window-frames cast by the street lamps on the high ceiling. His eyes, growing accustomed to the darkness, perceived the carving of the white panelled walls and mantelpiece. There was a door in the room, another door than the one which the doctor had left open. Roger did not like open doors. The other door, however, was closed. He wondered where it led, and whether it were locked. Presently he got up to see. It was locked. He lay down again.

His arm gave him no pain, and the night's adventure did not seem to have overset his nerves. He felt, on the contrary, calm, confident, extraordinarily at ease, and master of himself. The trouble—how could that ever have seemed important? This calmness—it felt like the calmness that precedes sleep. Yet sleep was far from him. What was it that kept sleep away? The bed was comfortable—the pillows soft. What was it? It came to him presently that it was the scent which distracted him, worrying him with a memory that he could not define. A faint scent of—what was it? Perfumery? Yes—and camphor—and something else—something vaguely disquieting. He had not noticed it before he had risen and tried the handle of that other door. But now— He covered his face with the sheet, but through the sheet he smelt it still. He rose and threw back one of the long French windows. It opened with a click and a jar, and he looked across the dark well of the courtyard. He leaned out, breathing the chill pure air of the May night, but when he withdrew his head the scent was there again. Camphor—perfume—and something else. What was it that it reminded him of?

He stood up and went, with carefully-controlled swiftness, towards the open door. He wanted light and a human voice. The doctor was in the room upstairs; he—

The doctor was face to face with him on the landing, not a yard away, moving towards him quietly in shoeless feet.

"I can't sleep," said Wroxham, a little wildly; "it's too dark and—"

"Come upstairs," said the doctor, and Wroxham went.

There was comfort in the large, lighted room. A green-shaded lamp stood on the table.

"What's behind that door," said Wroxham, abruptly—"that door downstairs?"

"Specimens," the doctor answered; "preserved specimens. My line is physiological research. You understand?"

So that was it.

"I feel quite well, you know," said Wroxham, laboriously explaining—"fit as any man —only I can't sleep."

"I see," said the doctor.

"It's the scent from your specimens, I think," Wroxham went on; "there's something about that scent—"

"Yes," said the doctor.

"It's very odd." Wroxham was leaning his elbow on his knee and his chin on his hand.

"I feel so frightfully well—and yet— There's a strange feeling—"

"Yes," said the doctor. "Yes, tell me exactly how you feel."

"I feel," said Wroxham, slowly, "like a man on the crest of a wave."

The doctor stood up.

"You feel well, happy, full of life and energy—as though you could walk to the world's end, and yet—"

"And yet," said Roger, "as though my next step might be my last—as though I might step into a grave."

He shuddered.

"Do you," asked the doctor, anxiously—"do you feel thrills of pleasure—something like the first waves of chloroform—thrills running from your hair to your feet?"

"I felt all that," said Roger, slowly, "downstairs before I opened the window."

The doctor looked at his watch, frowned, and got up quickly. "There is very little time," he said.

Suddenly Roger felt an unexplained thrill of pain.

The doctor went to a long laboratory bench with bottle-filled shelves above it, and on it crucibles and retorts, test tubes, beakers—all a chemist's apparatus—reached a bottle from a shelf, and measured out certain drops into a graduated glass, added water, and stirred it with a glass rod.

"Drink that," he said.

"You may be giving me poison," Roger gasped, his hands at his heart.

"I may," said the doctor. "What do you suppose poison makes you feel like? What do you feel like now?"

"I feel," said Roger, "like death."

Every nerve, every muscle thrilled to a pain not too intense to be underlined by a shuddering nausea.

"Like death," he said again.

"Then drink," cried the doctor, in tones of such cordial entreaty, such evident anxiety, that Wroxham half held his hand out for the glass.

"Drink! Believe me, it is your only chance."

Again the pain swept through him like an electric current. The beads of sweat sprang out on his forehead.

"That wound," the doctor pleaded, standing over him with the glass held out. "For Heaven's sake, drink! Don't you understand, man? You are poisoned. Your wound—"

"The knife?" Wroxham murmured, and as he spoke his eyes seemed to swell in his head, and his head itself to grow enormous. "Do you know the poison—and its antidote?"

"I know all." The doctor soothed him. "Drink, then, my friend."

As the pain caught him again in a clasp more close than any lover's he clutched at the glass and drank. The drug met the pain and mastered it. Roger, in the ecstasy of pain's cessation, saw the world fade and go out in a haze of vivid violet.

II

Faint films of lassitude shot with contentment wrapped him round. He lay passive as a man lies in the convalescence that follows a long fight with Death.

"I'm better now," he said, in a voice that was a whisper—tried to raise his hand from where it lay helpless in his sight, failed, and lay looking at it in confident repose—"much better."

"Yes," said the doctor, and his pleasant, soft voice had grown softer, pleasanter. "You are now in the second stage. An interval is necessary before you can pass to the third. I will enliven the interval by conversation. Is there anything you would like to know?"

"Nothing," said Roger; "I am quite happy—quite contented."

"This is very interesting," said the doctor. "Tell me exactly how you feel."

Roger faintly and slowly told him.

"Ah!" the doctor said, "I have not before heard this. You are the only one of them all who ever passed the first stage. The others—"

"The others?" said Roger, but he did not care much about the others.

"The others," said the doctor, frowning, "were unsound. Decadent students, degenerate Apaches. You are highly trained—in fine physical condition. And your brain! The Lord be good to the Apaches who so delicately excited it to just the degree of activity needed for my purpose."

"The others?" Wroxham insisted.

"The others? They are in the room whose door was locked. Look—you should be able to see them. The second drug should lay your consciousness before me like a sheet of white paper on which I can write what I choose. If I choose that you should see my specimens— *Allons donc*. I have no secrets from you now. Look—look—strain your eyes. In theory I know all that you can do and feel and see in this second stage. But practically— Enlighten me—look—shut your eyes and look!"

Roger closed his eyes and looked. He saw the gaunt, uncarpeted staircase, the open doors of the big rooms, passed to the locked door, and it opened at his touch. The room inside was, like the other, spacious and panelled. A lighted lamp with a blue shade hung from the ceiling, and below it an effect of spread whiteness. Roger looked. There were things to be seen.

With a shudder he opened his eyes on the doctor's delightful room, the doctor's intent face.

"What did you see?" the doctor asked. "Tell me!"

"Did you kill them all?" Roger asked back.

"They died—of their own inherent weakness," the doctor said. "And you saw them?"

"I saw," said Roger, "the quiet people lying all along the floor in their death clothes—the people who have come in at that door of yours that is a trap—for robbery, or curiosity, or shelter—and never gone out any more."

"Right," said the doctor. "Right. My theory is proved at every point. You can see what I choose you to see. Yes; decadents all. It was in embalming that I was a specialist before I began these other investigations."

"What," Roger whispered—"what is it all for?"

"To make the superman," said the doctor. "I will tell you."

He told. It was a long story—the story of a man's life, a man's work, a man's dreams, hopes, ambitions.

"The secret of life," the doctor ended. "That is what all the alchemists sought. They sought it where Fate pleased. I sought it where I have found it—in death."

"And the secret is?" asked Roger.

"I have told you," said the doctor, impatiently; "it is in the third drug that life—splendid, superhuman life—is found. I have tried it on animals. Always they became perfect, all that an animal should be. And more, too—much more. They were too perfect, too near humanity. They looked at me with human eyes. I could not let them live. Such animals it is not necessary to embalm. I had a laboratory in those days—and assistants. They called me the Prince of Vivisectors."

The man on the sofa shuddered.

"What is the third drug?" Roger asked, lying limp and flat on his couch.

"It is the Elixir of Life," said the doctor. "I am not its discoverer; the old alchemists knew it well, but they failed because they sought to apply the elixir to a normal—that is, a diseased and faulty—body. I knew better. One must have first a body abnormally healthy, abnormally strong. Then, not the elixir, but the two drugs that prepare. The first excites prematurely the natural conflict between the principles of life and death, and then, just at the point where Death is about to win his victory, the second drug intensifies life so that it conquers—intensifies, and yet chastens. Then the whole life of the subject, risen to an ecstasy, falls prone in an almost voluntary submission to the coming super-life. Submission—submission!

The garrison must surrender before the splendid conqueror can enter and make the citadel his own. Do you understand? Do you submit?"

"I submit," said Roger, for, indeed, he did. "But—soon—quite soon—I will not submit."

He was too weak to be wise, or those words had remained unspoken.

The doctor sprang to his feet.

"It works too quickly!" he cried. "Everything works too quickly with you. Your condition is too perfect. So now I bind you."

From a drawer beneath the bench where the bottles gleamed the doctor drew rolls of bandages—violet, like the haze that had drowned, at the urgence of the second drug, the consciousness of Roger. He moved, faintly resistant, on his couch. The doctor's hands, most gently, most irresistibly, controlled his movement.

"Lie still," said the gentle, charming voice. "Lie still; all is well." The clever, soft hands were unrolling the bandages—passing them round arms and throat—under and over the soft narrow couch. "I cannot risk your life, my poor boy. The least movement of yours might ruin everything. The third drug, like the first, must be offered directly to the blood which absorbs it. I bound the first drug as an unguent upon your knife-wound."

The swift hands passed the soft bandages back and forth, over and under—flashes of violet passed to and fro in the air like the shuttle of a weaver through his warp. As the bandage clasped his knees Roger moved.

"For Heaven's sake, no!" the doctor cried; "the time is so near. If you cease to submit it is death."

With an incredible accelerated swiftness he swept the bandages round and round knees and ankles, drew a deep breath—stood upright.

"I must make an incision," he said—"in the head this time. It will not hurt. See! I spray it with the Constantia Nepenthe; that also I discovered. My boy, in a moment you know all things—you are as a god. Be patient. Preserve your submission."

Roger did not feel the knife that made the cross cut on his temple, but he felt the hot spurt of blood that followed the cut; he felt the cool flap of a plaster spread with some sweet, clean-smelling unguent that met the blood and stanched it. There was a moment—or was it hours?—of nothingness. Then from that cut on his forehead there seemed to radiate threads of infinite length, and of a strength that one could trust to—threads that linked one to all knowledge past and present. He felt that he controlled all wisdom, as a driver controls his four-in-hand. Knowledge, he perceived, belonged to him, as the air belongs to the eagle. He swam in it, as a great fish, in a limitless ocean.

He opened his eyes and met those of the doctor, who sighed as one to whom breath has grown difficult.

"Ah, all goes well. Oh, my boy, was it not worth it? What do you feel?"

"I. Know. Everything," said Roger, with full stops between the words.

"Everything? The future?"

"No. I know all that man has ever known."

"Look back—into the past. See someone. See Pharaoh. You see him—on his throne?"

"Not on his throne. He is whispering in a corner of his great gardens to a girl who is the daughter of a water-carrier."

"Bah! Any poet of my dozen decadents who lie so still could have told me that. Tell me secrets—the *Masque de Fer*."

The other told a tale, wild and incredible, but it satisfied the listener.

"That too—it might be imagination. Tell me the name of the woman I loved and—"

The echo of the name of the anæsthetic came to Roger, and "Constantia," said he, in an even voice.

"Ah!" the doctor cried, "now I see you know all things. It was not murder. I hoped to dower her with all the splendors of the super-life."

"Her bones lie under the lilacs, where you used to kiss her in the spring," said Roger, quite without knowing what it was that he was going to say.

"It is enough," the doctor cried. He sprang up, ranged certain bottles and glasses on a table convenient to his chair. "You know all things. It was not a dream, this, the dream of my life. It is true. It is a fact accomplished. Now I, too, will know all things. I will be as the gods."

He sought among leather cases on a far table and came back swiftly into the circle of light that lay below the green-shaded lamp.

Roger, floating contentedly on the new sea of knowledge that seemed to support him, turned eyes on the trouble that had driven him out of that large, empty studio so long ago, so far away. His new-found wisdom laughed at that problem, laughed and solved it. "To end that trouble I must do so-and-so, say such-and-such," Roger told himself again and again.

And now the doctor, standing by the table, laid on it his pale, plump hand outspread. He drew a knife from a case—a long, shiny knife—and scored his hand across and across its back, as a cook scores pork for cooking. The slow blood followed the cuts in beads and lines.

Into the cuts he dropped a green liquid from a little bottle, replaced its stopper, bound up his hand, and sat down.

"The beginning of the first stage," he said; "almost at once I shall begin to be a new man. It will work quickly. My body, like yours, is sane and healthy."

There was a long silence.

"Oh, but this is good," the doctor broke in to say. "I feel the hand of Life sweeping my nerves like harp-strings."

Roger had been thinking, the old common sense that guides an ordinary man breaking through this consciousness of illimitable wisdom. "You had better," he said, "unbind me; when the hand of Death sweeps your nerves you may need help."

"No," the doctor said, and no, and no, and no many times. "I am afraid of you. You know all things, and even in your body you are stronger than I."

And then suddenly and irresistibly the pain caught him. Roger saw his face contorted with agony, his hands clench on the arm of his chair; and it seemed that either this man was less able to bear pain than he, or that the pain was much more violent than had been his own. And the plump, pale hand, writhing and distorted by anguish, again and again drew near to take the glass that stood ready on the table, and with convulsive self-restraint again and again drew back without it.

The short May night was waning—the shiver of dawn rustled the leaves of the plant whose leaves were like red misshaped hearts.

"Now!" The doctor screamed the word, grasped the glass, drained it, and sank back in his chair. His hand struck the table beside him. Looking at his limp body and head thrown back one could almost see the cessation of pain, the coming of kind oblivion.

III

The dawn had grown to daylight, a poor, grey, rain-stained daylight, not strong enough to pierce the curtains and persiennes, and yet not so weak but that it could mock the lamp, now burnt low and smelling vilely.

Roger lay very still on his couch, a man wounded, anxious, and extravagantly tired. In those hours of long, slow dawning, face to face with the unconscious figure in the chair, he had felt, slowly and little by little, the recession of that sea of knowledge on which he had felt himself float in such large content. The sea had withdrawn itself, leaving him high and dry on the shore of the normal. The only relic that he had clung to and that he still grasped was the answer to the problem of the trouble—the only wisdom that he had put into words. These words remained to him, and he knew that they held wisdom—very simple wisdom, too.

"To end the trouble I must do so-and-so and say such-and-such."

Slowly a dampness spread itself over Wroxham's forehead and tingled among the roots of his hair. He writhed in his bonds. They held fast. He could not move hand or foot. Only his head could turn a little, so that he could at will see the doctor or not see him. A shaft of desolate light pierced the persienne at its hinge and rested on the table, where an overturned glass lay.

Wroxham thrilled from head to foot. The body in the chair stirred—hardly stirred—shivered, rather—and a very faint, far-away voice said:—

"Now the third—give me the third."

"What?" said Roger, stupidly; and he had to clear his throat twice before he could say even that

"The moment is now," said the doctor. "I remember all. I made you a god. Give me the third drug."

"Where is it?" Roger asked.

"It is at my elbow," the doctor murmured. "I submit—I submit. Give me the third drug, and let me be as you are."

"As I am?" said Roger. "You forget, I am bound."

"Break your bonds," the doctor urged, in a quick, small voice. "I trust you now. You are stronger than all men, as you are wiser. Stretch your muscles, and the bandages will fall asunder like snow-wreaths."

"It is too late," Wroxham said, and laughed; "all that is over. I am not wise any more, and I have only the strength of a man. I am tired and wounded. I cannot break my bonds—I cannot help you!"

"But if you cannot help me—it is death," said the doctor.

"It is death," said Roger. "Do you feel it coming on you?"

"I feel life returning," said the doctor; "it is now the moment—the one possible moment. And I cannot reach it. Oh, give it me—give it me!"

Then Roger cried out suddenly, in a loud voice: "Now, by all that's sacred, you infernal decadent, I am glad that I cannot give it. Yes, if it costs me my life, it's worth it, you madman, so that your life ends too. Now be silent, and die like a man if you have it in you."

Roger lay and watched him, and presently he writhed from the chair to the floor, tearing feebly at it with his fingers, moaned, shuddered, and lay very still.

Of all that befell Roger in that house the worst was now. For now he knew that he was alone with the dead, and between him and death stretched certain hours and days. For the *porte cochère* was locked; the doors of the house itself were locked—heavy doors and the locks new.

"I am alone in the house," the doctor had said. "No one comes here but me."

No one would come. He would die there—he, Roger Wroxham—"poor old Roger Wroxham, who was no one's enemy but his own." Tears pricked his eyes. He shook his head impatiently and they fell from his lashes.

"You fool," he said, "can't *you* die like a man either ?"

Then he set his teeth and made himself lie still. It seemed to him that now Despair laid her hand on his heart. But, to speak truth, it was Hope whose hand lay there. This was so much more than a man should be called on to bear—it could not be true. It was an evil dream. He would awake presently. Or if it were, indeed, real—then someone would come, someone must come. God could not let nobody come to save him.

And late at night, when heart and brain had been stretched almost to the point where both break and let in the sea of madness, someone came.

The interminable day had worn itself out. Roger had screamed, yelled, shouted till his throat was dried up, his lips baked and cracked. No one heard. How should they? The twilight had thickened and thickened till at last it made a shroud for the dead man on the floor by the chair. And there were other dead men in that house; and as Roger ceased to see the one he saw the others—the quiet, awful faces, the lean hands, the straight, stiff limbs laid out one beyond another in the room of death. They at least were not bound. If they should rise in their white wrappings and, crossing that empty sleeping-chamber very softly, come slowly up the stairs—

A stair creaked.

His ears, strained with hours of listening, thought themselves befooled. But his cowering heart knew better.

Again a stair creaked. There was a hand on the door.

"Then it is all over," said Roger in the darkness, "and I am mad."

The door opened very slowly, very cautiously. There was no light. Only the sound of soft feet and draperies that rustled.

Then suddenly a match spurted—light struck at his eyes; a flicker of lit candle-wick steadying to flame. And the things that had come were not those quiet people creeping up to match their death with his death in life, but human creatures, alive, breathing, with eyes that moved and glittered, lips that breathed and spoke.

"He must be here," one said. "Lisette watched all day; he never came out. He must be here—there is nowhere else."

Then they set up the candle-end on the table, and he saw their faces. They were the Apaches who had set on him in that lonely street, and who had sought him here—to set on him again.

He sucked his dry tongue, licked his dry lips, and cried aloud:—

"Here I am! Oh, kill me! For the love of Heaven, brothers, kill me *now*!"

And even before he spoke they had seen him, and seen what lay on the floor.

"He died this morning. I am bound. Kill me, brothers; I cannot die slowly here alone. Oh, kill me, for pity's sake!"

But already the three were pressing on each other at a doorway suddenly grown too narrow. They could kill a living man, but they could not face death, quiet, enthroned.

"For the love of Heaven," Roger screamed, "have pity! Kill me outright! Come back—come back!"

And then, since even Apaches are human, they did come back. One of them caught up the candle and bent over Roger, knife in hand.

"Make sure," said Roger, through set teeth.

"Nom d'un nom," said the Apache, with worse words, and cut the bandages here, and here, and here again, and there, and lower, to the very feet.

Then between them the three men carried the other out and slammed the outer door, and presently set him against a gate post in another street, and went their wicked ways.

And after a time a girl with furtive eyes brought brandy and hoarse muttered kindnesses, and slid away in the shadows.

Against that gate-post the police came upon him. They took him to the address they found on him. When they came to question him he said, "Apaches," and his variations on that theme were deemed sufficient, though not one of them touched truth or spoke of the third drug.

There has never been anything in the papers about that house. I think it is still closed, and inside it still lie in the locked room the very quiet people; and above, there is the room with the narrow couch and the scattered, cut, violet bandages, and the Thing on the floor by the chair, under the lamp that burned itself out in that May dawning.

PART FOUR

From Automatons to Robots

THE NEW FRANKENSTEIN

(1838, abridged)

Anonymous
(attributed to William Maginn)

At the Lazaretto of Genoa, by good fortune, I met with a German who was travelling to the Vatican, in search of Palimpsests. He was scarcely thirty, though he might have passed for ten years older, as is often observed to be the case with those who have devoted much of their time to intense study. His shoulders inclined forward, and his light, flaxen hair hung much below his travelling cap. In his eye there were a wildness, and a glassiness, that bespoke, if not alienation of mind, at least eccentricity.

During our captivity in quarantine, we endeavored to kill time by relating our several adventures; and, one evening, the German, having been called upon to continue our *soirées*, looked round for a while, as though he were waiting for the dictation of some familiar spirit—some monitor, like a second

Socrates; and, with a voice not unresembling a cracked instrument, without preface, in his own idiomatic language, which I will endeavor to translate, thus commenced. [...]

At twelve years of age I was sent to the university of Leipsic, and at fifteen was thoroughly master of the dead languages; but my favorite author was Apuleius, the most romantic of all the ancient writers; and I had got almost by heart the first book of the *Golden Ass*, fully believing in all the wild traditions, the fantastic fables, and visions that it embodied. I thus early divided the life of man into two sets of sensation, but not of equal value in my eyes—a waking sleep, and a sleeping sleep; for it seemed to me, that no one could dispute the superior advantages of the latter in perceiving the only world that is worth perceiving—the imaginary one. But more on this subject hereafter. I only mention it *en passant*, to show that natural philosophy was the great object of my pursuit; and it must be confessed that my tutor—for I had a private one, and seldom attended the public lectures—was admirably qualified to direct this branch of my studies. [...H]e was a man in whose company I never felt quite at ease, and yet was attracted to him by a kind of resistless impetus. Though his features were good, his face was a continual mask; his eyes, dark and lustrous, had in them an extraordinary and supernatural power of inquisition. There was an expression in his countenance the most gloomy, a desolateness the most revolting; the depravity of human nature seemed to him a delight. He was never known to laugh but at what would have moved others to tears. Though he watched over me as if his own life depended on mine, there was hardly a drunken orgy, or a duel, its natural consequence (for you know such take place daily at our universities), that Starnstein—for that was his name—was not the exciting cause. [...]

Being destined for a physician, I repaired, after taking my degree, to Paris, for the purpose of attending the anatomical school. There, however, the only dissections in which I took an interest were those of the brain, which opened to me a new world of speculations,—one of which was, that all our sentiments are nothing more than a subtle kind of mind, and that mind itself is only a modification of matter. [...]

This is a long preface, but it is not foreign to my purpose. I pass over several years of my life, and find myself, in the summer of 18—, at Manheim. It is a curious old town; but I shall not stop to describe it. There it was that I first met with a German translation of that very ingenious history of Frankenstein. Such was my predisposition to a belief in what might have seemed to others prodigious, that I read it without a question or suspicion of its being a fiction. The part, however, that most interested me was the creation; the scene that riveted me most, the creation scene. One night I had the passage open in my hand, when who should walk into the room, arm-in-arm, but my old tutor and that anatomical man—that identical phantasmagoric hero. Starnstein, after having posted him against the oak panelling, turned towards me with one of his old Sardonic grins, pointed to his *protégé*, and slipped off before I could have detained him. [...] Thus he was standing in *propriâ personâ*—the human monster—the restored ruin—the living phantom—the creature without a name. I put my hand before my eyes more than once, to convince myself that it was only a vision such as a feverish imagination conjured up. No rattle-snake could have more fascinated its victim. Yes, there he stood in all his horrible disproportion. His back, as I said, was against the oak wainscot, and his face turned towards me.

Every one knows the effect produced at Guy's Hospital on the medical students, when the corpse of a criminal, under the effect of a powerful galvanic battery, opened its eyes, made one step from the table against which he was placed, erect, and stiff, and fell among them. Such was the feeling I experienced, lest he should advance. Horrible sensations for a time came over me; there was a lurid glare on all the objects in the room. Every thing took, or seemed to take, forms the most fantastic, and to bear some mysterious relation to the strange being before me. But by degrees I became familiarized with his person, and at length thought I should not dislike his company; I therefore took up the lamp, which was one of that classical construction common in Italy, with three depending wicks, and with measured and stealthy steps began to approach my visitor. But this rashness had nearly proved fatal; for that which had given him life had well nigh caused my death: so powerful was the galvanism with which he had been charged, that the shock struck me to the ground like a forked flash of lightning. How long I lay I know not; but, on recovering had learned sufficient prudence to keep a respectful distance from my uninvited guest. There he was in the self-same state. I now examined him steadily; but, instead of his being gifted with the faculties assigned to him by the fair authoress, I found he had only a talismanic existence—was a mere automaton—a machine—a plant without the faculty of motion. His eyes—those yellow eyes so graphically depicted—rolled pendulously in their sunken sockets with a clicking sound not unresembling that of a clock; there was a mechanical trepidation of all his fibers; his nerves quivered, but not with sensibility, and his whole frame had a convulsive motion; whilst his head moved from left to right and right to left, like that of a Chinese mandarin. [...] I pitied him, and said to myself,

I will be a new Frankenstein, and a greater. Like Prospero, I will have my Ariel. I will have my Paradox as Rousseau had his Paradox: the Paradox of Jean-Jacques was the hate of all mankind; mine shall be its admiration, envy, and despair. Frankenstein has left his work imperfect; he has resuscitated a corpse: I will make him what Thyestes was. Yes, I will give him a mind—a mind; yes, with a frantic joy I shouted, till the room re-echoed in loud vibrations, "I will create a mind for you, and such a mind as man, till now, never possessed!" But, how to begin? Would Columbus have discovered the New World had he not overcome all the difficulties he had to encounter from the elements? The *elements*; yes, I had to contend, with elements also. But, how to bring them into subjection was a question might well give me pause. Such an undertaking, till within the last twenty years, would have seemed preposterous and absurd. But, what were all the physicians and metaphysicians of old compared to the philosophers of the new school? There are only two sciences worth cultivating—phrenology and animal magnetism; and it was by their means that I hoped to accomplish the great arcanum.

> [The narrator learns to extract into "phials" the transcendental mental essence of Goethe, Percy Shelley, Samuel Taylor Coleridge, and other supposed great thinkers.]

And now, behold me back to Manheim. No miser, gloating over his stores—no devotee, the possessor of some relic of her patron saint—not Psyche herself, with her precious casket, felt half the raptures I enjoyed as I turned the key of my laboratory. I found my *humuncio* (which means, I believe, a great ugly follow, though not such did he seem to me) posted exactly where

I had left him, with the same mechanical clicking of the eyes, the same oscillation of the frame. And now for my reward.

One by one did I carefully unvalve my phials, and apply the contents to the portals of the brain. [...] Scarcely had I discharged through the olfactory nerves the subtle fluids, when I perceived a strange confusion—a chaos like that of the element, primeval—ensue; and it was easy to perceive that the late arrivals were dissatisfied with their new lodging, finding, doubtless, the apartments not to their taste—too spacious, or too confined for their operations. [...]

I observed a picture in one of the exhibitions at Paris, of I forget what year, the subject of which was Pygmalion and his statue. The artist has chosen the moment when the intensity of the sculptor's passion, which is impassable to love, warmed the marble into life. [...] We might almost see the roseate light of life and youth, as through an alabaster vase, gradually illuminating the perfect form of the nymphalept's creation; and the creator himself contemplating, with delight and wonder, the object of his adoration.

My feelings were different, though not less acute. Motionless as the sculptor, or almost turned to stone as one who had seen Medusa, I stood, all eyes and ears intently fixed on my phenomenon. I saw the glassy and unmeaning glare of *his* eyes give place to the fire of intelligence; the jaundiced, or, rather, livid hue of his cheek, disappear, like the gray of the morning at the uprising of the sun; and, as his lungs became inflated, I could distinctly hear...those sounds so expressive of inspiration and expiration—at measured intervals repeated. I now expected that his first impulse would be to fall down and worship me. But, far from this, what was my vexation and disappointment to mark the look of unutterable scorn and hate with which he regarded me. I think I now hear the floor ringing with his heavy tread, as he paced it backwards and forwards to give circulation to his blood, or as though waiting for the chaos of his thoughts to be reduced to form, ere he attempted to give them utterance. At length he found that distinguishing characteristic of man above all other animals—speech. His voice was hollow, hoarse, and unmodulated, resembling most a pair of asthmatic bellows, or a cracked bassoon, rather than aught human. At first, his utterance, like that of a newborn babe, consisted of inarticulate sounds; but, after running up and down the gamut of the vowels, he put together a variety of words, as by way of practice, and with a slow delivery, and a sort of telegraphic gestures, commenced an harangue. It was composed of all languages, which he called into requisition to express more fully his meaning, or no meaning. I have said, that his delivery was at first slow and difficult, but as he proceeded his facility of pronunciation, his volubility, increased. From a fountain, a rivulet, a river, he poured forth at last a torrent of eloquence, which it was impossible to stop, or almost to make intelligible in words. His merciless imagination flew with the speed of thought from subject to subject, from topic to topic, in a perpetual flux and reflux. It was a labyrinth inextricable—an ill-linked chain of sentences the most involved, parentheses within parentheses—a complication of images and figures the most *outré*. In short, imagine to yourselves the mysticism of Kant, the transcendental philosophy of Coleridge, the metaphysics of Shelley and Goethe, the poetry of Lycophron, mingled and massed together in one jargon, compounded of Greek, Latin, Italian, French, Spanish, German, and English, not to mention tongues known and unknown, and you may form some idea of his style; but of his barbarous pronunciation I can give you none. [...]

I now perceived, to my infinite sorrow, that I had done infinite mischief by this Phrengenesis. Its very creation weighed upon me like remorse upon the guilty. I had now the means of knowing that he had nothing to know, yet knew nothing.

Thus it was that I found out the Theosophs were right in separating entirely the mind from the soul, in considering them diametrically opposite relations—as different principles, as the physic and the phrenic. And I became satisfied that my paradox had no soul. What was to be done now? Should I leave the work imperfect, or endeavor to create one? Was it impious? I scarcely dared put the question. Was not Æsculapius struck dead by the balls of Jove for usurping his power? Were I to evoke the dead—call up the spirit of Adam himself—could he aid me in the undertaking? At which the imagination revolted, and shrank back in terror. Where lay the scent? Was there any tradition on the earth, below the earth, or above the earth, of the Psycogenesis? The more I reflected, the more was I lost and confounded. Abyssus, Abyssum. In the lowest deep there was yet a lower deep of mystery.

> [In order to solve the mystery of the soul, he determines to journey to Egypt.]

Yes, said I, it was in Osiris that the Egyptians supposed to reside all living beings, the genii and the souls of men. To Egypt, then!—there to unravel the mystery.

With my double, my second self, behold me journeying to Alexandria. We ascended the sacred stream of the Nile, and found ourselves among the ruins of ancient Thebes. My first visit was to the cavern in which Belzoni had abode for long twelve months. [...]

At the further extremity of the tomb, I discovered, hollowed out of the rock, a subterranean passage, that descend into the very bowels of the earth. With a delight unutterable, I led the way down the perpendicular stairs, till we came to a lofty door, the entrance to the Necropolis. On each side of this door crouched two colossal sphynxes, as though they were the guardians of the place.

No human foot had for three thousand years profaned the sanctity of that City of the Dead, into which our venturous steps were treading.

[Eventually, they find long hidden burial chambers of vast extent.]

And now for the great arcanum! With hands trembling at the sacrilege I was about to commit, I proceeded to lift off the lid of the sarcophagus. It yielded—slowly yielded—lost its equilibrium, and fell with a heavy crash on the floor. The sound was like that of thunder, and vibrated through the pitchy cavern in long echoes, which, from their repetition, proved it to be of vast extent—perhaps the hades of the Egyptians.

There lay the undecaying corpse of the Adamite king, enwrapt all save the face, in the winding sheet of death. Like to life he was—the hues of life were yet upon his cheek—his eyes were open, and glared on me with more than mortal luster; and, lit by that reflection, made more wan his lips, that moved and quivered, as though he was only waiting for me to address him, ere he replied in answer to my questions.

At that awful moment, the whole Necropolis rocked and shook, as though rent by an earthquake; and there appeared to rise on all sides, out of the ground, a multitude of hideous fiends, vibrating in their hands torches, from which the ruddy fire flew off in flakes. They came in crowds that seemed to thicken as they approached, and joining in one chorus. The words were these:—

"Papai Satan, Papai Satan, Aleppe!"

At that moment all the tombs opened with one accord, and the dead that had slept for ages rose slowly out of them in their shrouds, pressing forward in throngs from the depths of the streets that branched out on every side. They advanced as to a festival; and the light from their eyes was like that of a distant world, whose ashes are burning after it is extinct. [...]

Then, too, the earth seemed to open beneath my feet, and a red spiral flame issued forth, which by degrees assumed a form, a shape. It was, yet it was not, my old tutor. Then I awoke, and found it was—A DREAM.

EXCERPT FROM

THE STEAM MAN OF THE PRAIRIES

(1868)

Edward S. Ellis

Chapter I.
THE TERROR OF THE PRAIRIES

[Startled onlookers see an extraordinary "phenomenon."]

Several miles to the north, something like a gigantic man could be seen approaching. [...]

The distance was too great to scrutinize the phenomenon closely; but they could see that a black volume of smoke issued either from its mouth or the top of its head, while it was drawing behind it a sort of carriage, in which a single man was seated, who appeared to control the movements of the extraordinary being in front of him. [...]

Perhaps at this point a description of the singular mechanism should be given. It was about ten feet in height, measuring to the top of the 'stove-pipe hat,' which was fashioned after the common order of felt coverings, with a broad brim, all painted a shiny black. The face was made of iron, painted a black color, with a pair of fearful eyes, and a tremendous grinning mouth. A whistle-like contrivance was made to answer for the nose. The steam chest proper and boiler, were where the chest in a human being is generally supposed to be, extending also into a large knapsack arrangement over the shoulders and back. A pair of arms, like projections, held the shafts, and the broad flat feet were covered with sharp spikes, as though he were the monarch of base-ball players. The legs were quite long, and the step was natural, except when running, at which time, the bolt uprightness in the figure showed different from a human being.

In the knapsack were the valves, by which the steam or water was examined. In front was a painted imitation of a vest, in which a door opened to receive the fuel, which, together with the water, was carried in the wagon, a pipe running along the shaft and connecting with the boiler.

The lines which the driver held controlled the course of the steam man; thus, by pulling the strap on the right, a deflection was caused which turned it in that direction, and the same acted on the other side. A small rod, which ran along the right shaft, let out or shut off the steam, as was desired, while a cord, running along the left, controlled the whistle at the nose.

The legs of this extraordinary mechanism were fully a yard apart, so as to avoid the danger of its upsetting, and at the same time, there was given more room for the play of the delicate machinery within. Long, sharp, spike-like projections adorned those toes of the immense feet, so that there was little danger of its slipping, while the length of the legs showed that, under favorable circumstances, the steam man must be capable of very great speed. [...]

The door being opened in front, showed a mass of glowing coals lying in the capacious abdomen of the giant; the hissing valves in the knapsack made themselves apparent, and the top of the hat or smoke-stack had a sieve-like arrangement, such as is frequently seen on the locomotive.

There were other little conveniences in the way of creating a draft, and of shutting it off when too great, which could scarcely be understood without a scrutiny of the figure itself.

The steam man was a frightful looking object, being painted of a glossy black, with a pair of white stripes down its legs, and with a face which was intended to be of a flesh color, but, which was really a fearful red.

To give the machinery an abundance of room, the steam man was exceedingly corpulent, swelling out to aldermanic proportions, which, after all, was little out of harmony with its immense height.

The wagon dragged behind was an ordinary four-wheeled vehicle, with springs, and very strong wheels, a framework being arranged, so that when necessary it could be securely covered. To guard against the danger of upsetting it was very broad, with low wheels, which it may be safely said were made to 'hum' when the gentleman got fairly under way.

Such is a brief and imperfect description of this wonderful steam man, as it appeared on its first visit to the Western prairies. [...]

***

Chapter III. A GENIUS

Having progressed thus far in our story, or properly having began in the middle, it is now necessary that we should turn back to the proper starting point.

Several years since a widow woman resided in the outskirts of St. Louis, whose name was Brainerd. Her husband had been a mechanic, noted for his ingenuity, but was killed some five years before by the explosion of a steam boiler. He left behind him a son, hump-backed, dwarfed, but with an amiable disposition that made him a favorite with all with whom he came in contact.

If nature afflicts in one direction she frequently makes amends in another direction, and this dwarf, small and misshapen as he was, was gifted with a most wonderful mind. His mechanical ingenuity bordered on the marvelous. When he went to school, he was a general favorite with teachers and pupils. The former loved him for his sweetness of disposition, and his remarkable proficiency in all studies, while the latter based their affection chiefly upon the fact that he never refused to assist any of them at their tasks, while with the pocket-knife which he carried he constructed toys which were their delight. Some of these were so curious and amusing that, had they been securer by letters patent, they would have brought a competency to him and his widowed mother.

But Johnny never thought of patenting them, although the principal support of himself and mother came from one or two patents, which his father had secured upon inventions, not near the equal of his.

There seemed no limit to his inventive powers. He made a locomotive and then a steamboat, perfect in every part, even to the minutest, using nothing but his knife, hammer, and a small chisel. He constructed a clock with his jack-knife, which kept perfect time, and the articles which he made were wonderfully stared at at fairs, and in show windows, while Johnny modestly pegged away at some new idea. He became a master of the art of telegraphy without assistance from any one using merely a common school philosophy with which to acquire the alphabet. He then made a couple of batteries, ran a line from his window to a neighbor's, insulating it by means of the necks of some bottles, taught the other boy the alphabet, and thus they amused themselves sending messages back and forth.

Thus matters progressed until he was fifteen years of age, when he came home one day, and lay down on the settee by his mother, and gave a great sigh.

"What is the matter?" she inquired.

"I want to make something."

"Why, then, don't you make it?"

"Because I don't know what it shall be; I've fixed up everything I can think of."

"And you are like Alexander, sighing for more worlds to conquer. Is that it?"

"Not exactly, for there is plenty for one to do, if I could only find out what it is."

"Have you ever made a balloon?" The boy laughed.

"You were asking for the cat the other day, and wondering what had become of her. I didn't tell you that the last I saw of her was through the telescope, she being about two miles up in the clouds, and going about fifty miles an hour."

"I thought you looked as though you knew something about her," replied the mother, trying to speak reprovingly, and yet smiling in spite of herself.

"Can't you tell me something to make?" finally asked the boy.

"Yes; there is something I have often thought of, and wonder why it was not made long ago; but you are not smart enough to do it, Johnny."

"Maybe not; but tell me what it is."

"It is a man that shall go by steam!" The boy lay still several minutes without speaking a word and then sprung up. "By George! I'll do it!" And he started out of the room, and was not seen again until night. His mother felt no anxiety. She was pleased; for, when her boy was at work, he was happy, and she knew that he had enough now, to keep him engaged for months to come.

So it proved. He spent several weeks in thought, before he made the first effort toward constructing his greatest success of all. He then enlarged his workshop, and so arranged it, that he would not be in danger of being seen by any curious eyes. He wanted no disturbance while engaged upon this scheme.

From a neighboring foundry, whose proprietor took great interest in the boy, he secured all that he needed. He was allowed full liberty to make what castings he chose, and to construct whatever he wished. And so he began his work.

The great point was to obtain the peculiar motion of a man walking. This secured, the man himself could be easily made, and dressed up in any style required. Finally the boy believed that he had hit upon the true scheme.

So he plied harder than ever, scarcely pausing to take his meals. Finally he got the machine together, fired up, and with feelings somewhat akin to those, of Sir Isaac Newton, when demonstrating the truth or falsity of some of his greatest discoveries, he watched the result.

Soon the legs begin moving up and down, but never a step did they advance! The power was there, sufficient to run a saw-mill, every thing seemed to work, but the thing wouldn't go!

The boy was not ready to despair. He seated himself on the bench beside the machine, and keeping up a moderate supply of steam, throwing in bits of wood, and letting in water, when necessary, he carefully watched the movement for several hours.

Occasionally, Johnny walked slowly back and forth, and with his eyes upon the 'stately stepping,' endeavored to discover the precise nature of that which was lacking in his machine.

At length it came to him. He saw from the first that it was not merely required that the steam man should lift up its feet and put them down again, but there must be a powerful forward impulse at the same moment. This was the single remaining difficulty to be overcome. It required two weeks before Johnny Brainerd succeeded. But it all came clear and unmistakable at last, and in this simple manner:

(Ah! but we cannot be so unjust to the plodding genius as to divulge his secret. Our readers must be content to await the time when the young man sees fit to reveal it himself.)

When the rough figure was fairly in working order, the inventor removed everything from around it, so that it stood alone in the center of his shop. Then he carefully let on steam.

Before he could shut it off, the steam man walked clean through the side of his shop, and fetched up against the corner of the house, with a violence that shook it to its foundation. In considerable trepidation, the youngster dashed forward, shut off steam, and turned it round. As it was too cumbersome for him to manage in any other way, he very cautiously let on steam again, and persuaded it to walk back into the shop, passing through the same orifice through which it had emerged, and came very nigh going out on the opposite side again.

The great thing was now accomplished, and the boy devoted himself to bringing it as near perfection as possible. The principal thing to be feared was its getting out of order, since the slightest disarrangement would be sufficient to stop the progress of the man.

Johnny therefore made it of gigantic size, the body and limbs being no more than 'shells,' used as a sort of screen to conceal the working of the engine. This was carefully painted in the manner mentioned in another place, and the machinery was made as strong and durable as it was possible for it to be. It was so constructed as to withstand the severe jolting to which it necessarily would be subjected, and finally was brought as nearly perfect as it was possible to bring a thing not possessing human intelligence.

By suspending the machine so that its feet were clear of the floor, Johnny Brainerd ascertained that under favorable circumstances it could run very nearly sixty miles an hour. It could easily do that, and draw a car connected to it on the railroad, while on a common road it could make thirty miles, the highest rate at which he believed it possible for a wagon to be drawn upon land with any degree of safety.

It was the boy's intention to run at twenty miles an hour, while where everything was safe, he would demonstrate the power of the invention by occasionally making nearly double that.

As it was, he rightly calculated that when it came forth, it would make a great sensation throughout the entire United States.

THE NEW MOTHER

(1882)

LUCY LANE CLIFFORD

I

The children were always called Blue-Eyes and the Turkey, and they came by the names in this manner. The elder one was like her dear father who was far away at sea, and when the mother looked up she would often say, "Child, you have taken the pattern of your father's eyes," for the father had the bluest of Blue-Eyes, and so gradually his little girl came to be called after them. The younger one had once, while she was still almost a baby, cried bitterly because a turkey that lived near to the cottage, and sometimes wandered into the forest, suddenly vanished in the middle of the winter; and to console her she had been called by its name.

Now the mother and Blue-Eyes and the Turkey and the baby all lived in a lonely cottage on the edge of the forest. The forest was so near that the garden at the back seemed a part of it, and the tall fir-trees were so close that their big black arms stretched over the little thatched roof, and when the moon shone upon them their tangled shadows were all over the white-washed walls.

It was a long way to the village, nearly a mile and a half, and the mother had to work hard and had not time to go often herself to see if there was a letter at the post-office from the dear father, and so very often in the afternoon she used to send the two children. They were very proud of being able to go alone, and often ran half the way to the post office. When they came back tired with the long walk, there would be the mother waiting and watching for them, and the tea would be ready, and the baby crowing with delight; and if by any chance there was a letter from the sea, then they were happy indeed. The cottage room was so cosy: the walls were as white as snow inside as well as out, and against them hung the cake-tin and the baking dish, and the lid of a large saucepan that had been worn out long before the children could remember, and the fish-slice, all polished and shining as bright as silver. On one side of the fireplace, above the bellows hung the almanac, and on the other the clock that always struck the wrong hour and was always running down too soon, but it was a good clock, with a little picture on its face and sometimes ticked away for nearly a week without stopping. The baby's high chair stood in one corner, and in another there was a cupboard hung up high against the wall, in which the mother kept all manner of little surprises. The children often wondered how the things that came out of that cupboard had got into it, for they seldom saw them put there.

"Dear children," the mother said one afternoon late in the autumn, "it is very chilly for you to go to the village, but you must walk quickly, and who knows but what you may bring back a letter saying that dear father is already on his way to England." Then Blue-Eyes and the Turkey made haste and were soon ready to go. "Don't be long," the mother said, as she always did before they started. "Go the nearest way and don't look at any strangers you meet, and be sure you do not talk with them."

"No, mother," they answered; and then she kissed them and called them dear good children, and they joyfully started on their way.

The village was gayer than usual, for there had been a fair the day before, and the people who had made merry still hung about the street as if reluctant to own that their holiday was over.

"I wish we had come yesterday," Blue-Eyes said to the Turkey; "then we might have seen something."

"Look there," said the Turkey, and she pointed to a stall covered with gingerbread; but the children had no money. At the end of the street, close to the Blue Lion where the coaches stopped, an old man sat on the ground with his back resting against the wall of a house, and by him, with smart collars round their necks, were two dogs. Evidently they were dancing dogs, the children thought, and longed to see them perform, but they seemed as tired as their master, and sat quite still beside him, looking as if they had not even a single wag left in their tails.

"Oh, I *do* wish we had been here yesterday," Blue-Eyes said again as they went on to the grocer's, which was also the post-office. The post-mistress was very busy weighing out half-pounds of coffee, and when she had time to attend to the children she only just said, "No letter for you to-day," and went on with what she was doing. Then Blue-Eyes and the

Turkey turned away to go home. They went back slowly down the village street, past the man with the dogs again. One dog had roused himself and sat up rather crookedly with his head a good deal on one side, looking very melancholy and rather ridiculous; but on the children went towards the bridge and the fields that led to the forest.

They had left the village and walked some way, and then, just before they reached the bridge, they noticed, resting against a pile of stones by the wayside, a strange dark figure. At first they thought it was some one asleep, then they thought it was a poor woman ill and hungry, and then they saw that it was a strange wild-looking girl, who seemed very unhappy, and they felt sure that something was the matter. So they went and looked at her, and thought they would ask her if they could do anything to help her, for they were kind children and sorry indeed for any one in distress.

The girl seemed to be tall, and was about fifteen years old. She was dressed in very ragged clothes. Round her shoulders there was an old brown shawl, which was torn at the corner that hung down the middle of her back She wore no bonnet, and an old yellow handkerchief which she had tied round her head had fallen backwards and was all huddled up round her neck. Her hair was coal black and hung down uncombed and unfastened, just anyhow. It was not very long, but it was very shiny, and it seemed to match her bright black eyes and dark freckled skin. On her feet were coarse gray stockings and thick shabby boots, which she had evidently forgotten to lace up. She had something hidden away under her shawl, but the children did not know what it was. At first they thought it was a baby, but when, on seeing them coming towards her, she carefully put it under her and sat upon it, they thought they must be mistaken. She sat watching the children approach, and did not move or stir till they were within a yard of her; then she wiped her eyes just as if she had been crying bitterly, and looked up.

The children stood still in front of her for a moment, staring at her and wondering what they ought to do.

"Are you crying?" they asked shyly.

To their surprise she said in a most cheerful voice, "Oh dear, no! Quite the contrary. Are you?"

They thought it rather rude of her to reply in this way, for any one could see that they were not crying. They felt half in mind to walk away; but the girl looked at them so hard with her big black eyes, they did not like to do so till they had said something else.

"Perhaps you have lost yourself?" they said gently.

But the girl answered promptly, "Certainly not. Why, you have just found me. Besides," she added, "I live in the village."

The children were surprised at this, for they had never seen her before, and yet they thought they knew all the village folk by sight.

"We often go to the village," they said, thinking it might interest her.

"Indeed," she answered. That was all; and again they wondered what to do.

Then the Turkey, who had an inquiring mind, put a good straightforward question. "What are you sitting on?" she asked.

"On a peardrum," the girl answered, still speaking in a most cheerful voice, at which the children wondered, for she looked very cold and uncomfortable.

"What is a peardrum?" they asked.

"I am surprised at your not knowing," the girl answered. "Most people in good society have one." And then she pulled it out and showed it to them. It was a curious instrument, a good deal like a guitar in shape; it had three strings, but only two pegs by which to tune them. The third string was never tuned at all, and thus added to the singular effect produced by the village girl's music. And yet, oddly, the peardrum was not played by touching its strings, but by turning a little handle cunningly hidden on one side.

But the strange thing about the peardrum was not the music it made, or the strings, or the handle, but a little square box attached to one side. The box had a little flat lid that appeared to open by a spring. That was all the children could make out at first. They were most anxious to see inside the box, or to know what it contained, but they thought it might look curious to say so.

"It really is a most beautiful thing, is a peardrum," the girl said, looking at it, and speaking in a voice that was almost affectionate.

"Where did you get it?" the children asked.

"I bought it," the girl answered.

"Didn't it cost a great deal of money?" they asked.

"Yes," answered the girl slowly, nodding her head, "it cost a great deal of money. I am very rich," she added.

And this the children thought a really remarkable statement, for they had not supposed that rich people dressed in old clothes, or went about without bonnets. She might at least have done her hair, they thought; but they did not like to say so.

"You don't look rich," they said slowly, and in as polite a voice as possible.

"Perhaps not," the girl answered cheerfully.

At this the children gathered courage, and ventured to

remark, "You look rather shabby"—they did not like to say ragged.

"Indeed?" said the girl in the voice of one who had heard a pleasant but surprising statement. "A little shabbiness is very respectable," she added in a satisfied voice. "I must really tell them this," she continued. And the children wondered what she meant. She opened the little box by the side of the pear-drum, and said, just as if she were speaking to someone who could hear her, "They say I look rather shabby; it is quite lucky, isn't it?"

"Why, you are not speaking to any one!" they said, more surprised than ever.

"Oh dear, yes! I am speaking to them both."

"Both?" they said, wondering.

"Yes. I have here a little man dressed as a peasant, and wearing a wide slouch hat with a large feather, and a little woman to match, dressed in a red petticoat, and a white handkerchief pinned across her bosom. I put them on the lid of the box, and when I play they dance most beautifully. The little man takes off his hat and waves it in the air, and the little woman holds up her petticoat a little bit on one side with one hand, and with the other sends forward a kiss."

"Oh! Let us see; do let us see!" the children cried, both at once.

Then the village girl looked at them doubtfully.

"Let you see!" she said slowly. "Well, I am not sure that I can. Tell me, are you good?"

"Yes, yes," they answered eagerly, "we are very good!"

"Then it's quite impossible," she answered, and resolutely closed the lid of the box.

They stared at her in astonishment.

"But we are good," they cried, thinking she must have misunderstood them. "We are very good. Mother always says we are."

"So you remarked before," the girl said, speaking in a tone of decision.

Still the children did not understand.

"Then can't you let us see the little man and woman?" they asked.

"Oh dear, no!" the girl answered. "I only show them to naughty children."

"To naughty children!" they exclaimed.

"Yes, to naughty children," she answered; "and the worse the children the better do the man and woman dance."

She put the peardrum carefully under her ragged cloak, and prepared to go on her way.

"I really could not have believed that you were good," she said, reproachfully, as if they had accused themselves of some great crime. "Well, good day."

"Oh, but do show us the little man and woman," they cried.

"Certainly not. Good day," she said again.

"Oh, but we will be naughty," they said in despair.

"I am afraid you couldn't," she answered, shaking her head. "It requires a great deal of skill, especially to be naughty. Well, good day," she said for the third time. "Perhaps I shall see you in the village to-morrow."

And swiftly she walked away, while the children felt their eyes fill with tears, and their hearts ache with disappointment.

"If we had only been naughty," they said, "we should have seen them dance; we should have seen the little woman holding her red petticoat in her hand, and the little man waving his hat. Oh, what shall we do to make her let us see them?"

"Suppose," said the Turkey, "we try to be naughty to-day; perhaps she would let us see them tomorrow."

"But, oh!" said Blue-Eyes, "I don't know how to be naughty; no one ever taught me."

The Turkey thought for a few minutes in silence. "I think I can be naughty if I try," she said. "I'll try to-night."

And then poor Blue-Eyes burst into tears.

"Oh, don't be naughty without me!" she cried. "It would be so unkind of you. You know I want to see the little man and woman just as much as you do. You are very, very unkind." And she sobbed bitterly.

And so, quarrelling and crying, they reached their home.

Now, when their mother saw them, she was greatly astonished, and, fearing they were hurt, ran to meet them.

"Oh, my children, oh, my dear, dear children," she said; "what is the matter?"

But they did not dare tell their mother about the village girl and the little man and woman, so they answered, "Nothing is the matter; nothing at all is the matter," and cried all the more.

"But why are you crying?" she asked in surprise.

"Surely we may cry if we like," they sobbed. "We are very fond of crying."

"Poor children!" the mother said to herself. "They are tired, and perhaps they are hungry; after tea they will be better." And she went back to the cottage, and made the fire blaze, until its reflection danced about on the tin lids upon the wall; and she put the kettle on to boil, and set the tea-things on the table, and opened the window to let in the sweet fresh air, and made all things look bright. Then she went to the little cupboard, hung up high against the wall, and took out some bread and put it on the table, and said in a loving voice, "Dear little children, come and have your tea; it is all quite ready for you. And see, there is the baby waking up from her sleep; we will put her in the high chair, and she will crow at us while we eat."

But the children made no answer to the dear mother; they only stood still by the window and said nothing.

"Come, children," the mother said again. "Come, Blue-Eyes, and come, my Turkey; here is nice sweet bread for tea."

Then Blue-Eyes and the Turkey looked round, and when they saw the tall loaf, baked crisp and brown, and the cups all in a row, and the jug of milk, all waiting for them, they went to the table and sat down and felt a little happier; and the mother did not put the baby in the high chair after all, but took it on her knee, and danced it up and down, and sang little snatches of songs to it, and laughed, and looked content, and thought of the father far away at sea, and wondered what he would say to them all when he came home again. Then suddenly she looked up and saw that the Turkey's eyes were full of tears.

"Turkey!" she exclaimed, "my dear little Turkey! what is the matter? Come to mother, my sweet; come to own mother." And putting the baby down on the rug, she held out her arms, and the Turkey, getting up from her chair, ran swiftly into them.

"Oh, mother," she sobbed, "oh, dear mother! I do so want to be naughty."

"My dear child!" the mother exclaimed.

"Yes, mother," the child sobbed, more and more bitterly. "I do so want to be very, very naughty."

And then Blue-Eyes left her chair also, and, rubbing her face against the mother's shoulder, cried sadly. "And so do I, mother. Oh, I'd give anything to be very, very naughty."

"But, my dear children," said the mother, in astonishment, "why do you want to be naughty?"

"Because we do; oh, what shall we do?" they cried together.

"I should be very angry if you were naughty. But you could not be, for you love me," the mother answered.

"Why couldn't we be naughty because we love you?" they asked.

"Because it would make me very unhappy; and if you love me you couldn't make me unhappy."

"Why couldn't we?" they asked.

Then the mother thought a while before she answered; and when she did so they hardly understood, perhaps because she seemed to be speaking rather to herself than to them.

"Because if one loves well," she said gently, "one's love is stronger than all bad feelings in one, and conquers them. And this is the test whether love be real or false, unkindness and wickedness have no power over it."

"We don't know what you mean," they cried; "and we do love you; but we want to be naughty."

"Then I should know you did not love me," the mother said.

"And what should you do?" asked Blue-Eyes.

"I cannot tell. I should try to make you better."

"But if you couldn't? If we were very, very, very naughty, and wouldn't be good, what then?"

"Then," said the mother sadly—and while she spoke her eyes filled with tears, and a sob almost choked her—"then," she said, "I should have to go away and leave you, and to send home a new mother, with glass eyes and wooden tail."

"You couldn't," they cried.

"Yes, I could," she answered in a low voice; "but it would make me very unhappy, and I will never do it unless you are very, very naughty, and I am obliged."

"We won't be naughty," they cried; "we will be good. We should hate a new mother; and she shall never come here." And they clung to their own mother, and kissed her fondly.

But when they went to bed they sobbed bitterly, for they remembered the little man and woman, and longed more than ever to see them; but how could they bear to let their own mother go away, and a new one take her place?

II

"Good day," said the village girl, when she saw Blue-Eyes and the Turkey approach. She was again sitting by the heap of stones, and under her shawl the peardrum was hidden. She looked just as if she had not moved since the day before. "Good day," she said, in the same cheerful voice in which she had spoken yesterday; "the weather is really charming."

"Are the little man and woman there?" the children asked, taking no notice of her remark.

"Yes; thank you for inquiring after them," the girl answered; "they are both here and quite well. The little man is learning how to rattle the money in his pocket, and the little woman has heard a secret—she tells it while she dances."

"Oh, do let us see," they entreated.

"Quite impossible, I assure you," the girl answered promptly. "You see, you are good."

"Oh!" said Blue-Eyes, sadly, "but mother says if we are

naughty she will go away and send home a new mother, with glass eyes and a wooden tail."

"Indeed," said the girl, still speaking in the same unconcerned voice, "that is what they all say."

"What do you mean?" asked the Turkey.

"They all threaten that kind of thing. Of course really there are no mothers with glass eyes and wooden tails; they would be much too expensive to make." And the common sense of this remark the children, especially the Turkey, saw at once, but they merely said, half crying—

"We think you might let us see the little man and woman dance."

"The kind of thing you would think," remarked the village girl.

"But will you if we are naughty?" they asked in despair.

"I fear you could not be naughty—that is, really—even if you tried," she said scornfully.

"Oh, but we will try; we will indeed," they cried; "so do show them to us."

"Certainly not beforehand," answered the girl, getting up and preparing to walk away.

"But if we are very naughty to-night, will you let us see them to-morrow?"

"Questions asked to-day are always best answered to-morrow," the girl said, and turned round as if to walk on. "Good day," she said blithely; "I must really go and play a little to myself; good day," she repeated, and then suddenly she began to sing—

"Oh, sweet and fair's the lady-bird,
And so's the bumble-bee,

But I myself have long preferred
The gentle chimpanzee,
The gentle chimpanzee-ee,
The gentle chim—

"I beg your pardon," she said, stopping, and looking over her shoulder, "it's very rude to sing without leave before company. I won't do it again."

"Oh, do go on," the children said.

"I'm going," she said, and walked away.

"No, we meant go on singing," they explained, "and do let us just hear you play," they entreated, remembering that as yet they had not heard a single sound from the peardrum.

"Quite impossible," she called out as she went along. "You are good, as I remarked before. The pleasure of goodness centers in itself; the pleasures of naughtiness are many and varied. Good day," she shouted, for she was almost out of hearing.

For a few minutes the children stood still looking after her, then they broke down and cried.

"She might have let us see them," they sobbed.

The Turkey was the first to wipe away her tears.

"Let us go home and be very naughty," she said; "then perhaps she will let us see them tomorrow."

"But what shall we do?" asked Blue-Eyes, looking up. Then together all the way home they planned how to begin being naughty. And that afternoon the dear mother was sorely distressed, for, instead of sitting at their tea as usual with smiling happy faces, and then helping her to clear away and doing all she told them, they broke their mugs and threw their bread and butter on the floor, and when the mother told them to do one thing they carefully went and did another, and as for helping her to put away, they left her to do it all by herself, and only stamped their feet with rage when she told them to go upstairs until they were good.

"We won't be good," they cried. "We hate being good, and we always mean to be naughty. We like being naughty very much."

"Do you remember what I told you I should do if you were very very naughty?" she asked sadly.

"Yes, we know, but it isn't true," they cried. "There is no mother with a wooden tail and glass eyes, and if there were we should just stick pins into her and send her away; but there is none."

Then the mother became really angry at last, and sent them off to bed, but instead of crying and being sorry at her anger they laughed for joy, and when they were in bed they sat up and sang merry songs at the top of their voices.

The next morning quite early, without asking leave from the mother, the children got up and ran off as fast as they could over the fields towards the bridge to look for the village girl. She was sitting as usual by the heap of stones with the peardrum under her shawl.

"Now please show us the little man and woman," they cried, "and let us hear the peardrum. We were very naughty last night." But the girl kept the peardrum carefully hidden. "We were very naughty," the children cried again.

"Indeed," she said in precisely the same tone in which she had spoken yesterday.

"But we were," they repeated; "we were indeed."

"So you say," she answered. "You were not half naughty enough."

"Why, we were sent to bed!"

"Just so," said the girl, putting the other corner of the shawl over the peardrum. "If you had been really naughty you wouldn't have gone; but you can't help it, you see. As I remarked before, it requires a great deal of skill to be naughty well."

"But we broke our mugs, we threw our bread and butter on the floor, we did everything we could to be tiresome."

"Mere trifles," answered the village girl scornfully. "Did you throw cold water on the fire, did you break the clock, did you pull all the tins down from the walls, and throw them on the floor?"

"No!" exclaimed the children, aghast, "we did not do that."

"I thought not," the girl answered "So many people mistake a little noise and foolishness for real naughtiness; but, as I remarked before, it wants skill to do the thing properly. Well, good day," and before they could say another word she had vanished.

"We'll be much worse," the children cried, in despair. "We'll go and do all the things she says;" and then they went home and did all these things. They threw water on the fire; they pulled down the baking-dish and the cake-tin, the fish-slice, and the lid of the saucepan they had never seen, and banged them on the floor; they broke the clock and danced on the butter; they turned everything upside down; and then they sat still and wondered if they were naughty enough. And when the mother saw all that they had done she did not scold them as she had the day before or send them to bed, but she just broke down and cried, and then she looked at the children and said sadly—

"Unless you are good to-morrow, my poor Blue-Eyes and

Turkey, I shall indeed have to go away and come back no more, and the new mother I told you of will come to you."

They did not believe her; yet their hearts ached when they saw how unhappy she looked, and they thought within themselves that when they once had seen the little man and woman dance, they would be good to the dear mother for ever afterwards; but they could not be good now till they had heard the sound of the peardrum, seen the little man and woman dance, and heard the secret told—then they would be satisfied.

The next morning, before the birds were stirring, before the sun had climbed high enough to look in at their bedroom window, or the flowers had wiped their eyes ready for the day, the children got up and crept out of the cottage and ran across the fields. They did not think the village girl would be up so very early, but their hearts had ached so much at the sight of the mother's sad face that they had not been able to sleep, and they longed to know if they had been naughty enough, and if they might just once hear the peardrum and see the little man and woman, and then go home and be good for ever.

To their surprise they found the village girl sitting by the heap of stones, just as if it were her natural home. They ran fast when they saw her, and they noticed that the box containing the little man and woman was open, but she closed it quickly when she saw them, and they heard the clicking of the spring that kept it fast.

"We have been very naughty," they cried "We have done all the things you told us; now will you show us the little man and woman?" The girl looked at them curiously, then drew the yellow silk handkerchief she sometimes wore round her head out of her pocket, and began to smooth out the creases in it with her hands.

"You really seem quite excited," she said in her usual voice. "You should be calm; calmness gathers in and hides things like a big cloak, or like my shawl does here, for instance;" and she looked down at the ragged covering that hid the peardrum.

"We have done all the things you told us," the children cried again, "and we do so long to hear the secret;" but the girl only went on smoothing out her handkerchief.

"I am so very particular about my dress," she said. They could hardly listen to her in their excitement.

"But do tell if we may see the little man and woman," they entreated again. "We have been so very naughty, and mother says she will go away to-day and send home a new mother if we are not good."

"Indeed," said the girl, beginning to be interested and amused. "The things that people say are most singular and amusing. There is an endless variety in language." But the children did not understand, only entreated once more to see the little man and woman.

"Well, let me see," the girl said at last, just as if she were relenting. "When did your mother say she would go?"

"But if she goes what shall we do?" they cried in despair. "We don't want her to go; we love her very much. Oh! what shall we do if she goes?"

"People go and people come; first they go and then they come. Perhaps she will go before she comes; she couldn't come before she goes. You had better go back and be good," the girl added suddenly; "you are really not clever enough to be anything else; and the little woman's secret is very important; she never tells it for make-believe naughtiness."

"But we did do all the things you told us," the children cried, despairingly.

"You didn't throw the looking-glass out of window, or stand the baby on its head."

"No, we didn't do that," the children gasped.

"I thought not," the girl said triumphantly. "Well, good-day. I shall not be here to-morrow. Good-day."

"Oh, but don't go away," they cried. "We are so unhappy; do let us see them just once."

"Well, I shall go past your cottage at eleven o'clock this morning," the girl said. "Perhaps I shall play the peardrum as I go by."

"And will you show us the man and woman?" they asked.

"Quite impossible, unless you have really deserved it; make-believe naughtiness is only spoilt goodness. Now if you break the looking-glass and do the things that are desired—"

"Oh, we will," they cried. "We will be very naughty till we hear you coming."

"It's waste of time, I fear," the girl said politely; "but of course I should not like to interfere with you. You see the little man and woman, being used to the best society, are very particular. Good-day," she said, just as she always said, and then quickly turned away, but she looked back and called out, "Eleven o'clock, I shall be quite punctual; I am very particular about my engagements."

Then again the children went home, and were naughty, oh, so very very naughty that the dear mother's heart ached, and her eyes filled with tears, and at last she went upstairs and slowly put on her best gown and her new sun-bonnet, and she dressed the baby all in its Sunday clothes, and then she came down and stood before Blue-Eyes and the Turkey, and just as she did so the Turkey threw the looking-glass out of window, and it fell with a loud crash upon the ground.

"Good-bye, my children," the mother said sadly, kissing them. "Good-bye, my Blue-Eyes; good-bye, my Turkey; the new mother will be home presently. Oh, my poor children!" and then weeping bitterly the mother took the baby in her arms and turned to leave the house.

"But, mother," the children cried, "we are—" and then suddenly the broken clock struck half-past ten, and they knew that in half an hour the village girl would come by playing on the peardrum. "But, mother, we will be good at half-past eleven, come back at half-past eleven," they cried, "and we'll both be good, we will indeed; we must be naughty till eleven o'clock." But the mother only picked up the little bundle in which she had tied up her cotton apron and a pair of old shoes, and went slowly out at the door. It seemed as if the children were spellbound, and they could not follow her. They opened the window wide, and called after her—

"Mother! mother! oh, dear mother, come back again! We will be good, we will be good now, we will be good for evermore if you will come back" But the mother only looked round and shook her head, and they could see the tears falling down her cheeks.

"Come back, dear mother!" cried Blue-Eyes; but still the mother went on across the fields.

"Come back, come back!" cried the Turkey; but still the mother went on. Just by the corner of the field she stopped and turned, and waved her handkerchief, all wet with tears, to the children at the window; she made the baby kiss its hand; and in a moment mother and baby had vanished from their sight.

Then the children felt their hearts ache with sorrow, and they cried bitterly just as the mother had done, and yet they could not believe that she had gone. Surely she would come back, they thought; she would not leave them altogether; but, oh, if she did—if she did—if she did. And then the broken clock struck eleven, and suddenly there was a sound—a quick, clanging, jangling sound, with a strange discordant one at intervals; and they looked at each other, while their hearts stood still, for they knew it was the peardrum. They rushed to the open window, and there they saw the village girl coming towards them from the fields, dancing along and playing as she did so. Behind her, walking slowly, and yet ever keeping the same distance from her, was the man with the dogs whom they had seen asleep by the Blue Lion, on the day they first saw the girl with the peardrum. He was playing on a flute that had a strange shrill sound; they could hear it plainly above the jangling of the peardrum. After the man followed the two dogs, slowly waltzing round and round on their hind legs.

"We have done all you told us," the children called, when they had recovered from their astonishment. "Come and see; and now show us the little man and woman."

The girl did not cease her playing or her dancing, but she called out in a voice that was half speaking half singing, and seemed to keep time to the strange music of the peardrum.

"You did it all badly. You threw the water on the wrong side of the fire, the tin things were not quite in the middle of the room, the clock was not broken enough, you did not stand the baby on its head."

Then the children, still standing spellbound by the window, cried out, entreating and wringing their hands, "Oh, but we have done everything you told us, and mother has gone away. Show us the little man and woman now, and let us hear the secret."

As they said this the girl was just in front of the cottage, but she did not stop playing. The sound of the strings seemed to go through their hearts. She did not stop dancing; she was already passing the cottage by. She did not stop singing, and all she said sounded like part of a terrible song. And still the man followed her, always at the same distance, playing shrilly on his flute; and still the two dogs waltzed round and round after him—their tails motionless, their legs straight, their collars clear and white and stiff. On they went, all of them together.

"Oh, stop!" the children cried, "and show us the little man and woman now."

But the girl sang out loud and clear, while the string that was out of tune twanged above her voice.

"The little man and woman are far away. See, their box is empty."

And then for the first time the children saw that the lid of the box was raised and hanging back, and that no little man and woman were in it.

"I am going to my own land," the girl sang, "to the land where I was born." And she went on towards the long straight road that led to the city many many miles away.

"But our mother is gone," the children cried; "our dear mother, will she ever come back?"

"No," sang the girl; "she'll never come back, she'll never come back. I saw her by the bridge: she took a boat upon the river; she is sailing to the sea; she will meet your father once again, and they will go sailing on, sailing on to the countries far away."

And when they heard this, the children cried out, but could say no more, for their hearts seemed to be breaking.

Then the girl, her voice getting fainter and fainter in the distance, called out once more to them. But for the dread that sharpened their ears they would hardly have heard her, so far was she away, and so discordant was the music.

"Your new mother is coming. She is already on her way; but she only walks slowly, for her tail is rather long, and her spectacles are left behind; but she is coming, she is coming—coming—coming."

The last word died away; it was the last one they ever heard the village girl utter. On she went, dancing on; and on followed the man, they could see that he was still playing, but they could no longer hear the sound of his flute; and on went the dogs round and round and round. On they all went, farther and farther away, till they were separate things no more, till they were just a confused mass of faded color, till they were a dark misty object that nothing could define, till they had vanished altogether—altogether and forever.

Then the children turned, and looked at each other and at the little cottage home, that only a week before had been so bright and happy, so cosy and so spotless. The fire was out, and the water was still among the cinders; the baking-dish and cake-tin, the fish-slice and the saucepan lid, which the dear mother used to spend so much time in rubbing, were all pulled down from the nails on which they had hung so long, and were lying on the floor. And there was the clock all broken and spoilt, the little picture upon its face could be seen no more; and though it sometimes struck a stray hour, it was with the tone of a clock whose hours are numbered. And there was the baby's high chair, but no little baby to sit in it; there was the cupboard on the wall, and never a sweet loaf on its shelf; and there were the broken mugs, and the bits of bread tossed about, and the greasy boards which the mother had knelt down to scrub until they were white as snow. In the midst of all stood the children, looking at the wreck they had made, their hearts aching, their eyes blinded with tears, and their poor little hands clasped together in their misery.

"Oh, what shall we do?" cried Blue-Eyes. "I wish we had never seen the village girl and the nasty, nasty peardrum."

"Surely mother will come back," sobbed the Turkey. "I am sure we shall die if she doesn't come back."

"I don't know what we shall do if the new mother comes," cried Blue-Eyes. "I shall never, never like any other mother. I don't know what we shall do if that dreadful mother comes."

"We won't let her in," said the Turkey.

"But perhaps she'll walk in," sobbed Blue-Eyes.

Then Turkey stopped crying for a minute, to think what should be done.

"We will bolt the door," she said, "and shut the window; and we won't take any notice when she knocks."

So they bolted the door, and shut the window, and fastened it. And then, in spite of all they had said, they felt naughty again, and longed after the little man and woman they had never seen, far more than after the mother who had loved them all their lives. But then they did not really believe that their own mother would not come back, or that any new mother would take her place.

When it was dinner-time, they were very hungry, but they could only find some stale bread, and they had to be content with it.

"Oh, I wish we had heard the little woman's secret," cried the Turkey; "I wouldn't have cared then."

All through the afternoon they sat watching and listening for fear of the new mother; but they saw and heard nothing of her, and gradually they became less and less afraid lest she should come. Then they thought that perhaps when it was dark their own dear mother would come home; and perhaps if they asked her to forgive them she would. And then Blue-Eyes thought that if their mother did come she would be very cold, so they crept out at the back door and gathered in some wood, and at last, for the grate was wet, and it was a great deal of trouble to manage it, they made a fire. When they saw the bright fire burning, and the little flames leaping and playing among the wood and coal, they began to be happy again, and to feel certain that their own mother would return; and the sight of the pleasant fire reminded them of all the times she had waited for them to come from the post-office, and of how she had welcomed them, and comforted them, and given them nice warm tea and sweet bread, and talked to them. Oh, how sorry they were they had been naughty, and all for that nasty village girl! They did not care a bit about the little man and woman now, or want to hear the secret.

They fetched a pail of water and washed the floor; they found some rag, and rubbed the tins till they looked bright again, and, putting a footstool on a chair, they got up on it very carefully and hung up the things in their places; and then they picked up the broken mugs and made the room as neat as they could, till it looked more and more as if the dear mother's hands had been busy about it. They felt more and more certain she would return, she and the dear little baby together, and they thought they would set the tea-things for her, just as she had so often set them for her naughty children. They took down the tea-tray, and got out the cups, and put the kettle on the fire to boil, and made everything look as home-like as they could. There was no sweet loaf to put on the table, but perhaps the mother would bring something from the village, they thought. At last all was ready, and Blue-Eyes and the Turkey washed their faces and their hands, and then sat and waited, for of course they did not believe what the village girl had said about their mother sailing away.

Suddenly, while they were sitting by the fire, they heard a sound as of something heavy being dragged along the ground outside, and then there was a loud and terrible knocking at the door. The children felt their hearts stand still. They knew it could not be their own mother, for she would have turned the handle and tried to come in without any knocking at all.

"Oh, Turkey!" whispered Blue-Eyes, "if it should be the new mother, what shall we do?"

"We won't let her in," whispered the Turkey, for she was afraid to speak aloud, and again there came a long and loud and terrible knocking at the door.

"What shall we do? oh, what shall we do?" cried the children, in despair. "Oh, go away!" they called out. "Go away; we won't let you in; we will never be naughty anymore; go away, go away!"

But again there came a loud and terrible knocking.

"She'll break the door if she knocks so hard," cried Blue-Eyes.

"Go and put your back to it," whispered the Turkey," and I'll peep out of the window and try to see if it is really the new mother."

So in fear and trembling Blue-Eyes put her back against the door, and the Turkey went to the window, and, pressing her face against one side of the frame, peeped out. She could just see a black satin poke bonnet with a frill round the edge, and a long bony arm carrying a black leather bag. From beneath the bonnet there flashed a strange bright light, and Turkey's heart sank and her cheeks turned pale, for she knew it was the flashing of two glass eyes. She crept up to Blue-Eyes. "It is—it is—it is!" she whispered, her voice shaking with fear, "it is the new mother! She has come, and brought her luggage in a black leather bag that is hanging on her arm!"

"Oh, what shall we do?" wept Blue-Eyes; and again there was the terrible knocking.

"Come and put your back against the door too, Turkey," cried Blue-Eyes; "I am afraid it will break."

So together they stood with their two little backs against the door. There was a long pause. They thought perhaps the new mother had made up her mind that there was no one at home to let her in, and would go away, but presently the two children heard through the thin wooden door the new mother move a little, and then say to herself—"I must break open the door with my tail."

For one terrible moment all was still, but in it the children could almost hear her lift up her tail, and then, with a fearful blow, the little painted door was cracked and splintered.

With a shriek the children darted from the spot and fled through the cottage, and out at the back door into the forest beyond. All night long they stayed in the darkness and the cold, and all the next day and the next, and all through the cold, dreary days and the long dark nights that followed.

They are there still, my children. All through the long weeks and months have they been there, with only green rushes for their pillows and only the brown dead leaves to cover them, feeding on the wild strawberries in the summer, or on the nuts when they hang green; on the blackberries when they are no longer sour in the autumn, and in the winter on the little red berries that ripen in the snow. They wander about among the tall dark firs or beneath the great trees beyond. Sometimes they stay to rest beside the little pool near the copse where the ferns grow thickest, and they long and long, with a longing that is greater than words can say, to see their own dear mother again, just once again, to tell her that they'll be good for evermore—just once again.

And still the new mother stays in the little cottage, but the windows are closed and the doors are shut, and no one knows what the inside looks like. Now and then, when the darkness has fallen and the night is still, hand in hand Blue-Eyes and the Turkey creep up near to the home in which they once were so happy, and with beating hearts they watch and listen; sometimes a blinding flash comes through the window, and they know it is the light from the new mother's glass eyes, or they hear a strange muffled noise, and they know it is the sound of her wooden tail as she drags it along the floor.

THE DANCING PARTNER

(1893)

Jerome K. Jerome

"This story," commenced MacShaugnassy, "comes from Furtwangen, a small town in the Black Forest. There lived there a very wonderful old fellow named Nicholaus Geibel. His business was the making of mechanical toys, at which work he had acquired an almost European reputation. He made rabbits that would emerge from the heart of a cabbage, flop their ears, smooth their whiskers, and disappear again; cats that would wash their faces, and mew so naturally that dogs would mistake them for real cats, and fly at them; dolls, with phonographs concealed within them, that would raise their hats and say, 'Good morning; how do you do,' and some that would even sing a song.

"But he was something more than a mere mechanic; he was an artist. His work was with him a hobby, almost a passion. His shop was filled with all manner of strange things that never would, or could, be sold—things he had made for the pure love of making them. He had contrived a mechanical donkey that would trot for two hours by means of stored electricity, and trot, too, much faster than the live article, and with less need for exertion on the part of the driver; a bird that would shoot up into the air, fly round and round in a circle, and drop to earth at the exact spot from where it started; a skeleton that, supported by an upright iron bar, would dance a hornpipe; a life-size lady doll that could play the fiddle; and a gentleman with a hollow inside who could smoke a pipe and drink more lager beer than any three average German students put together, which is saying much.

"Indeed, it was the belief of the town that old Geibel could make a man capable of doing everything that a respectable man need want to do. One day he made a man who did too much, and it came about in this way.

"Young Doctor Follen had a baby, and the baby had a birthday. Its first birthday put Doctor Follen's household into somewhat of a flurry, but on the occasion of its second birthday, Mrs. Doctor Follen gave a ball in honor of the event. Old Geibel and his daughter Olga were among the guests.

"During the afternoon of the next day some three or four of Olga's bosom friends, who had also been present at the ball, dropped in to have a chat about it. They naturally fell to discussing the men, and to criticizing their dancing. Old Geibel was in the room, but he appeared to be absorbed in his newspaper, and the girls took no notice of him.

"'There seem to be fewer men who can dance at every ball you go to,' said one of the girls.

"'Yes, and don't the ones who can give themselves airs,' said another; 'they make quite a favour of asking you.'

"'And how stupidly they talk,' added a third. 'They always say exactly the same things: "How charming you are looking to-night." "Do you often go to Vienna? Oh, you should, it's delightful." "What a charming dress you have on." "What a warm day it has been." "Do you like Wagner?" I do wish they'd think of something new.'

"'Oh, I never mind how they talk,' said a fourth. 'If a man dances well he may be a fool for all I care.'

"'He generally is,' slipped in a thin girl, rather spitefully.

"'I go to a ball to dance,' continued the previous speaker, not noticing the interruption. 'All I ask of a partner is that he shall hold me firmly, take me round steadily, and not get tired before I do.'

"'A clockwork figure would be the thing for you,' said the girl who had interrupted.

"'Bravo!' cried one of the others, clapping her hands, 'what a capital idea!'

"'What's a capital idea?' they asked.

"'Why, a clockwork dancer, or, better still, one that would go by electricity and never run down.'

"The girls took up the idea with enthusiasm.

"'Oh, what a lovely partner he would make,' said one; 'he would never kick you, or tread on your toes.'

"'Or tear your dress,' said another.

"'Or get out of step.'

"'Or get giddy and lean on you.'

"'And he would never want to mop his face with his handkerchief. I do hate to see a man do that after every dance.'

"'And wouldn't want to spend the whole evening in the supper room.'

"'Why, with a phonograph inside him to grind out all the stock remarks, you would not be able to tell him from a real man,' said the girl who had first suggested the idea.

"'Oh, yes, you would,' said the thin girl, 'he would be so much nicer.'

"Old Geibel had laid down his paper, and was listening with both his ears. On one of the girls glancing in his direction, however, he hurriedly hid himself again behind it.

"After the girls were gone, he went into his workshop, where Olga heard him walking up and down, and every now and then chuckling to himself; and that night he talked to her a good deal about dancing and dancing men—asked what they usually said and did—what dances were most popular—what steps were gone through, with many other questions bearing on the subject.

"Then for a couple of weeks he kept much to his factory, and was very thoughtful and busy, though prone at unexpected moments to break into a quiet low laugh, as if enjoying a joke that nobody else knew of.

"A month later another ball took place in Furtwangen. On this occasion it was given by old Wenzel, the wealthy timber merchant, to celebrate his niece's betrothal, and Geibel and his daughter were again among the invited.

"When the hour arrived to set out, Olga sought her father. Not finding him in the house, she tapped at the door of his workshop. He appeared in his shirt-sleeves, looking hot but radiant.

"'Don't wait for me,' he said, 'you go on, I'll follow you. I've got something to finish.'

"As she turned to obey he called after her, 'Tell them I'm going to bring a young man with me—such a nice young man, and an excellent dancer. All the girls will like him.' Then he laughed and closed the door.

"Her father generally kept his doings secret from everybody, but she had a pretty shrewd suspicion of what he had been planning, and so, to a certain extent, was able to prepare the guests for what was coming. Anticipation ran high, and the arrival of the famous mechanist was eagerly awaited.

"At length the sound of wheels was heard outside, followed by a great commotion in the passage, and old Wenzel himself, his jolly face red with excitement and suppressed laughter, burst into the room and announced in stentorian tones:

"'Herr Geibel—and a friend.'

"Herr Geibel and his 'friend' entered, greeted with shouts of laughter and applause, and advanced to the centre of the room.

"'Allow me, ladies and gentlemen,' said Herr Geibel, 'to introduce you to my friend, Lieutenant Fritz. Fritz, my dear fellow, bow to the ladies and gentlemen.'

"Geibel placed his hand encouragingly on Fritz's shoulder, and the lieutenant bowed low, accompanying the action with a harsh clicking noise in his throat, unpleasantly suggestive of a death rattle. But that was only a detail.

"'He walks a little stiffly' (old Geibel took his arm and walked him forward a few steps. He certainly did walk stiffly), 'but then, walking is not his forte. He is essentially a dancing man. I have only been able to teach him the waltz as yet, but at that he is faultless. Come, which of you ladies may I introduce him to as a partner. He keeps perfect time; he never gets tired; he won't kick you or tread on your dress; he will hold you as firmly as you like, and go as quickly or as slowly as you please; he never gets giddy; and he is full of conversation. Come, speak up for yourself, my boy.'

"The old gentleman twisted one of the buttons at the back of his coat, and immediately Fritz opened his mouth, and in thin tones that appeared to proceed from the back of his head, remarked suddenly, 'May I have the pleasure?' and then shut his mouth again with a snap.

"That Lieutenant Fritz had made a strong impression on the company was undoubted, yet none of the girls seemed inclined to dance with him. They looked askance at his waxen face, with its staring eyes and fixed smile, and shuddered. At last old Geibel came to the girl who had conceived the idea.

"'It is your own suggestion, carried out to the letter,' said Geibel, 'an electric dancer. You owe it to the gentleman to give him a trial.'

"She was a bright, saucy little girl, fond of a frolic. Her host added his entreaties, and she consented.

"Herr Geibel fixed the figure to her. Its right arm was screwed round her waist, and held her firmly; its delicately jointed left hand was made to fasten itself upon her right. The old toymaker showed her how to regulate its speed, and how to stop it, and release herself.

"'It will take you round in a complete circle,' he explained; 'be careful that no one knocks against you, and alters its course.'

"The music struck up. Old Geibel put the current in motion, and Annette and her strange partner began to dance.

"For a while everyone stood watching them. The figure performed its purpose admirably. Keeping perfect time and step, and holding its little partner tight clasped in an unyielding embrace, it revolved steadily, pouring forth at the same time a constant flow of squeaky conversation, broken by brief intervals of grinding silence.

"'How charming you are looking to-night,' it remarked in its thin, far-away voice. 'What a lovely day it has been. Do you like dancing? How well our steps agree. You will give me another, won't you? Oh, don't be so cruel. What a charming gown you have on. Isn't waltzing delightful? I could go on dancing for ever—with you. Have you had supper?'

"As she grew more familiar with the uncanny creature, the girl's nervousness wore off, and she entered into the fun of the thing.

"'Oh, he's just lovely,' she cried, laughing, 'I could go on dancing with him all my life.'

"Couple after couple now joined them, and soon all the dancers in the room were whirling round behind them. Nicholaus Geibel stood looking on, beaming with childish delight at his success.

"Old Wenzel approached him, and whispered something in his ear. Geibel laughed, and nodded, and the two worked their way quietly towards the door.

"'This is the young people's house to-night,' said Wenzel, so soon as they were outside; 'you and I will have a quiet pipe and a glass of hock, over in the counting-house.'

"Meanwhile the dancing grew more fast and furious. Little Annette loosened the screw regulating her partner's rate of progress, and the figure flew round with her swifter and swifter. Couple after couple dropped out exhausted, but they only went the faster, till at length they remained dancing alone.

"Madder and madder became the waltz. The music lagged behind: the musicians, unable to keep pace, ceased, and sat staring. The younger guests applauded, but the older faces began to grow anxious.

"'Hadn't you better stop, dear,' said one of the women, 'you'll make yourself so tired.'

"But Annette did not answer.

"'I believe she's fainted,' cried out a girl who had caught sight of her face as it was swept by.

"One of the men sprang forward and clutched at the figure, but its impetus threw him down on to the floor, where its steel-cased feet laid bare his cheek. The thing evidently did not intend to part with its prize easily.

"Had anyone retained a cool head, the figure, one cannot help thinking, might easily have been stopped. Two or three men acting in concert might have lifted it bodily off the floor, or have jammed it into a corner. But few human heads are capable of remaining cool under excitement. Those who are not present think how stupid must have been those who were; those who are reflect afterwards how simple it would have been to do this, that, or the other, if only they had thought of it at the time.

"The women grew hysterical. The men shouted contradictory directions to one another. Two of them made a bungling rush at the figure, which had the result of forcing it out of its orbit in the centre of the room, and sending it crashing against the walls and furniture. A stream of blood showed itself down the girl's white frock, and followed her along the floor. The affair was becoming horrible. The women rushed screaming from the room. The men followed them.

"One sensible suggestion was made: 'Find Geibel—fetch Geibel.'

"No one had noticed him leave the room, no one knew where he was. A party went in search of him. The others, too unnerved to go back into the ball-room, crowded outside the door and listened. They could hear the steady whir of the wheels upon the polished floor as the thing spun round and round; the dull thud as every now and again it dashed itself and its burden against some opposing object and ricocheted off in a new direction.

"And everlastingly it talked in that thin ghostly voice, repeating over and over the same formula: 'How charming you are looking to-night. What a lovely day it has been. Oh, don't be so cruel. I could go on dancing for ever—with you. Have you had supper?'

"Of course they sought for Geibel everywhere but where he was. They looked in every room in the house, then they rushed off in a body to his own place, and spent precious minutes in waking up his deaf old housekeeper. At last it occurred to one of the party that Wenzel was missing also, and then the idea of the counting-house across the yard presented itself to them, and there they found him.

"He rose up, very pale, and followed them; and he and old Wenzel forced their way through the crowd of guests gathered outside, and entered the room, and locked the door behind them.

"From within there came the muffled sound of low voices and quick steps, followed by a confused scuffling noise, then silence, then the low voices again.

"After a time the door opened, and those near it pressed forward to enter, but old Wenzel's broad shoulders barred the way.

"'I want you—and you, Bekler,' he said, addressing a couple of the elder men. His voice was calm, but his face was deadly white. 'The rest of you, please go—get the women away as quickly as you can.'

"From that day old Nicholaus Geibel confined himself to the making of mechanical rabbits and cats that mewed and washed their faces."

A WIFE MANUFACTURED TO ORDER

(1895)

Alice W. Fuller

As I was going down G Street in the city of W— a strange sign attracted my attention. I stopped, looked, fairly rubbed my eyes to see if they were rightly focused; yes, there it was plainly lettered in gilt: "Wives made to order! Satisfaction guaranteed or money refunded."

Well! well! does some lunatic live here, I wonder? By Jove! I will investigate. I had inherited (I suppose from my mother) a bit of curiosity, and the truth of the matter was this: now nearing the age of forty, I thought it might be advisable to settle down in a home of my own; but alas! to settle down to a life of strife and turmoil, that would not be pleasant; and that I should have to do, I knew very well, if I should marry any of my numerous lady acquaintances—especially Florence Ward, the one I most admired. She unfortunately had strong-minded ways, and inclinations to be investigating woman's rights, politics, theosophy, and all that sort of thing. Bah! I could never endure it. I should be miserable, and the outcome would be a separation; I knew it. To be dictated to, perhaps found fault with—no, no, it would never do; better be a bachelor and at least live in peace. But—what does this sign mean? I'll find out for myself.

A ring of the bell brought a little white-haired, wiry sort of a man to the door. "Walk in, walk in, sir," he said.

I asked for an explanation of the strange sign over the door.

"Just step right in here and be seated, sir. My master is engaged at present, sir, with a great politician who had to separate from his wife; was so fractious, sir, got so many strange notions in her head; in fact, she wanted to hold the reins herself. You may have seen it—the papers have been full of it. Why, law bless you, sir, the poor man couldn't say his soul was his own, and he is here now making arrangements with master to make him a quieter sort of wife, some one to do the honors of the home without feelin' neglected if he happens to be a little courteous to some of his young lady friends. You see, master makes 'em to order, makes 'em to think just as you do, just as you want 'em to; then you've got a happy home, something to live for. Beautiful—golly! I've seen some of the beautifulest women turned out, 'most make your mouth water to look at." And so the old man rattled on until I was quite bewildered.

I interrupted him by asking if I could see his master.

"Oh, certainly, sir; you just make yourself comfortable and I will let you know when he is through."

I sat for some time like one in a dream, wondering if this could be so, and with many wonderful modern inventions in mind I began to think it possible. And then there was a vision of a happy home, a wife beautiful as a dream, gentle and loving, without a thought for anyone but me; one who would never reproach me if I didn't happen to get home just at what she thought was the proper time; one who would not ask me to go to church when she knew it was against my wishes; one who would never find fault with me if I wished to go to a base-ball game on Sunday, or bother me to take her to the theatre or opera. A man, you know, can't give much time to such things without interfering greatly with his comfort. Oh! could all this be realized? But just then my reverie was broken by the old man, who was saying: "Just step this way. Master, let me introduce you to Mr. Charles Fitzsimmons."

Short, thick-set, florid complexion, pale blue eyes with a sinister twinkle, was the description of Mr. Sharper, whom I confronted. Reaching out his hand, which was cold and clammy and reminded me very much of a piece of cold boiled pork, he said:

"Now, young man, what can I do for you? Want a life-companion, a pleasant one? Man of means, no doubt, and can enjoy yourself; a little fun now and then with the boys and no harm at all—none in the least. When a man comes home tired, doesn't like to be dictated to; want some one always to meet you with a smile, some one that doesn't expect you to be fondlin' and pettin' 'em all the time. I understand it—I know just how it is. Law bless my soul, I'e made more'n one man happy, and I've only been in the business a short time, too. Now, sir, I can get you up any style you want—*wax*, but can't be detected."

"Do you mean to say you manufacture a woman out of wax, who will talk?"

"That's just what I do; you give me the subjects you most enjoy talking upon, and tell me what kind of a looking wife you want, and leave the rest to me, and you will never regret it. I will furnish as many 'phones' as you wish; most men don't care for such a variety for a wife—too much talk, you know;" and he chuckled and laughed like a big baby.

"What are your prices, may I ask?"

"Well, it's owing a good deal to how they are got up—from five hundred to a thousand dollars."

"Well," I said, "I think that rather high."

"Dear man alive, a pleasant companion for life for a few hundred dollars! Most men don't grumble at all for the sake of having their own way and a pleasant home, and you see she ain't always asking for money." (Sure enough, I hadn't thought of that.)

"Very well, I will decide upon the matter and let you know."

"All right, young man; you'll come back. They all do, them as knows about it."

I went to my room at the hotel and thought it all out, thought of the pleasant evenings I could have with some one whose thoughts were like my own, some one who would not vex me by differing in opinion. I wondered what Florence would say. I really believed she cared for me, but she knew how I disliked so many of the topics she persisted in talking upon. What mattered it to me what Emerson said, or Edward Bellamy wrote, or Henry George, or Pentecost? what did I care about Hume or Huxley or Stuart Mill? any of those sciences, Christian Science or Divine Science or mind cure?—bah! it was all nonsense. The topics of the day were enough, and if I attended closely to my business I needed recreation, not such things as she would prescribe. Still Florence was interesting to talk to, and I rather liked her at times when she talked every-day talk; but I could not marry her, and it was her own fault. She knew my sentiments, and if she would persist in going on as she did I couldn't help it.

Yes, I decided I would have a home of my own, and a wife made to order at once. Before leaving the city I made all necessary arrangements, hurried home, rented a house, and went to see old Susan Tyler, whom I engaged as housekeeper; she was deaf and had an impediment in her speech, but she was a fine housekeeper. All my preparations made, the ideal home! Oh! how my heart beat as I looked around!—what happiness to do as I liked, a beautiful, uncomplaining wife ready to grant every wish and meet me with a smile! What would the boys say when, out a little late at night, I should be so perfectly at ease? I could just see jealousy on their faces, and I laughed outright for joy. To-morrow I was going for my bride. Side-looks and innuendos were thrust at me from all quarters, but I was too happy to demur or explain. When I reached the city I could scarcely wait for the appointed time.

Alighting from the carriage the door was opened, and I was ushered into the presence of the most beautiful creature I had ever beheld. The hands extended towards mine, the lips opened, and a low, sweet voice said, "Dear Charles, how glad I am you have come!" I stood spellbound, and only a chuckle from Mr. Sharper brought me to my senses.

"Kiss your affianced, why don't you?" he said, and chuckled again.

I felt as though I wanted to knock him down for speaking so in that beautiful creature's presence. And then a little soft rippling laugh, and she moved towards me. Oh, could I get that beast to leave the room! Why did he stand there chuckling in that manner?

"Sir," I said, "you will oblige me by leaving the room for a few moments."

With that he chuckled still louder and muttered, "Bless me, I really believe he thinks her alive." Then to me: "To be sure, to be sure, but you only have a short time before going to the minister's, and I must show you how to adjust her. When you get home"—and he chuckled again—"you can be just as sentimental as you please, but just now we will attend to business. Here are a box of tubes made to talk as you wished them. They are adjusted so. Place the one you wish in your sleeve. You can carelessly touch her right here if there is any one around. Here is a spring in each hand and the tips of her fingers. I will give you a book of instructions, and you will soon learn to arrange her with very little effort, just to suit yourself, and I am sure you will be very happy. Now, sir, the time is up; you can go to the minister's."

As I put her wraps around her and drew her arm through mine she murmured so sweetly, "Thank you, dear." How glad I was to get out of the presence of that vile man who was constantly pulling or pushing her; I could scarcely keep my hands off from him, and my serene Margurette—for I decided to call her that—would only smile and say, "Thank you!" "Oh, how lovely!" "Ah, indeed!" I was almost vexed with her to think she did not resent it. I wanted her all to myself where I could have the smiles, and thought I should be thankful when we were in our own home.

During our journey I could not help noticing the admiring glances from my fellow travellers, but my beautiful wife did not return any of their looks. In fact, I overheard a couple of young dudes say, "Just wait till that old codger's back is turned, and we shall see whether she will have no smiles for any but him." I had half a notion to adjust her to give them some cutting reply and then go into the smoker awhile, for I was sure they would try to get into conversation with her; but pshaw! I hadn't ordered any tubes of that kind. I believed I'd send and get one in case of an emergency. No, I wouldn't have such in the house; I wanted an amiable wife, and when we were once at home it would not be necessary. I wouldn't *have* to go with her anywhere unless I wanted to. Only think of that!—never feel that my wife would ask me to go with her and I have to refuse, then ten to one have her cry and make a fuss about it. I knew how it was, for I had seen too much of that sort of thing in the homes of my friends.

Business ran smoothly; everything was perfect harmony; my home was heaven on earth. I smoked when I wished to, I went to my base-ball games, I stayed out as long as I pleased, played cards when I wished, drank champagne or whatever I fancied, in fact had as good a time as I did before marriage. My male friends congratulated me upon my good fortune, and I was considered the luckiest man anywhere around. No one knew how I had made the good luck for myself.

There are some things in life I could never understand. One of them is that, when everything seems so prosperous, calamity is so often in the wake. And that was the case with me. After so many prosperous years a financial crash came. I tried to ward it off; I was up early and late. Margurette never complained, but was always sweet and smiling, with the same endearing words. Sometimes as the years went by I felt as though I would not object to her differing with me a little, for variety's sake; still it was best. When I would say, "Margurette, do you really think so?" and I would speak so cross to her often—I don't know but that I did so more than was necessary; still a man must have some place where he can be himself, and if he can't have that privilege at home, what's the use of having a home?—but she was never out of patience, and my wife would only say, "Yes, darling," so low and sweet. I remember once I said, when I was worried more than usual, "I am damned tired of this sort of thing," and she laughed so sweetly and called me her "own precious boy."

But the crash came, and there was no use trying to stay it any longer. I came home sick and tired. It was nine o'clock at night, with a cold, drizzling rain falling. Susan had gone to bed sick, and forgotten to light a fire in the grate. I went into the library, where Margurette always waited for me. No lights; I stumbled over a chair. I accidentally touched Margurette. She put up her lips to kiss me and laughingly said, "Precious darling, tired to-night?" Great God! I came very near striking her.

"Margurette, don't call me darling, talk to me; talk to me about something—anything sensible. Don't you know I am a ruined man? Everything I have got has been swept away from me."

"There, precious, I love you;" and she laughed again.

"Did you not hear what I said?" I screamed.

But she only laughed the more and said, "Oh, how lovely!"

I rushed from the house. I could not endure it longer; I was like one mad. My first thought was, Where can I go, to whom can I go for sympathy? I cannot stand this strain much longer, and to show weakness to men, I could never do that. I will go to Florence, I said. I will see what she says. Strange I should think of her just then!

I asked the servant who admitted me for Miss Florence.

"She is indisposed and cannot see anyone to-night."

"But," I said, writing on a card hastily, "take this to her."

Only a few moments elapsed and she came in, holding out her hand in an assuring and friendly way. "I am surprised to see you to-night, Mr. Fitzsimmons."

"O Florence!" I cried, "I am in trouble. I believe I shall lose my mind if I cannot have someone to go to; and you, dear Florence, you will know my needs; you can counsel, you can understand me."

"Sir!" Florence said, "are you mad, that you come here to insult me?"

"But I love you. I know it. I love the traits that I once thought I despised."

"Stop where you are! I did not receive you to hear such language. You forget yourself and me; you forget that you are a married man—shame upon you for humiliating me so!"

"Florence, Florence, I am not married; it is all a lie, a deception."

"Have you lost your reason, Mr. Fitzsimmons? Sit down, pray, and let me call my father. You are ill."

"Stop," I cried, "I do not need your father. I need you. Listen to me. I imagined I could never be happy with a wife who differed in opinion from me. In fact, I had almost decided to remain single all the rest of my days, until I came across a man who manufactured wives to order. Wait, Florence, until I have finished—do not look at me so. I am indeed sane. My wife was manufactured to my own ideas, a perfect human being as I supposed."

"Mr. Fitzsimmons, let me call my father." And Florence started towards the door. She was so pale that she frightened me, but I clutched her frantically.

"Listen," I said; "will you go with me? I will prove that all I have told you is true."

My earnestness seemed to reassure her. She stopped as if carefully thinking, then asked me to repeat what I had already told her. Finally she said yes, she would go.

We were soon in the presence of my beautiful Margurette, whom I literally hated—I could not endure her face. "Now, Florence, see," I cried; and I had my wife talk the namby-pamby lingo I once thought so sweet. "Oh! how I hate her!" and I glared at her like a madman. "Florence, save me. I am a ruined man. Everything has been swept away—the last to-day. I am a pauper, an egotist, a bigot, a selfish"—

"Stop!" cried Florence. "You wrong yourself; you are a man in your prime. What if your money has gone, you have your health and your faculties, I guess" (and there was a merry twinkle in her eyes); "the whole world is before you, and best of all, no one to interfere with you or argue on disagreeable topics."

"O Florence! I am punished enough for my selfishness. O God!" and I threw myself on the couch, "were I not a pauper, too, there might be some hope for happiness yet."

"You are not a pauper," said Florence; "you are the master of your fate, and if you are not happy it is your own fault."

"Florence, I can never be happy without you. I know now it is too late."

"Too late—never say that. But could you be happy with me, 'a woman wedded to an idea,' 'strongminded'? Why, Charles, I am liable to investigate all sorts of scientific subjects and reforms. And then supposing I should talk about it sometimes; if it was not for that I might think of the matter. As far as money is concerned, that would have little to do with my actions. Still, Charles, upon the whole I should be afraid to marry the 'divorced' husband of so amiable a wife as your present one is. I, with my faults and imperfections!—the contrast would be too great."

"Florence, Florence," I said, "say no more. All I ask is, can you overlook my folly and take me for better, for worse? I have learned my lesson. I see now it is only a petty and narrow type of man who would wish to live only with his own personal echo. I want a woman, one who retains her individuality, a thinking woman. Will you be mine?"

"I will consider the matter favorably," said Florence; "but we shall have to wait a year, for opinion's sake, as I suppose there are not many who know how you had your late wife manufactured to order."

And we both laughed.

THE LADY AUTOMATON

(1901)

E. E. Kellett

"Yes," said Arthur, "I feel very much inclined to try it."

The speaker, Arthur Moore was a man whom I was proud to call my friend. Early in life he had distinguished himself by many wonderful inventions. When a boy he had adorned his bedroom with all sorts of curious mechanical contrivances; pulleys for lifting unheard-of weights; rattraps which, by cunning devices, provided the captured animal with a silent and painless end; locomotives which, when once wound up, would run for a day; and numberless other treasures, which, if hardly useful or even ornamental, had yet the effect of inspiring the housemaid who made the bed with a mortal terror of everything in the room.

As he grew older he lost none of his skill. At the age of fifteen he had successfully emulated most of the feats of

Vaucanson; his mechanical ducks gobbled and digested their food so naturally that even the famous scientist, the Rev. Henry Forest, was for a moment taken in. He had been to College, but, after a year of University life, he had wearied of the dull routine, and had begged his father to let him start life on his own account.

His father need have had no fear for the result. Within a year young Moore's automatic chess player, that had played a draw with Steinitz himself, had attracted the awe-struck attention of the civilised world by the simplicity and daring of its mechanism. The chess player was followed in two years by a whist player, still more simply and boldly conceived; and after that time scarcely a year passed without being signalised by the appearance of new wonders from Moore's fertile brain and dexterous hand.

His last achievement had been a phonograph so perfectly constructed that people began to think that even Edison must soon begin to look to his laurels, or he would be eclipsed by the rising fame of this young man of thirty.

I had known him since he was a boy; and had kept my acquaintance with him in spite of the ever-widening difference between our paths and our beliefs. I had chosen the medical profession, and was already a fashionable doctor, pretty well known by the public.

It was just after the new phonograph had appeared that I had with Arthur the memorable and unfortunate conversation which I shall regret to the very end of my life.

"Well," I said, "a new and great success again. You will be one of the greatest benefactors of the century in a few years."

"Yes," he answered, for he had no false modesty. "I believe the phonograph is about as perfect as I can make it. Suppose we listen to it now." He produced the instrument, and I had the pleasure of listening to a speech of Lord Rosebery with the familiar tones and inflections of the great orator reproduced to the life. I could have believed I saw the President before me.

"Wonderful," I said. "It is indeed perfect. What a strange and almost uncanny thing it is! We shall soon have to be very careful what we say; for a bird of the air shall carry the voice, and that which hath wings shall tell the matter. Fancy what a preventive of crime a phonograph fastened on every lamp-post would be! It would be a kind of Magic Flute, forcing people to tell the truth whether they would or no. Jones might say, 'I said this,' but the phonograph would say, 'You said that.' Mere human fallible creatures will soon be banished from the witness box; judges and juries will content themselves with taking the evidence of unerring, unlying phonographs."

"Heaven save us," Moore replied; "all of us say many things that will hardly bear repeating; and if they are all to be recorded how dreadful it would be."

"Yes, you see you are after all but a doubtful benefactor of the human race; it is not everybody, who, like Job, can wish that his words were now written."

"Nor Job himself at all times," he answered; "perhaps he would hardly have wished to have recorded the words he used when he cursed his day."

"In fact," I said, "what is a phonograph after all but a tattling old woman, repeating whatever it hears without discrimination or tact?"

"Exactly," he said; "but with this difference; that the phonograph repeats what it hears without alteration or addition, whereas the old woman repeats it just as it suits her."

At this moment the fatal idea struck me, which now I would give worlds to have forgotten or suppressed before it came to the birth. Alas, we know not the result of our least words.

"Why," I said, "don't you try to make a kind of complement of a phonograph?"

"What do you mean?"

"Why, this. Your phonograph only repeats what it hears. Why not make an instrument which should not *repeat* words, but speak out the suitable answer to them? If, for instance, I were to say to it 'Good morning; have you used So-and-so's Soap?' then why should it not answer 'No, I use somebody else's,' instead of merely reiterating my words? At present your machine is nothing but an echo; glorious, I grant; a triumph of civilisation; but what an achievement it would be to contrive a sort of anti-phonograph, that should give the appropriate answer to each question I like to put!"

"Why, a thing that could do that would be nothing less than man."

"Well," I said, "what is man but a bundle of sensations—a machine that answers pretty accurately to the questions daily put to it?" For I was, or pretended to be, a full-blown materialist.

"It may be so," he answered, "yet it seems to me that he is a very complex machine for all that. He has taken thousands of years to evolve, if what Darwin says is true; you ask me to make him in at most a year or two."

"Listen to me," I said, half in irony, half in earnest. "When you made your whist player, what did you do but calculate on a certain number of actions, all theoretically possible, and arrange that the machine should give the proper answer to them?"

"True."

"And with your chess player, was it not the same?"

"Exactly."

"Well, then, the general principle is granted. Are there not practically infinite varieties of hands at whist? Yet your automaton never made a mistake. Are there not infinite varieties of number? Yet did that puzzle Babbage's calculating machine?

"You may be right, Phillips," he said, smiling at my earnestness. "I will think of it."

I took my leave, little dreaming that I had set in motion a mighty force which would bring misery to more than a few. Indeed, I completely forgot the whole conversation. It was not till several months later that, happening to meet Moore in the street, I was suddenly startled by hearing the words I have already mentioned.

"Yes, I feel very much inclined to try it."

"To try what?" I said, completely bewildered.

"Why, the thing we were talking of some months ago. Listen. Words are nothing but air-vibrations, are they?"

"Nothing," I answered.

"Well, then, it follows that words, if put in the proper positions, can generate motion."

"I follow you; a molecular windmill."

"Well," he said, "this is the idea of my machine. Words are spoken into the ear of my automaton. Passing through the ear they enter a machine you would call an anti-phonograph, and set in motion various processes which in a very short time produce the words constituting the proper answer."

"Wonderful," I said, "if true."

"Come and see then," he rejoined, "if you will be so sceptical."

I followed him to his workshop, and saw a small instrument, in its main external details exactly like a phonograph.

"This," said Moore, "is the centre of my automaton. Try it yourself. Ask it a question—anything you like."

Wondering, I did as he suggested. There was a tube on each side of the instrument, communicating with its centre, which I supposed would form the "ear" of the automaton when finished. I was at a loss how to begin the conversation, so called the weather to my aid.

"A very cold day," I remarked.

A sweet and beautifully modulated feminine voice answered.

"Yes; but hardly so cold as yesterday." I started, as though I had seen a ghost. Had I not been a doctor, old as I was, I should have precipitately fled. But it takes a good deal to shake the nerves of a physician. In an instant I recovered myself.

"Moore," I said, "you can't play with me. You are ventriloquising."

He was very indignant. "What do you think of me?" he said. "I to go playing the tricks of a strolling mountebank!

"Try it again. I will not open my mouth."

I tried again, a certain uncanny feeling still possessing me. Oh, for the inventive powers of a Frenchman, in order to begin the conversation naturally!

"That was a fine speech by Mr. Chamberlain yesterday evening."

"Yes," the delicate feminine voice again replied; "I didn't read it all, but the beginning and the end were very good, weren't they?"

Again the same eerie feeling came over me, followed as before by the conviction that some trickery must be at the bottom of this most unparalleled experience.

I tried yet a third time, determined to watch Moore's face during the whole operation.

"It looks as if there'll be war between China and Japan," I said rather inanely.

"Yes, and I fancy Japan will win," replied the voice, *precisely at the same moment as Moore was saying*:

"Two to one on the little 'un."

I was convinced by that. No human being ever spoke two sentences precisely at the same instant. Either there was somebody else in the room, or Moore had succeeded, marvellously succeeded. He had made an instrument that could not only imitate the tones of the human voice, but could keep up a conversation as constantly, if not as wittily, as Miss Notable and Mr. Neverout in Swift's "Polite Conversation."

"Satisfied, old fellow?" said Moore, rising from his chair and coming toward me.

"My dear fellow," I said, "I know you are incapable of deception. But this is extraordinary. I never heard anything like it."

"No more did I," he replied with pardonable vanity, "until a week or so ago. I had tried all kinds of devices to make the thing answer sensibly; she would answer, of course, long ago, but I wanted her to behave like a lady, not like a lunatic."

"So you mean your automaton to be a lady, do you?"

"Yes," he replied, drawing closer. "And I want her to be a lady that would deceive anyone. Not a thing that can only act when lifted into a chair, or stuck up on a platform; but a creature that will guide herself, answer questions, talk and eat like a rational being—in fact, perform the part of a society lady as well as the best bred of them all."

"Moore," I said, "you must be mad."

"Mad or not, I mean to try it. See here. Here is another automaton that can walk, eat, turn its head, shut its eyes. That is common enough. Here is the brain power, the 'anti-phonograph' that can speak and hear—indeed, do anything but think. What is wanted but that the two should be combined?"

"My dear fellow," I answered, "it is easy to talk like that. I am a materialist, and would grant you more than most; but even in my view the brain is more than a mere machine. A man guides himself; you have to guide this automaton. How are you to get inside her and make her do all these things together at the proper time?

"Take a very simple example; your thing has to be sure to open its mouth when it speaks. How are you to insure that the process which causes it to open its mouth, and the process which causes certain words to be uttered, shall take place simultaneously? Suppose the thing to say, 'I will sit down,' how are you to insure that, at the proper moment, she shall go through the proper motions involved in sitting down? Remember, an error of half a second in your mysterious clockwork may make all the difference between your lady occupying a dignified position in a chair and sprawling ingloriously on the floor.

"Why, think of the actions of but five minutes. She rises from a chair, she avoids the toes of the ladies and gentlemen in the room, she bows to a gentleman, she smiles—more or less hypocritically—at a lady, she makes a *bon-mot*, she laughs at somebody else's *bon-mots*; she even blows her nose. What countless simultaneous processes, not one of which must go wrong!"

Moore heard me through.

"Plausible enough," he said, when I had finished; "we shall soon see who is right."

"Who was it," he went on, "who lectured so vigorously on the folly of certain women of our time, and talked so largely about their utter inanity? 'The Society woman of our time,' you proclaimed, 'what is she but a doll? Her second-hand opinions, so daintily expressed, would not a parrot speak them as well?' You meant that for metaphor and eloquence, old fellow, and yet you object to my proving that it is all literal truth."

"Prove it first," I said.

"Only give me time," he answered. "But before you go," he said, with a sudden impulse, as he saw me nearing the door, "for Heaven's sake not a word of this until I give you leave."

"Make your mind easy," I replied, "a doctor knows how to keep a secret. When your lady goes out of order, send for a bottle of my emulsion, and I'll engage she'll trouble you no more."

During the next few months, I often thought of Moore and his hallucination; the picture of the poor fellow engaged on a hopelessly mad task often rose before my mind. I pitied him greatly. "Another fine brain wasted," I used to say. "A man that more than rivalled Edison spending the best years of his life over a mad chimera!"

I urged rest, a sea voyage, anything to cure him of his brain-sick folly. But he met me always with one reply: "Rest *then*; not before." Rest in the grave, poor fellow, I thought, as I noted his hectic cheek and staring bones. His fiery soul was fretting his body to decay.

At last, more than a year after our last conversation, amid the heap of letters lying on my table at breakfast, I came upon one that startled me. It was from Arthur Moore, short, but to the point.

"Success at last; come when you can."

As soon as my round of visits was finished, I drove to his rooms. Mounting the stairs, I was ushered into the room by the most beautiful girl I had ever seen; a creature with fair hair, bright eyes, and a doll-like childishness of expression.

"Can he have married?" I thought, as I looked at her. "How is Mr. Moore?" I said aloud.

"Poorly to-day," she replied. "He will be here in a minute."

Where and when had I heard that voice before? I seemed to know it, and yet I could not associate it with anybody. But I had no time to be perplexed, for in two or three seconds Moore appeared, looking ghastly and deathlike in his pallor.

"You are ill," I said, when the first greeting was over. "You have been overstraining yourself. You must really rest, or you will kill yourself."

"Yes, I must," he replied; "and I think I shall. It has been toilsome work. But I think it was worth it, don't you?"

"How should I know?" I answered. "I haven't seen it yet."

"Yes, you have," he said, smiling in spite of the pain that he must have been feeling.

I looked around, bewildered. I could see nothing but the same old room, and the strange girl sitting in an easy chair in the corner.

"You are mysterious," I said.

"Wait a moment," said Moore. Then, turning to the girl, he spoke a little louder.

"It looks as if there *has* been war between China and Japan," he said.

Again those clear, distinct, delicate tones, as the answer came.

"Yes, and I fancy Japan *has* won."

I saw it all now. That beautiful, lady-like girl that had ushered me into the room, whom I had taken for his wife, was an automaton! That doll-like expression was due to the fact that she was a doll. I was utterly astounded. Moore sat by, enjoying my bewilderment; for a moment his weakness left him.

"Come here," he said to the automaton.

The lady arose, after one second of apparent indecision, and approached him.

"Let me introduce to you Dr. Phillips," he said.

The lady smiled approval. (To this day I have never understood how Moore had managed to produce that smile—that fatal monotonous, fascinating smile.)

"Dr. Phillips, Miss Amelia Brooke."

The lady bowed, and extended her hand.

"I am most happy to meet one of whom I have so often heard," she said.

Could it be a reality? I felt more and more staggered. The lady stood perfectly still, her hands clasped before her. This fair creature not of flesh and blood? Impossible!

"You may go," said Moore.

The thing moved back to her place, and sat down.

"What do you think of her?" he said aloud.

Before answering, I looked round to see where she was.

"Don't mind," he said laughing; "she can't hear. I often have that feeling myself. You may discuss her as you please, and she won't be offended. She has one merit other women haven't; she is not touchy; but she has a failing the best of them have not; she can't blush. On the whole, however, I prefer her."

"I am still almost incredulous," I replied; "indeed, until I have dissected her, and found pulleys instead of a liver, and eccentrics instead of a spleen, I shall hardly believe she isn't a woman in reality."

"You can easily do so," he said. "Come here, Amelia." The creature rose, and came forward. "Let Dr. Phillips see your arm," he said. The lady showed me her arm, and turned up her sleeve. It did not need a moment's inspection to show me that this was not an arm of flesh and blood. What it actually was made of Moore would not tell me.

"Better than a waxwork figure, isn't it?" he said.

"Much better," I replied. "Might deceive anyone but a doctor."

Passing my hand down to her wrist, I noted an exactly-moving pulse. So wonderfully was the human pulse imitated, that I believe anybody but one, like myself, trained to accurate discrimination would have been deluded. I could not refrain from expressing my admiration.

"Yes," said Moore, "she will often have her arms bare, and there may be a good deal of hand-pressing and that sort of thing; so that I thought I ought to have everything right."

"Does her heart beat, too?" I asked.

"No," he said; "I wanted the space for other mechanism, so she has to do without a heart altogether. Besides," he added, smilingly, "I wanted her to be a Society lady."

"The thing will be worth thousands to you," I said, when I had finished the examination of the creature's cutaneous covering. It is uncanny enough, and I can't say I like it, but it will draw. What a pity Barnum has gone! He would have given you a million pounds for it."

Moore rose angrily.

"Do you think I will sell my own lifepower for money?" he cried. "That thing has cost me at least ten years of my life, and she shall never be exhibited like a twoheaded nightingale, or a creature with its legs growing out of its pockets! She shall walk drawing-rooms like a lady, or I will break her to pieces myself!"

"My dear fellow," I said, "you are overexcited and ill. Surely you cannot know what you are saying?"

"I know well enough," he answered doggedly. "I have made a lady, you can't deny it; and a lady she shall be.

"Phillips," he went on, all the force of his character coming out in his face, "I am determined that she shall be the beauty of the season. She shall eclipse them all! I tell you. What are they but dolls? and she is more than a doll; she is ME. I have breathed into her myself, and she all but lives; she understands and knows! Come, promise me you will not betray me."

"Of course I will not," I said; "but you must give up this mad scheme. Consider, as an automaton she will make you for life; as a lady she will be found out in five minutes, and you will be laughed at. For your own sake pause."

"Listen," he said fiercely. "You call her an automaton. I tell you she is alive. See!"

He called the thing to him.

"Amelia," he said, "I have made you, and you are mine. Are you grateful?"

The creature smiled—the one smile she possessed, which she had, as I knew afterwards, for prince or peasant, man or maid.

"I can never forget what I owe you," she replied.

"Kiss me, then," he said. The thing bent down and kissed him obediently.

"You see," he cried, "is *that* an automaton? Now, will you introduce her to Society as a lady?

"For the present she is perfect. I have taught her French—drawing-room French, I mean—and three songs. She can enter a room, bow, smile, and dance. If, with these accomplishments, she can't oust the other dolls and turn them green with jealousy for one season, I am much surprised. Now, will you help me?"

I tried to enter a feeble protest, but he overbore me. You ask how; I cannot tell. Call it magic—anything you like; but it overbore me. I yielded; I promised my assistance.

We sat like two mischief-making children far into the small hours of the night, plotting how we could carry out the plan best. Moore had enslaved me, body and mind; I was carried away in a kind of drunken enthusiasm and almost as feverishly excited as Moore himself. Nothing would now have stopped me. Would Frankenstein have paused the very hour before his creature took life? As for Moore, I believe he would have gone on with his designs in the very midst of the thunders of the Judgment Day itself.

Why should I linger over the early triumphs of our Phantasm? I was a fashionable doctor; I brought Miss Amelia Brooke out as a niece of mine. The Countess of Lorimer, one of my patients, undertook to pilot her through the first shoals of real life.

Never shall I forget that first evening. Scarcely had she entered the room—it was at Mrs. Vandeleur's when the eyes of all seemed, as if by magic, to be turned towards her. Exquisitely dressed, with a proud demeanour, with the step of a queen, she swept into the ball-room. She was my niece; I ought to have been proud of her, but I hated her with an intense loathing. Moore could do much with me, but he could not make me like this creature. Yet I was bound in nature to do all I could for her.

"Who is she?" said young Harry Burton to me. "By Jove, she looks like a born queen."

"You flatter me," I replied. "She is my niece. Good Heavens," I went on to myself, "would that she were a born anything, instead of a made doll!"

"Oh," rejoined Burton, "lucky man that you are! Introduce me, will you?"

"With pleasure," I answered. I took him up and introduced him. During the ceremony I watched the creature carefully. No, there was no doubt about it. Such acting would deceive the Master of the Ceremonies in the Court of Louis XIV himself. Every motion, every word, was exactly as it should be. How on earth had Moore managed it? I was almost deceived myself. Could this be after all a real creature of flesh and blood, substituted for the Phantasm? No; that detestable, beautiful smile was there—a smile which no woman ever wore, yet which none the less would be the bane of more than one man's existence.

Harry Burton danced many dances with her that night. When it closed, he was head over ears in love.

"Phillips," he said in a brief interval, "she is divine."

"Fiendish, rather," I thought. "Yes," I said aloud, "I think she is good looking."

"Good looking!" he cried. "What are all these painted dolls to her? *They* have nothing to say for themselves, *they* are mere bundles of conventionality; but *she*—she is all soul."

"My boy," I said warningly, "you are evidently all heart. Be careful. Don't do anything rash. Dance with her, talk to her—do anything but fall in love with her."

"Who talked of falling in love?" he said, astonished at my earnestness. "I said nothing but that she was the finest girl in the room, and so she is, by Jove!"

At this moment a new dance began, and Burton ran off to claim his partner. I remained, absorbed in not very pleasant reflections. Things were getting involved already. Moore had only told me he was making a woman; I had never calculated that he would make a coquette. What would come of it? I sat and watched her as she danced, dancing beautifully but a little mechanically, I thought, saying always the right things, answering questions always in the same way, and wearing at pretty regular intervals the same detestable smile.

If I hated her before, I hated her tenfold now. I would speak to Moore, and put an end to it. A sudden cold—ordered to the South of France—and never let her come back. Good Heavens, this creature never had a cold, never had a headache, never felt out of sorts; yet Moore said he had made a woman.

Slowly the evening dragged to its close—the most wearisome evening I had ever spent. The creature did not seem to tire; one dance or twenty was the same to her. The monotony of it all became at length intolerable to me. At the earliest decent opportunity I took my leave.

Moore had never been a Society man. Even to witness his own triumph he had refused to be drawn out of his retirement, and it was with a feverish eagerness that he waited for the story of her successes from my lips.

"How did it go off?" he said anxiously, as I made my promised call to tell him.

"As an experiment, very well," I answered. "There was no hitch, no failure. The success was only too monotonous. Human beings sometimes put their foot in it; she never. Would to Heaven she might show now and then a little proneness to error!"

"You are queer," Moore answered. "Why should you grudge her her victories?"

"Arthur," I said, "the joke has gone quite far enough. Put a stop to it. Why go further? Think of the chances of detection—no, think of the far worse chances of success! Can't you see that the more skillful the deception the more dangerous will its consequences be? Already, more than one young fellow has fallen head over ears in love with her. It is horrible to think of!"

"The fools!" he said, with a rather cynical smile. "That is just the way with young fellows—never looking below the surface, looking only at the face. Why, Phillips, if they are taken in in that way they deserve to be taken in. I shall do nothing."

So the thing went on, new developments constantly arising. I hasten to the fatal ending.

Among the many deserters from the shrines of other goddesses who thronged to pay their court to this new and strange divinity, two seemed to hold the divided first place in her favour. One was my young friend Harry Burton; the other was handsome, impulsive, universally-liked Dick Calder. These two had been firm friends before, in spite of the fact that they had often flirted with the same girl. But it was impossible for two young fellows to love Amelia and continue to love each other.

To do Amelia justice, she was rigidly impartial between

Burton and Calder. For both she had the same silvery tones, for both the same fascinating smile. To both, if they asked the same questions, she returned identically the same answers. To both she sang the same songs, with the crescendo on the same passages, and both, at the conclusion of the songs, received the same languishing, irresistible smile over the right shoulder, which made them her slaves on the spot.

One evening, a curious incident happened. Burton and Calder were as usual basking in the rays of their divinity, when by some mischance Amelia's brooch fell to the ground. Both the swains stooped to pick it up, but Burton was successful. Delighted at his triumph over his rival he solicited the honour of refastening it. Calder watched him with jealous eyes. Suddenly a clumsy pair of waltzers, not looking where they were going, came hard into Burton. The brooch pin was driven deep into the fair throat of Amelia. Burton started in horror; he began a savage oath, but stopping in time he pulled out the pin. Amelia had not uttered a sound.

Burton, speechless with dismay, was taking out his handkerchief to staunch the blood; a little crowd was gathering round them; when I, suddenly recollecting myself, rushed in. With the speed of lightning I slipped out my handkerchief and tied it round Amelia's neck.

"Stand back, all of you!" I said in a tone of command. Even Burton and Calder fell back a little. "My niece is very sensitive," I said. "The hurt is not great, but it would be as well that she should go home at once." A terror had possessed me; an overmastering fear of detection held me as in a vice.

"I assure you, uncle, that I am not hurt at all," said Amelia.

"Come along," I said sternly.

I hurried her off, finding just time to bid my adieus to my hostess, and to console the dumfounded Burton by saying there was no danger.

We drove, not home, but direct to Moore's lodgings. Hurriedly we went upstairs. Moore was still up. He seemed surprised to see us.

"What do you want," he said.

"Fools that we are," I answered. "Why, we were within a hair's breadth of detection. *The creature can't bleed.*"

"Why, what need has she to bleed?" he said.

"Every need," I answered. "Doesn't a girl bleed when a pin is driven a good inch into her throat?"

"What do you mean?"

I explained the circumstances, and how I hoped I had for this once staved off discovery. I had been just in time.

"No," he said, when I had finished. "I never thought she would need to bleed. Strange that I should have forgotten that. They say that murderers always forget just one thing, just one little thing. But they take pains to get rid of the blood, and I ought to take pains to have it there."

"Give it up, Moore," I said.

"Give it up! Never!" he shouted. "Give it up for a few drops of blood! Rather would I drain my own veins into hers. Rather go out and kill somebody. What did Mephistopheles say? 'Blood is a peculiar sort of juice.' But I will make it."

Miss Brooke was "ill" for a few weeks from "shock to the system." At the end of that time I saw Moore again. He and the Phantasm were in the room together. He gave me a pin.

"Prick her," he said. I obeyed, not unwillingly; and to my horror something very like bleeding began. "Yes," said Moore! "I have done it. I have looked up Shakespeare. Do you remember what Shylock says, to prove that a Jew is, after all, a man? 'Hath not a Jew eyes? Hath not a Jew hands, organs, dimensions, senses, affections, passions? Fed with the same food! hurt with the same weapons! subject to the same diseases, healed by the same means, warmed and cooled by the same winter and summer, as a Christian is? If you prick us, do we not bleed? If you tickle us, do we not laugh? If you poison us, do we not die?' Now every one of these marks my Amelia has; so I say she is a genuine woman. Why, if you tickle her, she will laugh!"

"No one is likely to tickle her," I said.

"No; but after our last experience it is well to be prepared for all emergencies."

In this case, however, I did not make an experiment. Moore's word was enough. If the creature's smile was so detestable, what must her laugh be like?

After her time of seclusion, Amelia again appeared in Society, and was again the cynosure of all eyes, chiefly, however, of the four owned by Burton and Calder. These latter had never ceased to make inquiries after her health.

I had often wondered whether Burton had noticed that the scratch of the pin had drawn no blood; but his conduct afterwards set me at ease. If he had seen it he had probably thought that his Venus was too ethereal to bleed even the thinnest celestial ichor.

Though Amelia certainly could not feel, yet there was no doubt that in the future she would bleed if pricked, and I was free from anxiety on that score. But there was one thing which caused me considerable uneasiness. She was a girl of originality—indeed, I venture to think that there has never been a girl quite like her—yet there was a sameness, an artificiality, about her which puzzled and alarmed me. To the same question she always and inevitably returned the same answer. On topics of the day she always had the same opinion, expressed in the same words. My rival, Sir John Bolas, who didn't like her for some reason or other, used to say that in her company he always felt as if talking to a very well-trained parrot. She uttered her opinions as if they had been learnt verbatim from someone else.

The time drew near for Calder and Burton to declare themselves. I need not say that, closely as I watched the doings of Amelia, I was not present on these auspicious occasions. But I can distinctly assert, nevertheless, from my knowledge of human nature, that the language of Calder, who came second, was almost precisely the same as that of Burton, who had the first chance. Hence it followed, with mathematical certainty, that Amelia's reply would be the same to both.

Here was a pretty predicament! What I had blamed in her was her unwomanly constancy; but this very constancy had led—as I was sure both *a priori* and from the happy faces of the two young men—to a display of fickleness unparalleled in the whole history of womankind. Within an hour after accepting Burton the faithless creature accepted Calder in almost identically the same terms. Even the most heartless of coquettes had surely never been guilty of such conduct as this.

All this, however, was for the present merely a plausible conjecture, based upon a more or less certain knowledge of character. To make sure of it, I determined to ask. The result but too sadly confirmed my fears. Burton was almost delirious with joy.

"She is mine," he said; "and that beast Calder was never in it with her. To think that I should ever have been afraid of a cad like that!"

I congratulated him, as in duty bound, and spent an hour with him, which may have been pleasant to him, but became very tedious to me, so difficult was it to get him off his one eternal topic and induce him to talk like a rational being. At last, however, I managed to effect my escape, and made my way to Calder. He also received me very graciously.

"Old man," he said, "I have good news to tell you. Amelia has just consented to be engaged to me!"

"Indeed!" I replied; "I am very pleased to hear it. You are a happy man, Dick."

"Yes!" he said! "happier than I deserve. But what delights me almost as much as having won her is that she never gave a thought to that fellow Burton. If I had had any sense I must have seen that a girl like her could never be taken in by a wretched fellow like him; but somehow I managed to be jealous of him. Well, that's all over! thank goodness. I really believe I shall get to like him now I'm sure he can do me no harm."

And so the young fellow chatted on, cutting me to the heart with almost every sentence that he uttered. What a dreadful awakening I was preparing for him! For of course, the awful truth must be told him, that he and his rival had fallen in love with a sham. It would be an awkward moment for both of us. Should I tell him now, and get it over? On the whole I preferred to put it off, and consult Moore first. His fertile brain would suggest a way out of the difficulty. Perhaps he would make a second automaton that would do for one of the rival suitors, while the other kept to Amelia. At any rate! I preferred to get his advice before acting. He had made the Phantasm bleed; might he not get us out of this still more unpleasant position?

I told him of the new complication. To my surprise he made light of it.

"Well?" he said, when I had finished my recital.

"Well?" I replied, "I should think that was enough."

"Why," he said, "I can see nothing wonderful in that. The wonder would be if they *hadn't* proposed to her. Women have had offers before now."

"But you can't intend to let things go on as they are?" I cried.

"That's exactly what I *do* intend," he answered. "Why should I interfere?"

"But think of it for one moment," I said. "Two men in love with the same automaton; two men in the position of accepted lovers at the same moment! Think of even one man in that position! How awful it is—why, it is too dreadful to think of!"

"Then I shan't think of it," he answered coolly. "My dear fellow, what is there so strange in it all? Men have been in love with stone-like women before this. Men have given themselves up to heartless and soulless abstractions before this. Anyone who gets my Amelia will get *something*, at any rate, not a mere doll."

The plain fact dawned on me that Moore's extraordinary success had turned his brain. He had put so much of himself into his automaton that he had positively begun to regard her as a real living being, in whose veins flowed his own blood, in whose nostrils was his own breath. Eve was not more truly bone of Adam's bone than this Amelia was part and parcel of Moore's life.

There was a mysterious union between them which gave me an uncanny feeling of sorcery. Could it be that by some unholy means Moore had succeeded in conveying some portion of his own life to this creature of his brain? I tried to dismiss the thought, for I am a man of science; yet it recurred again and again.

Burton and Calder were engaged to Amelia. It may be easily understood that now and then they came into collision. Sometimes things looked strange to them. Calder once demanded an explanation of his *fiancée* as to the frequency of Burton's visits. She gave him an account that satisfied him, and sealed it with a smile and a kiss that made him feel like a villain forever doubting her. People wondered at the confidence with which both the young men asserted that they were the favoured suitors, and admired the daring skill with which Amelia played off one against the other. No one warned the young men; it was none of our business to interfere with them.

In such matters one young man is remarkably similar to another. Their very modes of speech tend to become the same. In asking Amelia to fix the day, need it be wondered at that they used precisely the same terms as have been used by all young men from the day when that nameless suitor of "pretty Jane" promised to buy the ring for his beloved? The result may be easily foreseen. Amelia, by some hidden law of her being, for which not she but perhaps Moore was to blame, could not help fixing the same day for both. Had a third candidate appeared on the scene, she would have fixed the same day for him also.

When I had heard this fatal *dénouement*, I confess that even Moore's influence could not keep me from taking a step on my own account. I would not destroy Amelia, much as I hated her for the trouble she had caused me. Something seemed to tell me that her death would be the certain death of Moore, whose life was bound up in hers as closely as the life of Jacob was bound up in that of Benjamin.

By some subtle process, every time danger threatened Amelia, Moore's spirits seemed to sink; every time she surmounted the danger his spirits rose again. He had put himself into her. I would not destroy her; but I went to Calder and I gave him a pretty plain hint as to the position of affairs between her and Burton. He would not believe me.

"If I thought she was false," he said, "I would stab her where she stood, were it at the very altar. But it cannot be. She has pledged herself to me, and mine she is!"

"I know it for a fact," I answered, "that she has promised to marry Burton on the 29th of February."

"The twenty-ninth," he cried. "Why, that is my day, the day on which she promised to marry me."

"Precisely so," I said. "What she means to do I don't know."

"But I know what I mean to do," he answered gloomily. "I will have it out with her."

"No violence."

"None at all. Don't fear me. By Heaven, what a heartless creature. But it can't be true. You are deceiving me."

"Too true. But find out for yourself." I took my leave, and went home. I afterwards ascertained what Calder's plan was. He made no inquiry from Amelia; he simply went and begged her to put off the day of his marriage a month, from the twenty-ninth of February to the last day of March. She readily agreed. He then went off and bought a sharp Spanish dagger.

The day of the marriage drew near, and nearer. Every preparation was completed. It was to be fashionable. The church was got ready in expectation of a large assemblage of people. At length the eventful morning dawned. I was to give the bride away to Burton, as after the postponement of Calder's wedding he was the only bridegroom left in the race. We came out and stood before the altar.

As I passed along I noticed two figures in different parts of the building, both familiar to me. They were Moore and Calder. The former was untidy, evidently excited and restless. The latter was scrupulously neat; but he had a strangely determined look on his face. One hand was hidden under the breast of his frock coat.

The service proceeded. Fancy a girl like this being told she was a daughter of Abraham, so long as she was not afraid with any amazement! Certainly a cooler, less perturbed daughter of the patriarch I never saw. She gave the response in a clear, musical voice. They came to the fatal question—"Wilt thou have this man to be thy husband?"

Before she could answer "I will," there was a sudden confusion; a man rushed forward, drew forth a dagger from his breast and shouting, "You shall not!" stabbed Amelia to the heart—or rather through the left side of her bodice. She fell to the ground, striking her head heavily as she fell against the rail. There was a whirr, a rush. The anti-phonograph was broken. I bent over her, and opened her dress to staunch the wound. Moore had made no provision for her bleeding *there*. As I drew out the dagger, it was followed by a rush of sawdust.

In the confusion of the strange discovery, no one noticed that a real death was taking place not twenty feet away. As the sexton was clearing out the church, he noticed a man asleep in one of the pews, leaning against a pillar. He went up and touched him; but there was no answer. He shook him; but the man was as heedless as Baal. It was Arthur Moore, and he was dead. He had put his life into his masterpiece; his wonderful toy was broken, and the cord of Moore's life was broken with it.

And as for me, why, I am no longer a fashionable physician. As I write, there are men about me, who talk of me as a *patient*.

Acknowledgments

I would like to acknowledge all the scholars who came before me, who have built an edifice to Shelley's novel that is quite recent but now of great extent—yet no more than her work deserves, in my opinion. What I say in the introduction here comes from or in reaction to what others have done and the many smart approaches to her "hideous progeny" that I deeply admire.

I also want to thank my students from numerous classes for the work they put in on the Frankenstein Meme Project, which we stitched together from 2016 to 2018 in time for the 200-year anniversary of the novel. Together we built a website to house an online searchable database of works influenced by Frankenstein, 1818–2018. That work led directly to the book you hold now. I appreciate them for putting up with my obsession, and for all they achieved in reading and writing entries (and proofing and editing them) for the database. I also want to acknowledge the support of University Archives and Special Collections and the Patrons of the Library at my campus,

California State University, Fullerton, in the Frankenstein Meme Project. The website for the Project is still live, and you can check it out at frankensteinmeme.com.

I also want to acknowledge the great work of Christine Neulieb, Feliza Casano, Amanda Thomas, and all the people at Lanternfish. The gorgeous look and feel of the Clockwork Editions series inspired me to pitch this book—and I'm so glad I did.

Finally, I want to acknowledge Amy and Adele, for just everything.

ABOUT THE AUTHOR

DR. DAVID SANDNER is a Mythopoeic Award–nominated scholar of the fantastic and teaches at California State University, Fullerton. His books include *Critical Approaches to the Fantastic, 1712-1831*; *Fantastic Literature: A Critical Reader*; and *Philip K. Dick: Essays of the Here and Now*, among other books and essays. He digitally mapped Mary Shelley's other SF work, *The Last Man*, for *Space(s) of the Fantastic* and founded an online database, *The Frankenstein Meme*, to study Shelley's literary influence. As a writer, he publishes fiction and poetry and is a member of the Science Fiction and Fantasy Writers Association and the Horror Writers Association. Learn more at davidsandner.com.